Jean Saunders began her career as a writer of short stories in 1965. Since then she has published many novels and over 600 short stories, under various pseudonyms, in both Britain and America. She has also written two books in the Allison & Busby Writers' Guide series – *The Craft of Writing Romance* and *Writing Step By Step*. A member of the Romantic Novelists' Association and the West Country Writers' Association, she lectures widely and takes an active part in writers' groups and conferences. She is also a committee member of the Writers' Summer School. Jean is married and writes full time at her West Country home.

JEAN SAUNDERS

To Love and Honour

2 To Love and Honour

This title first published in Great Britain in 1992 by
Severn House Publishers Ltd.
First published in any format in the U.S.A. 1993
by Severn House Publishers Inc, by arrangement with
HarperCollins Publishers
This edition licensed by Severn House Publishers Ltd,
produced by Magpie Books Ltd, and published by Parragon
Book Service Ltd in 1995.

A copy of the British Library CIP data is available
from the British Library.

ISBN: 0 75251 269 2

Printed and Bound in Great Britain

1

Amy decided that summer was definitely the worst of seasons, simply because it meant going out without a coat. In winter, snuggled into cheap rabbit-fur collars, their felt cloche hats pulled down around the flattering kiss-curls, nobody could guess what was underneath all the layers . . . but none of that bothered her friend Tess, of course, fashionably thin as a reed.

Saturday afternoon was the highlight of their week, and the Roxy cinema in Baltimore Street drew them like moths to a flame. They did themselves up in their best clothes and went off in search of romance, bangles and beads jangling, skimpy floral frock for Tess and low-waisted navy cotton for Amy, which she fondly hoped did something to disguise her over-indulgence in below-stairs snacks.

They were comfortably settled in the plush seats at the Roxy that afternoon, when Amy felt her heart jolt.

'Tess, he's here again,' she breathed.

Her friend was too enthralled by the exploits of Mr Douglas Fairbanks on the cinema screen to care who Amy had seen. Their hero was wickedly handsome as Don Q, son of Zorro, sending curious thrills through their bodies, although they were seeing him in the new role for the third time.

'Who's here again?' Tess said, unwilling to blink her eyes away from the silver screen for a single moment.

'Your admirer! Oh, now he's turned away. You'll have to wait until the next interval to see him. He's in the second row from the front. I wish you'd seen the way he looked at you. He's real nice-looking –'

Tess compressed her lips. 'He's not my admirer. And if

he can only afford front seats, I'm sure I don't want to know him!'

She stuck her nose in the air, managing to look superior without even trying. The two of them might only be downstairs maids, but Tess had ambitions, and the determination to go places, as she grandly called it. She was already several rungs up the ladder from Amy, although they'd started in service at the big house in Aveley Square on the very same day, forging a bond that had seen them through plenty of scrapes.

Tess was already lost in the film again, while Amy looked about restlessly. She was becoming a bit bored watching a film they knew off by heart.

She glanced at Tess's rapt face and sighed. There was a lot about Tess that Amy could have envied if they weren't such friends. Chocolate-box good looks, if a little hard and shallow, gloriously flat shape, cornflower-blue eyes and reddish-blonde hair, and a flirty way of looking at a chap from beneath her eyelashes.

Even the Honourable Giles Beaumont had apparently nodded and passed the time of day with Tess on the stairs. And Amy had agreed that from somebody as snooty as young Mr Giles, that was definitely a compliment.

She was cheerfully aware that few noticed her in the same way. Amy was a little brown mouse, Bert Figgins once told her, but a cuddly one that fitted very nicely into a chap's arms.

It was flattering, of course, especially to a girl like Amy, who'd known from the very beginning that she wasn't quite like other girls. Her grandmother had informed her as soon as she was able to understand that her mother had been one of the unfortunates who'd loved a man too well and carried the consequences, namely Amy, and died in childbirth.

Tess's mother led a free and dubious life, but Amy still envied the fact that Tess *had* a mother.

6

It looked as if Tess had this new admirer too. The one that seemed to turn up at the Roxy every time they were there, and kept staring round as if he looked for Tess especially. He'd never spoken to them yet. but that could be due to the annoying fact that they always had to rush out of the cinema as soon as the film ended to catch the tram back to Hampstead.

Amy thought longingly that it must be nice to be rich and not have to bother about trams and things. To have a uniformed chauffeur like Bert Figgins bring a sleek limousine round to the front of the cinema when the film ended and have the crowds gawping with envy as you stepped elegantly into it.

The comical picture of the Beaumonts' chauffeur doing any such thing for the likes of Amy Moore and Tess Loveridge made her chuckle right in the middle of one of Don Q's most torrid moments, and Tess glared at her.

'Shut up, Amy. You're spoiling it.'

She stifled her giggles in a handkerchief. Really, Tess was going daft over this Douglas Fairbanks lately. Who was he, for God's sake, but a celluloid image on a bit of canvas that went blank as soon as the man in a little room at the back switched off his projection thing!

Bert had explained all about it on a picnic by the river one day, having an enthusiasm for anything mechanical, and attempting to blind Amy with science to persuade her to let him sneak a quick look at her knickers.

It had worked too, she thought with a wicked little thrill of shamed recollection. Bert might not be the man of her dreams, but he wasn't such a bad bloke . . . a downstairs maid could do a lot worse.

She gazed unseeingly at the flickering screen, wondering why some folk had to be rich and others so lowly. Wondering why she couldn't have been born looking like Clara Bow and having all the men in Hollywood falling in love with her. Amy grinned. Fat chance. All the same . . .

7

Without too much effort, in her dreaming moments Amy managed to see herself transported to the silver screen, her small mouth exaggerated into the harsh bow lips by bright red tango lipstick, the long lashes circling her doe eyes fluttering invitingly at her adoring new leading man . . .

In one of his amorous moods, Bert had told Amy with enthusiasm that she had all the equipment that could drive a bloke wild, but she knew what he was after, and told him severely not to be so daft.

She and Tess had recently seen Clara Bow in *Kiss Me Again*, and both had immediately had their hair bobbed. Tess's was now looking a suspiciously brighter and somewhat redder colour than was natural.

It was all right for her, whose flighty mother didn't object to such things. Amy's grandmother had told her in no uncertain terms that she'd be a fool to act as fast as Tess, and to get herself a friend who didn't have a mother no better than she should be, with hair that owed more to the dye-bottle than to natural black roots.

Gran Moore frequently said severely that wishing you were somebody else was a waste of good living time, and nobody had time enough on this earth for that . . .

'Oh Tess, he's coming this way!' Amy said in a fright, as the lights went up in the second interval and everyone in the cinema blinked like moles newly exposed to the daylight.

'Who is?' Tess said, foraging in her bag for the penny twist of boiled delights she'd bought at the corner shop. A sharp sweet was just what she needed to moisten up the dryness of her mouth after the exciting events of the picture-so-far.

'Your admirer! He's *ever* so good-looking, Tess. I'm sure he's going to speak to you.'

'Well, I shall just ignore him if he does. I've no intention of picking up a chap in the cinema,' Tess said airily, with

8

all the confidence of a girl who could have any young man she wanted. 'It's so common.'

Amy grinned. Tess's mother was the commonest woman for miles around, and it was a bit ludicrous for Tess to be so hoity-toity. But the young man with the nice angular face was definitely coming their way, and looking as if he was going to sit in the empty seat next to Amy. She wondered if he'd suggest changing places with her to sit beside Tess, and just what she was supposed to say if he did.

Her heart seemed to be doing all kinds of somersaults, even though this was 1925 and Hollywood was doing its best to promote women who were fast and glamorous. Except that the clamminess of Amy's own hands was proving abysmally that she for one definitely didn't have the self-confidence of a Clara Bow . . .

'Don't you dare let him speak to me, Amy,' Tess said out of the side of her mouth, like a movie gangster. 'I choose who I want to walk out with . . .'

Her voice faded into nothing as the young man took the empty seat beside Amy. The girls stared rigidly ahead. After a few minutes' silence the pianist at the front of the theatre, abandoning the crashing chords of the film for the time being, burst into a more recognizable popular tune of the moment.

'She's my once-a-week love, my once-in-a-dream-time love, all so del-i-cate and lovely . . .'

It struck Amy's romantic heart immediately that nothing could be more wonderfully, poignantly appropriate. And all Tess could do was stick her nose in the air and ignore this young man who was daring to approach her.

'Hello,' he said, and although his voice was quite subdued, it was very strong and masculine.

Amy didn't move a muscle, feeling the dig of Tess's fingers in her arm. Tess needn't worry. She had no intention of acting as go-between. It was so – so degrading. She might be destined to remain a downstairs maid, but

9

she still had her pride. She lifted her chin, wishing it were as square-cut as Tess's, wishing there wasn't that irritating little fold of plump flesh beneath it.

'Forgive me if I'm intruding. I don't mean to offend you, but I've seen you in here most weeks, and I've been wondering whether to come and talk to you. We must be the best Saturday customers of the Roxy. I bet we could get a yearly ticket at a cheap rate if we enquired together – your friend too, of course. What do you think?'

Amy turned her head slowly. Her gaze met two of the friendliest eyes she had ever seen. They were an undefinable colour in the gas-light. It made them velvety-dark, and there were little creases at the sides when they smiled at her. At *her*, not at Tess.

The miracle of it penetrated her senses. The intriguing young man was smiling at, looking at, admiring *her*, Amy Moore.

She felt the dig in her ribs from the other side.

'What's he saying?' Tess mouthed.

For the first time in her life, Amy ignored her, turning slightly away from her friend to look more closely at the newcomer and answer his question.

'Well, I don't know. I suppose they might.'

Oh, why couldn't she be bright and articulate, the way Tess would be! Why couldn't she think of something far more witty and clever to say than the boring reply she'd just given! The young man chuckled, as if she'd truly said something wonderful.

'Let's ask at the end of the show. They can only throw us out on our ears for our cheek.'

Tess suddenly dropped her bag of boiled delights. It split, and the sweets rolled about like marbles among the seats, just as the pianist came to the end of his impromptu session and began to play more dramatically in keeping with Don Q's progress on the screen.

The lights went down, but not before she'd leaned

10

forward to look more fully into the face of the stranger who'd come to sit beside Amy, when all these weeks both girls had been quite certain that as usual it was Tess he had pined for from afar.

The usherette appeared from nowhere, shushing people from talking as the overhead beam of smoky white light fractured with dust motes shone forth from the projectionist's room above, and the next part of the tense film story began to unfold.

Tess sat stiffly, indignation mixed with amazement seeping into her very bones. She hadn't wanted the insufferable attentions of the young man, but it was a knock to her self-esteem to realize it was Amy he'd been looking at after all. *Amy*, with the fudge-coloured doe eyes and unfashionably generous curves . . . when all the time, Tess had been rehearsing in her best femme-fatale manner how she would give him the boot. It needed thinking about. It certainly did.

And that quick glance, when she'd deliberately let her favourite sweets go in the cause of research, had been enough to tell her that perhaps she'd been too quick to condemn him. He wasn't Douglas Fairbanks, but he wasn't Bert Figgins either.

Amy was mesmerizingly aware of the stranger's arm next to hers between the cinema seats. Not that he pressed against hers in any over-familiar way, but she could just feel the warmth of another arm, with only the thickness of his coat between his skin and hers. Summer, she thought, could be an extra-specially nice time of the year after all.

If she moved away, it would seem too obvious that she was being rude, so she did nothing at all, except to enjoy the unexpected contact of this man who had made a point of coming to sit beside her. And since she was also aware of Tess's suppressed anger and disbelief, to try not to let it all go to her head.

Although she registered little of the remainder of the

film, she was sorry when it ended and the lights came up again. The pianist changed key and roared into the strains of 'God Save The King', while everyone stood in united reverence until the final notes faded away. Tess turned to Amy at once.

'Come on. We'll have to hurry to get a tram.'

'Oh. Yes, yes, of course.'

Amy was thoroughly disoriented, still caught up in the stranger's delightful suggestion of getting some kind of reduction for good attendance out of the cinema management. Had he meant it or not? Or was it all just an excuse to speak to her, to sit with her? She was almost delirious with the thought.

'Unless you've got other plans, of course,' Tess said nastily when she didn't move.

The young man was moving along the line of seats away from them. Out of their lives . . . until the next Saturday, presumably, *if* he bothered to turn up again. Amy felt her shoulders wilt. It had probably all meant nothing, and she'd been a fool to get so excited over a meaningless piece of chatter in a darkened cinema, which everybody knew was a hot-bed of all sorts of disreputable rogues if you weren't very careful.

'Of course not,' she said crossly. 'Let's get out of here. I'm starving, and Cook promised to save us some of her apple pie for supper.'

Tess's mouth curved into a small smile as she heard Amy's inevitable remedy for disappointment. They pushed through the crush of people, and Amy tried not to mind that the young man had disappeared as quickly as he'd moved to her side. Everyone was out for a fast bit of excitement these days.

Older people said it was the aftermath of the war . . . but if excitement had been the only reason he'd sought her out, she pushed down the guilty thought that she was as keen for it as anyone. She was twenty-one and as yet

12

innocent about men – apart from Bert Figgins, whom she considered she could handle well enough.

'Well! It looks as though your beau's known in high places.' Tess commented as they went into the foyer, still seething at not having heard any of their conversation.

Amy looked around sharply. She'd taken off one shoe in the cinema, and the button still wasn't fastened properly, and the shoe felt in danger of parting company with her foot. She hobbled to the nearest wall and bent down to fix it, her eyes searching to where Tess was pointing.

He was talking to a bullish elderly man they both recognized at once. The owner-manager of the Roxy cinema always stood by the box-office at the end of every performance, like a ship's captain, assessing the audience's reaction to the entertainment. He was a keen entrepreneur. If the crowd was very enthusiastic, he retained the film for one more week, or tantalized them by advance notices that it would be brought back at some future date. If they were dissatisfied, he cut his losses and brought in a newer offering to keep the customers happy.

The young man caught sight of his target and weaved his way back towards Amy.

'All arranged,' he said cheerfully. 'Three yearly tickets on a cut-price basis –'

'How wonderful –' Amy said in delight.

'How ridiculous,' Tess snapped. 'How can anybody be sure they can come every week for a whole year!'

He looked at Tess properly for the first time. He was even better looking than she'd thought at first, Tess realized with a mild shock, but it didn't make her feel any better. She had no wish to reveal to this – this whoever-he-was – that they didn't have much money and were merely housemaids. He wasn't real class, she surmised, but he was no down-and-out either. He spoke well enough, even if he wasn't on the Honourable Giles Beaumont's level.

13

'We can't always manage it, you see,' she heard Amy say apologetically. 'We –'

'We have to look after our aged parents some Saturday afternoons when the maids have their day off,' Tess put in grandly.

'Oh, I see,' he replied without showing any surprise. 'What a pity. Still, if you mention my name at the box-office, I'm sure it will be all right for you to come for half price when you can, on account of your being such good customers. My name's Daniel Easton.'

It sounded vaguely familiar.

'That's very kind of you, Mr Easton.'

Tess had taken control of the conversation now, while Amy stood by in stunned embarrassment, knowing she was being forced to share the lie Tess had told. Knowing too, that however much she had imagined, even for a moment, that Daniel Easton might want to see her again, she could hardly admit to him now that she didn't have aged parents to care for, and that she was one of the maids in question!

Sometimes Tess infuriated her, and what was more, out of the corner of her eye she saw their tram begin to trundle past the cinema, and knew that they didn't have a snowball's chance in Hades of catching it.

'Tess, there's our tram –' she began despairingly.

Daniel Easton looked concerned. 'I say, have you missed it? It's all my fault for keeping you talking. But if you'll allow me, I'd be more than happy to drive you wherever it is you want to go.'

Amy saw her friend's eyes widen still more. Few men could not resist her when she treated them to that innocent look that lightened the hardness in her face. Tess put on her class-conscious voice.

'Do you have a car? How spiffing. We accept, don't we, Amy? But only if you promise to drop us at the corner of Aveley Square. Our parents are rather stuffy about that

14

kind of thing, and we insist on walking the last bit. It's Hampstead. Not too far, I hope?' She spoke coolly, like one well used to being driven about.

'Anywhere you say, miss.' Daniel grinned, clearly seeing in Tess the archetypal dutiful daughter. 'If you'll both kindly wait here, I'll have the car round the front in a jiffy.'

They watched him go, sparing a few words to the Roxy manager as he left. The crowds had thinned out, and the portly manager glanced at them before he went inside his box-office to count up the day's takings in his podgy little fingers.

'Odious little man,' Tess breathed, as they stood on the pavement outside the cinema.

'Not as odious as you!' Amy flared. 'How could you be so mean and deceitful, Tess? You've ruined everything for me now.'

Tess stared at her in exasperation.

'Why? Because I told a little white lie to the boyfriend? Do you think he'd have looked twice at you if he knew we were housemaids, ninny?'

'He'd already looked twice at me,' Amy said in a strangled voice. 'That's what's really got you in a twist, isn't it? He looked at me, not you!'

Tess began to laugh. 'Don't be potty. Do you think I care if the chap fancies you? I've already got plenty of them panting after me.'

'But this one fancied *me*,' Amy said wildly. 'Leave him alone, Tess – please.'

Whatever she might have said in answer to that was stopped by the roar of a car's engine as the black Austin twelve stopped right outside the cinema. It wasn't the Beaumonts' Rolls-Royce, but it was a more exclusive vehicle than the stuffy tram, and the two girls moved together towards the pavement as Daniel Easton swept out and opened the rear passenger door.

15

'I'm sure you'll find it comfortable.' He smiled at Tess, as Amy automatically allowed her to get in first. To her sheer amazement, Daniel Easton slammed the door shut behind Tess, who was still fussing to make her floral skirts sit prettily around her in case anyone should be watching. He opened the front passenger door with a flourish, and smiled straight into Amy's startled eyes.

'For you, my lady,' he grinned. 'I promise it's quite safe to sit beside the driver.'

She stepped inside, thinking this must be a dream. She had never sat in the front seat of a car in her life. Cars rarely came down Stratford Lane, where her grandmother lived, a street so narrow that the sun seldom lit the cobbles. And in Hampstead, cars were for the toffs, not for the likes of her and Tess. Even when Bert had taken her out, she'd had to sit beside him on the jolting tram and then walk the rest of the way to the river.

In the driving mirror she caught sight of Tess's face as Daniel started up the engine again. She was furious at being relegated to the back seat. Amy looked away quickly, her heart thumping. Her new friend glanced at her and smiled as the Austin eased its way out into the middle of the road.

His hand reached for some sort of lever just as Amy smoothed down her navy cotton skirt with hands that were not quite steady. Their fingers brushed together, and the small contact sent the blood rushing to her cheeks.

She was acting like a simpleton and she knew it. But for the rest of that heady journey, everything looked new and different from the front seat of the car. And even the grubby streets of London could seem magical and exciting when someone with an enthusiastic male voice was pointing out places of interest she'd hardly noticed before. Through it all, the strains of a brand-new popular song kept running through Amy's head.

'She's my once-a-week love, my once-in-a-dream-time love, all so del-i-cate and lovely . . .'

It was ridiculous, impossible, and everybody knew that dreams rarely came true for the likes of a girl from Stratford Lane . . . but then, before today she'd have said that all of this was impossible too, and she was blowed if she was going to pinch herself in case she found that it wasn't really happening.

2

Tess related the incident to anyone who would listen, as if to underline the unlikelihood of such a thing.

'Amy's got herself a gentleman friend.'

The huge kitchen of the Beaumont mansion was wringing with steam, and Cook raised her flushed face in irritation at the cocky tones of the parlour maid. Cook and the butler had been discussing her that afternoon.

'She's getting far too uppity for her own good,' Cook had said in aggrieved tones, 'especially since she's taken the eye of Lady Beaumont. Next thing we know, Tess Loveridge will be wheedling her way into being lady's maid for her ladyship and putting Miss Phipps out of a job, and then she'll be impossible.'

Mr Allen had been cynical.

'Well, if it happens, at least Tess won't be bothering us so much. Miss Phipps is getting too old to be much use to her ladyship any more, if the truth was told. And that nice young Amy Moore would be far better off without Tess goading her all the time!'

They both registered what Tess was telling them now.

'A gentleman friend, is it? Since when did you girls have time for walking out with young gentlemen?'

Despite the fact that she'd normally be pleased for Amy, Cook was still fussing over the fact that the Saturday roast was done a mite too well for Lady Beaumont's delicate digestion.

'I'm not walking out with anyone,' Amy said shortly. 'It's just that I – we – met this chap in the cinema –'

'And what kind of place Is the cinema for a proper introduction? You want to mind yourself, ducks. No good

18

ever came of young men who put propositions to gels in dark places,' Cook said meaningly.

'He wasn't at all improper.' Amy was annoyed at the way her lovely moments were being diminished so rapidly. She glared at Tess, angry with her for mentioning it at all. Her feet hurt from the long walk from the corner of the square, where they had insisted Daniel let them out of the car, and she was sure there was a blister on her toe.

'Did you know him before today, Amy?' Mr Allen put in. He was tall and square-faced and could be as stiff-backed as the Beaumonts when he wanted to be. But he had a protective fondness for the smaller, rounder housemaid, and Amy shook her head.

'We've *seen* him before, though, lots of times. He always seems to be at the Roxy when we're there. We thought he'd taken a fancy to Tess –' She stopped, as Cook and Mr Allen glanced at one another.

'And instead o' that, he took a fancy to you,' Cook finished triumphantly as Tess scowled. 'Well, it's like I always say, gel. Good wins out in the end.'

'What's that supposed to mean?' Tess snapped.

'Nothin',' Cook chuckled. 'Only that our Amy here deserves a boy of her own, that's all, and I hope he's a good 'un.'

'What's his name?' Mr Allen persisted.

'Daniel. Daniel Easton.'

Just saying it made her heartbeats do a little dance of pleasure. It was such a nice name. It flowed. It was musical, like the song that still burned in her brain . . .

'Easton. Seems to me I've heard that name somewhere.' Mr Allen frowned. 'It'll come to me soon.'

Amy was tired of being quizzed about it all. The excitement of the car-ride was already fading a little, and all she wanted was to take off her shoes and be alone for a while. She wanted time to think about Daniel Easton and to savour the magic of him wanting to know her, before she put on her serviceable maid's dress and got back to the kitchen on proper duty.

It was Tess who'd insisted on popping in here first, before they went up to their attic room, and now she knew why. She'd wanted to make Amy look silly.

Sometimes Amy wondered why she considered Tess such a friend. If she hadn't suspected that beneath all the gloss and veneer Tess was as insecure and vulnerable as herself, she'd probably have run a mile from her.

'Has he asked you to walk out with him?'

The young scullery maid put in her penn'orth from the corner of the kitchen where she was diligently scrubbing the soup tureen.

'No,' Amy said miserably. 'He's getting us cut-price tickets at the Roxy though, Fanny. I never knew anyone who could get blood out of a stone before –'

'That's where I heard the name,' the butler said. 'Easton. The owner of the Roxy's called Easton, and he's a wily old fox for drumming up trade if I ever met one. I bet your young man's his son. No wonder he could get you cheap-rate tickets. It's good for business, and makes sure you'll go back there again.'

He couldn't have said anything to make her spirits plummet faster. That, and the fact that Tess was finding it hard not to smile. It was obvious what Tess thought. Daniel had probably sized up the two of them and decided that Amy was the more gullible of the two. What did a couple of cut-price tickets mean to a man like the owner of the Roxy? It ensured their faithfulness, and if he enlisted his son to snare likely customers . . .

Her imagination ran away with her. Never mind that the Roxy was always full, and there was no need for giving away cut-price tickets. Never mind that Daniel had been looking out for her for several weeks, and had seemed so nice. Never mind that he'd said he hoped to see her at the cinema next week – without making any other kind of arrangement, she noted painfully now.

All her pleasure in the afternoon was gone, and with a stifled sound in her throat, she rushed out of the kitchen and up the servants' stairs. Seconds later Tess came storming into their tiny room behind her.

'What's got into you now, for God's sake?'

'You just don't see, do you?' Amy burst out. 'This lovely day was all for nothing. You spoiled half of it with your stupid lies, and now that I know the truth, it's *all* spoiled.'

'What's spoiled about it?' Tess said crossly. 'Is it just because your Daniel's not some big city gent, and only the son of that pig-eyed Roxy owner? You're getting ambitious in your old age, aren't you? Anyway, he didn't let on who he was, either. So what's the difference?'

Amy glared, her face flushed with misery.

'I wouldn't care what he was if he wanted me for myself.'

'Well, why shouldn't he want you for yourself? You're not bad-looking. In fact, with a bit of colour in your face you can be pretty enough,' Tess said generously. 'I'll tell you what. You can borrow my rouge for next week if you like.'

'I'm not going next week.'

Tess pulled the floral frock over her head and sat down on her own bed in her petticoat. She was as flat and fashionable as a boy, thanks to rigid dieting. She only allowed herself the one bag of sweets at the Roxy every Saturday, and more often than not, Amy finished those.

'Why ever not? He'll expect to see you again, and he's probably the best catch you'll ever get.'

'Thanks very much.'

Amy tried not to believe that it was probably true. Thoroughly depressed now, she felt fat and frumpy. She wished she had Tess's bone structure. She wished she had three fewer inches all round her body and three extra inches of height. She wished she had Tess's airs, and that she wasn't just – Amy. And knew full well that wishing never got anybody anywhere.

'I didn't mean it like that,' Tess said impatiently. 'You could be a stunner if you took the trouble, and there's not many other girls I'd say that to.'

They both knew that was the truth. Why be stupid enough to hand out compliments to the opposition? But in Amy's case it was different. The poor mutt needed a helping hand, and for once, Tess was about to give it.

'Look, I'll help you doll yourself up a bit for next week, and you can borrow one of my frocks.'

'I'd never fit into it,' Amy muttered.

Tess clicked her small white teeth. 'Then it's time you did something about it. You don't want to end up an old maid because you're too fat for a chap to get his arms around you, do you?'

Amy glared. But Tess was right. She enjoyed her food too much, and it showed.

'All right. I'll starve myself all the week if you think it'll do any good.'

'That's the spirit. It's time you learnt to be bright and witty too. I'm going to take you in hand, and by the time you see Mr Daniel Easton again, you'll be a different girl.'

'Not too different, then. If I change myself too drastically, he might lose interest.'

Tess gave a superior smile. 'What rubbish. I never saw a gent yet who wasn't bowled over by a bit of powder and paint on a girl.'

'Just as long as you don't make me look like a tart,' Amy said doggedly. 'Me gran wouldn't give me house-room if I went indoors looking like one of them Chinese floosies in all the mystery pictures.'

Tess screamed with laughter.

22

'That'd be the day! You'd need to lose half your weight to look Chinese. Besides, Chinese girls have slanting black eyes, not whopping great fudgy ones.'

'They're hazel, and I didn't mean it literally,' Amy said crossly. 'Sometimes you're so daft, Tess.'

She changed out of her frock quickly, and the faint odour of ashes-of-roses wafted out of the material. Amy believed in keeping herself clean and fresh. She hung the frock in the narrow wall closet, smoothing out the creases, and slid her maid's frock over her head, while Tess watched her jerky movements, arms crossed behind her head as she lay on her bed.

'You know your trouble, don't you, Amy Moore?' she said at last.

'No, but I'm sure you're going to tell me.'

'You need a proper love affair to put some life into you, gel. Bert Figgins is all right for a bit of slap and tickle, but he ain't never going anywhere. You might do all right with this Daniel, so I've decided to let you have him without a fight. I can't say fairer than that, can I?'

Amy looked at her in silence for a minute, and then she was struck by the utter bloody comical conceit of it. Tess Loveridge really believed what she was saying. She'd discard any thought of having Daniel Easton for herself – as if he'd ever fancied her anyway! – and would graciously bestow him on her little friend.

'Well, thank you kindly,' Amy said, barely able to contain her mirth at Tess's sauce. 'I'll be sure and tell him I've got your blessing.'

Tess sat up at once. 'You'll do no such thing,' she began, and then stopped as Amy doubled up with laughter, because Tess looked so funny, sitting there in her petticoat with that look of indignation on her face and her hair all mussed up.

For once, Amy felt completely superior. She was the

one Daniel Easton had sought out, and nothing was going to take away the glow of that.

Daniel cleared his throat for the third time. He'd quickly made up his mind about Amy Moore. After his initial attraction towards the other girl, he realized it was Amy he liked enormously and wanted to know better. He always found it easy to come to a decision, but not so easy to carry it out when there was the usual tension in the house. His father put down his knife and fork with a clatter, while his mother looked up nervously.

'Look, boy, if there's something on your mind, let's have it. You've been sitting there like a cat on hot bricks for the last fifteen minutes, so for God's sake come straight out with it. I can't abide atmospheres in the house. You haven't been toying with some young girl and don't have the guts to tell us, have you?'

'Frank, please. There's no call for such talk,' Helen Easton murmured, scarlet-faced.

He looked at his beige little wife, wondering why on earth he had ever married her. He was a man of ambition, and it had seemed useful to have a woman at his side who said little and opposed him not at all. Long before the marriage was a year old, Frank Easton realized what a mistake he had made. Helen wasn't just amiable. She was a cabbage, a nonentity, and he found it hard not to despise her more as the years went by.

The only capable thing she'd done in her life was to give him a son. She'd taken long enough over that too, he thought sourly. She was old, and he easily overlooked the fact that he was two years older. And she doted on their son in a way that made him puke, never seeing that all the affection she lacked from her husband was returned to her a hundredfold from her darling boy.

Frank saw the boy put a restraining hand on his mother's arm now, and scowled. The two of them had a closeness

24

he'd never had from anyone. The fact that his ineffectual wife and his handsome son were on such good terms made it all the more galling to him. Daniel was far from being the blessing he had expected a son to be, and they were often at each other's throats.

'I want to ask a girl home for tea next Sunday.'

Frank's mouth dropped open. Whatever had been fidgeting Daniel, he hadn't expected it to be this. He wished now he hadn't made the caustic remark about getting a girl in trouble. It was high time Daniel was interested in girls, and the remark had merely hidden Frank's unease that a son of his might be turning into a nancy-boy. He beamed across the table.

'Well, there's nothing wrong in that, boy. It's time you brought a nice girl home for Sunday tea, isn't it, Mother?'

Helen had long given up the dry response that she wasn't Frank's mother. She'd made it often enough over the years and he'd never heeded it. He rarely listened when she spoke, not proper listening, in the shared way two people considered each other's feelings and opinions.

'Who is this girl, Daniel? Do we know her?' she said instead, with a mother's concern.

Daniel smiled at her with genuine affection. Privately he considered his father a fool for not seeing the gentleness in his pretty mother. He hated him for treating her like the wallpaper and even more for dallying with fancy-fluffs whenever he got the chance. Frank thought no one knew about the late nights at the cinema when it wasn't work that kept him behind, but Daniel knew, and hated him for it.

'Dad's seen her, though he probably won't remember her. She's a regular on Saturday afternoons and comes with her friend. They live in Hampstead –'

'Hampstead, eh?' Frank put in, his eyes calculating. 'Then she's probably quite well-to-do. We can do with a bit of class in the family, so you lay on a good spread, Mother, and don't let us down by any silly female talk.'

'The girl's a female, isn't she? She won't want to be bored by hearing about the state of the nation or the ups and downs of your box-office takings on a Sunday afternoon,' Helen was stung into saying. 'What's her name, Daniel?'

'It's Amy. Amy Moore.'

Frank sniffed. 'Don't sound too posh to me. It'll be short for one of them upper-crust names, I dare say.'

Daniel felt the usual anger with this oafish social-climber of a man.

'I don't give a d – anything whether she's rich or poor. We've only just met. She's a nice girl, but don't go making any daft plans in your head. I haven't even said anything to her about coming to tea yet. I shan't see her again until next Saturday.'

Frank snorted. 'You mean you're waiting a whole week before getting your oar in? What the devil are you made of, boy? Sometimes I wonder if you really are a son of mine.'

Daniel jumped up from the supper table. 'For God's sake! One minute you're accusing me of getting some girl into trouble, and the next you're as good as telling me to get on with it. There's no pleasing you, is there?'

Frank's bushy brows drew together in a fury.

'Don't you talk to me in those tones!' he bellowed. 'I'm still your father, whether you're twenty-two years old or not, and you'll treat me with respect.'

'A bit of respect from you wouldn't go amiss either,' Daniel snapped back.

'Stop it, both of you,' Helen's quiet voice broke in. 'Can't we have one meal without the two of you wrangling all the time? And can't you be pleased for Daniel that he's met a nice girl, Frank? I'm delighted, and I'll make her very welcome, darling.'

Frank turned his anger on her, his tone sneering.

'Well, no doubt you'll be singing a different tune if he marries her and brings her here to live. You'll be relegated to second place in your own kitchen then, Mother, and it's about the only place you have any say in things.'

'Shut up, can't you?' Incensed, Daniel put himself between his tearful mother and his father. 'I told you I've only just met the girl and you're interfering already. If I ever ask her or anybody else to marry me, rest assured I'll never bring a wife to live under your roof!'

'And if you don't, you can say good-bye to your inheritance,' Frank put in triumphantly. 'There'll be no Roxy for you, boy. You'll be out on your own with your little bit of fluff, and you'll be barred from this house from then on. There'll be no little chit-chats with your mother again neither. How does that fit in with your plans, heh?'

'Daniel,' Helen said fearfully, 'your father means what he says. He's always said that families should stick together –'

'Like one big happy family, you mean?' he said savagely. He put his arm round his mother's thin shoulders, feeling them shake, and was angry at being made to feel guilty at his part in this scene.

'Don't worry, Mother, I'd never leave you. Not if it meant leaving you with him.'

He kissed her soft cheek. It would be somebody very special who took on his father as well as himself, he realized. Somebody who loved him very much. Somebody like Amy Moore.

Housemaids weren't allowed to be ill. Mr Allen had said so time and again, just as if his will was strong enough to influence cold and flu germs flying about the place. They struck Tess down on the following Saturday. She awoke with streaming eyes and a head that felt like a bucket full of sand. She informed Amy that she ached from head to toe, and nobody was going to get her out of her bed.

'You can't be ill!' Amy said. 'It'll mean I've got to do both our jobs, and I'll never get away to the pictures this afternoon.'

'Well, that's nice, that is,' Tess croaked. 'Here's me with a throat like a gravel pit and all you care about is yourself –'

'Oh Tess, you know that's not true!' She was all contrition. 'But this is my big day and you were going to help me get ready.'

Tess looked at her from her puffed-up face, not prepared to be sociable.

'You didn't stick to your diet, did you? You ain't lost an ounce all week, I bet. You'll have to wear your own frock and just hope that your gent prefers 'em cuddly.'

She turned over on to her stomach and closed her eyes, refusing to say another word. Amy left her there, rushing down the servants' stairs two at a time to inform Cook and Mr Allen that Tess would have to stay in bed for the rest of the day. Cook would be obliged to climb the stairs for herself to check that Tess was as ill as she said, and Amy would have to do all the brasses and run up and down with breakfast trays as well as doing her own work before she had any thoughts of going out for the afternoon.

She was still going through everything in her mind when she cannoned straight into someone at the foot of the stairs. Her face went brilliant red as she looked up into the arrogant eyes of Giles Beaumont. Her hands had gone out to save herself, and Giles's arms had reached out just as automatically to catch her.

'What's the rush? Is there a fire or something?' he said, with a smile playing around his wide mouth.

'I'm sorry, sir,' Amy gasped. 'I didn't expect to see you so early in the morning. Tess has a cold and I'll have to do her work as well as mine, you see.'

She closed her eyes for a brief moment as the inconsequential words tripped out. She had never come close to Giles Beaumont before, let alone spoken to him. What must he think of her, this elegant young man who couldn't care less about the doings of maids?

'Poor Tess.' Giles was still smiling. 'But if her indisposition meant this delightful little encounter, then Allah give praise to the common cold.'

'Yes, sir. Thank you, sir,' Amy twittered, not understanding half that he said. His accent was so royal it was almost laughable, and Tess had said some of his obscure phrases were terribly clever. When she'd tried to repeat them Amy thought they were just plain daft.

Lots of things were just plain daft to Amy, which probably meant she didn't have the sense to sort out the gold from the dross. Or so Tess was always telling her.

'What's your name?'

Amy became aware that Giles Beaumont was still holding her. He was looking down at her in a way that made a sudden shiver run through her. She would have wriggled free of the unexpected embrace, had it not seemed less embarrassing to stay exactly where she was.

'Amy, sir,' she said primly. 'Amy Moore.'

'And what does Amy Moore do here?'

She looked up in astonishment, and then realized that there was no earthly reason why the likes of Giles Beaumont should know what she did! The household ran smoothly and efficiently, and those upstairs had no knowledge of the skivvies below who spent their lives rushing about to do their bidding.

'I'm a housemaid, sir, below stairs.'

His grip on her arm tightened a little as he threw back his head and laughed. His aristocratic head, with the light brown hair that curved over his scalp in little ridged waves that looked as if they had been crimped with an iron every morning . . .

'Well, below-stairs Amy, I'd better let you go before I'm accused of abducting you, hadn't I?'

'Yes, sir. Thank you, sir.'

She scuttled away from him, aware of him watching her with amusement. She was as useless as a bent ha'penny, she thought dismally. Tess would have flirted and enjoyed the moment, while she . . . She dashed into the kitchen, cheeks scarlet. While she had merely felt her heart move at the dark brown eyes that had smiled down into hers.

'Lord above, gel, calm yourself. Not sickening for summat, are you?' Cook scolded her. 'You're as red as a turkey-cock, and where's that other lazy miss?'

'Tess is in bed with a cold, and there's nothing wrong with me.'

Nothing except that in the space of a week she'd met and spoken with two young men from very different backgrounds, and it was dawning on her that each of them had the power to make her heart beat faster. She liked the one enormously, while the other, even in those brief moments, had made her feel distinctly uneasy.

3

Amy had never been to the Roxy on her own before. Her grandmother harped on about nice girls never going to the cinema alone. She wished to blazes that her gran's sayings didn't keep spinning in and out of her brain. She didn't want to think about Gran, or about Tess pining away in bed, or the rights and wrongs of knowing how much she was looking forward to seeing Daniel Easton again. One minute she was guiltily glad at the thought that Tess wasn't here, and the next she was frantically nervous without her.

She'd hoped to see Daniel waiting in the cinema entrance for her and Tess, but he wasn't there. After five minutes of fidgeting with her gloves and trying to ignore the curious glances of the girls and fellows going in, she gave up the waiting game and bought her own ticket, too embarrassed to say anything about a cut rate. Inside, the gloom of the cinema surrounded her in anonymity and hid her acute disappointment.

For once, she hardly noticed what was happening on the flickering screen. She had a job to fight back the tears as time passed and there was no sign of Daniel. She'd been in such a hurry to get here she hadn't had time to experiment with Tess's rouge. Her self-confidence was slipping by the second.

Whenever she got upset her skin went blotchy and her eyes puffed up, and she knew that she was probably looking a mess by now, and then Daniel wouldn't want to be bothered with her anyway . . . in fact, she wasn't sure that she wanted to see him either, not now when she knew she must look so awful.

31

Somebody slid into the seat beside her, but her eyes were too blurred to care who it was. She sniffed noisily, and shoved her hand up her sleeve for her handkerchief, when one was thrust in front of her face.

'Will this do? It's perfectly clean. I'm awfully sorry I'm so late. My mother isn't well, and I waited until the doctor came to be sure she was all right.'

When the voice stopped whispering, Amy held her breath for one last second before turning her head in the darkened cinema. Daniel looked at her anxiously, and not knowing what else to do with it, she blew her nose into his handkerchief. Since she could hardly give it back to him in its soiled state, she balled it up in her hand and simply stared at him.

'Are you all right, Amy? Mother's got this wretched influenza that's going around. Don't say you're coming down with it too.'

Unwittingly, he gave her the lead she needed.

'It's just a cold. Tess has got it, and I'm probably catching hers. She's stayed home today.'

Daniel's face broke into a smile.

'Bad luck for her, but not for me, because now I've got you all to myself.'

People around them began shushing, and Amy tried to concentrate on the picture. But she couldn't concentrate on much because Daniel was sitting beside her at last, his arm comfortably close to hers, and he'd said he was glad Tess wasn't here. Her heart sang at the joy of it, and by the time the performance was over, her skin had lost its blotches, her eyes sparkled, and no artificial colour was needed to put the glow in her cheeks.

She moved out of the cinema in the long file of people. She was just ahead of Daniel, aware of his guiding hand on her elbow. Once in the foyer, she stood uncertainly, wondering whether to mention the cut-price tickets. His father was busy speculating on the success of this week's picture, and didn't appear to notice them at all. It didn't seem her place to make the first move, and without the protective ambience of the cinema all around them, she felt shyness begin to overwhelm her again.

'Do you fancy some tea and cakes?' Daniel said. 'There's a nice little tea-room not far from here. We could walk there if you like, and then I'd be happy to drive you home, Amy. Or at least to the end of the road,' he finished with a smile.

She flushed, remembering Tess's silly comment about their status. She turned the tables on him before giving him an answer.

'Why didn't you tell us who you were?' she accused. 'You never said you were the manager's son!'

'What difference does it make? I'm still me and you're still you, so are we going to have some tea or aren't we?' he said half-teasingly.

She thought for a minute, and then nodded. It was true. They were the same people who clearly liked each other, regardless of their backgrounds. And just for a little while it was all that mattered.

'All right. Tea and cakes would be lovely,' she said, relieved to be actually doing something.

There was a special delight in walking along the road in the company of this tall young man who offered her his arm just like the toffs did, after side-stepping quickly to walk on the outside of the pavement so that her skirts wouldn't be splashed by the motors going by. And she, Amy Moore, accepting it all as coolly and graciously as a lady born to such civilities.

'I had something to ask you today, Amy,' Daniel said, when they were sitting opposite one another in the tea-room with the lace tablecloths and glass-domed cake servers, and the atmosphere made cosy and intimate by wide window-ledges so thickly adorned with potted plants you could hardly see out.

'Were you?' she said, her heart thudding.

It was the first time she'd been out with a young man, unchaperoned, except for Bert Figgins. And since he was always sniffing around for anything in skirts, she hardly counted him. He wasn't a proper gent, like Daniel.

The waitress brought them a pot of tea and a serving-plate of fancies, and Daniel waited for Amy to pour, while she prayed that her hands wouldn't shake and spill it all over him. It was usually Amy who was doing the fetching and carrying, and this was a novelty.

But he wouldn't know that, of course. Because of Tess's fibs, he thought she lived in a house with maids of her own, and with every minute that passed she knew she couldn't bear to disillusion him.

'I was supposed to ask you to tea tomorrow, but now that my mother's ill, we'll have to postpone it,' he said regretfully. 'Would you have come, Amy?'

Her face flushed, and he thought he had never seen anything so beautiful. She was transparently lovely, natural and innocent, not like her friend. Attractive though Tess undoubtedly was, Daniel suspected that she was a bit of a tart. For him, Amy had the kind of innocence that was its own protection.

'I – I think so,' she said dubiously, her glance unconsciously arch, and they both laughed, delighting in the game of flirtation that had hardly begun.

'But you can't help wondering if I really do have a mother, and if I'm respectable, or if I secretly mean to carry you away to my tent in the desert,' he said dramatically.

Amy giggled. 'Like Rudolph Valentino in *The Sheik*,' she said. 'Wasn't he simply wonderful?'

'If you say so. But don't say it too often or I shall get jealous.'

Amy took a sip of tea, watching him from above the rim of her cup. He had lovely dark eyes. He wasn't so unlike Valentino, not as far as she was concerned anyway.

'Will you really? But he's only an image on the silver screen, and you're right here,' she said before she stopped to think, and blushed scarlet immediately.

'That's the best thing anyone's ever said to me,' Daniel said with a smile. 'And to reassure you about my mother, I have a note written in her hand last week inviting you. But unfortunately, it will have to wait now until a later date.'

Amy took the note, and felt his fingers brush hers as she did so. Just as before, that brief delicious sensation of fire ran through her at his touch. She read quickly. It seemed perfectly all right. She tucked it in her purse, savouring it because it was a link with him.

'I hope your mother will recover very soon, and please tell her how much I shall look forward to meeting her,' she said formally.

Daniel looked delighted and put his hand across the tablecloth to take hers.

'I'm so happy to hear you say so, Amy. I know you'll like one another, and as soon as she's better we'll have that tea-party.'

Amy withdrew her hand reluctantly as the waitress stood beside them with the bill. She didn't know how important this invitation was meant to be. She didn't know if it meant she was walking out with Daniel Easton or not. She only knew that she felt more alive when she was with him than she had ever felt before. She was somewhere up among the stars, and the dank kitchen of the Beaumont mansion seemed a million miles away from here.

'What's wrong?' she heard him say in sudden concern, and she cursed the mobility of her face that made her feelings so obvious.

'Nothing at all,' she said, refusing to end the day by confessing that she wasn't who he thought she was. 'I just had a shiver, that's all. I told you, I'm probably catching Tess's cold.'

It was more than likely that she would, since they shared the small cramped bedroom . . .

'Then I'd better get you home,' he said, and stupidly, Amy knew she'd brought the day to an end sooner than need be. 'Come on, I can't have my girl catching cold. The car's parked between here and the Roxy, so it won't be long before you're tucked up inside.'

One phrase made her pause before standing up. One sweetly beautiful phrase . . . She looked into the face that was becoming so dear to her, her hazel eyes searching for the truth.

'Am I your girl, Daniel?' She could hardly breathe as she asked the question.

He pretended to look all around him, considering.

'I don't see any other to take my fancy, so I suppose you'll have to do,' he teased. 'Unless you've got any objections, Miss Moore?'

'I don't believe I have, Mr Easton,' she said with a catch in her throat.

And what a tale she'd have to tell Tess Loveridge when she got back!

The excitement of it all stayed with her until Daniel left her at the corner of her road again. He'd leaned forward to kiss her cheek, and she could still feel the tingling in her veins as the slight roughness of his skin touched hers.

She had a young man, and was going to meet his parents as soon as his mother was well again. And that must mean his intentions towards her were serious and honourable.

But even before she reached the steps leading down to the servants' entrance of the mansion, anxiety was washing over her. If she met Daniel's people, then presumably he'd want to meet hers. His parents would want to know all about the girl who'd taken their son's fancy, and what would they think when it was discovered that she wasn't rich or even middle-class, that she didn't live in indolence and luxury like Lady Beaumont, but existed in the harsh reality of a servant's lot?

How would the Eastons react when she tried to describe her grandmother and the miserable if clean rooms in the tall cramped house in Stratford Lane? Her eyes blurred, remembering how she used to dream of inheriting pots of money. Or that Gran had been saving up for a rainy day, and they'd turn out rich after all. Daft, of course. If it wasn't, Gran wouldn't have sent Amy out in service . . .

'Here, mind where you're walking, gel. That floor's just been scrubbed,' she heard Cook's voice say crossly, and realized she had blundered into the kitchen unseeingly, too intent on thinking how the effects of a simple lie could spread like the ripples of a whirlpool to notice where she was putting her feet.

'She's still taken up with seeing her young man at the pictures,' Fanny said cheekily. 'Are those stars in her eyes, d'you think, Cook?'

'You mind your work, miss, and watch your tongue.'

Cook had no truck with scullery maids who tried to be familiar with her. Besides . . . She looked keenly at Amy's sensitive face. She guessed unerringly that something wasn't quite right, and any other time she'd dearly like to know what it was. But what with being short-handed, and that young Tess giving her an earful when she'd gone upstairs to check up on her, Cook wasn't in the best of humours.

'And Amy, best get out of that nice frock and into your working clothes. You'll have to stand in for Tess tonight and help Mr Allen, upstairs.'

Amy gulped, all thoughts of Daniel forgotten. She'd only once served at dinner in the big dining-room, and it had terrified her. The room was so large and the table so long, and the Beaumonts and their guests had either stared at her all together or ignored her so humiliatingly that she'd felt like a piece of furniture.

She still didn't know which was worse. Her hands had been so sweaty, her fingers had been all thumbs and the extra shilling Mr Allen had given her for her help hadn't compensated one bit. The only time she'd relaxed was when she'd gone home on Sunday morning and made Gran laugh fit to split her sides by imitating Lady Beaumont's plummy tones so magnificently.

She raced up the stairs, with Cook's voice still in her ears. Perhaps Tess was better, she thought desperately. Perhaps she wouldn't want to miss her evening serving-up of dinner for the family, which she seemed to think so important. But one look at Tess's body burrowing beneath the bedclothes, and Amy knew it was all up to her.

'How are you, Tess? Did Cook come and see you?'

'You mean did the old bag check up on me? What do you think?'

Tess's voice was muffled until she raised her head a fraction. Her hair stuck up like orange spikes, the remnants of her make-up streaked across her face like a clown. Amy thought she looked a proper fright, though no doubt Tess would have called it vivacious.

'Never mind about me. What happened today? Did he show up, and did you get the tickets?'

Amy had completely forgotten about any cinema tickets by now. She shook her head.

'He was there and we went for tea afterwards, but he didn't say anything about the tickets.'

'Why didn't you ask then? Honestly, you are a ninny, Amy.' Tess could still be impatient even if she was ill, Amy thought crossly. She wrinkled her nose at the stale, almost pungent smell she couldn't readily define. It was probably due to having too little air in the room. Amy went to the small window and dragged it open, breathing in fresh air before hurriedly changing her clothes.

'For God's sake, shut that window. Do you want me to die of pneumonia? There's a lot of flu about, in case you haven't heard.'

'Of course I have. Daniel's mother's got it. If she hadn't I'd be going there for tea tomorrow,' Amy snapped without triumph.

Tess sat bolt upright in bed. Her mouth looked swollen and she dragged the bedclothes up around her.

'What have you done to your neck?' Amy said, staring. 'It looks bruised –'

'It's nothing. D'you mean he's asked you to meet his folks already? That's a turn-up. What did you say? You accepted, I hope.'

'It's all off because his mother's ill, but I shall go when she's better. She wrote me a note. Do you want to see it?'

'I'm too tired. Shut the bleedin' window, Amy, and let me get back to sleep. And if you're waiting table tonight, you'd better borrow my cap and apron – and see that you keep it clean.'

She turned her back and burrowed down beneath the bedclothes again. Amy remembered that reading wasn't one of Tess's best accomplishments. She just got by without disgracing herself, and that was all.

Somewhere in the house a bell tinkled, and Amy forgot everything but the coming ordeal. She washed herself quickly at the small marble washstand and splashed ashes-of-roses scent under her armpits and between her legs. It would be the most terrible thing to give offence in the Beaumonts' dining-room. Some girls might not be fussy, but Amy wasn't one of them. She put on the better of her two work frocks and Tess's cap and apron, and smoothed her hair back behind her ears to look as neat and tidy as possible. She wasn't Tess, but they'd just have to do with what they'd got for tonight.

*   *   *

'You'll do,' Mr Allen said kindly when he saw her. 'Just keep your eyes lowered and make yourself as invisible as you can while you're upstairs. There's only two guests tonight, so there'll be five altogether. There's cauliflower soup to start, so mind you're not careless with it. Just stay calm and go about things quietly.'

She'd be a lot better if her heart didn't thump so much, she thought. She caught sight of Fanny eyeing her enviously, took a deep breath and lifted her chin. At least it would be something to tell Gran about tomorrow. She must try to record it all in her mind to amuse the old lady.

And after all it wasn't so bad. The starchiness of the dining-room compared with the hustle and bustle below stairs was almost comical. But in a strange way, the very orderliness of the Beaumonts affected Amy in a similar way. She was able to respond with quiet efficiency. She didn't drop anything, or spill the soup, or make herself obtrusive in any way, and she could tell by Mr Allen's silent approval that he was pleased with her.

After the meal the gentlemen went to the library for their coffee, and she carried in the tray as if she'd always done it. The air was already thick with cigar smoke, and under cover of handing him his coffee cup, young Mr Giles Beaumont gave her a gigantic wink. Amy gave a half-smile back, then froze for a second as the aroma of his cigar wafted into her nostrils.

She had smelled it before. Only then it had been stale, still lingering in a room long after Giles Beaumont had left it. She remembered swollen lips and tender bruises on a white neck. And she knew immediately that Cook hadn't been the only caller on Tess that afternoon.

Amy lay on her back in her own bed, shoulders still aching from lifting the heavy tureens and serving-plates. Tess was snoring gently. She smelled stale, Amy noted, and wondered briefly if Giles Beaumont had minded that she was careless about personal cleanliness. Perhaps in the height of passion it was something a man overlooked.

Amy sat up against her hard pillow, trying to fathom out her own feelings. Shock, yes. Disgust, perhaps. Envy – she wasn't sure. Passion was something she hadn't experienced as yet. She discounted the clumsy fumblings of Bert Figgins. She hadn't wanted his hands on her. She was saving herself, she'd told Tess grandly, ignoring the hoots of derision.

All the same, for all Tess's worldly-wise manner, she'd always thought her as innocent of men as herself. She'd never have believed Tess would allow a man into her room – *their* room – and especially not the son of the house, which seemed the epitome of folly.

Tess stirred restlessly, her eyes suddenly wide open as if she sensed someone staring at her.

'Good God, I thought you were a ghost,' she croaked. 'How'd it go, then? Tired you out, did they?'

'You don't sound very ill,' Amy said suspiciously. She was seeing all sorts of things she hadn't seen before. Like using a cold as a ruse to get the room to herself on a Saturday afternoon, so she could have a gentleman caller. If it were so, Tess was her mother all over again . . .

Tess gave a token cough. 'I'm much better. These summer colds don't last long. But what's up with you? You look funny peculiar.'

'Who's been up here, Tess?' Amy burst out. 'This afternoon while I was out, I mean.'

'While you were at the pictures with your young man?' Tess said. 'Nobody, only Cook, o' course –'

'I never saw Cook smoke cigars, nor leave the smell of 'em about the place,' Amy said accusingly. 'Nor leave marks on somebody's neck either, unless she's turning into a vampire in her old age.'

Tess stared at her. In the stark bright moonlight from the window, Amy could see her face go a dull red.

'All right, so Giles came to see how I was getting on. What's wrong with it?'

'You *know* what's wrong with it. You're playing a dangerous game, Tess! He'll only want you for one thing – and since when did you start calling him Giles?'

Tess threw off the bedclothes and padded across to the washstand in her bare feet to pour out a glass of water. In the cool of the night, she held her cotton nightgown tautly around her. Without the flattener she habitually wore by day to give her her boyish figure, her small firm breasts peaked against the fabric. Amy avoided looking at them, not wanting to imagine Giles Beaumont's hands caressing them.

'Amy, you're such a child. I could hardly be so formal as to call him Mr Beaumont when he was making passionate love to me, now could I?'

Amy's mouth went dry. Tess spoke with a kind of false bravado, a haughty pseudo-sophistication that perhaps hid a real fear of what she'd done. Amy couldn't be sure. She only knew that today Tess had moved into another kind of world that she didn't yet know. Unless she had already been there before . . . She felt sudden anger that this room should be used for such a purpose.

'Was this the first time?' she asked. 'Or is he in the habit of calling on you every minute I'm occupied elsewhere? Cleaning the brasses or running errands, or –'

'Oh Amy, of course it was the first time!' Tess's composure slipped, and she looked young and comical with her make-up still smudged across her face. 'And I'll tell you something. It was nothing like as wonderful as the medical book tells you. It hurt and it made me bleed and I thought I was dying until Giles told me not to be so silly and that it would be better next time.'

'Next time! You're not going to let him do it to you again, are you?'

'I don't know yet. It can't be so bad when you get used to it, or people wouldn't keep doing it, would they?'

People like Tess's mother, Amy added silently, people who were well known for entertaining men. Dear God, she never thought Tess would go the same way. Tess with her fine ambitions . . . Amy got out of bed and ran to put her arms around her friend. She knew she was right about the uncertainty in Tess. She could feel it in every shivering nerve in her body. And suddenly, for the first time in her life, she felt the wise one.

'Let's forget it and go to sleep, Tess. We have to be up early if we don't want Cook bellowing at us, and I'm off home in the afternoon. Gran will want to know all about Daniel and the Beaumonts' dinner-party.'

They parted, both awkward at the rare show of affection, and got back into bed. Tess curled up, trying to ignore the burning sensation that still lingered between her legs from Giles Beaumont's roughness.

Now that the shock of her discovery was receding, Amy was slowly beginning to wonder how it felt to have a lover's arms holding her in the most intimate of embraces. And naturally transferred every romantic dream in her head towards Daniel Easton.

4

The Beaumonts went to the country on Sundays, and the housemaids were usually free in the afternoons unless Cook had any special jobs for them to do. Tess had recovered remarkably quickly from her cold, and went to make her monthly duty visit to her mother.

Amy set out from the house to catch the nearest tram to take her home, though she'd have to walk the first mile and the last. Trams didn't go down the elegant tree-lined squares where the Beaumonts lived, nor into the maze of narrow cobbled streets leading to Stratford Lane.

'Amy. Hey, Amy. Want a lift?'

She turned as she heard her name called. Bert Figgins was pedalling furiously along the wide square, incongruous in his bicycling plus fours and cap, and looking less impressive than in his grey chauffeur's uniform.

She stepped back from the edge of the pavement as he whizzed to a halt beside her. He wasn't bad-looking, she conceded, for anyone who liked pale-faced men with sandy-coloured hair and eyes the same colour, and lips that were a bit too full to be really masculine.

'You're not expecting me to ride on that thing, are you?' she laughed. 'It's not even a bicycle made for two!'

'You can sit on the cross-bar. It'll be quite safe, and it'll get you to the tram-stop in record time. Come on, Amy. I bet Tess wouldn't refuse the offer.'

Tess rarely refused anything, Amy thought dryly. But Bert's words were the challenge he intended them to be, and after a glance around to see there was no one about, she sat gingerly on the cross-bar of the bicycle. On Bert's instruction she leaned against him, and felt the machine wobble precariously along the street as he regained his balance.

'This is a lark, isn't it, Amy? The rich folk don't know what they're missing!'

He broke into a tuneless whistle in her ear. Bert was cheery and fun, and everything was a lark to him, and Amy began to feel as reckless as he as she clung on to the middle of the handlebars for dear life with one hand, and clutched Bert around the waist with the other. She gave a little squeal as she was bumped against his chest, and she could hear his heart beating fast. She caught sight of his cheeky grin as he glanced down at her.

'You never let me get this close to you before, Amy, not even by the river. You're a lovely soft bundle, better than that skinny Tess, and don't let anybody tell you otherwise.'

She felt his arms imprisoning her and her breast was squashed against him. She felt uncomfortable at the contact, especially as they were coming out of the square and there were a few more people about.

'You'd better just let me down now, Bert Figgins,' she said severely. 'I don't want my reputation ruined by being seen held tight by a young man on a cycling machine.'

'All right,' he said regretfully. 'But if you want to change your mind about visiting your gran, we could always go to the park instead. It's a nice day for it.'

His grin told her it wasn't just the weather he was talking about, and Amy flushed, remembering the time she'd let him be more familiar than she'd intended.

She wasn't sure whether she really liked him all that much, but at least he listened when she talked, as if she said something intelligent, which was more than Tess did. Daniel was attentive too, and she was still trying not to be too disappointed over the fact that if his mother had been well enough, she'd have been spending this afternoon with him and his family.

45

Bert let her off the bicycle reluctantly. She was a sweet little thing all right, and a real smasher with her cheeks rosy-red and her eyes sparkling from the fun of the ride. He'd like to give her another kind of ride, he thought, feeling a flicker of lust stirring down below. Bert welcomed every scrap of attraction he felt towards a woman, because it diminished those other darker desires he tried to keep strictly under control.

'Perhaps when you're free again, we could take another picnic,' he suggested. 'I could borrow a bike for you next time. I'd soon teach you to ride it.'

'I don't think so,' Amy smiled. 'But thanks for asking, Bert.'

She walked on down the street, and he watched her go, seeing the swing of her hips and the shapeliness of her legs. He frowned. There'd been a funny look in her eyes as she'd refused him, as if she was thinking of something else – or somebody else. And the thought was enough to make his lustful urges stronger than ever.

He definitely had manly feelings towards Amy Moore, he thought jubilantly, and he leapt on the saddle of his machine and felt the rough tweed cloth of his plus fours move exquisitely against the half-hard bulge inside them.

Gran Moore waited expectantly for Amy to come home. Her granddaughter was a good girl, not like that flighty piece she'd palled up with at the big house where she worked. Gran sniffed. Her own daughter had been deflowered and disgraced, even though the whole family had managed to hush it up at the time, and she dreaded the thought of such a thing ever happening to little Amy . . .

But it wasn't for her to say who Amy picked for her friends, and one day if she was lucky, she'd see her treasure marry a good man and live happily ever after. She doubted very much if she'd live to see great-grandchildren. These Sunday afternoons that they shared were precious, and

46

now she suspected they were numbered, she appreciated them all the more.

She pushed such gloomy thoughts out of her mind, and set about putting cups and saucers on the table and arranging a plate of the biscuits she'd laboriously made that morning. And when she heard Amy's tapping footsteps on the cobbles, she gave a sigh of gladness, and poked at the fire beneath the kettle.

They might still be enjoying the long days of summer, but Gran liked her warmth and comfort, and was rarely without a fire in the hearth. Besides, it saved using the new-fangled gas-stove that she still didn't understand and which frightened her every time it popped and hissed.

She'd never used the oven part yet. There was nothing like food cooked on an open fire in her old black cooking-pot and stews done long and slow in the range beside it, but at least the gas-oven was a useful place for keeping her bits and pieces.

'So here you are at last, gel. Thought you'd got lost,' she greeted Amy, because it wasn't her way to let the pleasure show. Amy kissed the corrugated cheek, knowing her too well to be upset by the apparent lack of emotion.

'Here I am, Gran,' she said cheerfully, trying not to let her nose wrinkle at the cloying smells inside the room. 'And I've got such a lot to tell you.'

At that, the old woman couldn't stop a smile crossing her face.

'A juicy bit of gossip about those hoity-toity employers of yours, I hope?'

Amy laughed. What would her gran say if she told her that the only bit of gossip concerning the Beaumonts was that Giles Beaumont had made love to Tess in the room her granddaughter shared? That would wipe the smile off Gran Moore's face all right.

'No, it's not,' she said sternly. 'But I served at dinner

47

for them and two guests last night because Tess had a cold. What do you think of that?'

'Not much, unless you're going to say the old boy got apoplexy at the table and left you a fortune in his will, and I doubt that! Is that all you've got to tell me?'

'No, it's not.' Amy grinned. 'Though I thought you'd be interested to know that the guests were another lord and his daughter, and Mr Allen reckons they're planning to make a match between her and Mr Giles.'

It was something she'd forgotten to mention to Tess, what with everything else. But Gran wasn't interested in matchmaking, and Amy told her the real news.

'You remember I told you about meeting a young man called Daniel Easton at the Roxy the other week?'

Gran's knowing little eyes looked more keenly as Amy busied herself making the tea.

'Did he get over-familiar, my gel? I warned you –'

'No, he didn't! And if you're not going to listen I won't tell you any more!'

Amy banged the kettle down on the hearth when she'd filled the tea-pot. Drops of water spurted out, spluttering on the coals and making them sizzle.

Amy looked at the prim little figure of her grandmother, solid as the Bank of England, Sunday-aproned and hair-curled, and felt a rush of love for her. She moved swiftly across the tiny parlour and knelt on the floor, taking the old woman's arthritic hands in hers.

'He's asked me home for Sunday tea when his mother gets over her flu. We had tea and cakes together in a tea-room yesterday, all proper and correct, and I think he's serious about me, Gran.'

The old woman's eyes softened as she looked at the glowing face level with hers. She remembered fleet-ingly when little Amy was only this high, 'knee-high to a flea' she had called her. Then she'd grown up and overtaken her old gran, and now she was crouching at eye-level on the floor, still anxiously needing approval of her young man. It was right. It was the way things should be.

'And why shouldn't he be serious? There's no finer young woman than my Amy, and that's all the praise you're going to get from me, my gel, so don't go looking for more.'

Amy felt her throat thicken. It was praise indeed from this stoical, wiry old lady with matchstick arms and legs, who'd once presided over a family. Now they only had each other. Amy gave her a quick hug, knowing Gran would be embarrassed by more.

'When are you going to bring him to see me?'

Amy got up and poured the tea and handed Gran her cup with two biscuits in the saucer. They didn't stand on ceremony in Stratford Lane.

'Soon,' she said. 'Very soon.'

'Not ashamed of me, are you, gel?' Gran was always irritatingly direct, always probing at the heart of things.

'Of course I'm not. It's just that – well, he doesn't know what I do – exactly.'

Gran's cup clattered in the saucer. 'What does that mean, for God's sake? Either he knows or he don't.'

Amy felt resentment wash over her, but not towards Gran this time . . .

'It was Tess's fault –'

'I mighta known.'

'Tess let him think we lived in a posh house and had maids. I – just haven't told him the truth yet.'

Gran's mouth dropped open. Her few remaining teeth clicked together.

'What a daft 'a'porth of nothing you are! Letting that little tart get away with it was one thing, but not telling the boy the truth is the daftest thing I ever heard. He won't thank you for it.'

'I know,' Amy said miserably. 'And I'll tell him next

time I see him, even if it means he won't take me home to tea after all.'

Gran looked at her silently before slurping her tea noisily out of the saucer where the biscuits had got satisfyingly soggy.

'If he don't, he ain't worth bothering about. What is he, the king of England or summat?'

'No. His father owns the Roxy though. I don't know what Daniel does.'

'It's time you found out then. You can't marry a chap without knowing what he's bringing into the house.'

'Nobody said anything about marrying him, Gran.' But she began to laugh, because she couldn't deny that the thought of marrying Daniel Easton had figured heavily in her day-dreams lately.

'Tell that to the birds,' Gran said dryly. 'When you seeing him again?'

'He didn't say anything about that, but if I go to the Roxy next Saturday I'm sure he'll be there.'

The old woman snorted. 'You want to get things sorted more definitely than that, gel. Mind that other tart don't step in and snap him up from under your nose.'

'Tess wouldn't do that!'

Hadn't she told her so? In that airy way of hers, Tess had handed Daniel over to Amy without a qualm . . . without even trying to get him for herself, which in Tess's mind she could do very easily.

All the way back on the tram Amy tried to think why she felt unaccountably deflated. Usually she enjoyed her little chats with her grandmother, but today she was unsettled and jittery, and not only because of the doubts in her mind over Daniel's intentions.

Gran hadn't looked well, and Amy hadn't even commented on it. She'd looked pinched and yellow, and the room was a bit of a dirt-heap, but Amy knew that if she'd suggested tidying up for her, Gran would have told her sharply that as long as she drew breath she'd stand on her own pins and look after herself, and nobody was messing about with her things until she was dead and gone. And when that happened, she wouldn't care what they did after they'd carried her out in a wooden overcoat, feet first.

There was a flurry of excitement at the Beaumonts that evening. Word filtered down from upstairs that there was definitely an engagement in the offing.

'Miss Phipps is all of a twitter,' Mr Allen told the downstairs staff. 'Apparently young Mr Giles and the Honourable Thelma Parkes-Leighton are going to make a match of it. It was her and her father at dinner last night, Amy, and they all spent today together at the estate in Norfolk.'

'That'll be an occasion to celebrate then,' Cook said, beaming.

There was a sort of choking sound from someone standing behind her, seconds before a great pile of china plates went crashing to the kitchen floor.

Cook jumped, her hand clutching her heart, and a loud screech left her lips as she turned on Tess.

'What the devil do you think you're doing, you stupid baggage? You made my heart stop altogether. You clear this mess up at once, and think yourself lucky if you aren't stopped every penny for that china out of your wages.'

'A fat chance I'd have of doing that,' Tess howled back at her. 'It'd take me a hundred years to pay for it out of my pittance, so don't talk so stupid.'

She felt a stinging blow from the back of Cook's ample hand.

'Don't you speak that way to your betters, miss. Get down on your knees and clear up that mess this instant before I report you to Madam and get you sent packing.'

'I'll help you, Tess,' Amy said at once, rushing for the

51

dustpan and brush, since Tess seemed unable to move for the moment.

'So will I,' Fanny said in a fright, never having seen Cook strike anyone before.

'And I'll get Cook a drop of brandy and sit her down to recover before we all lose our tempers completely,' Mr Allen said shortly, steering Cook well out of the way of the scurrying housemaids.

'Amy, how *could* he?' Tess was white with tears and temper among the clatter of broken china as they swept furiously. 'It was only yesterday that he – that we –'

'Tess, shut *up*,' Amy hissed at her as Fanny came rushing back with a tray for the broken bits of china. 'Do you want everyone to know what happened? We'll talk about it later.'

They cleared up the debris, and the others took Tess's dishevelled face to mean that she was sorry for the trouble she'd caused, which mollified Cook a little. It was only Amy who realized with a shock that Tess too must have been weaving romantic dreams . . . crazy, ambitious dreams about the son of the house, of all people, which were never going to come true.

It was very late that night, when they finally went wearily to bed, that they were at last able to talk freely.

'Tess, I never thought you could be so daft,' Amy said frankly. 'You must have known he was only dallying with you. Girls like us can't expect anything more.'

'You talk for yourself, Amy Moore,' Tess bawled at her angrily. 'You might be content to settle for a two-bit chauffeur or a chap whose dad owns a cinema, but that ain't everything. Some of us want more, and had every chance of getting it too!'

'Tess, you never stood a chance in a million with Giles Beaumont! Why won't you listen to sense?'

'Because I was here on this bed with Giles and you

weren't, that's why. Because I heard the things he promised me if I'd do what he wanted, and he gave me a shilling on account too. I was the one he kissed and held, and I was the one who felt his body next to mine and had him inside me.' She stopped for a second, and then rushed on. 'And if all that was for nothing, then I just wish I could die!'

Amy looked at her helplessly as she sobbed into the bedclothes.

'He never promised to marry you, did he?'

'He said he loved me, and that's the same thing,' Tess said in a strangled voice.

'Oh Tess, it's not. You know it's not. Any man can say that and not mean it. How could you be so daft!'

Tess sat up furiously, glaring at her.

'If you tell me I'm daft one more time, I shall throw something at you, Amy. I'm not daft. It's you who's daft for making so much of going to stupid tea with stupid Daniel Easton's family.'

Amy felt her face flush and defended herself.

'At least it's all above board and respectable. At least he didn't come sneaking to my room when everybody else was out just to have his way with me and then throw me over for the Honourable Thelma double-barrel! At least Daniel *respects* me.'

She turned out the gas-light savagely and climbed into bed, ignoring the snivelling sounds. Tess was being perfectly ridiculous. She must have known nothing could come from a brief bit of slap and tickle with Giles Beaumont. That was all it was to him, and the sooner Tess realized it the better. Amy would never have believed she could be so naïve as to think anything different.

Half an hour later, when neither of them had been asleep, there were muffled words from the other bed.

'I've had a rotten day. I wasn't going to tell you, but I might as well. My mother's gone. Run off with an Italian chap and left me to pay her last month's rent. I couldn't have paid a penny towards that bloody broken china, and they'd have had to send me to jail first. You're right about one thing though. What man in his right senses would want to marry somebody like me? A fine pedigree I've got!'

Amy was contrite at once. She tip-toed over to Tess's bed as if the girl was bereaved, wanting to put her arms around her and comfort her. For all her mother's faults, Tess had been fond of her, and this double blow today had hit her very hard. But the last thing she wanted was Amy's concern.

'Just leave me alone, will you?' she said harshly. 'Get back to your dreams of soppy Daniel, for all the good they'll do you.'

During the next days, Tess kept her lips tightly compressed and hardly spoke to anyone. Amy tried not to be resentful over Tess's scathing remarks about Daniel.

Tess had thought him tasty enough before she'd taken Giles Beaumont's eye, and she'd been pretty put out when Daniel had wanted Amy in the front seat of his Austin car beside him instead of Tess. In her mind, she was quite sure it was Tess who'd first attracted him. Why wouldn't she? Tess was smarter, louder, better looking and certainly slimmer than herself.

And Tess was also the one who'd told him the lie, she reminded herself with a sigh, and it was Amy who was going to have to put that right. The sooner the better.

'Shall we go to the Roxy on Saturday?' she asked Tess a few days later.

'If you like.' Tess shrugged.

'Oh come on, Tess, look on the bright side. It's not the end of the world.'

The other girl's look told her that for her, it was.

'I'll share Daniel with you if you like,' she went on generously. 'He can sit between us.'

'Thanks for nothing,' Tess said sarcastically. 'When I

need any help from you to get a chap, I'll ask for it.'

'I'm only trying to cheer you up.'

'Well don't. I don't want to be cheered up. I want to enjoy being miserable.'

But by Saturday it was a different matter. It was as if she had taken Amy's comments to heart, and decided to share Daniel's attentions. He had obtained the cut-price tickets for them now, and Amy whispered to him that Tess was suffering from a touch of the broken hearts, and that if she seemed more brash than usual it was only to hide her true feelings. After the performance, Daniel took charge.

'Shall we go and have some tea in that little place again, Amy? All three of us, of course,' he said.

'Oh yes. I've heard all about that,' Tess said, and threaded her arm through his at once. Amy felt a stab of anger. There was no need to go this far! But Daniel was holding out his other arm to her, so that Amy was the one obliged to walk on the outside edge, while Tess was cherished on the inside.

'Is your mother well again?' Tess asked politely when they were sitting together in the little tea-room.

'Yes, thank you. And that reminds me – Amy, you're invited to tea tomorrow. You will come, won't you?'

'Oh yes, of course.'

The sun seemed suddenly brighter, and the days of summer were suddenly glorious again, because the invitation excluded Tess. Even though she had infiltrated this place that Amy thought of as exclusively their own, it was she and not Tess who was invited to tea with the Eastons.

'Do you think you'll be able to get time off, Amy?' Tess said with studied casualness.

There was a sudden silence between them. Daniel had a frown between his brows, and Amy looked at Tess in a fury.

55

'Time off?' Daniel asked with a smile as Tess clapped her hands to her mouth.

'Oh Amy, forgive me. You know how my tongue runs away with me sometimes.'

She stretched out her hand and put it on Daniel's for a moment. 'You'll think us terrible, Daniel, but it's a little game we sometimes play. Amy and I don't have maids. In fact, we both started work for the Beaumonts as housemaids, though I expect to be Lady Beaumont's personal maid quite soon.'

Somehow, without really saying so, she managed to put the charade squarely on Amy's shoulders. In the midst of Amy's frozen horror, she heard Daniel start to laugh, his dark eyes tender on her face.

'Is that all? I thought you were going to tell me something terrible.'

Amy gulped. 'Are you saying it doesn't matter?'

He shook off Tess's hand and took Amy's in his.

'It doesn't matter a damn to me. I'd guessed something of the sort, anyway. Ladies of quality don't have such red hands, my love. But whatever kind of work you do, you'll always be a lady to me.'

He turned over her captive hand, and in front of everyone in the tea-room he raised her palm to his lips and kissed it. And in her confused pleasure, Amy barely registered the look of pure hatred that Tess gave her.

5

'Sometimes you can be a prize bitch, Tess!' Amy burst out when Daniel had been allowed to drive them right outside the Beaumonts' house that afternoon.

'Why? You kept saying he had to know the truth, and you heard what he said. You'll always be a lady to him!' she mimicked nastily, her eyes widening in mock surprise at being told off.

'I wanted to tell him in my own way and in my own time,' Amy said, furiously close to tears. 'You must have known that.'

'Oh, for God's sake, don't go on about it. You're the one invited to tea, so make the most of it.'

'And you're not, so stop looking so annoyed.'

Tess stopped walking, her slender foot on the top step of the stairs leading down to the kitchen. She looked Amy up and down in a way that would normally have quelled her, but Amy was in no mood to be quelled by anyone today.

'Annoyed! If I wanted to go to tea with the Eastons, I'd soon get an invitation, believe me.'

Amy pushed past her. She might be righteously angry with Tess, but those words were the ones most calculated to set off the little flutter of fear inside her breast. It wouldn't be the first time Tess had stolen a sweetheart from under another girl's nose, and if she once set her sights on Daniel . . .

Even though Amy was sure he was falling in love with her, Tess had a way of worming her way into a chap's heart before he even knew it. And whatever she said, Amy knew that Tess still hadn't got over the fact that Giles Beaumont's engagement announcement was about to be splashed all over the society columns of the best newspapers.

It was the timing of it that galled her. The fact that she'd given up her virginity to him on the very day that his lady-love was coming to dinner to settle the bloody betrothal. What was more natural than Tess seeking to get a new chap at the earliest opportunity in order to salvage her wounded pride? Whatever was available.

Angrily, Amy refused to worry about it. There was tomorrow to think about, anyway. She'd warned Gran that she might not be going home that weekend if Mrs Easton was well again and the tea-party was on, but that she'd nip down to Stratford Lane the next time she was sent to the market for vegetables, and tell her all about Daniel's family.

'What are you doing tomorrow afternoon, Tess?' Amy said when they went to bed that night. Tess had given her the silent treatment since coming home, and Amy was bored by it. If it meant sinking a bit of pride, she wanted to restore the old friendship between them.

Tess snorted. 'I might go to the park and listen to the bands. There's always plenty of people there. I shan't have my mother to visit, and you'll be busy, so I'll have to make other arrangements, won't I?'

Amy bit her lip and counted a baker's dozen. It had been the other way round so many times. Tess would be dressing up to the nines to go out walking with some new beau, or Tess's mother would be 'entertaining' and there'd be an impromptu party going on in her untidy rooms. Or Tess simply couldn't be bothered to spend her free time with Amy, who wasn't fast or smart and didn't care about being seen in all the right places where some exciting city gent might take a girl's eye. Amy couldn't even dance very well, and what use was a girl these days if she couldn't even do the charleston!

'I'm sure you'll have a good time whatever you do,' Amy began encouragingly.

'I'm sure I shall,' Tess said, and turned her back on her, shutting her out.

By morning Amy had given up worrying about Tess, and was more concerned with making the most of herself for Sunday tea with the Eastons. She knew she was being paraded for their inspection, so she had to look her best.

She refused absolutely to borrow anything of Tess's, or to doll herself up with more make-up than her usual discreet touches. Daniel liked her as she was, and that was how she was going to be.

And sharp at four o'clock, she stood outside the house in the warm summer sunshine, and her heart gave a surge of happiness as Daniel's black Austin turned into the square and stopped beside her. Daniel leapt out and opened the front passenger door for her.

'Your taxi, my lady,' he said gallantly, and Amy laughed and swept inside it, bold as brass. Once in the seclusion of the car, he leaned over and touched her lips with his for a second.

'You look perfect,' he said simply. 'My mother will love you.'

'Will she? I'm very nervous, Daniel.'

'Well, don't be. You know me, and you've already seen my father.' He glanced at her and laughed. 'All right, but Mother's not in the least like him. She's gentle and kind – very much like you, Amy. Perhaps that's why I was attracted to you in the first place.'

'And in the second?' she asked daringly.

'I'm not sure that I should turn your head by saying I fell for your beauty and charm and all the rest of it – even if it's true!' he said teasingly.

'Is it?' She was enchanted at all this flattery. 'Is it really, Daniel?'

'Why are you such a doubting Thomas? Hasn't anybody else ever told you how lovely you are?'

'Well, not many,' she said frankly, at which he burst out laughing again.

'Oh Amy, that's one of the things I love about you. You're so appallingly honest!'

She couldn't make head or tail of why this should be so amusing to him. Weren't most people honest? And she certainly hadn't been honest when she'd shared in Tess's lie. But that was something it seemed he was willing to overlook. And it reminded her of something else.

'Do you know that I have no idea what you do for a living?' she said as they drove through the sunlit streets.

'Nor you don't. If my father had his way I'd be working as a projectionist at the cinema to keep it all in the family, but I couldn't face seeing the same picture over and over again. I work at the penny lending library in Albert Square.'

'Oh.'

Somehow she had never expected this. She wasn't exactly disappointed, but it didn't sound very glamorous . . . and what could be more glamorous than being able to watch the silver screen six nights a week and a Wednesday matinée performance too!

They were passing the Roxy now, all shut up for Sunday and looking somehow forlorn with only its posters advertising the latest Hollywood epic, and no customers clamouring to get inside its doors.

'The house isn't far from here,' Daniel said, and Amy was immediately beset by nerves again. She twisted the long string of amber beads that lay against her best yellow print frock, and prayed her stockings were straight and Mrs Easton wasn't going to think she was too dowdy or too fast or just too awful for her son . . .

'Daniel, I'm scared. I'm not sure that I can go through with it,' she said in a panic as the car turned into a side road

60

and came to rest outside a pleasantly middle-class house. He squeezed her hand tightly. This wasn't the moment to let her know he was scared too. Damn scared of what his father might say or do to undermine this lovely girl's fragile confidence.

'It's only tea, Amy. They won't bite you. Just be your sweet and natural self, and you won't go far wrong. You're the first girl I've brought home, you know.'

'Really?' That was enough to stop her feeling of panic for a second, because now she saw the little nerves twitching at the sides of Daniel's mouth, and guessed more than he let on. He was nervous too. He wanted to show off his girl, and he'd want her to make a good impression.

For Daniel's sake, she held her head high and pulled in her stomach muscles, then let them out again a bit. Partly because she couldn't breathe like that, and partly because it made her bosom stick out too much. And it was too late now to wish that she'd gone on that diet . . .

For the first half-hour it wasn't so bad. The house was comfortably furnished with a plum-coloured velour sofa and matching chairs, all complemented with antimacassars of beige Nottingham lace. There were lots of dark-leaved plants in heavy china containers, and patriotic pictures of the royal family alongside family portraits on the walls, and one of Mr Easton standing pompously and importantly outside the Roxy cinema.

She warmed to Daniel's mother at once, seeing far more than the rather pretty, if colourless, woman revealed. Helen Easton welcomed Amy into the house with grace and gentility. But it wasn't difficult to assess quite quickly how much she was dominated by her bull of a husband, and that Daniel was a bit intimidated by him too, however much he tried to hide it. Or perhaps inhibited was the better word, Amy thought. She didn't really care to think that Daniel was intimidated by anyone.

Anybody would be though, Amy thought fervently, as the four of them sat around the tea-table, spread with dainty sandwiches and home-made pastries.

Frank Easton tried to decide just what his son saw in this girl with the big eyes and the expression of a frightened fawn, and the nicely rounded curves that were out of fashion. Not that that bothered Frank. He liked a woman to be a woman and to blazes with fads.

She was pretty enough, but nothing like that more vivacious friend of hers he'd seen coming out of the Roxy a couple of times. Frank had fondly hoped it was the other one Daniel was taking up with. She wouldn't be averse to a little fun on the side, while this one . . .

'So what does your family do, Amy?'

Frank put the question when all the niceties were over and they were halfway through their tea. He was finding it hellish hard to restrain himself from giving a huge belch, since Daniel had said this girl was from a nice home in Hampstead and had maids to wait on her. Well, if she married into the Eastons, she'd have to make do with this house and learn to cook and clean, he thought with relish.

Amy went cold all over.

'My family?' She found herself stammering and reddening and looked desperately at Daniel. Dear God, he hadn't continued the farce with his father, had he?

Daniel gave her a warning look and spoke up before she could gather her thoughts together.

'I forgot to put you right about the game we were playing, Father. Amy works for a rich family in Hampstead and lives in. There's only her grandmother, who lives very modestly.'

Frank's eyes bulged with rage at what he considered this deception. It wasn't hard to guess what kind of job she did if she lived in. A common skivvy! The girl had probably got around his son with her soft doe eyes and sweet face, but she wasn't getting around him. Not if she was no more than a skivvy! That wasn't the sort of daughter-in-law he intended being brought into his family, when he'd dragged himself up by the short and curlies to get where he was. And the sooner Daniel got shot of her the better.

'You mean you're no more than a bloody servant? And all this talk about having maids waiting on you hand and foot was a load of lies, was it?'

'Frank, for heaven's sake!' his wife put in, clearly distressed at the look of horror on the girl's face. 'Amy's a guest in our home, and I won't have you speaking to her like that.'

'Why not? And don't tell me what to do, woman. I'll ask her to bring in the bloody coals if I choose to. No doubt she's used to doing it.'

Amy felt her face burn. From the little she'd seen of him, she'd never liked the man, but now she loathed him. She heard Daniel scrape back his chair in a fury.

'You'll apologize to Amy this minute, Father –'

'Don't you tell me what to do in my own house either, you young whippet. I thought you'd have had more sense than to get tangled up with the likes of –'

'Nobody needs to apologize to me.' Amy's clear young voice rose vibrantly above them both. 'I'm the one who should apologize to Mrs Easton for upsetting her lovely afternoon. I know what hard work it is to set a fine table for those who never appreciate such things. And yes, Mr Easton, it was very wrong of me to pretend to be what I'm not, but I'm quite convinced now that I'd rather be a housemaid doing menial jobs than acting pompously above my station. If you prefer that I leave your house right away, I can probably get a tram somewhere near and go and see my grandmother, where at least I'm treated like a human being.'

'You'll do no such thing,' Daniel began angrily, when to Amy's astonishment his father let out a bellow of laughter and thumped the table so hard that the plates rang. His voice held grudging admiration.

'By God, but you've got some spunk, girl, I'll say that for you. And no guest in this house ever left here to catch a tram before they'd eaten their fill. You came to tea and you'll stay to tea, and I suppose you'll do well enough for this son of mine unless he can find something better. What do you say, Mother?'

Amy hardly dared look at Daniel at this insulting statement. She was furious at the brashness of the man, and wondered how on earth his gentle wife ever tolerated him.

Helen Easton spoke with perfect control that hid a lifetime's subjection to her husband's whims.

'I say that it's entirely Daniel and Amy's business, and if you've quite finished acting like a company sergeant-major, perhaps we can finish our tea in peace. Would you like some more boiled bacon, Amy?'

'Thank you,' she replied, hardly able to register that she was holding out her plate now and having it filled quite calmly with meat and being offered a dish of pickles as if nothing untoward had happened.

She sipped her tea and managed to ignore Frank Easton for the rest of the meal. Was this the normal style of this household? she thought in disbelief. It made the frequent display of temperament below stairs at the Beaumonts' no more than a fly-buzz.

'So you're a servant,' Frank couldn't resist goading again when they'd left the tea-table.

'I'm a housemaid,' Amy told him with quiet dignity, looking him straight in the eyes.

By God, but those eyes were quite something when they were flashing, he thought, startled. She could be quite a beauty. But his small burst of admiration left him just as quickly. She definitely irritated him. She might look a docile one, but beneath it all there was

64

plenty of fire. She wouldn't be dominated like Helen. It surprised him to realize it. He wondered if she even realized it herself. Given different circumstances, Amy Moore could probably be somebody to reckon with.

'All right. So you're a housemaid and you have a grandmother. Any more relatives to speak of?'

'Not to speak of,' she said, tongue in cheek. 'I had an uncle who went to Australia when I was about four years old. We never mention him.'

'You never told me about that,' Daniel said.

'You never asked,' she answered, smiling for the first time since the upheaval began.

It was odd how that bit of conversation stuck in her mind for a long time afterwards. Perhaps it was to shut out the unpleasantness of Frank Easton that she thought more about her uncle Tommy than the awkwardness at the Easton house and Daniel's clumsy attempts to apologize for his father later. She hadn't thought about her uncle for years.

She'd been too young to know what happened, but she remembered Gran's closed face and the certainty that Uncle Tommy was to be a taboo subject from then on. She wondered now if Gran ever missed him. Could you love a son all your life and then push him out of your mind as if he'd never lived? Amy was sure it was an impossibility.

She tried to picture her mother's brother as she remembered him before he stormed out of the narrow house in Stratford Lane. She'd been hiding under the stairs, terrified at the raised voices. Uncle Tommy was tall and thin, and to the young Amy, very dashing. When her gran told her where he'd gone, Amy cried, but she thought he was very brave, travelling all those thousands of miles across the sea. She said as much, and Gran hit her for the first and only time in her life.

In the soft darkness of her room at the Beaumonts,

Amy moved restlessly, wishing she'd known more about the reasons for Uncle Tommy's departure at the time. Wishing the memories were more than mere distorted fragments in her mind, and not really understanding why it should even matter to her.

In the distance she heard a church bell and counted the chimes. It was already dark and Tess hadn't come in yet. She'd be for it if Mr Allen discovered how late she was. Tess had been so miserable since Giles Beaumont's engagement and her mother's disappearance. She hadn't intended telling her about the awfulness of tea at the Eastons, but she decided that she would. It would probably cheer Tess up enormously.

Amy drifted off to sleep, still waiting for Tess to come home. It was daylight when she awoke and time to start the day. Tess must have come in very quietly. She was hunched up in bed, and Amy woke her cautiously. Her face was streaked with tears, and Amy felt alarmed, because it was so unlike Tess.

'What's happened now?' she asked.

'That bitch,' Tess spat out. 'Leaving me to pay all her debts. I've been halfway across London trying to sort things out. The woman in the room upstairs said she was living in Notting Hill and I tried just about every street but I couldn't find her.'

'But I thought you'd paid her rent.' Amy put the disjointed sentences together and presumed it was Tess's mother they were talking about.

'It's not just the rent! The tally-man was sitting outside and refused to budge till he'd got something on account, and on a Sunday too. She's shamed me that much, Amy. She's run up bills for drink at the public, and at the betting-shop. I tell you, I'll swing for her one of these days. I'll have to settle it in weeklies or they'll be after me as well, though God knows how I'm going to manage it.'

'Oh Tess, I wish I could help. I can let you have a couple of shillings.'

Tess gave a short laugh. 'A fat help that'll be. I've been racking me brains trying to find a way. Short of going on the streets, I can't think of nothing else.'

Amy felt shock run through her. 'Tess, you wouldn't! You didn't – last night –'

'No, I didn't,' she scowled. 'Not that I didn't think of it, mind. When you've done it once, what's the bleedin' difference?'

Amy ignored that. 'What are you going to do?'

Tess shrugged. 'I'm not going to prison for her, that's for sure. I'll have to see if I can get some money – on account. Giles said he'd see me all right. It's the only thing I can think of – and it's not like going on the streets, is it?'

'You mean you'd ask him to pay you – for favours?'

Tess's eyes flashed. 'Can you think of another way?'

'But he's getting engaged.'

Tess gave a harsh laugh. 'Oh Amy, you're so naïve. Any man who can get a bit on the side isn't going to say no, especially one like Mr Giles, who likes plenty! It'll be all right. And if I don't go to the Roxy for the next few weeks, I'll be entertaining instead.'

There was nothing that Amy could say to dissuade her, and neither referred to the subject again. But all through the month of August and into September, Tess stayed away from the Roxy on Saturday afternoons, and Amy gave her a quick resumé of the pictures so that she could make her usual colourful comments about them to Cook, and pretend everything was the way it had always been.

Amy never asked what went on in the little bedroom she shared with Tess, and refrained from going into it for as long as possible when Daniel took her home. When she did, she always opened the window to rid the room of the smell of Giles Beaumont, and she tried not to notice that Tess didn't look exactly happy at the arrangement.

The only thing that Tess told her tersely was that her mother's debts had been paid. A week or so later there was even money to spare to buy a new frock and shoes. The fact that it coincided with the weekend that Giles Beaumont's engagement was formally announced didn't appear to bother Tess in the least.

Amy's growing attachment to Daniel Easton was blissful and gradual, the way all good love stories should be, she thought romantically. Nothing hurried, nothing rushed, with all the time in the world to get to know one another. She went to his home several more times and grew very fond of his mother, and found it remarkably easy to ignore his hateful father. And a few weeks after their first meeting, she anxiously took him home to Stratford Lane to meet her grandmother.

'Now I'm the one who's nervous.' Daniel grinned as he stopped the car at the narrow entrance of the cobbled street, his eyes daring the urchins to lay a finger on it until they returned.

'Don't be daft.' Amy grinned back. 'Who'd be scared of my gran! She's very keen to meet you, Daniel.'

'Keen to inspect me, you mean,' he said, tucking her hand in his arm as they went down the street. Amy glanced up at him speculatively, as if seeing him for the first time and trying to be impartial about what she saw.

'Well, you look all right to me. Not too flashy in those new Oxford bags, a clean white shirt, hair slicked down and not too untidy, and good teeth and legs –'

'Here, I'm not a horse, old thing.'

'And I'm not an old thing,' she said pertly.

He laughed. 'That you're not. You're my lovely Amy.'

He squeezed her arm to his side, and she thrilled at the tenderness in his glance. He hadn't spoken of love to her yet, but love was in his every glance and every gesture. Love flowed between them unspoken and perfect, as unsullied as the love between any hero and heroine on the silver screen. And Saturday afternoons at the Roxy now were extra special because Amy shared them with him.

'Here we are. Gran will have been watching out for us and the kettle will be just coming up to the boil,' Amy said, seeing the old house now through Daniel's eyes, and wishing it wasn't quite so shabby.

It wasn't posh, and neither were they. Daniel would have to take them both as they were, for better or worse, she thought in a little burst of defiance. The phrase made her heart leap, as she realized it came from the marriage service. Happily, she hoped and believed that one day in the deliciously hazy and not-too-distant future she and Daniel Easton would be repeating the words to one another.

6

Daniel was taking her to a tea-dance on the first Saturday afternoon in October. Amy was all of a twitter about it, and Tess scowled as she watched her get ready, changing from one frock to another until Tess could have screamed at her indecision.

'For pity's sake, it's only a rotten tea-dance at Flannery's! You won't be meeting *royalty* there.'

'I know. But they're giving a lesson in the shimmy-shake and I know I shall be just *useless*,' Amy retorted. But there was an underlying complacency beneath the shivering excitement because by now she was perfectly sure that whatever her feet did, Daniel wouldn't find her useless at all. Daniel would simply adore her mistakes the way he adored everything else about her. She didn't need to be a clairvoyant to know that!

Tess eyed her in annoyance. Amy had blossomed in the last few months. She wore a bit more lipstick now, and her curves had fined down to a gently rounded shape. Daniel looked better on romance too. More dashing, more alive . . . Tess had already decided that she might have slipped up there. She could have had him with one crook of her little finger, and instead she'd been dazzled by the attentions of the Honourable Giles Beaumont, which were getting her precisely nowhere.

Not that she'd expected marriage, but nor had she expected him to be losing interest so soon after his engagement. There was no need, and Tess had been enjoying the little presents and the sneaking excitement of him coming to her room of a Saturday afternoon.

Once, they'd even gone into the master bedroom when

Lord and Lady Beaumont were away for the weekend. and Tess had thought herself a real toff making love on silken sheets, and catching sight of her own naked thighs entwined with Giles's thick-set ones in a huge flawless mirror.

It had all been as intoxicating as the wine Giles had brought to the bedroom, which always made her slightly silly and abandoned, and seemed to excite him more. But now there was the nagging worry . . .

'Are you going to the Roxy this afternoon, Tess? They're showing *The Sheik* again,' Amy said as she finally surveyed herself in the black-spotted looking-glass above the wash-stand.

She wore a soft pink frock with handkerchief points at the hem, a matching headband around her forehead and shiny black beads and matching bangles. On her legs were white stockings and black low-heeled court shoes with the latest cut-out fronts. She quite fancied herself, she thought with a grin. It was almost a pity she had to put on the long jacket with the waist-length lapels over the top to hide it all until she got to Flannery's.

'I might,' Tess said lazily. 'You never know who you might pick up at the cinema these days.'

Amy refused to be annoyed with her. Tess was edgy these days and even more sarcastic than usual, but it wasn't going to spoil her lovely day. Daniel would be calling for her in five minutes, and she blew Tess a kiss and clattered down the stairs in a flurry of nerves and pleasure.

Daniel was already waiting outside. He opened the car door in his gallant way and she slid inside, laughing.

'What's so funny?' he asked, pressing one finger to his own lips and then to hers so he wouldn't smudge her lipstick, a consideration that she found quite adorable.

'You're a proper Sir Galahad. aren't you?' She giggled, remembering how he'd enchanted her with tales of King Arthur and his knights. He'd borrowed the book from

71

the penny library for her, and she'd quickly picked up the stories. Daniel was ever so clever, she'd thought admiringly, and she strived to keep up with him.

'And you're my queen. How'd you fancy being a queen, Amy?' he said, as the car began its lurch along the square.

'I'm happy enough as I am,' she said. She was more than content, knowing that the fact of being Daniel's girl had given her a special aura of late. Cook and Mr Allen had taken to calling her their sunny girl, while what they called Tess was best left unsaid.

'We can't always stay the same though.' Daniel was obviously in one of his more serious moods as he steered the car into the more densely packed streets. 'You don't want to stay a housemaid for ever, do you, Amy?'

'I hadn't thought,' she said, her heart beginning to do somersaults. Right now, life was pleasant, life was easy. And she was a little afraid of change. 'What about you? Are you always going to stay a librarian?'

Daniel gave a short laugh. 'Well, of course I'm destined to be a property owner, though I can't imagine my father handing over his precious pile of sticks and stones before he takes his last breath.'

Amy looked at his handsome profile. Perhaps she wasn't very bright, but she'd never even thought about him inheriting anything as grand as the Roxy. It slightly embarrassed her.

'My word, I'll have to watch my Ps and Qs in future, won't I? I didn't know you were going to be so important.'

'More important than a librarian, eh?' He grinned wryly, and she saw that he'd guessed how she felt about that. She was shame-faced, knowing that it took somebody clever to deal with books and hand out the ones that customers wanted – and who was she to think it was less glamorous than the owner of a cinema! But she did. Guiltily, she knew she did. Anybody would.

She suddenly hugged his arm, causing him to pull at the steering-wheel, and he yelled at her to be careful or she'd have them in the side of a tram in a minute.

'I'm sorry,' she said, letting go at once. 'It's just that I don't care to think about change. Let's enjoy things as they are for now, Daniel – please?'

'All right.' He grinned. 'Why not? I can't think of anything nicer than going to a tea-dance with my best girl. Nobody's going to change anything, Amy love.'

They drove on blissfully, their love still a tender plant that could only grow stronger. But neither of them had reckoned with Tess Loveridge.

She dressed carefully. There was no chance of seeing Giles that weekend. He'd gone to the country to stay with the Honourable Thelma and her father, and she was left twiddling her thumbs, which was something Tess Loveridge didn't care to do. For one thing it gave her too much time to think. And what she was beginning to think was happening *couldn't* be happening. Could it? Fearfully, she counted back and then counted again. Even more fearfully she pressed the new green frock against her belly, trying to see if there was the slightest bulge there. There wasn't.

How could there be, if the thing she feared the most had only been there for six weeks at most? She felt a gut fear run through her. Fear and then anger. Why the hell wasn't her mother around to help her through this? Her mother would know what to do, Tess had no doubt of it, but her mother had vanished from the face of the earth with her Italian lover, and Tess was left to face the music alone, if there was any music to face.

She wasn't even certain. Yes, she'd felt a little queasy these last few mornings, and yes, her breasts that were normally small had felt a bit tender and surely they looked bigger beneath the green bodice of her frock?

The flattener definitely felt tighter this afternoon. Tess swore colourfully. She was imagining things. She had to be. That bastard Giles hadn't put a baby in her belly.

He'd been careful, like he always said he'd be. Only what with the wine and the way it made her go all woozy in the head, she was never sure quite what he did by the end of their love sessions. She only knew she felt sore and unhappy, and even the few shillings he always left her now weren't enough compensation for the feeling of being used.

'Shit on you, Giles Beaumont,' she said aloud to the looking-glass because it made her feel better. 'If you've done for me, I'll make you pay and no mistake.'

Her own face looked back dismally. How could toffs like Giles Beaumont be made to pay? He'd simply deny being with her, and Amy's word wouldn't count for much. There weren't exactly any witnesses to what went on. If she went to Lord Beaumont she'd assuredly be dismissed for trying it on. She knew it, because there were rumours of such a thing happening once before to a parlour-maid before her time.

The fear made her senses swim for a minute. Her eyes were huge and shadowy and she put more powder beneath them to disguise the fact that she wasn't sleeping too well. Those pigs in the kitchen didn't help, always praising up Amy and getting at her. She put more of the bright tango lipstick on her cupid's bow mouth and fluffed up the kiss-curls. Once she'd done that she felt better. She slung her jacket with the rabbit fur collar around her shoulders and took herself off to get the tram for the Roxy. Like she'd said to Amy, you never knew who you might pick up at the cinema these days.

Frank Easton saw her approach. He watched the slim boyish hips do their usual swing as she realized someone was watching her study the posters, and felt a surge of lust in his loins. She was a cracker all right, and he wouldn't mind getting his arms round that one, for all that she didn't have as much up top as the one Daniel had taken up with. With a practised eye, he assessed her, knowing the young things wore flatteners these days, so there was probably more there than at first appeared. His fingers positively itched to undo the fastenings and find out for himself.

'Good afternoon, my dear.' He stepped out in front of Tess as she wandered up the steps of the Roxy. 'Got your cut-price ticket ready, have you?'

'Oh, Mr Easton, you gave me quite a fright,' Tess said, fluttering her eyelashes and putting one hand to her chest. 'I didn't see you there.'

He smiled, knowing very well that she had. She'd be a third of his age, he guessed, but that didn't mean a thing in these days of fast living and the way people were being swayed by their Hollywood idols.

'Come to see our Rudolph, have you?' he said in the over-familiar way of one almost on intimate terms with the stars of the silver screen because of his position.

'Yes. I've seen it before, but there was so much chattering going on I missed half of it,' Tess invented.

Frank beamed. 'Well now, how'd you like a ringside seat, no charge?'

Tess widened her eyes in her best Clara Bow manner.

'I'm not sure that I should,' she began, and they both knew that she would.

Ten minutes later, she was seated prettily in one of the cinema boxes with the manager breathing heavily beside her. She was perfectly well aware of his hand sliding around her shoulders, and for the moment she allowed it to stay there before leaning forward so that he wasn't touching her.

He fair gave her the creeps, Tess thought with a shudder, but a plan was unfolding in her mind that might very well need his assistance, and she couldn't afford to be unsociable towards him until she knew for certain whether she needed to put it into action.

Just for the time being, she decided to play it very coolly, and she gave him a dazzling smile in the smoky darkness.

'Mr Easton, I'm sure you know I'm not that kind of a girl,' she said coyly, shifting his hand from her knee very gently.

He laughed, knowing from her tone that he could bide his time, and thinking himself a clever fellow indeed. He just had to go steady with this one, and this little encounter could be every Saturday afternoon, if he was lucky . . .

'I'll bet your friend don't say such things to that son of mine,' he whispered in her ear. Tess gave a small sigh, deciding to plant the seeds anyway, just in case . . .

'You know, I thought it was going to be Daniel and me.' She allowed her breath to catch in her throat. 'I saw him first, and I'm sure it was me he really wanted. It was me he –' She paused meaningfully. 'But things don't always turn out the way you want, do they? Just as long as there's no harm done.'

Out of the corner of her eye she saw him frown as he digested this bit of ambiguity. But she mustn't go too far too fast. It might all be for nothing. Daringly, she put her own small hand on his knee to return the pressure of his own on hers, and then removed it.

'Never mind. I'm enjoying myself now, and it's all thanks to you, Mr Easton.'

'Call me Frank,' he said, forgetting everything for the moment but the warm feeling still lingering on his knee where her hand had been.

Amy was sure she'd never get the hang of the shimmy-shake. The entire group of young men and girls at Flannery's were in a high old state of fun that was approaching hysteria by the end of the afternoon, and the couple trying to teach them the rudiments were trying hard not to become impatient.

The flappers were more intent on showing their legs off in their short skirts than learning to dance, and they screamed with excitement every time their ridiculously long strings of beads hit their partners in the eye.

'Let's get out of here,' Amy gasped finally. 'I can't take any more, Daniel. I shall collapse if I try to twist my feet into any more impossible shapes.'

'Thank goodness for that.' He grinned. 'I'm in need of refreshment anyway. Come on.'

They tore away from the dance-floor like fugitives from justice. Flannery's was exhausting on a Saturday afternoon, but it was great fun all the same, and when Daniel suggested coming back next week, Amy groaned in mock horror and said yes.

The waitress brought them their pot of tea and cakes, and once she'd laid out the cups and saucers, Amy poured. Daniel leaned back in his chair and smiled at her.

'Penny for them,' she said, her cheeks slightly colouring at his fond glance.

'I was just thinking of the first time you poured tea for me. You were all fingers and thumbs, weren't you? And how confidently you do it now.'

'That's because I know how you like it,' she said, expertly dropping in two lumps of sugar and handing him his tea with a flourish.

He reached for her hand, and she recognized a new look in his eyes. A look that took them farther than they'd been before.

'No you don't, Amy. You don't yet know the heart and soul of me, nor I of you.'

She felt her mouth go dry, but she was mesmerized by his dark eyes and couldn't draw her hand away to sip at her tea. Besides, it would spoil this fragile. special moment that she knew instinctively was very important to them both.

He gave a sudden groan and it was he who removed his hand, leaving her feeling suddenly cold.

'God, Amy, do you know what you do to me when you gaze at me with those soft eyes of yours? You tear me apart.'

'What do you mean? I don't mean to hurt you,' she began in bewilderment.

'I *want* you, Amy,' he said in a low voice, because there were others from the dancing class coming into the tea-room now. 'Do you know what I mean? I want more than just kisses. I want to know every part of you.'

He stopped abruptly. A young couple came across to them and asked if they could join them. Amy still felt her senses spin. She knew exactly what Daniel meant, and she didn't know whether to feel glad or insulted by it. Why hadn't he also said he loved her? If only he'd said he loved her, it might have made all the difference to her feelings right now. Saying the words meant a lot to a woman, even if a man seemed to think it was taken for granted. She needed the words, and the tenderness . . . and oh, she needed his love . . . and yes, she wanted him too . . .

'It wasn't that bad, was it, Amy?' the other girl, introduced informally at the dance-class as Jane, said laughingly. 'Don't tell me old twinkletoes managed to reduce you to tears!'

Amy realized her eyes had filled and she dashed the blurring away and laughed back, more shrilly than she intended.

'Not likely. The smoke gets in my eyes, that's all.'

'I'm so sorry,' the girl said, waving away the smoke from her long cigarette holder. 'Would you like one? They help to calm the nerves, and I have a spare holder in my bag. Do try one, Amy.'

'I'm not sure if I should.' And she was sure her Gran wouldn't approve. She seemed to be on the brink of doing a lot of things she hadn't done before . . .

'Oh, go on. Don't be a chick!'

Without another thought Amy took the holder Jane offered and fixed the cigarette into it. Her companion, a man with a thin black moustache and well-cut clothes worn with patent-leather dancing shoes, held Amy's hand still as he flipped open a gold-coloured cigarette lighter and lit the end of the cigarette for her.

She took a few experimental puffs and immediately had a coughing fit. Daniel rushed around to pat her on the back and glower at the others.

'Can't you see she's not used to smoking? You could have warned her not to draw on it so deeply.'

'I say, I'm sorry, old man, but how were we to know?' the man said in a cultured voice that took them both by surprise. 'Sorry, Amy, old thing, but better luck next time, eh? Try a more gentle puff, and it might be an idea to pick up the thing before you burn a hole in the tablecloth.'

Amy gasped, her eyes truly stinging now. She didn't want the cigarette. She didn't like the taste of it, and she told the man, who she remembered was called Ronald, that she'd rather not.

'All right,' he said cheerfully. 'Every one to his own, I say. And I sense that perhaps we interrupted something, Jane, old girl,' he said in a stage aside to his companion.

He fished in the pocket of his jacket for a card and put it on the table. 'Just to show there are no hard feelings, any time you fancy a spot of fishing or riding in the country, give me a tinkle on the old blower and we could perhaps make up a foursome. We may see you here again, of course. It was a hoot, wasn't it? Dashed nice to have met you both anyway.'

They both stared after the couple as they swept out, and wordlessly, Amy picked up the card from the table and read out the name and address, embossed in gilt letters.

'Ronald Derbisham, The Gables, Lower Witterley, Sussex. Telephone Witterley 34.' She looked at Daniel. 'Well, what do you make of that? Do you think he was somebody important?'

Daniel didn't care. Whatever Ronald Derbisham was or did, he had ruined a magic moment as far as Daniel was concerned, and one that wouldn't be recaptured now that the place was filling up with people calling to one another and laughing over the hectic afternoon they'd shared. Strangers or friends, they were united by a common cause, and if Amy and Daniel weren't to seem completely standoffish, they were obliged to be drawn into the lively discussion.

Amy was glad there were other people around, because somehow there was a small barrier between them that hadn't been there before. She couldn't explain what it was. If Daniel's proposal, of whatever kind, had been brought to some kind of conclusion, there wouldn't have been this feeling of restraint between them. But it hadn't. It hung in the air between them like an intruder and neither knew how to get close again.

When he drove her home, each of them making the most inane small talk, she sat awkwardly for a moment.

'I have to go and see Gran tomorrow. She's not at all well. Will you come, Daniel?'

'Do you mind if I cry off this week? I promised Mother I'd take her to Hyde Park, and before the weather gets too cold . . .'

'Of course. I understand. Next week then?'

'Oh rather. Next week. We'll decide then what we want to do. You never know, I might pop in to see you before then. Will it be all right, do you think?'

Amy gave a small smile. 'Yes! I don't think Cook believes my young man really exists.' She had to use the words, to remind herself that it was real, and that Daniel wasn't slipping away from her for reasons she couldn't even understand. One minute he'd said he *wanted* her in that most romantic fashion that made her toes curl, and the next . . .

All the way home in the car, Daniel was cursing himself. What a damn fool he'd been, rushing her like that. The look of relief in her eyes when those others had joined them was almost pathetic. And then the tears . . . He was a young man with normal urges, but by God, that had made them dwindle fast enough.

It was obvious that it would be marriage or nothing, as far as Miss Amy Moore was concerned, and since he didn't feel himself ready for marriage yet, not until he was at least made chief librarian, he must just go more slowly and keep his instincts to himself. He owed his lovely Amy that much. Not for worlds would he do anything to hurt her . . .

He caught the flash of a bright green skirt beneath a long jacket as he turned the corner to pass the Roxy on his way home, and someone was waving gaily at him. He felt obliged to stop and pass the time of day, knowing unerringly that at least there was no need to watch what he said to this girl.

She might be a bit flashy, but at least she was uncomplicated and made it plain when she liked a chap. Without being aware of it, he was comparing Tess with Amy as he opened the car door and on impulse asked if she wanted a lift. She accepted at once, and he watched her slide in beside him with quite a show of leg.

Tess thanked him prettily, triumphant at sitting in the front seat beside him at last. And before he knew it the short lift to the tram-stop that he'd intended had extended all the way back to Hampstead. That was the artful thing about Tess. She had a knack of persuading men to do things before they even realized it.

7

Summer had merged into a crisp autumn, the kind that had people scurrying to and fro on frosty mornings, pulling coat collars up around their necks and grumbling at the abundance of crackling leaves whipped from the trees by the capricious wind in streets and squares alike.

Amy tied a light scarf around her throat on Sunday afternoon to ward off any ill effects of a smart walk between tram-stops in a cold wind. The trams were all of a crush that day, as if nobody wanted to be out and about on such a day with the swirling leaves and road-dust stinging their eyes and catching their breaths. She hoped Gran had a good fire going.

As soon as she got to the house in Stratford Lane she knew that something was wrong. There was no kettle boiling cheerily on the fire, and the embers were low. The room struck a chill in her the minute she entered it, and she called her grandmother's name anxiously. The weak voice answered from the bedroom and Amy rushed in, pulling off hat, gloves and scarf as she did so and flinging them on to a chair.

'Gran, what's wrong with you? Have you had the doctor?' she said in alarm to the tiny figure that made hardly a bump in the bedclothes.

'Don't fuss, my gel,' Gran Moore said feebly. 'There's no doctor can get rid of the flu before it's ready to go, so stop your fretting and fussing and make me some tea, for Gawd's sake. I'm fair parched.'

'How long have you been like this?' Amy demanded.

The old woman scowled, eyes like coals in her yellow parchment face.

'Coupla days, that's all. I didn't take to me bed until today, knowing you were coming. Old Mother Coggins next door made me some soup, but I couldn't eat the stuff. Tasted like last week's dishwater.'

She probably wasn't as bad as she looked if she was grumbling so heartily, Amy thought hopefully.

'You stay right where you are and I'll get you some proper food and stoke up the fire. It's freezing in here.'

'Make the tea first,' Gran bawled with the last of her strength.

Amy did as she was told, using the top of the gas-stove for speed and jumping back in fright as the thing popped into life. No wonder Gran was scared of it. The landlord had installed it for his own prestige among neighbouring landlords, and so he could increase the rent, but it was enough to give an elderly woman heart failure.

In half an hour the fire was giving out a cosy heat, and Gran had drunk two large cups of tea and was tucking into fried eggs and bread cooked in bacon fat. Amy eyed her surreptitiously. There was hardly anything of her in the huge nightgown that covered her from head to toe.

'What did the doctor say?' she asked, having discovered that Mrs Coggins had sent for him two nights ago.

Gran snorted. 'No more'n I already knew. I'm old, gel, and there's no cure for that. But a bit of flu ain't going to kill me, and I'll be as right as ninepence tomorrow.'

She didn't bother telling Amy it was the other thing that was going to kill her. The thing that was growing faster'n the rising sun in her belly and eating her up. Sometimes she couldn't get food past it, but today she tried hard for Amy's sake, and was thankful to get something good and greasy inside her.

'I have to go to the market tomorrow, so I'll come and see to you again,' Amy said. 'You just stay in bed until I get here, do you hear? I'll ask Mrs Coggins to look in on you, and I don't want any arguments.'

She should have guessed there was something more to it than flu by the docile way Gran leaned back against the pillow with a satisfied belch as she finished the food, but it never crossed her mind at the time.

'You're a good gel, Amy, even if you're a bit of a bully like my Tommy used to be.'

Amy was startled. Gran hadn't mentioned the runaway son in years. She might have asked her about him, since his name had cropped up so unexpectedly the first time she'd gone to Daniel's home, but Gran's eyes were closing and her head lolling sideways, so Amy merely tucked the bedclothes up around her neck and busied herself in clearing away the crocks and tidying up a bit.

'Don't you dare touch my bits and pieces,' a thin voice screeched at her from the bedroom. 'You leave things just as they are so I know where to find 'em, miss.'

'All right, Gran,' Amy said with a smile, resisting the temptation to wrench open the oven door that was probably stuck fast by now, and see what treasures were inside.

When she was finished, Gran said tetchily that all she wanted was to be left in peace and not have to listen to a lot of tip-toeing footsteps and clatter that was disturbing her sleep.

Amy stood looking down at the old lady. 'I'm off now then, Gran, but I'll see you tomorrow.'

'That's right. I'll see you tomorrow. You're a good gel, and don't let nobody tell you different. 'Tain't your fault. None of it's your fault . . .'

Her voice faded away as she fell immediately into a deep sleep, as she often did these days. Amy smiled wanly, knowing the waay Gran's thoughts were going when she started rambling about none of it being Amy's fault. She kissed the creased old cheek gently and crept out.

No, she thought, going back to Hampstead on the tram in the late afternoon. None of it was her fault. It wasn't her fault her mother had borne her out of wedlock and then died as a result. It was a long time since she'd wanted to die of shame every time she thought of it.

Gran had explained that none of the blame was hers and it was a waste of time worrying about things that couldn't be changed. But sometimes in very private moments, it still made Amy feel less than human to know she was a bastard. It still made her flinch to let the very word come into her head. Bastard. Bastard. It was ugly and hateful, and if she ever got to feeling uppity, she only had to recall it . . .

One thing she was very sure about. The last thing she ever wanted was to come face to face with her unknown father. He'd never done anything for her, and she wasn't going to start concerning herself with him in his old age.

But she wondered uneasily if it was something she should have told Daniel, or if it was something he need never know. Who was to tell him when there was only herself and Gran who knew the truth? And Gran wasn't likely to go blabbing and spoil her chances.

Perhaps her uncle Tommy knew the facts as well, but he was God knew where in Australia, and was never likely to figure in her life again. It was best to leave well alone. She knew it was what Tess would have advised, and Tess was far more worldly-wise than she.

Tess hadn't been able to resist telling Amy that her young man had given her a lift home in his Austin car. She made it sound far more than it was, teasing Amy with arch comments about how comfortable the back seat was, and then laughing when Amy got all red-faced, saying didn't Amy remember how Tess had been relegated there on that first Saturday afternoon?

And never *quite* satisfying Amy that she hadn't shared the back seat with Daniel that very day . . . Then, bored with her teasing, she asked Amy lazily about the afternoon at Flannery's, and discovered that her friend wasn't seeing Daniel again that weekend.

More than that, she was told exactly where Daniel was going to be. Somewhat guiltily, she knew she was using Daniel Easton as a prop to her ebbing self-confidence and that Amy was going to be sorely put out if she knew it. But as if by accident, Tess managed to bump into Daniel and his mother as they stood listening to one of the soap-box speakers in Hyde Park that Sunday afternoon.

'Well, hello. It is you, isn't it?' Tess said as if in delighted surprise as she stood alongside Daniel.

He turned at hearing the female voice, and then gave a start. It was Tess, Amy's friend, and yet it didn't look like the Tess he remembered. She was dressed less flamboyantly than usual, her make-up more subtle, everything about her more subdued than before. Except for the eyes, still wide, blue and captivating.

Even Tess, in her determination to appear a most personable young woman, couldn't suppress the flirtatious allure of those eyes.

'How nice to see you,' Daniel said, surprised by this vision. When she continued to stand smilingly beside him, he was obliged to introduce her to Helen. 'Mother, this is Amy's friend, Tess Loveridge.'

'It's lovely to meet you, Mrs Easton,' Tess said, with just the right amount of pleasure in her voice. 'I've heard so much about you from Amy.'

Helen smiled. 'Do you often come to hear the speakers in the park, Miss Loveridge?'

'Oh yes,' nodded Tess earnestly. 'I think it's so important to widen one's horizons by listening to men of authority, don't you?'

Helen Easton was impressed. The girl was pretty and obviously intelligent. Amy had never mentioned coming to the park to listen to the speakers, and it was something

Daniel was quite keen about. It paid to know what was going on in the world.

She saw Daniel's slightly crooked smile. If she could have read his mind she'd know he was thinking that he'd never heard Tess express an interest in anything but the heroes of the silent screen! But then he didn't really know her. He'd never had the chance to speak to her on any serious subject.

'What do you think of the miners and their problems then, Tess?' Daniel challenged, having listened to the impassioned speech from the soap-box for the last half-hour.

Tess had prepared herself for this by discreetly questioning Mr Allen, who fancied himself as an amateur politician.

'Well, it stands to reason that anybody who does a job for the good of the community should get proper wages,' she declared righteously. 'If the only way to get it is to strike, then they'll have to strike. Even the King was reported to have said that he couldn't see how they could avoid it, and you can't get no higher opinion than that now, can you?'

'My word, you are knowledgeable, Miss Loveridge,' Helen Easton said in some surprise.

'Oh, but you shouldn't believe all you hear, Tess. All that was back in July,' Daniel commented, 'and nothing's happened yet.'

'I bet it will, though,' Tess argued, feeling no end of a clever one for having stirred up this little bit of intellectual interest while knowing less than nothing about the true facts. She glanced at the red-faced speaker, beginning to bluster now as the park hecklers became more raucous. Daniel saw his mother give a small shiver and came to a decision.

'Anyway, I think we've heard enough for today. Mother's getting cold.'

'Oh, what a shame,' Tess said apologetically. 'I'm sorry to have kept you standing about.'

'It's perfectly all right,' Helen protested. 'And it's a pity the tea-rooms are closed on Sundays. We could have continued the discussion over some tea and biscuits.'

'That would have been nice.' Tess put a heavy note of regret into her voice. 'Perhaps another time, Mrs Easton.'

'Well, why not come back to the house and join us for afternoon tea instead?' Helen said suddenly. 'I'm sure Daniel will take you back to Hampstead afterwards.'

Tess felt triumphant, but still managed a look of vague embarrassment towards Daniel. 'I'm not sure that I should. Amy might be upset . . .'

Helen put her hand on Tess's arm. 'My dear, you're invited as *my* guest. A cup of tea to warm you on this blustery day isn't going to upset Amy, surely? She's not a petty type of girl.'

It was so easy to plant the seeds in people's minds, Tess thought jubilantly as the three of them walked together towards Daniel's parked car. It still might all be unnecessary. It was simply insurance, just in case she needed it . . . With this performance, she should have been on the stage, Tess was thinking, and in any case Daniel was definitely a better bet than being thrown out on the streets . . .

And because of her artless acting, by the time Daniel dropped her outside the Beaumonts' house, he was grudgingly thinking that maybe Tess wasn't as scarlet as she was painted, after all. His father had tried hard not to show his patent delight at seeing the vivacious young woman again, and his mother had begun to call her Tess.

And there was no way she could resist telling Amy that she'd been invited to tea at the Eastons because of the friendship that had sprung up between her and Helen Easton – and that Daniel had brought her home the long way round. And later, despite Daniel bluntly telling her

88

the truth of it, another seed of doubt was planted very firmly in Amy's mind.

Wasn't there some saying about the lady protesting too much . . . ? Amy didn't see why it shouldn't apply to gentlemen as well.

Four weeks later, Tess knew the worry wasn't going to go away, and she would have to confront Giles Beaumont. Amy was off to Flannery's with Daniel and her new friends again, and when Giles had lifted his eyebrows at her at breakfast that morning, she'd given a small nod which told him the coast was clear. And early that Saturday afternoon she heard the stairs creak outside her bedroom door and knew he was here.

He opened the door without knocking, carrying a bottle of wine in his hand. Tess groaned beneath her breath. She knew all too well how silly and amorous she got after only one small glass, and she certainly needed to keep her head clear today.

But Giles Beaumont wasn't a man to argue with. He'd come here for one purpose, and until he'd had his way there'd be no chance of wheedling anything out of him. Tess's heart beat extra fast as he encouraged her to drink the wine until her head reeled. His greedy hands roamed all over her until the bottle was empty.

'Now, my girl,' he said hoarsely, entering her pliant body and wasting no more time. Tess knew that there was something she had to say. Through the muddle of her senses and her dry, thickened tongue, there was something important . . .

She finally got the words out in a great rush while he still panted above her. 'Giles, you've got me in trouble, and you'll have to help me.'

She couldn't have diminished his ardour quicker if she'd thrown iced water over him. He jerked up his head, and she felt him shrink inside her before he slid away, shoving her legs together roughly as if the action could rid his mind of the words he'd just heard.

'What trick is this?' he snarled.

'It's no trick,' Tess said shrilly. 'It's the truth, and you're responsible.'

He glared down at her furiously. 'If you think you can blackmail me, bitch, don't waste your time. Nobody knows I've been here, and it'll be my word against yours.'

'Well, that's rich,' Tess screeched, her heart racing sickeningly.

'And if you think I'd marry a little tart like you, you must want certifying.'

He was off the bed and shrugging into his clothes so fast Tess could hardly get her senses together. Then she heard herself screaming at him.

'Marry *you*? That's the last thing I'd do. You're not even good at it, and your bride is welcome to you –'

She didn't get any farther. She felt the back of his hand across her face. He wore a heavy ring, and the corners of it were sharp. She felt the sting of blood on her cheek.

'I hope you'll enjoy the work-house, because that's where you'll end up, you little slut,' he said, incensed, and tore out of the room, banging the door behind him.

Tess stayed exactly where she was for a long time, numbed and shocked. She didn't really know what she'd expected of Giles, but now she knew she had to harden her feelings and put the second plan into action fast.

Amy was miserably unhappy. Daniel had been honest enough about meeting Tess in Hyde Park, though he hadn't told her about it until the next Saturday. He said quite freely that his mother had invited Tess home for tea, stressing that it had been all Helen's idea. He still protested that part of it too defensively to Amy's sensitive mind, and she couldn't forget Tess's sly remarks about the back seat of the Austin car.

She was hardly allowed to forget, since Tess constantly crowed about in the darkness of their attic room, despite the number of times Amy said angrily that she knew Tess was just having her on. It was just a kindness, a lift home in a car . . .

'You always was a gullible one, Amy. Besides, you don't own Daniel Easton, and so what if he may or may not have kissed me a few times?' she lied, her tone intimating that there had been far more than kisses without ever actually saying so.

Amy stared into the darkness, numbed by the words and the picture they evoked.

Tess went on recklessly. 'Anyway, I don't probe into everything you do, do I? You don't tell me details of your new friends, do you? This la-di-da chap you met at Flannery's with the plum in his mouth – who's he, for God's sake? You're going up in the world now, with your dancing and your posh friends with their business cards.'

Amy drew a ragged breath. 'Shut *up*, Tess. You know none of it means anything to me compared with Daniel. And if you – if you –'

'If I what?' Tess challenged.

'If you take him away from me, I'll never speak to you again.'

Tess laughed. 'If he thinks that much of you, I shan't be able to, shall I?'

'You'll try though, if you've a mind to,' Amy said bitterly. 'I know you will.'

'Well, we'll just have to see which of us he likes best, won't we? Anyway, me and his mother are the best of mates now, and I reckon our Daniel takes after his old man. He's got an eye for the girls too,' she went on, twisting the knife so that Amy couldn't fail to know how far Tess had already gone in worming her way into the Eastons' lives.

Amy had too much pride to ask Daniel outright if he

was going to see Tess again. It was hiding her head in the sand, but she just couldn't bear to know, and besides, it wasn't something a girl should really be asking a chap.

She certainly couldn't deny the fact that the Eastons were now well acquainted with Tess, Amy thought miserably. Amy had been there to tea once more since the Sunday in Hyde Park, and Frank had made no bones about mentioning her bright little friend, while Helen had agreed that Tess was more intelligent than she'd thought at first. It was just as if they too were intent on wounding her without even knowing it.

As for Tess being intelligent . . . Amy's stomach had almost curdled at the word. All Tess's intelligence was between her legs, she thought with rare crudity, and she'd be no asset to a man in line to be chief librarian at the penny library! She couldn't even read and write properly. She stopped her spinning thoughts, appalled to realize she was as good as accepting that her own chances of becoming Daniel's wife were fading, while Tess's were riding high . . .

But Amy had worries of a different kind. In her last few weekly visits to Stratford Lane, she'd seen all too clearly that her grandmother was slipping fast. She was eaten up with anxiety on Gran's behalf, wondering how she was going to get through another winter.

Daniel came with her on her next visit and, not having seen her for a while, he was clearly shocked too. Because of their mutual concern, she felt closer to him than she'd been for ages.

When they left, Amy turned to Daniel in the misty seclusion of the car, tears dampening her cheeks as he held her in his arms and tried to comfort her.

'I know she's going to die,' she sobbed. 'And she's all I've got left in the world.'

'Love, don't upset yourself. We all have to die, and she'd

be the first to say she's lived her life. As for her being the only one you've got in the world, that's not true. You've got me, Amy, and you know how I feel about you.'

She lifted her swollen eyes to his.

'No, I don't,' she said in an angry, brittle voice. 'I don't know because you've never told me.'

Daniel held her so close that she couldn't tell which of their heartbeats was his and which was hers.

'Amy,' he said hoarsely. 'Did I really need to say it in words? It may be easy for Douglas Fairbanks to say all the smooth words to a woman in the pictures, but a real live man can't always bare his feelings like that. But for pity's sake, what do you think I've been telling you all these months? You must have seen the love spilling out of me every time I looked at you, every time I touched you. Sometimes I've had to hide the strength of my own feelings because I was afraid they'd be too much for you.'

She felt the sting of tears again.

'I'm not so daft that I believe everything I see on the screen, Daniel. And did you think I was so soft that I couldn't appreciate a bit of loving?' she said in a small quavering voice. 'A woman has feelings and needs too. And – I won't break if you hold me. I know all about – love.'

He crushed her to him. She buried her scarlet face in his tweed-clad shoulder, because in reality she knew absolutely nothing about the ways of love. She only knew that her feelings for this man were deep and strong, and that she would love him until the day she died.

Emotionally she was as experienced as anyone. Physically, she had everything to learn, especially when it came to living with a man and giving him the very essence of herself.

Fleetingly, she remembered the shadowy story of her own mother and her unknown father. She remembered the lust Giles Beaumont had shown towards Tess. Giving

93

everything to the wrong man could be ugly and result in misery . . . but she still believed fervently that it could also be beautiful, the way it was portrayed on the silver screen.

'Amy, this isn't the time and place, and perhaps it's too soon, but do you think you could love me too? Enough to last a lifetime?'

Her arms went around him so tightly he could hardly breathe, and he was stunned by the passion in this girl whose beauty had opened up so gradually that he had hardly noticed how exquisite she really was, like a fragile flower opening in the sun.

'Oh Daniel, I love you so much already. I could never love anyone more. You're my strength, and I'm going to need you so much. Gran's been both mother and father to me, and I shall miss her so much when I'm alone.'

He felt his throat tighten as he held her. 'You haven't been listening to me properly, darling. I'm never going to let you be alone again,' he said.

And at that moment the spite of Tess Loveridge was the farthest thing from either of their minds.

After a sleepless night, Amy decided she was going back to Stratford Lane just as soon as she could get permission from Mr Allen. She had to stay with Gran until the end, no matter how awful it might be to watch her die. It was the last thing you could do for someone you loved, Amy thought – be with them and hold their hand until they slipped from this world to the next.

Cook saw at once that there was something wrong, saying that the whole household seemed to be going topsy-turvy lately. What with Tess hardly being civil to anyone, barging about and losing her temper over the slightest thing, and now this . . .

'Not that I'm blaming you, gel. You must see to your

94

own, and I'm sure Mr Allen will put things right with them upstairs for a few days.'

'I doubt that it'll be more, and I'll go just as soon as Tess comes down from serving breakfast,' Amy said, fighting to hold back the tears. The next minute she had given up the fight and was clasped to Cook's ample bosom, because nobody could know just how much she was going to miss her old grandmother.

'There's somebody here to see you, Amy,' Fanny said in a scared voice, and seconds later Daniel came into the big Beaumont kitchen, large and awkward in the unfamiliar surroundings. Amy's heart leapt at the sight of him, and she could see Fanny's admiring glance and the quizzical look from Cook. None of it mattered except that he was here, for whatever reason. He came and took her hands.

'Can we go somewhere alone for a minute, Amy? I've got something to say.'

A nod from Cook gave her permission, and when she and Daniel were alone on the outside steps, Amy shivered in the cold November morning.

'This is for your grandmother, to make her last days comfortable,' he said, pushing an envelope into her hands. 'I'm driving you to Stratford Lane right now and we're getting her into hospital.'

Amy opened the envelope and gasped. There was money inside, and to Amy it seemed like a year's wages.

'I can't take this,' she said at once. 'I never owed a penny, any more than Gran did –'

'You'll take it for her,' he said roughly. 'It's not a loan, it's a gift, and don't give me any arguments. Or do you want her to die in that miserable place?'

It didn't take more than a moment then for Amy to give in. All this was for Gran. She knew she was about to lose the prop of her life, but now she had Daniel. He was the best thing that had ever happened to her, and she thanked God for him.

8

Tess knew now that she had to put on an act such as she had never done before. She daren't wait any longer. She had no one to confide in, and if the truth was known, she'd never felt so alone or so terrified. She and Amy were barely speaking, and she knew damn well she was about to shatter all her friend's dreams, but fear drove her on.

Amy would get over it. She still had choices, while Tess did not, and she was sick with panic every time she wondered what the hell she was going to do without a man to stand by her. A girl in her position *had* to have a man to help her out, or she'd be done for. Giles Beaumont would deny everything, and she knew that the rotten stinking bastard had started rumours upstairs that she was a flighty baggage.

Lord Beaumont had been sharp with her at breakfast over nothing, and she'd got flustered and dropped a dish of marmalade all over the damask tablecloth. What with that and Giles smirking at the far side of the table, she'd lost her temper at the unfairness of everything and nearly blabbed out the truth. Instead of which, she'd let fly with some pretty ripe language.

It had all ended up with her ladyship getting pink and upset and his lordship telling her she could pack her things and get out.

She flounced downstairs, where Cook and Mr Allen were bemoaning the fate of poor Amy's grandmother, and that just about did it. She banged the silver tray down on the table and tore off her cap and apron.

'What in blazes has got into you, my gel?' Cook said at once.

'Nothing that need bother you any more,' Tess yelled. 'I'm leaving right now and good riddance to the lot of you. I'm going one better than working my fingers to a pulp for them ungrateful buggers, thank you very much.'

'Here, less of the language, miss, and just where'd do you think you're going? Don't you go leaving us in the lurch. Amy's gone to be with her gran, and where will we be if you just walk out?'

'Up to your arses in greasy dishes, for all I care!' she screamed, and stormed out of the kitchen and up to the attic room.

She was shaking with fury as she dragged her battered cardboard suitcase from the bottom of the cupboard and stuffed everything she owned into it. It was bad luck about Amy's gran being ill, but it was no concern of hers, and she had her own problems. Her mother had gone off with her fancy-man, so a fat lot of help she'd be, and there was only one place left for her to go. She had always known it, half-planned it, but now that the moment was here, she was shit-scared.

She marched off down the square until she reached the tram-stop and got a fare to near the Easton house. She knocked at the front door, aware that her heart was pounding.

A small unexpected stab of conscience almost made her turn turtle. Amy had been her friend for a long time, and she was about to do the dirty on her . . . but it was her survival or Amy's. It was too late now, anyway, because Helen Easton was opening the door, smiling in surprise. And then she saw the suitcase . . .

Frank's bullet head appeared behind his wife's, and Tess immediately decided that tears might be the best defence. They began to swim in her eyes as she started to babble, and she was hastily drawn into the house before any of the neighbours heard the rumpus.

*　　*　　*

The hospital ward for elderly incurables was painted dark green and smelled of sickly antiseptic, urine and approaching death. Amy kept her nostrils pinched as tightly as she could and tried not to register any of these smells as she watched the stretcher taking the small figure of Gran Moore to a bed in the corner.

Then she and Daniel were told brusquely by a woman in a crunchy starched apron and cap to stay in the corridor until the patient was in bed. Gran was no longer a person with a name. She was the patient. Amy held Daniel's hand tightly.

'I've never been in a place like this before,' she whispered through dry lips. 'It's – awful.'

It made her want to cry. She was very grateful for Daniel's kindness in insisting on paying for Gran to be cared for, but in her heart she knew Gran would have preferred Amy's way – to die at home in her own bed, with Amy holding her hand and letting her go . . .

But Gran wasn't in any condition to say what she wanted any more. When they'd got to Stratford Lane a small group of neighbours was standing outside Gran's house, and there was uproar coming from inside. Gran was having a fit, raving and fighting with herself as pain ravaged her. The thin body was covered with innocently self-inflicted wounds, and Amy knew she couldn't be left there.

So now she was here, and the raving had stopped and Gran was in some kind of coma. The ironic thought filled her head that they probably wouldn't need much of Daniel's money for treatment after all, except to bury her.

'Why didn't she tell me how ill she was?' Amy wept. 'Why didn't she let me do more for her before it was too late?'

'Call it pride,' Daniel said. 'When people get old, it's all they have left. You're a lot like her, Amy. I know she was proud of you.' He tried to avert her thoughts from the inevitable.

'Why should she be?' Amy looked up at him, tears shimmering on her lashes. 'A housemaid's nothing to be proud of.'

Daniel raised her cold hands to his lips. 'It doesn't matter a damn what you do to earn an honest living. It's what's inside that counts, and you know you'll always be a lady to me. So you were to her, Amy.'

It was so tempting, in those intimate moments, when they were seemingly alone in this mausoleum of a place, to tell Daniel that she was anything but a lady. That she didn't even know who her father had been, and the name that society would label her with was *bastard* . . . but the words stuck in her gullet and the secret remained her own.

Soon, she would be the only one in the world who knew it, except for Uncle Tommy, and the man who had fathered her – and he didn't count.

'I wonder if I should try to get in touch with my uncle after – afterwards,' she muttered, since his name had come into her head. 'He'll have a right to know about his mother, won't he?'

'Let's think about that when the time comes. I won't fill you with false hopes and say she might pull through yet, because we both know that she won't. But don't worry yourself over what's to be done later.'

'What else do I have to think about? I don't want to think about what's going on in there!' She jerked her head towards the crowded hospital ward, where groans and shrieks and the occasional scuffle told a grim story.

Daniel could think of nothing else to do to comfort her, and they sat there holding hands for more than an hour, and nobody came to tell them anything. Finally a nurse bustled along the corridor, and Amy stood up stiffly.

'Can I please see my grandmother now? It's Mrs Moore. Mrs Daphne Moore. We brought her in earlier.'

'Just a minute. I'll see,' the nurse said importantly. 'We've been very busy today.'

So had Gran, Amy thought. Busy dying.

A short while later the nurse came back to them.

'You can come through. She won't know you, and the doctor says it can only be minutes now.'

The shock of it almost knocked Amy over. *Minutes!* And if she hadn't asked this nurse about Gran, she would have died all alone. She rushed down the ward to the end bed, ignoring the nurse's sharp instruction not to run. She reached the bed where Gran breathed in shallow little bursts. She looked tiny, old and very tired. Amy took her hand and caressed it lovingly.

'I'm here, Gran.' She leaned forward and said urgently, 'I won't leave you.'

At first there was no response, then very slowly the old woman's eyes opened. She looked straight into Amy's eyes and there was the smallest pressure from her fingers.

'Not your fault, gel. None of it was.'

The words were as thready as her pulse, and then both were gone. The nurse hovered by, and said quietly that it was all over and would they please wait outside as the hospital would need all particulars.

Amy didn't move for a few minutes. The grip on her hand had stopped and the wizened features had slackened, but this was still her gran whom she loved, and how dared this woman tell her to go away before she'd made her final peace?

'Just a few more minutes,' she mumbled.

She was dimly aware that Daniel spoke sharply to the nurse and then Amy was left alone by the bed.

'I'll try to find him for you, Gran. I know it's what you'd want me to do. I'll tell him.'

She was too blinded by tears to say anything more. She bent and kissed Gran Moore and stumbled away to where Daniel waited for her. They were taken to a small room where someone waited to speak with them, and she went through the ordeal of giving particulars and agreeing to the suggested arrangements for burial, still too stunned at the outcome of this day to take in any of it.

Outside the hospital, the November air was keen and damp. Trams and buses went by, and cars honked their horns. Leaves scurried about bent figures and legs wearing winter boots, and everyday life still went on. Amy took a deep breath and tried to believe that today had really happened.

'I'm taking you home,' Daniel said. 'Father's got some brandy, and it's what you need.'

'*No*. I'm going back to Stratford Lane. There are things to do and people to tell.'

'Not today, Amy, for God's sake.'

'Don't you see that if I don't go back there at once, I'll be too scared ever to go back there again? I'll stay there tonight, Daniel, and tomorrow I'll start going through her things. There may be some clue to Uncle Tommy's address.' She was suddenly strong and determined, and he gave a small sigh, seeing the glitter in her tear-filled eyes.

'Don't become obsessed with this Uncle Tommy business, Amy. It'll probably do no good. Anyway, if you don't find anything, your best bet is to see a lawyer and get him to do the search. I'll help you financially if you're really set on it. I don't want to upset you today of all days, but you've got to be reasonable about all this, and I can't see the sense in spending money indefinitely on a wild-goose chase.'

Her cheeks burned. 'Is that how it seems to you? How can you be so heartless?'

She quickened her footsteps, rushing away from him, and then realized she had no idea where to go. This part of London was unknown to her. She stopped running, helpless as a kitten until he caught up with her, gripping her beneath the elbow so she couldn't take flight again.

'I'm not heartless, but we have to think of ourselves, of our lives, Amy. We have a future.'

'I can't think of that now! I can only think of what *she* would want.'

Privately, Daniel thought that if Gran Moore hadn't tried to contact her son all these years, it was hardly likely she'd want him contacted now. But there was a frenzied light in Amy's eyes, and he knew she was in no condition to be reasonable.

'Let's get back to the car. It's cold standing about,' he said practically. 'Amy, our family lawyer is Charles Rugby of Welles Street. Remember the name, and go to him for the best advice.'

The name went into her head and out again. What would she want with lawyers? There must be a forwarding address somewhere. The more she thought about it, the more she persuaded herself that Gran must have had some idea where Tommy had gone. Just because she never spoke of him didn't mean she never thought of him, and she'd been too much of a matriarch to let go of what was hers.

Her son Tommy and her daughter Emily – Amy's mother. Gran had lost them both, and the least Amy could do was to trace Uncle Tommy. He was her last link with a family of her own.

She refused to go back to Aveley Square. Her place was at Stratford Lane, and there was nothing he could do to dissuade her. He tried not to look surreptitiously at his pocket watch. He'd taken the whole day off from the library without explanation so far, and he'd be in trouble if he didn't report there soon. He dreaded leaving Amy in the house alone, but it was obvious it was what she wanted.

Once there, a few neighbours hovered around, asking for news, and when it was known that Gran Moore was dead they drifted away quickly. Only Mrs Coggins stood fast, her old eyes filled with moist tears.

'You'll be clearing out her bits and pieces then, gel,' she

stated. 'I'll be right next door, and you're to shout if you want anything at all. Don't get scared.'

'What's to be scared of? Gran wouldn't scare me if she was laid out in her own bed,' Amy said baldly. 'She's still my gran wherever she is. I want to be here on my own for a bit, thanks all the same, Mrs Coggins.'

The woman had no truck with any hints of an afterlife and the like, and glanced at Daniel.

'Will she be all right?' she mouthed, as if Amy couldn't hear.

'Yes. She insists on staying, but I'll come back and see her sometime tomorrow. Will you keep an eye on her?'

''Course I will. Known her since we moved in here right after the end of the war.'

For a moment Amy stopped her restless fingering of Gran's ornaments, Gran's fading pictures on the wall that were forever slipping sideways, Gran's wire-rimmed glasses left behind when they took her to the hospital . . . She wouldn't need them now. She wouldn't need any of it again.

Daniel was obviously getting fidgety and she gave him a crooked smile.

'Why don't you go? I know I've kept you from your work, and there's nothing else you can do here.'

He was her love and she needed his strength. But in some weird way his physical presence was coming between her and her memories. More than she needed him at that moment, she needed to be alone with the memories, here in Gran's house where she had been born.

He was filled with guilt and unease. He wanted to get away from this cloying place with its unhealthy atmosphere and the stale smell of old age that would probably linger until everything of Gran Moore's was cleared out. Yet he wanted to stay, because Amy looked so strange with that burning light in her eyes, as if she'd gone somewhere where he couldn't reach her.

Daniel was an uncomplicated man, and Amy's own straightforward nature was what had drawn her to him first of all. He wanted her to stay as uncomplicated as himself. He was uncomfortable with this new Amy who intended looking for a lost cause that could only end in heartbreak and disillusion.

He made up his mind. He kissed her gently while Mrs Coggins turned discreetly away, an unwilling chaperon.

'Take care, darling,' Daniel whispered in her ear. It was on the tip of his tongue to make the usual kind of platitude about Gran having had a good life, but he resisted it quickly.

It was obvious she'd never had a good life. Who would, living here? It wasn't a hovel, but it wasn't Aveley Square either, and Daniel's own home was somewhere between the two. He'd be glad to take Amy away from here, but she was a girl of determination, and he knew it had to be when she was ready.

Amy watched him walk away from Stratford Lane and listened for the engine of the Austin to start up. She turned to Mrs Coggins, who was wondering how soon she could decently get away to start her old man's supper.

'Did Gran ever mention my uncle Tommy to you, Mrs Coggins?'

The question startled the woman. She'd expected tears, or even a collapse now that the young man had gone. She'd been prepared to fuss around making tea for the girl and maybe even offer her a bit of pork pie and mash since she probably hadn't eaten all day. She hadn't expected this.

'Good Gawd almighty, gel, whatever made you think of 'im? I 'eard tell of 'im once when I first moved 'ere. Rumours and such, I dare say, but the person who spoke about 'im moved away, and nobody ever mentioned 'im since.'

'Not even Gran?'

The woman's face softened, suddenly recognizing the need in the girl to have someone of her own to relate to.

'I'm sorry, my duck, but I 'eard tell that your gran wiped 'im out of her life after 'e left. She was only a little 'un, but she had strength enough for that. She just forgot 'e existed, and there's no point in anybody tryin' to resurrect the dead!'

She clapped her hand to her mouth at once, puce with embarrassment considering that Gran Moore had just died, but Amy was too sick with disappointment to notice. She'd only wanted one clue . . .

"Course, the doctor might know summat. Your gran was always thick wiv 'im. Should my Len go to tell 'im she's gone? He can run round there after tea.'

'Oh – yes – thank you.' She breathed deeply. 'I think I'll get started now. There's a lot to do. If there's any little thing of Gran's you'd like, we'll talk about it tomorrow. You were a good friend.'

'All right ducks.' She tried not to let her eyes wander to the picture of wild geese she'd always fancied.

Tomorrow was time enough, and the poor little bugger looked as if she'd had enough for one day.

Daniel couldn't concentrate on anything. First he called at Aveley Square to tell Cook that Amy's grandmother had died, and that she'd be staying at Stratford Lane for a few days. And since it was near to five o'clock in the afternoon, he took the rest of the day off and went home.

He was met by an avalanche of noise. At first he couldn't make head or tail of it. All he knew was that his father was in one of his rages and his mother was shocked and weeping. And Tess Loveridge was sitting awkwardly upright on the sofa, with a scared look in her eyes as if she hadn't known what she was letting herself in for.

'What's happened?' Daniel spoke directly to his mother, an instinct that had his father's lip curling.

'You young whelp! It won't help you to hide behind your mother's skirts this time. I thought you'd have had more sense than to play around with one girl while all the time you were putting t'other one in the puddin' club! We're not going to have Amy Moore rushing round here with a similar tale, are we? One bastard's enough for any man to cope with, let alone two.'

Daniel felt as if he was being knocked sideways as the words were hurled at him. Helen's weeping got noisier, and Tess began shouting in a fright that Frank was only making matters worse. It was too late now to go back on the lies she'd told him, though the realization dawning on Daniel's face was beginning to make her quake.

'What the hell has she told you?' he roared back at his father. His mother's hands fluttered towards him in a futile gesture.

'Darling, it's no use trying to bluff it out. Tess had no choice but to come to us when she found out she was in trouble, and it was only right that she did.' She couldn't say more, her shaking hands dabbing an entirely inadequate handkerchief to her eyes.

The shock of what Tess had done almost floored him for a minute. Tess was supposed to be Amy's *friend* . . . he wouldn't have believed anybody could be despicable enough to drum up this story, but it was clear that his parents were completely taken in by her lies. He turned on her, a murderous look in his eyes.

'What have you told them, you lying bitch?'

Tess flinched at the look. She'd known all along it would cause an uproar, but she simply hadn't prepared for it. Typically, she hadn't thought beyond the moment and saving her own skin. She hadn't reckoned on such blatant hate from Daniel.

She tried to gather her wits, still believing that he'd

always secretly fancied her. Men always did. They fancied her far more than plain little Amy . . . she counted on that. He wasn't a bad catch after all, and with her to mould him . . .

Once he got used to the idea, he'd soon forget Amy and they could have a cosy life together. It was as far as her terrified thoughts had gone. She ran to him, clutching at his arms.

'Daniel, don't turn against me, please! For the baby's sake, if for nothing else.'

She used the full power of her blue eyes on him, begging him not to let her down. He shook her off as if she was a clinging insect, incredulous at her gall.

'I've put no baby in you and you know it! I've never touched you. Admit it, for Christ's sake!'

'You always wanted me.' Tess sidestepped the demand, starting to sob now as she saw her security slipping away. 'You know you did, far more than you wanted Amy.'

'You make me sick!' Daniel said furiously. 'And you're not getting away with it.'

One minute he was ranting at her, and the next he was lying full length on the floor as his father rushed to him and knocked him down, catching him off balance. Frank stood over him like a Colossus.

'Don't try and cover lies with more lies, boy. If the child's your responsibility you'll do what's right by the girl, or –'

Daniel hauled himself up, tasting blood in his mouth. He was blinded by rage and wrenched at his father's throat until Frank's eyes bulged.

'I'm telling you the child's not mine. Are you prepared to believe a trollop before your own son?'

'Daniel, let him go,' Helen screamed as her husband began choking. 'You're killing him!'

Daniel let go with a thrust that had his father staggering.

'It's no more than he's been doing to you for as long as I can remember,' he shouted.

He picked up Tess's suitcase and threw it at her. 'Get out of here and find some other fool to take care of your bastard.'

Tess's eyes filled again. It wasn't difficult now, because she could see all her careful plans coming to nothing. She tried desperately to gauge whose will would be the stronger, the son's or the father's. Helen had shrunk back on the sofa, seemingly too afraid to say any more to either of them, and Frank was still hawking to catch his breath.

Finally, he let out a gravelly roar. It held all the cunning of a tiger who'd been stalking his prey for long enough and had finally cornered him.

'The girl's come here as the result of your lust, boy, and you'll do the honourable thing and marry her. Otherwise you can get out of this house.'

Daniel heard his mother moan, and his gut twisted. The old bastard. He knew exactly how Helen would react to this ultimatum, but he'd be damned if he'd be blackmailed into this. If ever he needed to be strong, it was now.

He heard Tess give a small cry as she dropped her suitcase and ran to him, winding her arms about his neck.

'Oh, Daniel, I know everything will be all right,' Tess cried against his face. 'The little baby will keep us together, and once we're married no one need ever know that it wasn't born prematurely.'

He shook her off. 'How much longer are you going on with this? You know the baby's not mine,' he snapped.

She was crying again. 'How can you be so cruel? My mother's run off and I've no one else to turn to. I know you were fond of Amy, but –'

'You'll never know the truth of that,' he said bitterly. 'Nor what this will do to her, after what's happened.'

'What do you mean? What's happened?' she said suspiciously. The little fool hadn't got herself up the spout as well, had she?

'Her grandmother died today.'

'Oh. The poor little bugger.' For once, Tess spoke with genuine feeling. The old woman might have been a tartar, but she and Amy were as close as feathers on a duck, and this was a hell of a time for it to happen. Perhaps if Tess had known, she'd have waited to spring her surprise, but she hadn't known, and it was too late now.

'Exactly. The poor little bugger,' Daniel said icily 'And even if you've managed to persuade my father into believing your lies, you'd never get Amy to believe them.'

Frank gave a snort, tired of all this hedging about.

'It don't matter what Amy believes or don't believe. She's got nothing to do with it, but you two have got to make a go of it for the kid's sake. I'm not having my good name dragged down.'

Good name? Daniel was tempted to shout at him that his own ogling eyes for young women made a mockery of all his sanctimoniousness. But Frank always lived by one rule for himself and another for the rest of them.

'Daniel,' his mother said fearfully. 'You know you must do what's right.'

So she didn't believe him either. It only took one persuasive girl to put about a lie, and the whole world took her word for it.

Frank was soothing Tess now, patting her hand, and to Daniel it was a continuing nightmare. And for the first time he wondered briefly if Amy too would take Tess's word against his. He couldn't believe she would, but it was something that didn't bear thinking about. He glowered at his father, ignoring Tess completely.

'I won't be blackmailed into this,' he said savagely. 'The child's not mine and if you can't accept my word for it I'll get out right now.'

'No!' Helen gasped.

He took her cold hands in his.

'Come with me, Mother, then he'll have no more hold over you. You'll be free of his bullying once and for all. We'll find rooms and I'll look after you.'

Slowly, to his complete disbelief, she shook her head. Frank Easton had dominated her all these years, but she couldn't let go.

'I can't. He's my husband,' she whispered, and he knew that the strange bond that kept them together was still there. And both of them were completely taken in by Tess. His face hardened.

'Then I'll go alone. I'll be in touch with you as soon as I'm settled, Mother.'

'You're not leaving this house,' Frank blustered, seeing the initiative taken away from him.

'It will take a better man than you to stop me.'

He took the stairs two at a time until he reached his own room. He had every intention of doing exactly as he said, and when he was in rented rooms, he would do his utmost to persuade his mother to change her mind about going with him.

He reckoned shrewdly that once Tess saw that she had met her match in Daniel Easton, she would be obliged to turn to some other fool to get her out of her trouble. Nothing would make Daniel remain in this house now until it was settled, and nobody was throwing him out. He saw his action as the only way to deal with an impossible situation. Savagely, he threw a few essentials into a travelling bag and was gone from the house within minutes.

9

Amy lit the gas-mantle with shaking fingers and stoked up the fire. If she was going to stay at the house in Stratford Lane that night, there was no point in freezing and being scared of shadows where there were none. She swallowed the lump in her throat and tied one of Gran's aprons around her waist.

Bedroom first. Strip the bed and bundle all the bed-clothes together for sending to the charity. They'd boil the sheets and sort them through, regardless of their condition. Right now that was something Amy just couldn't do. Then methodically sort everything into bags, some to keep for herself, some to give away to Gran's good neighbours. There was pitifully little. The furniture belonged to the landlord and the odds and ends of personal belongings were shabby or broken.

Amy had never really noticed how frugally Gran had kept herself. There had always been a welcome for her, a kettle boiling, thick crusty bread crisped on a finger-nipping toasting fork in front of the fire and then made delicious with oozing dripping, and an endless pot of nourishing soup made from butchers' scraps.

She made her mind a blank as much as possible until the bedroom was bare and anonymous, as if Gran Moore had never been a living, breathing part of it. She closed the door on it and turned to the parlour. This was going to take more time. The tiny kitchenette where the gas-stove stood in all its glory could come last.

The kettle was beginning to sing in the hearth, and before she did anything else, Amy made herself some tea. The milk was slightly off, but she didn't care. The drink was steaming hot and dark, the way Gran always made it. For a moment, she felt that she *was* Gran, that she'd somehow slipped into her skin and assumed her place. She shivered, pushing the weird thought away, and deliberately thinking of something else.

Daniel. She wondered what Daniel was doing now. He'd have told his parents about today, and Helen would be all sympathy and sadness for Amy. Frank Easton – well, Amy hardly cared what he thought. He was a great bully of a man, and the only thing she dreaded about marrying Daniel – *if* he ever asked her, she thought, crossing her fingers and touching wood for extra security – was that he might expect her to move in with them.

It would be so lovely, she thought dreamily, to have a little house of her own. A cottage perhaps, with roses around the door, and just herself and Daniel to share it, although eventually there would be babies too . . .

She stopped dreaming abruptly. It was wicked and shameful to be thinking about her own future on such a day as this with Gran hardly cold. And the parlour was a bit of a muddle and would take ages. The old sofa could be turned into a bed, and she was going to sleep on it tonight. Not for worlds could she have slept in Gran's room.

Finally, Amy eyed the gas-stove. The Beaumonts had had a splendid one installed in their large kitchen and it was Cook's pride and joy. Gran had always mistrusted hers, but it had been cleaned and polished regularly until her eyes had got too bad to bother. It was looking decidedly lacklustre now, Amy thought, and it would be letting Gran down to leave it in such a state for the landlord to gossip about to his new tenants.

She took the hob apart and washed the iron bits in a bowl of hot soapy water. She finished it all off with a good rub with a cleaning-rag and some spit and polish. It wasn't too badly neglected, and it came up shining enough to see her face in it. The oven should be clean inside, since Gran had never used it except to store bits and pieces.

The door handle was very stiff, and Amy had to wrench at it to get it open. The door creaked on its hinges, and a great tumble of envelopes and bits of paper poured out at Amy's feet. For a moment she felt sick and unable to move. This collection, whatever it was, was essentially Gran. This was private, sacred even, and meant for Gran's eyes alone. Amy was tempted to throw the whole lot on the fire without going through it at all.

But how could she do that? She was too curious, and whatever was here was part of her life too . . .

'Are you all right in there, ducks?'

Amy jumped at the sound of the voice, and saw the shadowy shape of Mrs Coggins outside the curtained window. She got up quickly, spilling half the contents of the oven around her. The bead curtain swung back across the kitchenette area as she went to meet the neighbour at the front door.

'I'm all right, Mrs Coggins. Still tidying up.' She tried to sound as calm as she could.

'You've done 'er proud by the looks of it, gel,' the woman said, trying not to make her nosiness too obvious as she looked past Amy. 'Don't go knocking yourself up now. You're still a bit white round the gills, and a drop o' brandy's what you need. Got a coupla glasses, have you?'

Amy saw the bottle in the woman's hand and hid a sigh, knowing she meant to be kind. She opened the door wider, and fetched two glasses from the cupboard. Mrs Coggins poured a generous splash of brandy into each and raised her glass.

'To your old gran, Gawd bless 'er. They don't make 'em like 'er no more,' she said, and Amy felt her throat convulse as she did likewise.

'Now you're here, you may as well take this picture

113

you always liked, Mrs Coggins,' Amy said, to cover the silent moment. The picture was already down off the wall, leaving a pale patch on the discoloured wallpaper. The woman clucked her teeth.

'I hope you don't think I came 'ere for that, Amy, though it'd be summat to remember 'er by.'

'Yes,' Amy said, hoping she wouldn't stay too long. Then she had a thought. 'Mrs Coggins, did the postman bring Gran many letters?'

'Letters? Nobody gets letters round here, ducks. Who'd want to write to us when half of us can't read!' she finished with a chuckle.

'Gran could,' Amy said, with a trace of pride. Which made it all the more odd that all the envelopes inside the gas-stove were unopened. And suddenly she was feverishly impatient to get back to them.

'Ah well, there's them that likes learning and them that don't,' Mrs Coggins said comfortably. She drained her glass and picked up her picture. At the door she turned back to Amy.

'By the way, my Len's been to tell Doctor O'Neil your gran's passed over. I dare say he'll be round to see you soon. Sleep tight, gel, and get that brandy down you.'

Amy thanked her, verging on hysteria. Why didn't people say what was what instead of being so daft about it? *Gran had gone. Gran had passed over.* Gran was *dead*, for God's sake, and no fancy words were going to change that or bring her back.

She drained the glass of brandy, aware that she probably needed it. She felt its bitter sting all the way down to her stomach, and then she went back through the bead curtain.

The floor in front of the gas-stove was littered with the unopened envelopes. The bits of paper were mostly scribbled notes, old bills, half a lifetime's flotsam. In her haste to answer the door, Amy hadn't noticed that there were also a few fading photographs among the souvenirs. Or perhaps they'd just been face-down at the time. She picked up one of the sepia-tinted portraits and gazed at a face she hadn't seen for years. Uncle Tommy.

Amy felt her heart turn over. It was such a good-looking face, smiling and happy. It was a young face, as young as Daniel's, and had obviously been taken a long time ago. There was a great family likeness. His eyes were the same shape as her own, and the hair, although not coloured in the photograph, was probably a light brown, like hers, with the same tendency to wave. On the back of the photo the scrawled inscription was almost indistinct where the ink had faded.

To my dearest Mother. Your loving son, Tommy.

Amy's eyes prickled. Whatever had happened between them, it was obvious that Tommy had loved her. She picked up another photo. It was a young woman this time. It could have been Amy herself, although she knew it wasn't. She drew in her breath as she turned the photo over. From the spidery scrawl, she saw it was Gran's writing.

Emily. Died 15 June, 1904.

It was also the day Amy was born. And Emily was her mother. The stark words evoked more pain than any flowery obituary. Amy's tears flowed freely, and she dropped the photo with trembling hands. The trauma of losing a daughter and a son was obviously too great for Gran to keep the photos on the mantelpiece.

There were still the letters. Their presence nagged at her. There must have been a reason for leaving them unopened. Gran wasn't illiterate, and neither was she.

She picked one of them up. There was an unfamiliar stamp on the front of it. Australian. It was addressed to Gran, but sent to a post office box number for collection. Amy wondered who had collected it. Her breath came raggedly, because she knew who must have sent it. Uncle Tommy.

The other letters looked similar, except for the dates on the postmarks. The earliest was dated 1909, then there was a long gap until 1918. After that, they seemed to have come more regularly until three years ago.

Methodically, as if she would still put off the moment when she opened them and revealed Gran's secret, she set about sorting the letters, until she had the earliest ones on top. What still puzzled her was that all the time she'd lived with Gran she'd never known about them. As Mrs Coggins said, the postman never came to Stratford Lane.

Slowly, Amy slit open the first envelope with her finger-nail. The address at the top of the letter was a place called Woollamalloo, which sounded daft and made-up. She began to read the words, and as her heart began to beat sickeningly, Amy knew that the terrible thing she was discovering could never have been made up by anyone.

My dear Mother,
By the time you get this I shall be on my way to Australia. It's for the best, though it grieves me very much to leave you and my sweet Amy and know I shall never see either of you again. I don't ask you to forgive me for living a lie, Mother. I know you never will. Neither of us will forget or forgive that I caused the death of my beloved Emily.

Amy gasped, seeing her mother's name so unexpectedly. She read on, her breath tight in her chest.

You must believe that Emily and I truly loved each other. We knew it was a forbidden love, but for one brief summer, we were everything to each other. We knew it mustn't continue, and when I went to work at the docks for a while, it was to spare us the agony of seeing each other and not being able to express our love.

116

Then came your letter, telling me Emily was in trouble and refusing to name the man. She wrote to me too. She begged me to stay away and say nothing, because she'd die rather than confess that her own brother was the father of her child. She knew it would mean prison for me, and she loved me too much for that.

Amy felt the room sway and blur and the tortured words swam in front of her eyes. Dear God, *dear God* . . .

When Emily died, I hated the child at first, because she'd taken my bright lovely girl from me. You never knew how I hated Amy. I never even wanted to see her. But I had to support the two of you and gradually Amy found her own place in my heart. I grew to love her as my own, because she *was* my own. She was Emily all over again.

You were never meant to know the truth. I'd vowed to keep our secret for ever, but I hadn't reckoned on you, Mother. Your eyes always saw too much, and that last time you saw Amy and me together, I knew you'd guessed. I never expected quite so much venom from you, and it was something I couldn't live with. I've hurt two of the women I loved, and I couldn't risk hurting a third. Amy will never know the truth, and that's the only thing I can do for her, unless I make good in Australia. If I do, I'll send money for you both, but I won't write again unless I have an answer.

Ever your devoted son, *Tommy*.

Amy sat as if frozen, with the letter on her lap. She was Tommy Moore's daughter. He wasn't her uncle, dashing, daring and exciting. He was her father, and Amy was the result of his incest with his sister. And Gran Moore had had too much pride even to open the letter and know what agony her son suffered.

She began to shake as the truth of it hammered into her brain. She was sick with shame. It wasn't her shame, yet she shared it. She was part of it. And Gran had known. All these years she had hidden the terrible secret and never revealed it.

Gran could so easily have turned against her, the product of such wickedness, but she never had. She had always adored the child, even though it was never her way to say so. But the love had been there all the same, and somehow Amy had always known that it was a special kind of love. A compensating kind of love, she saw now. And now Gran had died, and it was too late for Amy ever to tell her how much she had loved her too.

Well, now she knew the truth, and there was no changing anything. She didn't know how she felt towards Tommy yet. She was too numb with shock. But since there could be nothing in these other envelopes half as bad as this, she might as well open them and skim through the letters. Tommy had obviously changed his mind and begun writing again . . .

Inside the first envelope was a small bundle of bank-notes. Australian pounds. Amy stared at them in disbelief. She had no idea of their value, but there seemed to be a lot of them. She ripped open the other envelopes. More notes fluttered out. There were no letters, just money.

How long she sat there on the floor, smothered in money, Amy couldn't have said. Her head was in a complete daze. She couldn't think straight. When she heard the knocking on the door again she was tempted to ignore it. She couldn't cope with any more of Mrs Coggins tonight.

'Amy, it's Dr O'Neil,' she heard the gruff voice say a few seconds later.

He opened the front door quietly and let himself in. Doors were never locked in Stratford Lane. Neighbours all knew one another, and who would steal from such a place where there was nothing to steal? Nothing but a small fortune in the gas-stove of old Gran Moore . . .

Amy began to laugh wildly. A small fortune, here all the time. Or perhaps it wasn't that much. It looked a great

118

deal, enough for Gran to have lived in luxury instead of watching every penny.

'Mother of God,' the silver-haired doctor said, the Irish in him more pronounced at the sight of Amy sitting in front of the open gas-stove, but his voice was more reverent than surprised. 'So this is what she did with the letters.'

Amy stopped the hysterical laughing.

'You knew about them?'

'I collected them for her, me love. She swore me to secrecy, and you know what a stubborn old cuss that one could be,' he said with rough affection. 'She wanted no one to know anything. 'Twas the shame, you see. Her own son running off like that.'

'You don't need to pretend any more. I *know*,' Amy said woodenly. 'I know all of it, and I think you do too.'

She handed him the one letter Tommy had written. He glanced through it and sighed deeply.

'Yes, I knew,' he said sadly. 'The poor wee loves, both of them.'

Amy felt her face burn. 'They committed a *crime*, and it was me and Gran who suffered because of them! How can you feel pity for *them*? And now I've got to try and find *him*. Before I knew all this, I was going to do it, because he was the only one I had left in the world. Now all I want to do is send back his blood-money. It belongs to him.'

'No, me darlin'. It belongs to you. Tommy's dead,' Dr O'Neil said quietly.

Seconds before, she had been burning up. Now she felt the colour drain away from her face. It was too much. All this, and two deaths in one day. But of course, Tommy hadn't died today . . .

'When? About three years ago?' she said jerkily, guessing.

'That's right. When no more letters arrived, I asked a lawyer to trace Tommy Moore. He never married and he died without issue in Victoria.'

'Without issue?'

'Children,' Dr O'Neil said, immediately realizing his mistake.

'He had me,' Amy said bitterly.

'So he did, and all of this is now yours. Don't be foolish with it, Amy. Make something of yourself now you've got the chance.'

She looked at him dully. Make something of herself? She was what she had always been, a bastard. Only now she was something worse that probably didn't even have a name. She flinched away from the thought.

'Your gran told me you have a young man,' the doctor said encouragingly. 'Perhaps when you and he get married, you could go into some little business with him. A shop or something. You could do a lot worse, Amy.'

'I suppose.' She couldn't think about it. She didn't want to think about it. The notes crackled every time she moved, and she didn't want them either, but she wasn't daft enough to deny that money made anybody's life a bit easier.

'If you'll allow me, I'll take this money home with me for safe keeping,' he went on, seeing that she seemed incapable of thinking for herself. 'We'll go to the bank tomorrow and get it changed into British currency, and they can tell you what it's worth. I dare say the bank will want you to open an account.'

Amy stared at him blankly. All this talk of bank accounts was beyond her comprehension. She'd never had any truck with such things.

'If you think it's best,' she said, knowing she could trust him.

'I do. And meanwhile you go and make us a nice cup of tea, and before I go I shall give you something to make you sleep tonight.'

She felt so exhausted, mentally and physically, she was sure she wouldn't need it. But she did as he said. She was a leaf in the wind, ready to do whatever she was told, as long as she didn't have to think.

'Are you and that friend of yours still as mad on the moving pictures as ever?' Dr O'Neil decided to make light conversation once he'd ascertained which hospital Gran Moore was in, and the funeral arrangements.

'Yes, I suppose so. Well, Tess doesn't go as much now, and Daniel and me have been going dancing on Saturday afternoons. To Flannery's. A nice class of people go there, far posher than me. We've got friendly with a man called Ronald Derbisham who's got a business-card written in gilt letters, ever so swish, and his girlfriend smokes cigarettes in long holders and wears turbans round her head, and such short frocks it's a wonder her knees don't freeze.'

The words rushed out and stopped abruptly. It was one of Gran's sayings that they both recognized. *It's a wonder your knees don't freeze, gel, and I'm a poet and don't know it!*

The tears ran unheeded down her face and the doctor calmly sipped his tea and let her cry.

'Is that young feller of yours going to show up again tonight, Amy?'

'No.' She shook her head, dragging her thoughts together with an effort. 'He's been with me all day, and he had to be up early tomorrow.'

'Somebody should be with you. What about that friend who works with you at Aveley Square?'

'I don't want anybody. I'm best on my own. Besides, everybody has their own work to see to.'

He patted her shoulder. 'Well, you needn't concern yourself with thoughts of work, Amy. You just stay here as long as you think necessary, and then tell your employers to give your job to some other girl who needs the money more than you do.'

She listened to him with polite attention, not really taking in all that his words implied. She had always needed

121

the money from her job, however lowly it might seem. It had helped Gran out . . . She looked down at her hands, idle in her lap for once, and the tears threatened again.

Dr O'Neil hoped fervently that her young man would show up in the morning, and was slightly surprised he hadn't come back tonight, knowing the girl would be all alone and at her most vulnerable.

Amy said he'd been with her most of the day, but he wouldn't know about this money business yet, nor the truth about Gran Moore's son and daughter.

It was a rotten thing for Amy to find out. Dr O'Neil had known the truth all these years, and respected the old lady's confidence, and would go on doing so. It wasn't for him to reveal it to anybody else, and he hoped briefly that Amy wouldn't let the burden of it fester inside her.

He knew of old that Amy had the same fierce pride as her grandmother. She was a survivor . . . but in his professional experience, it didn't always do to bottle everything up. Eventually things had a habit of bursting out.

As he prepared to leave Stratford Lane, he decided that perhaps the boyfriend's presence tonight would have made Amy even more emotional after all. It might be best for Amy to find her own way of getting over all the shocks she'd had today. Alone and in the dark. maybe, like an animal crawling away to lick its wounds.

10

Dr O'Neil called on Amy again the next day, uneasy in his mind about her reactions to all the shocks she'd received in one day, and suggesting that she came to the bank with him to sort out her new financial status. He said it as much to get her away from the gloomy atmosphere in the house as anything.

For Amy the hours were still passing hazily. She still couldn't reconcile herself to the pain of Gran's death, and she dutifully took the doctor's recommended pills, which she didn't want but was too bewildered to refuse. He was being kind and helpful in trying to lift her out of her depression, and she was too disciplined to argue. But in reality it all washed over her and she felt as if she was moving and responding in a dream-world.

The people at the bank were quite deferential when they knew the purpose of the visit. The money wasn't a fortune, but as Dr O'Neil kept telling her, it was a nice little nest-egg and would give her a bit of independence. The stiff-necked young bank teller had tried to explain the exchange of currency to Amy, but she didn't have the patience to try and fathom out the reason for Australian money being any different from English money. A pound was a pound, and Amy now possessed what still seemed to her like riches.

She had money to pay the rent for Gran's old home if she wanted to take it on, and meanwhile she could look around for a better class of work. Unless, of course, Dr O'Neil stressed, she and her young man were thinking of getting married right away. Nobody would think ill of her on her gran's account if she did, he added.

'I can't marry him unless he asks me, and he hasn't done that yet,' Amy said flatly.

She believed in facing the truth, and the truth of it was, Daniel still hadn't come to Stratford Lane by the end of the second day when Dr O'Neil looked in on her again. She told him she was all right, but as far as Daniel was concerned, something definitely wasn't right, she thought privately, and she felt bitterly hurt and let down.

She needed Daniel's support. She needed him here. The funeral was tomorrow, and she'd expected to have his arm to cling to while they buried Gran. There would be few enough mourners for an old woman who'd hardly ever ventured far from home in a miserable back street that rarely saw the sunlight. It was a rotten enough send-off for anybody.

'Anyway,' she went on, pushing the thoughts away, 'why shouldn't I go on working for the Beaumonts? It's the only work I know, and there's no shame in it.'

'Sure, and there's not,' the doctor agreed steadily, changing the subject at the quick flare of pride in her eyes, and doggedly refusing to let her think there might not be any marriage.

'But perhaps your Daniel won't want you to continue working when you've tied the knot. A sweet girl like yourself deserves a good husband and children. Once you have your man to lean on, you'll be able to forget the sorrow of these days, me love, and the sooner the better.'

She felt wanly that there was no prop at all for her to lean on right now. Only the old doctor, who cared about her as he would any lost child.

But early that evening when her thoughts were still wrapped up in the past, and she was too afraid to look into the future, she heard a step outside her door and knew that it was Daniel. She rushed to open it, and as soon as she saw him all the pent-up emotions came flooding out.

The second he stepped inside and closed the door behind him, she clung to him blindly.

'Oh, if you knew how I've missed you! I was so afraid you'd had an accident or your mother was ill, and that I'd be going to the funeral tomorrow with no one of my own at all to help me get through it. I didn't know how I was going to bear it, Daniel, I really didn't.'

She gabbled against his chest, without even seeing the look on his face, or noticing that he hadn't yet said a word. He didn't get a chance as Amy keened against him, finding a kind of solace for the first time since Gran had died, just because he was here, so dear and warm.

And Daniel let her weep, holding her in his arms and loving her, and holding back from bursting out the news of Tess Loveridge's treachery.

He'd tried desperately to think of a way of telling her about Tess's wicked lies, praying that he wouldn't read any suspicion in her eyes. He hadn't been able to face it yesterday. He knew Amy's feelings would still be too raw after her grandmother's death to deal with anything else.

'Why haven't you come until now?' She wept against him. 'I needed you so.'

'Amy, I'm so sorry. There's been a hell of a row at home and I've moved out. It took me a long search to find some decent rooms and move in. And I've been back home while my father was at work, trying to persuade my mother to change her mind and move in with me, but she won't.'

He stopped abruptly, aware of her brimming eyes staring at him. His own words sounded so feeble, weighed against the enormity of her loss . . . but then, she didn't know the rest of it.

And here was his sweet Amy in his arms, whom he loved and wanted more than he had ever wanted any woman, and he didn't yet know how deep her trust went. He wouldn't even blame her if she wondered, just a little . . . .

'Amy, love.' He heard his own voice, thick with guilt that wasn't even his. 'There's something I've got to tell you . . .'

Her eyes were wild.

'Don't say you can't get time off to come to Gran's funeral! She'd have wanted you there as much as me. She thought such a lot of you, and I just can't face it without you.'

The tears spilled out again.

Gawd almighty, gel, she seemed to hear Gran Moore say severely, *where's all these waterworks coming from? You tryin' to drown us or summat?*

'Of course I'll be there,' Daniel said quickly. 'I'll pick you up here at ten o'clock. That'll be time enough, won't it?'

'Yes.' She spoke jerkily, sensing something, and not knowing what. 'They're taking Gran straight from the hospital layin'-out room to the cemetery. Afterwards we'll come back here for a bit of cold ham and pickles. I'll ask Mrs Coggins and the doctor as well. That'll be enough of a wake. Gran wouldn't have wanted a big show.'

He listened to her tragic voice with something like horror welling up in him. He couldn't tell her yet, after all. It wasn't the right time. He'd tell her tomorrow, after the cold ham and pickles. He knew he was putting it off as much for himself as for her. She couldn't cope with learning about Tess's wickedness just yet, and he didn't have the stomach to tell her. For a little while longer, it was kinder not to let her know.

'I can't stay long, Amy,' he said in a low voice. 'I just wanted to be sure that you were all right.'

'I'm all right, I suppose. Dr O'Neil's been looking after me.'

She moved slightly away from him. Something was wrong. She didn't yet know what it was, but in some indefinable way, Daniel had gone away from her. Physically he was here, but in some funny peculiar way he might have been in another world.

Something awful had happened to Gran, and ever since then she had been unnaturally perceptive to anything else of an awful nature. There was something bad, inside Daniel, and he was keeping it from her. And a flicker of that bloody false pride that grew out of struggling to get a share of the sun from the dark back streets such as Stratford Lane wouldn't let her ask him what it was.

'Do you have time to stay for a cup of tea?' Without meaning it to, the question came out sarcastically.

'Of course I do!' He recognized her hurt and added, 'Amy, I haven't stopped thinking about you for a single minute –'

'Thinking about somebody's not the same as being with them when you're needed. Gran always said thought was cheap. It's actions that mean summat. P'raps we'll both feel a bit more settled after tomorrow.'

Head high, she swept through the bead curtain to the kitchenette, hearing the clack-clack of the wooden beads as they swung to and fro behind her. She didn't know why she was almost trying to pick a quarrel with Daniel. Perhaps because she wanted to feel anger and to goad him into anger too. Wanting to feel that she was still alive, instead of the numb creature that was taking her over.

She hadn't even told him her own news yet. That she wasn't penniless. That she could grandly return the money he'd given her for Gran's hospital bill and not even notice the dent in her brand-new bank account, thank you very much.

'Dearest Amy, I wish tomorrow would never come,' she thought she heard him mutter.

She frowned, not understanding this daftness, and turned to the kettle that was beginning to sing on top of the gas-stove. She used it deliberately now, as if to prove to herself that she was a modern young woman of some means and could deal with new-fangled things perfectly well.

In minutes she had dumped the tray on the parlour table and poured out two cups of tea without letting it brew properly. The liquid was pale and hot and they drank it down, both aware of an embarrassment and restraint that had never existed between them before.

'Thanks for the tea,' Daniel said when he'd emptied his cup, ignoring the fact that there had been no sugar offered. He rose to go, his angular face strained in the popping gas-light. He hardly knew what to say to this darling girl to whom he had felt so close, and who now seemed so far away from him.

'I'll see you in the morning then,' Amy said.

'See you then,' he answered. He kissed her upturned lips, and turned away swiftly before he blurted out everything here and now.

Whatever happened, he wasn't going to be forced into marrying Tess Loveridge, and far from pushing him out of his own home, he felt he'd made a stand for his independence that was long overdue. Somehow he'd find a way to make her tell the truth, but that hardly seemed the issue now.

With Amy looking so pale and drawn, and the dread of telling her of Tess's treachery, he felt as strangely trapped as if he really had betrayed Amy. It was a feeling that enraged him, but one that he couldn't escape.

Amy closed the door slowly behind him. She'd never thought Daniel was one of those people so trammelled by bereavement that he couldn't give her any comfort. How could he have changed so quickly? She didn't understand what was happening. She only knew that she had ached for him and longed for him, with a physical need for his closeness that was almost shameful, in the circumstances.

But now that he'd been and gone she felt more alone than before.

Mrs Coggins called next, coming into the house with the briefest of knocks on the door and not bothering to wait for an answer. Mrs Coggins kept checking on her 'as a kindness', but this time she was in a flurry of excitement.

'Amy,' she hissed. 'There's a gent with one of them big Roller motors blocking the end of the lane. I 'eard him ask somebody where you lived as I was coming back from the public with my Len's tonic bottle. If it's somebody you don't want to see, you just say so an' I'll stay.'

'Hello, Amy,' said Bert Figgins' voice, his grey shadowy figure filling the doorway. He'd taken off his chauffeur's cap, and his sandy hair looked like spun gold in the light. He gave a small smile, looking very handsome in his uniform, the grey gauntlet gloves fitting his fingers like a second skin.

'Bert! You're a bit out of place round here, aren't you?' It was all Amy could think to say in the confusion of seeing him.

'I had to drop Lord Beaumont at his club and it wasn't worth taking the motor back to Aveley Square, so I thought I'd look you up. We were all ever so sorry to hear your sad news, Amy. Very sorry indeed.'

She felt her eyes fill with tears at this unexpected kindness. And then she was aware of Mrs Coggins eyeing the two of them in a way that Amy found almost comical. As if she was wondering just how many more beaux the quiet little Amy Moore was going to have up her sleeve!

'Thank you for coming in, Mrs Coggins. I'll see you in the morning, shall I?' she said firmly. 'The doctor said he'd take you to the cemetery, and you'll come in for a bite afterwards, of course.'

'Oh, yes, of course,' the woman said, reluctantly backing

out of the door. Amy gave Bert her first real smile for three days.

'Salt of the earth, some say, and others speak the truth,' she said, making a feeble joke of it. 'My reputation's probably gone for a packet of pins now. My young man's just been to see me, and now you're here too. But it's very good of you to bother, Bert.'

'We were all shocked to hear about your gran,' he said. 'I dare say Tess would be too if she knew about it.'

Amy stared at him. 'For goodness' sake sit down and tell me what you mean, Bert. Why doesn't Tess know?'

She'd wondered why Tess hadn't been to Stratford Lane. It might be a bit beneath her, but it wouldn't have hurt her to make the tram journey in the circumstances . . .

'I was forgetting you hadn't heard,' Bert said. 'Miss high-and-mighty Loveridge got her knickers in a twist over a bit of a fuss upstairs and then Cook having a go at her. Next thing we knew, she'd packed her things and gone, and nobody knows where.'

Amy stared. Tess had threatened to walk out so many times that nobody took her seriously. Tess had got so strange and secretive lately. Amy hoped she wasn't turning out like her mother, after all. *A bad apple, that Tess*, Gran always said. *You just be careful of her* . . .

'Is that tea in the pot?' Bert said hopefully. 'It's a cold night, Amy.'

He removed the elegant gauntlets and rubbed his hands together. His nails were kept short and clean, considering he tinkered with the engine of the Rolls-Royce whenever he could, but then, Bert fancied himself a bit of a ladies' man. It was a wonder she and Daniel had never seen him at Flannery's doing the light fantastic, she thought, and realized that because he was taking her mind off Daniel's odd behaviour, she was beginning to feel slightly better.

'I'll make some fresh. It won't take a minute on the gas,'

she told him. 'There might be a bit of cold pie left too, if you fancy a bite.'

'Why not? It's right cosy here, Amy. Not a palace, but homely and clean. I bet you've been scrubbing your fingers to the bone these last few days to keep yourself occupied.'

He followed her through the bead curtain, watching her movements. She was still shocked, anybody could see that, and she probably hadn't eaten anything for three days. She looked thinner already. He remembered how she'd felt in his arms the few times they'd had a cuddle, and hoped she wouldn't get too thin.

'Miss her, do you?' he asked. 'I know you used to come out here a lot.'

She swallowed. The question might have been intrusive, but somehow it wasn't. Bert was being kind. Bert had taken the trouble to seek her out when she was nothing to him, nor he to her. He was just a friend, and she needed friends. She didn't have Tess any more, and tonight she had felt that she didn't have Daniel either. Her mouth quivered and Bert moved forward, his arm on her shoulders.

'Come on, old girl, you cry on good old Bert's shoulder if you've a need. Don't they say crying's good for the soul or summat?'

Amy sniffed against his shoulder, finding comfort in the smooth grey cloth of the chauffeur's uniform, while Bert found these odd moments quite endearing. Poor little bugger with no one to turn to, he thought. If he'd been the boyfriend, he'd have made bloody sure he'd got his feet under the table by now.

'And if you're short of a few bob,' Bert added magnanimously, as a new thought struck him, 'I can let you have some readies. Funerals don't come cheap, I dare say, and knowing you, you wouldn't want your old gran to be planted by the charity.'

'She won't be,' Amy said in a wobbly voice. 'She's

131

having the best walnut coffin with brass handles that Greyson's can supply.'

Bert blinked. This wasn't what he'd expected to hear at all. Since when was a housemaid like Amy Moore able to spend money on walnut coffins with brass handles? An extravagance that Bert Figgins privately thought a waste of good money, since unless you were planted in a lead box, the worms eventually chewed through the wood, whatever it was.

Amy hadn't intended saying so much, although anyone who went to the funeral would see the splendid coffin tomorrow. Word would get around that Gran Moore hadn't exactly been given a pauper's send-off. It was the first thing Amy had insisted on seeing to when Dr O'Neil had sorted out her bank account.

She gave a small shrug as Bert took the tea tray out of her hands and took it back to the parlour. He undid the buttons on his jacket now, and looked relaxed and easy in front of the roaring fire.

'You're doing her proud, Amy,' Bert remarked. 'But you make sure you leave enough for yourself.'

He took a sip of the tea she handed him. His instincts told him there was something to sniff out here. Curiosity was fair bursting out of him, but he was canny enough not to probe. He heard her cup sit noisily in her saucer, and despite her trauma, her cheeks flushed in the firelight.

'I've got to tell somebody, Bert, and as long as I can trust you . . .'

'Amy darling, you know that without asking,' he said earnestly. 'I've always had a fondness for you, and if ever I can do anything to help – well, I'm here now, aren't I?'

She gave him a grateful glance. They'd shared some good times together, and it was true he'd always been affectionate towards her. If she'd sometimes thought he was inclined to be *too* affectionate and too forward, none of that mattered now. As he said, he was here. He'd cared enough to come.

'Well then, what would you say if I told you I was rich, Bert?' she spoke in a hushed voice that hid her sudden excitement. Saying the words out loud made them real. She was rich! A legacy of nearly five hundred pounds was hers, and suddenly she didn't give a tinker's cuss that the man who'd sent the money halfway around the world had sent it on account of his own guilt and shame. Reasons didn't matter. It had been sent for herself and Gran, and now it was all hers. She heard Bert Figgins laugh.

'Oh yes. Pull the other one, sweetheart,' he said with lazy indulgence.

'It's true!' Amy said. 'If you don't believe me, I'll prove it to you.'

She pulled open a drawer in the sideboard and got out the pristine new bank account book. She hadn't looked at it since she and the doctor came home from the undertakers', with just the one entry deducted from the vast amount. She shoved it under Bert Figgins' nose.

'What do you think of that then?' she said triumphantly.

He stared at it in silence for a full two minutes, his imagination doing his thinking for him. And then he handed the book back to her, pretending no more than a mild interest in her sudden good fortune.

'What did you do, rob a bank?' He grinned. He'd helped himself to a piece of cold pie and lavishly adorned it with pickles, and he scraped the plate with his fork, sorry when it was finished.

'Of course not. My – a relative left it to me. Well, to Gran and me both, really, only I didn't discover it until after she died.'

The glow and the excitement faded at once. Here she was, chattering away about a legacy in that grand way, when none of it altered the fact that Gran was dead. She

133

should be ashamed. Tommy was dead too, she thought fleetingly, but she couldn't feel anything towards him at all. Not one single thing.

Bert was quick to note the change of expression on her face, and capitalized on it.

'You did the best you could for your gran when she was alive, and not everybody can say that. I'm sure she'd be happy to know that you're taken care of, Amy.'

He got to his feet while she was still appreciating his thoughtfulness in making her feel better.

'It's time I was off, or his lordship will be sending for the bobbies, thinking I've run off with his Roller.' He hesitated. 'You'll have people around you tomorrow, Amy, but if there's ever anything I can do, well, you know where I am. And you'll be coming back to Aveley Square to pick up your things sometime, won't you?'

'Oh yes. Yes, of course,' she said vaguely. Why did everyone assume that she wouldn't be working there any more? She couldn't shake off the past two years of her life that easily, even if Tess could. But Tess was Tess and she was Amy. They were poles apart, really, she thought, only she'd never really seen it before.

'Goodbye, love. Keep your pecker up.'

Before she knew what was happening, Bert had put his arms around her and kissed her full on the mouth. His lips were soft and his kiss wasn't as firm as Daniel's, but she responded simply because it was so good to have people caring about her.

She hardly remembered a thing about the funeral. Daniel arrived, looking uncomfortable and solemn, and there was no pleasure in this sad drive in his Austin car. The doctor took Mrs Coggins along in his bone-shaker, since it was too undignified to go to a funeral on a tram. It couldn't have been a more mournful day, starting off with a yellow pea-souper that made the streets eerie and silent except for the inching traffic and the occasional sight of the sparks from the overhead tram-lines.

But by the time the walnut coffin was lowered into the ground, the fog had lifted and the November day reverted to its usual grey. And once it was over, the little group of people went back to Stratford Lane and sat drinking tea and eating boiled ham and pickles, making whispered conversation so as not to upset Amy. And inside, most of them were wondering how soon they could decently get away and go back to normal everyday living.

11

Daniel had only been given the morning off, and Mr Jenkins had been a bit scratchy about letting him have that. Gran Moore hadn't been a relative, after all . . . It wasn't a good morning for him. He ached for Amy's distress at burying her grandmother, but even more he dreaded the moment he'd have to tell her about Tess.

He'd found some miserable rooms quite near to the penny library, but Amy didn't even know about that yet. There were secrets between them now, when everything had seemed so open and honest before.

They held hands tightly throughout the brief burial, and afterwards. But Amy had the strangest feeling that he wasn't really with her. They couldn't even talk properly until the others had gone from the house, and still Amy couldn't seem to reach him. When they were finally alone, she couldn't stand it any longer.

'Are you going to tell me what's wrong? I thought you were meant to be cheering me up, but you've got a face longer than a penny whistle.'

She was already facing the future and preparing to be strong. Gran was gone now, and she'd decided stoically that she had to get on with living, and her crying was done. But all morning she'd sensed that Daniel's thoughts were elsewhere, and the feeling was still there. She hadn't expected him to be the type that couldn't take funerals. Even the simple folk around Stratford Lane knew that birthing and dying were things that nobody could escape.

Amy certainly didn't think Daniel was a weak-livered sort of chap. But somehow he looked hunted, as if he couldn't wait to get out of this dark house with the drawn curtains that Amy was pulling back now.

They both needed something to lift them out of the depression of the last days. Perhaps if she told Daniel about Tommy – not all of it, even to him – it would bring a smile to his face and her own too, by telling him about wrenching open the gas-stove and seeing all the stuff come tumbling out. If it had been a scene at the pictures, it would have looked quite comical. Buster Keaton would have made a big production out of it.

She didn't even see the irony of trying to cheer Daniel up, when she was the one who was bereaved. Fretting about Daniel made her somehow able to pretend that everything was all right between them, and that she wasn't about to hear something dreadful.

He broke into her spinning thoughts. 'Amy, will you listen to what I've got to say without interrupting?'

She licked her dry lips. It was obviously something terrible. Her imagination soared to the worst that she could think about. He was dying. He had some incurable, hereditary disease that meant he could never marry her or anyone.

'Tess came to our house the day your grandmother died, Amy. She was there when I got home.'

He saw the blankness in her face. Whatever she had expected, it wasn't this.

'*Tess*?'

'You said you wouldn't interrupt –'

'No I didn't.'

Daniel breathed harshly. How could he expect her not to burst through his garbled words, when he still didn't know how he was going to find the right ones? There *were* no right ones. There seemed no other way than the cruel, stark way of coming straight out with it.

'She'd got to my father before I arrived home. She'd told him she was in trouble, and that I was responsible.'

137

He heard her strangled gasp, all the colour leaving her face, save for the two hazel pools of her eyes.

'No! Oh, God, *no*.'

Her hand went to her throat, and by Christ, now he knew how it felt to be betrayed. He thought he'd known it before, when that bitch did the dirty on him, but that was nothing compared to the way he felt now. He seized Amy's icy hands, feeling them lifeless in his own.

'You know damn well it's not true. I've never touched her or looked at her in that way. You've always known it's you I love!'

Any hope of her not interrupting him now was lost on both of them. It seemed as if she hadn't heard him.

'I didn't know she was in trouble. She never told me.' Her voice shook. 'I never dreamed – oh, how *could* you?'

Somehow she couldn't think of anything else for the moment. It seemed there was space in her head for only one thought at a time.

His voice was ragged. 'I was praying it wasn't true. There's been no proof, no doctor's say-so, but my father's gone off half-cocked, trying to make me marry her.'

'*What*?' Amy said. She felt her senses rock. She felt as though someone had punched her in the stomach and knocked all the innards out of her. She was totally out of balance.

Though why should she be surprised? Hadn't she known it was going to be something awful? And hadn't Gran always told her to be careful of Tess Loveridge, saying she'd go the way her mother had gone, the shameless hussy?

Amy felt her teeth chatter as if she had a violent chill, and knew that not even Gran's death had been such a terrible shock as this.

'Amy, it's not my child. You know that, don't you? *Amy*?' She heard Daniel's hoarse voice through a haze.

She tried to speak, but words wouldn't come. Her heart pounded so fast she was sure she was going to die. Yet there were no tears. The hurt was too great for tears. It burned like a flame, and then she gave out a great cry like an animal in severe pain. It was exactly how she felt. Her heart was breaking, and the pain was devouring her.

Next door, Mrs Coggins heard the cry and sent her Len off in a flurry of fear for the doctor. In her opinion, whatever ailed Amy Moore now was summat needing medical attention, and wasn't to be interfered with.

'It's best that you go and leave her to me,' Dr O'Neil said quietly to Daniel, looking at Amy's pupils and feeling her racing pulse. 'It's probably delayed shock. She's had a lot to take in since the old lady died. I'll take her home with me tonight, and my wife will take care of her. Come and see her in a couple of days.'

They heard Amy gathering up breath and both looked at her in some apprehension.

'*No.*' The hoarse sound seemed to be dragged out. 'I don't ever want to see him again.'

Daniel looked stricken, and the doctor was clearly alarmed at Amy's reaction. Her young man was the person he'd expected her to lean on most. But shock took folk in strange ways, and he'd seen plenty in his time. He shrugged his shoulders and nudged Daniel to the door.

'Give her time. Her spirit's at rock-bottom, but she's young and she'll recover.'

Helplessly, Daniel knew there was no point in staying. He wished he dared confide in the doctor, but if he stayed any longer, it was obvious, even to him, that Amy might go right over the edge.

He drove home in a blind rage. How he missed hitting lamp-posts and other vehicles he didn't know. A guardian angel must have been looking over him. He wished

139

it hadn't. He wished he need never face another day, knowing Amy had decided that everything was over between them.

The doctor's wife insisted that Amy stayed in their spare room for as long as necessary. She knew there had been a bust-up of sorts between her and her young man.

That gossip Mrs Coggins had confided there'd been another chap visiting Amy, ever so posh-looking, with a great Roller motor blocking the end of Stratford Lane. Kathleen O'Neil guessed it had probably been a chauffeur. Chauffeurs! Mother of God, what were they! Poncing about like male tarts in their uniforms, playing at being the rich ones. Kathleen had no time for the likes of them.

But on the third day of Amy's stay with the O'Neils, the Rolls-Royce slid smoothly to a stop outside the doctor's house, and the sandy-haired young man came knocking on the door. Kathleen had known at once that this wasn't a patient come for a cough bottle or a liniment rub.

'Miss Amy Moore, please,' Bert said smoothly. 'I've a message from friends where she works.'

Kathleen eyed him up and down, barring his way at the front door, a small efficient barrel of humanity.

'Give me your name, and I'll ask if she's up to seein' visitors,' she said in her best County Galway voice. This one might wear a uniform and have a smile like the angels, but he was still no more than a servant and he'd wait to be invited before he set foot across her threshold. She went directly to Amy, who was supposedly reading in the parlour.

'You've a visitor, love. Do you want to see him?' Kathleen said.

'Him?' She didn't want to see Daniel. She couldn't *bear* to see him and know he probably belonged to Tess by now. She couldn't turn love on and off like a tap, and she wasn't strong enough to see him yet. If she did she'd be tempted to fall into his arms and beg him to tell her the nightmare wasn't true. And she knew it had to be true . . .

''Tis a fine fellow in a chauffeur's uniform,' Kathleen added, trying not to sniff.

'Bert Figgins,' she murmured. 'Yes, I'll see him.'

Bert came into the room, trying to hide his shock at the sight of Amy. She'd reverted to being a little brown mouse again, he thought, the hair untidy, the face white except for those huge eyes, and he could see she hadn't been eating. The extra flesh she'd always hated so much seemed to have rolled off her. She was hardly a catch for a wide-awake chap such as himself – except for the money, of course . . .

'Amy, I had the devil's own job to find you,' he said, sliding into a chair. 'When I saw the house all shut up I thought you'd done a bunk, until the big woman sent me up here. How've you been?'

She looked at him mutely, and he said hastily, 'Sorry. Daft question. I can see you ain't exactly in the pink. Cook wanted me to bring you this, in case you weren't eating properly.'

He produced an apple pie from the cardboard box beneath his arm, like a magician with a rabbit in a hat. Amy felt her eyes fill with tears.

'That's lovely of her, Bert. Thank her for me, won't you? I haven't had much appetite lately.'

'I can see that. You're wasting away, gel. How about if we have a piece now? I'm partial to a bit of apple pie meself. Let's have a midnight feast in the afternoon.'

'If you like. I'll get some plates,' she said quickly, and he watched her go, his eyes thoughtful. He remembered her looks when she first had this chap of hers. She'd been quite tasty then, Bert remembered, with a real bloom on her. And she could be that way again, once she'd got over this little lot.

141

Amy came back with plates and spoons and a tray of tea, and she picked at the pastry out of politeness.

'What you doing here then, gel?' Bert asked. 'Couldn't you face it in your gran's old place after all?'

'Not exactly,' she mumbled, and then convulsing sobs tore her apart, and Bert was rocking her in his arms in embarrassment, and bits of apple pie were flying everywhere.

'Gawd, Amy, I didn't mean to upset you!' Bert said, when he could disentangle himself. He tried not to make it too obvious that he was dabbing at the apple stains on his smart grey double-breasted jacket.

'You didn't,' she sobbed. 'I'm sorry about the mess on your coat. I'll clean it for you in a minute.'

'It don't matter a bit,' he lied. 'Cook will see to it in a jiffy when I get back. We miss you there, Amy,' he remembered to say. 'We've got two new girls to replace you and Tess, but one's only temporary until you come back.'

'I shan't be coming back, Bert.'

Until that moment she hadn't even thought about it properly. But how could she go back to Aveley Square, where everyone had known her and Tess? How could she work alongside them, knowing that they'd get to know, if they didn't know already, that Tess had stolen her boy? They'd be whispering about her, comparing her to those other sad women resigned to growing old without their men who'd died in the Great War.

Bert put an arm loosely around her shoulders, the caring friend who knew damn well that there was something more going on here than just normal grief. There was despair too, and Amy should have got over that by now, especially with the nice little legacy the old duck had left her.

'Well, you're probably doing the right thing, Amy,' he said. 'You don't need to work your fingers to the bone any more, so why should you? You can take things easy

142

until you know what you're going to do with the money, can't you?'

'I wouldn't care a fig about the money,' she muttered. 'I'd give it all away tomorrow if only I could turn back the clock and stop –'

'Stop what, gel? I dunno what it is that's torturing you, but you know what they say: a trouble shared is a trouble halved, and they always said I had such big ears I ought to be a good listener.'

He was jocular and considerate, trying to make her smile again. Amy saw the older brother, the friend, the confidant that Tess had been. When she spoke again, her voice was bitter. Her eyes were shadowed and she didn't look at Bert, not wanting to see his pity.

'It's Daniel – and Tess. She says there's a baby . . .'

It wasn't what she'd meant to say, and even now she still didn't know whether she believed it. Common sense told her it was almost certainly Giles Beaumont's child . . . but a fat lot of good that knowledge was going to do her. It didn't change the fact that Tess had gone to Daniel, expecting him to do right by her, and in Amy's innocent head that could only prove that Daniel must have *been* with her.

Bert wasn't stupid. He saw everything in an instant. So that little tart had got herself up the spout and the boyfriend had been turning two birds, had he? Amy obviously couldn't say the words, but she didn't need to. Nor did she need to look any further for someone to take care of her. Amy and her five hundred pounds were suddenly a dazzling package to a chap like Bert Figgins.

'If that's the kind of chap he is, then don't waste your time on him, gel,' he said, with just the right amount of sympathy and indignation mixed in. 'Your old gran wouldn't have wanted you mooning about over what can't be changed, would she?'

He'd heard enough of Gran Moore's philosophy in the past to know just how to handle this.

He saw her shake her head. She raised her swimming eyes to his. She was flushed now, and with those eyes full of tears she looked – she looked stunning, Bert thought in surprise. He'd thought her a little maggot when he arrived, but it only needed a touch of colour and the mouse quickly turned into a delicate fawn. He'd never realized what a mobile face Amy had. Every expression was clearly inscribed there, which could be an advantage or not, he thought.

'I'm not the type of chap to heave another one out of the limelight,' Bert said earnestly, thankful that he could hide anything behind his own bland features. 'But if what you say is true, then that leaves me free to say what I've wanted to say for a long time, Amy –'

'Don't, please, Bert,' she said quickly, not sure how she suddenly came to be sitting with Bert Figgins' arm around her, for all the world as though they were courting. 'I can't think of anything like that yet.'

'Of course you can't.' He took his arm away at once. 'But you can't mourn for ever, gel. Not your gran, nor your chap's infidelity.'

He chose the word deliberately and saw her flinch. He mustn't go too fast, but there was no harm in reminding her that that was how the rest of the world would see it.

'I know,' Amy answered in a low voice. 'But I need time to get used to – everything.'

'A week,' Bert said briskly. 'And then I'm taking you out. What'll it be? The pictures? I know that was always your favourite, and I heard they're showing Charlie Chaplin in *The Gold Rush* again at the Arcadia –'

'*No!*' Amy said sharply, bright spots of colour in each cheek as images of Daniel leaning towards her in the darkened cinema on that first day spun through her mind.

Daniel, wanting her, admiring *her*, not Tess . . . 'Not the pictures, Bert.'

'All right then, how about dancing?'

Before she knew it she was smiling. Dear kind Bert, coming all this way to cheer her up, when she was nothing to him. It made her feel better to know that she probably *could* be something to him, if she wanted to be. But she didn't, she thought fervently. She didn't want anyone making up to her or trying to take Daniel's place.

She realized with a shock that it didn't matter what he had done, she still loved Daniel. But forgiving was easier than forgetting, and she wasn't sure she would ever be able to do that. It was far better to put it all in the past and start building a life without him as soon as possible. And she couldn't do that by shutting herself away from the world.

'I just *might* go dancing with you, Bert,' she said finally. 'Just as long as you don't read anything more into it. It's just dancing – and it's good of you to ask me. I'm not much company at the moment.'

'Of course it's just dancing.' He beamed, ignoring the rest.

And what better way to work himself into a girl's good books than by tripping round the polished floor of a ballroom with her in his arms! From his arms it would be but a short step to his bed and his life, though with Amy Moore Bert Figgins had the certain feeling that it would have to be a trip up the aisle as well.

He hadn't really bargained on that, not with Amy or anyone else. He wasn't the type for settling down, and girls to him were really just pretty accessories to wear on a chap's arm . . . but the lure of that five hundred pounds was like a red rag to a bull. And even if it meant the ultimate sacrifice and marrying Amy Moore, he was prepared to do it if there was no other way of getting his hands on it.

12

After a few more days under Kathleen O'Neil's somewhat claustrophobic care, Amy knew she had to stand on her own feet. Bert's visit had put a lot of things into perspective. She was grateful to him, and a little surprised. Whatever else she may have thought about Bert Figgins, she'd never seen him in the role of counsellor. But it was time she decided what she was going to do, and the first thing was to see the landlord of Gran's rooms and arrange to continue with the let for the time being. The next was to take her courage in her hands and go back to Aveley Square and inform the Beaumonts that she could no longer work for them. It would take courage, because she'd be retracing all the steps in which Daniel had still been a part of her life. And Tess too. She resolutely refused to think about Tess. A friend who could do what Tess had done to her was the worst kind of enemy.

Amy thought it might be eerie, coming back to Gran's rooms, but it wasn't. She had done a good job of the clearing-out, and the rooms were fresh and clean and sweet-smelling. It wasn't that Gran's presence had gone. To Amy, the place would always be essentially Gran, but there was nothing upsetting about that. And remembering the day of the funeral, when Daniel had broken her heart, was something she just had to endure.

She packed away her black mourning frock and put on a pale grey blouse with a picot-edged collar and a darker grey low-waisted skirt. She looked thinner than she'd ever looked before. She allowed the thought to give her a moment's pleasure before pushing her arms into her tweed top-coat and pulling the cloche hat around her ears.

It was cold and damp outside, and it was a long walk to the tram. Her cheap side-buttoned boots didn't keep out much of the wet. She reminded herself that she could buy new ones if she wanted to. She could buy anything she liked. She was a woman of independent means, and the thought of it could still take her by surprise.

By the time she left the house in Stratford Lane, Amy Moore was actually smiling, and walking with a little lift in her step. As Gran would have said, you couldn't mourn for ever. Bert Figgins had said it too, she remembered suddenly.

Cook was embarrassingly pleased to see her, throwing her ample arms around Amy as if she was a long-lost relative. Mr Allen too, in his stiff way, left her in no doubt that he was glad to see she was getting over things, as he quaintly put it. The new housemaids eyed her warily, clearly wondering if she was about to take over their jobs that minute, and Fanny sulked in the corner, patently put out about something, as usual.

'Did that Bert Figgins give you the apple pie I baked special for you? He ain't been down here to tell us, and I hope he didn't upset you in your time o' sadness.'

'Yes, he came to see me, and it was sweet of you to have sent it,' Amy said. 'Bert was very kind too.'

Cook snorted at that. Only ever out for the main chance was that one, she thought keenly. 'You need feeding up, by the looks of you. So when you coming back, my duck? We can do with a bit of your elbow-grease around here.'

The new girls muttered indignantly at the slight, and Amy said swiftly, 'That's what I've come to say, Cook. I shan't be coming back. My gran left me provided for, you see.' She felt a small frisson of pride as she said the words.

'Well, I never,' Cook said, staring. 'Left you provided for, did she?'

It wasn't something that happened every day to a housemaid, particularly one from Stratford Lane.

'That's good to hear, Amy.' Mr Allen smiled at her. 'And how's that other young miss faring?'

For once Amy didn't let her face betray her feelings. She kept the smile firmly fixed on her face. No one would have known what it cost her to do it.

'I don't know. I don't see Tess any more,' she said with a shrug.

'And a good thing too,' Cook said approvingly.

'Well, I'd better see if I can speak to Lady Beaumont, and then collect my things,' Amy said in the small awkward silence when none of them quite knew how to conclude the visit. 'It was good to see you again.'

She escaped with their good wishes still ringing in her ears. As one of the new girls escorted her to the main part of the house like company, she realized she felt very nervous. Lady Beaumont spent most mornings in the sewing-room with her embroidery, and it wasn't a place that downstairs housemaids frequented. But she wasn't a housemaid now, Amy reminded herself. She lifted her chin as the girl tapped on the door, opened it at Lady Beaumont's call, and stood back for Amy to go inside.

Lady Beaumont looked up in surprise, frowning slightly. There was something familiar about the girl standing diffidently by the door in the cheap coat with the rabbit fur collar up around her neck. She was pretty enough, but Lady Beaumont couldn't place her . . .

'It's Amy Moore, my lady,' Amy obliged her. 'I am – was – your housemaid.'

'Which is it then?' Lady Beaumont smiled. 'Are or were?'

Amy smiled back. It didn't occur to her to find it odd that her mistress didn't even seem aware that Amy had been away or suffered a bereavement. The domestic doings of servants didn't concern those upstairs as long as the household continued to be run smoothly.

'That's what I've come to tell you. I'm afraid I have to leave right away. Me – my grandmother died recently and left me provided for, so I'm – I'm going into business.'

The words tripped out before she'd properly prepared them. The first thing that came into her head was what the doctor had said. But he'd suggested she and Daniel could set up a nice little business together . . .

Lady Beaumont's eyes widened slightly, but good breeding made her recover instantly.

'That's very good news, and I'm happy for you, my dear. I wish you luck in your new venture.'

She was dismissed. There was nothing more for either of them to say. Thank goodness, Amy thought fervently. It would have served her right for being so daft if Lady Beaumont had asked all about the so-called business, and caught her out for being a liar. She got out of the room quickly, and sighed with relief.

She made her way quickly to the servants' stairs and the room she and Tess used to share. The other girls would be using it now, and she guessed that her things would be put ready in the shabby carpet-bag she'd brought them in. She stepped inside awkwardly, seeing the marks of occupation that didn't belong to her. Nor to Tess, she thought gladly. There was nothing here in the poky little room to remind her of either of them.

She saw her bag on top of the clothes cupboard and pulled it down. Her things had been stuffed inside without much care, but it didn't matter. Amy glanced around, as if seeing for the first time how mean and small this room really was. It was one setting for the rich and another for the poor, she thought, comparing it with the elegant little sewing-room she had just left.

Suddenly she wanted to get out of there. The room was stifling her. And if she stayed she'd start thinking too much, remembering that it was here that she and Tess had shared their dreams, pouring out their hearts to one another and never thinking it would all end so terribly. Not for Tess though, Amy thought bitterly. Tess had presumably got what she wanted, and Daniel would be pushed into marrying her in the end. If it was all true, he'd *have* to do it, for his good name as well as hers. Tess would have security and a name for her baby instead of being disgraced and ostracized, even if she didn't have love.

In the heart and soul of her, Amy knew that Daniel still loved her and would always love her . . . at least, that was the way it would be played out in all the best Hollywood pictures, a beautiful tragic love that was destined never to be fulfilled.

She shivered. She'd gone off the pictures good and proper. It was all a sham, all the beautiful play-acting and the dramatically printed words on the screen that had had her and Tess sobbing into their sodden handkerchiefs with as much pleasure as pain. Because afterwards they could emerge into the afternoon sunlight and link arms and run to catch their tram, and exist on a diet of dreams of romantic heroes carrying them off into the sunset, until the next Saturday and a new programme, when it would begin all over again.

No more, Amy thought, taking her time walking down the stairs instead of the old frantic hurry to escape Cook's wrath. She'd done with the pictures. They only put ideas in a girl's head that no real man could live up to. Not the men she knew, anyway. The bastards like Giles Beaumont, and those trapped by circumstances like Daniel . . . and Bert Figgins, who was hardly a Rudolph Valentino, and could be as irritating as a hornet. Bert had his better moments, she thought grudgingly, remembering the kindness he'd shown her, but really she was in no mood to think the best of any of them.

Amy straightened her shoulders. Today she was going to

walk out of the front door into Aveley Square. She wasn't scuttling up into the daylight from the back stairs. She was going out like a lady. A woman of means.

She put up her hand to open it when it opened from the other side, and Giles Beaumont nearly walked into her. His brief irritation vanished as he stared at her.

'Good God, it's young downstairs Amy, isn't it?' he said in that plummy voice of his. 'Lost your way, have you? The servants' stairs are that way.'

He waved vaguely. Servants' quarters were of no concern to him, except when he was creeping up the stairs to ravish some unsuspecting housemaid. Amy's face burned with memory of the marks on Tess's neck, and the lingering scent of Giles Beaumont's cigar in the room they'd shared.

'I'm not a servant any more – sir,' she said haughtily. 'And if you'll let me pass . . .'

He barred her way.

'Got some young tearaway to marry you then, have you?' he taunted. 'It's the usual way you skivvies get out of doing your duties, isn't it?'

'Is it? I was under the impression that housemaids get left in the lurch when they're in trouble – sir. Not that *I'm* in that state. I've too much respect for myself to be any man's plaything – sir.'

She couldn't believe she'd really said it. But the words had been whipped out of her mouth before she could stop them. She saw Giles's eyes narrow and she stared back unblinkingly. For a minute she thought he was going to strike her for her insolence. In the same instant the feeling that of course Tess was carrying this bastard's child and not Daniel's became overwhelming.

But she should have known that the Giles Beaumonts of this world had no need for violence or bluffing. They simply ignored what they did to ruin a girl's life. The thought ran through her mind that if she wasn't careful she was going to start feeling sorry for Tess, and she hardened her heart immediately.

'I'm pleased to hear you no longer work for us,' Giles said smoothly. 'It saves me the bother of sacking you. Now get back to the dirt where you belong.'

'Where *you* belong, you mean,' Amy said, before she ducked beneath his raised arm and ran down the front steps of the house, her heart pounding.

After a few minutes her feet slowed, and she swung her carpet-bag in her hand, keeping her head up and her dignity intact. She felt oddly lighter and freer, and even though she knew the feeling wouldn't last, it was enough to keep her spirits moderately high until she reached the tram-stop again and went back to Stratford Lane.

Tears of reaction overcame her as soon as she stepped inside her own front door. Amy blinked them back, and as she did so she saw a letter on the rag rug. She picked it up and knew the handwriting at once. It belonged to Daniel's mother. She sat and looked at it for five full minutes before tearing the envelope open, not wanting to know what the letter contained, but curiosity was stronger than the dread of wondering what Helen Easton could possibly want with her now.

Amy my dear, I wanted to tell you personally how very sad I was to hear of your grandmother's death. It is unlikely that we shall meet again, but I do want you to know that you are often in my thoughts. We're both victims of circumstance, Amy, and we can only go on, and survive as best we can. My very best wishes for the future, and my regrets once again. *Helen Easton*.

It was a sad, guarded little letter, saying nothing and yet everything. It spoke of a lifetime of martyrdom, and Helen clearly saw Amy cast in a similar mould. Only in her case, Amy didn't even have the status of being a married

152

woman. Amy was a cast-off, betrayed by her best friend, and destined to become one of life's old maids . . .

Well, she'd be damned if she was going to sit down and just let it happen to her, Amy thought, suddenly bristling with rage and self-respect. She might never marry – she thought it highly unlikely that she would – but she wasn't going to turn into some sort of cabbage, patiently waiting for old age and then death, with nothing to her credit with St Peter but memories of what might have been. That wasn't what she'd been put on this earth for, she thought savagely, knowing that Gran would have approved.

On Saturday afternoon, Bert Figgins came to take her dancing. He knew a chap who'd wanted a bit of tinkering done with his car engine, and Bert had begged the loan of the machine for a couple of weekends instead of payment. Small though it was, it still wouldn't go down Stratford Lane, but he'd parked it out of sight at the end of the road, and when Amy had walked carefully over the cobbles in her best shoes, expecting to be walking all the way to the tram-stop, Bert bent low like Sir Walter Raleigh and with a flourish opened the door of the car standing at the kerbside.

'Is this yours?' she exclaimed. 'Not come into money, have you, Bert?'

Not yet, he thought with dry amusement. He felt elated, knowing he was pulling Amy out of her misery and that she'd be thinking soon that she owed him something. She looked a fair picture this afternoon, obviously having made a bit of an effort. The dark shadows beneath her eyes were still there, but they didn't detract from her looks. They enhanced them if anything, giving interesting planes of light and shade to her face.

She wore brighter lipstick than she used to, and her cheeks were quite pink. Rouged, Bert suspected, which was quite a turn-up for plain little Amy. She'd discarded her drab clothes and wore a frock of pinks and blues beneath the thick winter coat she was snuggling into. She was quite a catch after all. Bert decided he was cleverer than he'd thought. All this and money too.

'Well? Is it yours?' she repeated when he'd got the engine started and the car was bouncing along nicely.

'No. Borrowed it from a friend to take my best girl dancing,' he said cheekily, trying out the words to see the effect it would have on her.

She didn't say anything, just stared ahead, wondering where they were going. Not to Flannery's, she hoped, wishing she'd thought to say so before. But she doubted if Bert would go there. Not up West . . . but if it was, she'd grin and bear it, because it was the only way to exorcize from her mind all the places she associated with Daniel. Anywhere except the Roxy. That was the one place that was definitely taboo.

'Sorry it's not the Rolls,' he went on.

'It beats walking,' Amy said, glad that it wasn't an Austin Twelve either. He glanced at her.

'You look much better,' he said. 'Beginning to get over things, are you, love?'

It was almost what Mr Allen had said. She'd agreed then, because it made other people feel better and less embarrassed at dealing with bereavements or broken hearts. It was crazy how you always considered other people's feelings when your own were in tatters, Amy thought in surprise. But with Bert she felt she could be more honest, and he wasn't perceptive enough to notice the brittleness in her voice.

'I miss Gran a lot, and I'll probably never get over Daniel, but I know I've got to accept things as they are. It's not the same thing as getting over them, but it's better than feeling as if I'm being washed down the drain with the soap-suds.'

'That's the ticket,' Bert said, relieved. It would have

been no fun dragging little Miss Misery round the dance-floor. But now that she was cheering up there was no reason why they couldn't have a good time. He wasn't going to rush her, but there was no harm in planting a few seeds.

'I heard you'd been to the house and told them you've finished,' he went on. 'You're doing the right thing, Amy. Start afresh and see what you can make of yourself.'

'The trouble is, I don't know what I do want to make of myself. I can't do much, except cook and clean, and there's no point in exchanging one skivvying job for another.' She gave a brief smile. 'You should have heard me talking to Lady Beaumont the other day, Bert. Proper toffee-nosed I was for a minute, telling her I was leaving because I was provided for now, and going into business. You should have seen her face!'

Bert laughed with her, rejoicing because unwittingly she'd given him the lead he wanted.

'You know, that's not such a bad idea, old girl,' he said with sudden enthusiasm, as if the idea had only just occurred to him. 'Investing your money in a proper business, all legal and above-board, could be just the thing for you.'

'Oh yes?' she said sceptically. 'And what would I know about investing money in a business? No, it was all pie-in-the-sky, Bert. Forget I ever mentioned it.'

But he didn't, and neither did she. Though for the present it went out of her mind as she saw that they were pulling up outside Flannery's dance-hall and tea-room. It was too late to say she never wanted to set foot in there again, knowing that there was no time like the present for showing a brave face and putting her new plan of exorcism into operation before she lost her nerve.

'Amy, *darling*! How marvellous to see you. We quite thought you'd vanished off the face of the earth, didn't we, Ronald!' The melodious voice greeted her almost as soon as she went through the doors and into the warmth and brightness of the dance-hall, and she was hugged to Jane Broome's flattened chest.

'Amy, my dear.' Ronald was less effusive, but none the less sincere. He looked his usual immaculate self, his hair glossed to the same dark perfection as his patent leather shoes. It would have given some men the look of a gigolo. On Ronald it sat like a mark of wealth and landed gentry, and Bert Figgins moved in like a homing pigeon.

'It's good to be here,' Amy said, her voice betraying none of the trembling inside. Despite all her fine new resolution, Flannery's would be forever linked in her mind with Daniel.

'I haven't been too well, but I'm fine now,' she went on, seeing no reason to burden these nice people with her personal troubles. 'You don't know Bert, do you?'

She made swift introductions, then listened in open-mouthed amazement as Bert expertly guided the conversation around to motor-cars. Jane smiled at Amy.

'It's always the same, isn't it? Shall we leave them to it and go and powder our noses before it all begins?'

She linked arms with Amy, and for a minute it was Amy and Tess, the way it used to be, before any of the nightmare began. Amy blinked the image away.

'Now tell me what's really been happening,' Jane said softly, when they were alone in the ladies' powder room. 'You don't fool me, darling, even though that attractive loss of weight suits you very well. But that's not the man you came with before, is it? This one seems quite dashing, but what happened to the other one?'

'It all came to nothing, the way these things do,' Amy said brightly, applying more lipstick to lips that were already carmine-red. 'My grandmother died, and since then, Bert's been a good friend to me, and that's just about all there is to tell. It's still a bit painful to talk about, so I'd rather not, if you don't mind. Let's go and join the others, shall we? I can hear the music starting up.'

'Poor Amy,' Jane said sympathetically, accepting that the subject was closed. She didn't seem to be *too* upset though, she thought, completely misinterpreting the artificial brightness of Amy's voice and the brilliant smile on Amy's face, and later, the way Amy threw herself into the shimmy-shake with all the energy of a young colt.

When the afternoon's dancing had them all glowing, the four of them went into the tea-room together. Again, Amy pushed away the memory that this was where Daniel had revealed how passionately he thought of her. That sweet, fragile moment when she knew they had been on the brink of love, when each had known how dear the other was . . . and however nobly she tried to believe that she was privileged enough to have known such sweetness, even for a moment, nothing prepared her for the sudden surge of passion inside her. Because, desperately, blindly, she wanted him back. He was hers, and had always been hers, and the pain of losing him threatened to choke her again.

'Are you all right, Amy?' Bert was leaning towards her, and she realized she had been staring into space with blank eyes. 'Ronald was telling me about his brother.'

'Oh?' She forced herself to be attentive. 'I didn't know you had a brother, Ronald.'

'There's no reason why you should,' he laughed. 'I was just saying to Bert that he should meet Archie. They'd have a great deal in common, Bert with his interest in machines, and Archie with his present fad for aeroplanes.'

'Couldn't they come down next weekend, Ronald?' Jane said suddenly, raising her eyebrows slightly.

'Yes, why not?' he exclaimed. 'Jane and I are getting engaged next weekend and having a bit of a shindig at the old homestead. If you'd like to be house-guests, we'd love to have you. Come on Saturday and stay overnight. There's plenty of room, and you and Archie can get your heads together, Bert. I'm sure you'll find him amusing.'

He handed Bert one of his cards and gave him directions to The Gables, leaving Bert wondering just what he was getting into. Whatever it was, it couldn't be bad. Moving into better circles never hurt anybody, and these two seemed the least class-conscious of any toffs he'd ever met. It would do Amy good too, he remembered as an afterthought.

13

'We can't possibly go!' Amy said furiously when they were driving back to Stratford Lane in the twilight and she began to think sensibly about the invitation.

'Why not?' Bert demanded.

'Because we won't fit in, that's why. A housemaid and a chauffeur going to some big posh house in the country and joining in with the nobs! Have some sense, Bert.'

'Listen, Amy Moore. You're no housemaid any longer, and there's nothing wrong with being a chauffeur – not that I see any reason for telling anybody what I do . . .'

'You see? You're ashamed of it.'

'I'm bloody well not, but it won't hurt them to think I'm starting up me own car-selling business soon, which is something I've always wanted.'

'Is it?' she said, her thoughts diverted for a moment. 'I never knew you had any ambitions, Bert.'

'Anybody with any gumption's got ambitions,' he said brazenly. 'I don't intend touching my cap to that snot-nosed Giles Beaumont any longer than necessary, I can tell you.'

'Amen to that,' Amy said feelingly.

He pricked up his ears. 'Don't tell me he tried anything on with you, gel,' he said indignantly.

'No he didn't,' she said, and then got him tickled pink by telling him what had happened the day she marched out of the house in Aveley Square.

At the end of it he gave a deep sigh. Fate was playing right into his hands, and Bert wasn't one to turn up his nose at the chance.

'I envy you being able to put him in his place. All I

need is a few hundred quid to start me off, and I'd be out like a long-shot. That's all it'd take, a few hundred quid. That's peanuts to folk like the Beaumonts – and to Ronald Derbisham too, I dare say – but it can make all the difference between holding your head up and being somebody, and wiping somebody's arse for 'em, begging your pardon for being so coarse. But forget about my pipe-dreams, Amy. The important thing is you, and what's to stop you getting yourself togged up with posh new clothes for a weekend in the country? We've got the use of this car, and we can pretend to be real toffs. My walking-out togs ain't so bad, and if there's dancing, I reckon we can show 'em all a fancy step or two by now. So why the bloody hell not?'

So why not? On Monday she took the tram up to the big shopping emporiums and bought a glittery bronze evening frock that just reached her knees. Its matching headband made her look like a vamp, but the plum-voiced salesgirl assured her it was the very latest thing. To go with it she bought a string of pearls so long that she could twist it into a knot and still have a good loop hanging below her waist. And a gilt bangle for her upper arm, into which she'd tuck a wisp of chiffon hanky. The heady excitement of spending money as she'd never spent it before made her even more reckless. She bought two new woollen day frocks with stockings and shoes to go with them. Her old coat had seen better days, so she treated herself to a long-lapelled one in the latest camel-beige colour.

'My Gawd, gel!' Bert was awestruck when he came to call one afternoon while Lord Beaumont was at his club, and she paraded round for him in the bronze finery. 'You'll dim the stars, no danger, in that little lot.'

'It's not too – well, tarty, is it?' Amy said anxiously.

Bert caught her round the waist, pulling her into him. She felt soft and warm in his arms, and he smiled down admiringly into her small flushed face.

'You could never looked tarty if you tried, sweetheart. You look like a million pounds, and I'll be as proud as Punch to escort you to the ball!'

'Oh Bert, you are daft.' She started to laugh at his theatricals. And then she wasn't laughing any more as Bert's mouth descended on hers, seeking her lips and pressing them to his. His hand was behind her head so that she couldn't move away as she'd instinctively intended. She didn't want any man kissing her other than Daniel . . . but as the kiss went on, she surrendered to it helplessly. It wasn't Daniel's kiss, but perhaps she could just pretend for a moment that it was. Foolishly, recklessly, she let herself dream, and found herself melting against Bert Figgins' body in a way that he had never expected and hardly knew what to do with.

When they broke away, they looked at each other, both a little shaken.

'Well!' Bert said.

'Well,' she said in a small voice, the shame of it sending the wild colour to her cheeks. Pressing herself against a man like that, like a wanton hussy, and feeling the tingling inside her at his hard masculine reaction . . .

'We'd better have some tea,' she said, flustered.

'Take your finery off first,' he suggested, and at the frightened look in her eyes, he laughed, and teased her. 'Don't be daft, our Amy, I only meant you don't want to mess it up! I'll put the kettle on while you get changed, and then we'd better think about things.'

She went into the bedroom and changed into her old frock, her hands trembling. What was there to think about? Nothing had changed. Though there *had* been something on her mind these last few days. When she had composed herself she went back into the parlour, hearing Bert whistle as he prepared the tea. He was quite domesticated, she thought. He'd make some woman a decent enough husband. Not as exciting as he liked to

161

think, perhaps, but a girl could do a lot worse. She tried to imagine a lifetime married to Bert Figgins, and put the thought away from her at once.

'Now then.' Bert said when he'd poured them both a cup of steaming tea. 'I've got a proposition to make to you, and you can throw me out if you don't agree with it.'

She looked at him apprehensively. She didn't want to hurt his feelings, but she didn't want to marry him either. She wasn't ready to be caught on the rebound, like a rubber ball that had lost its spring.

'Don't look so worried.' Bert grinned. 'It's only a *business* proposition I'm suggesting, not a trip to Australia to find out if any of your elusive uncle's relatives are still lurking about in the bush.'

He said it to make her laugh, but from the look on her face, Bert knew he'd made some kind of mistake.

'Oh, come on, love, it was only a joke,' he said, hoping she wasn't heading for another depression, and plunged in. 'How'd you like to be the business partner of Figgins' Motor Sales? That's the proposition I'm – er – proposing.'

He floundered as her shoulders began to shake. For a minute he thought she was going to scream at him that she'd known all along that he was only after her money. That measly five hundred quid that wasn't going to set the Thames on fire, but could certainly get Bert Figgins started . . . and then he saw that she was laughing. Laughing and crying too, and he felt a stab of hope.

'Oh, I'm sorry, Bert,' she gasped, wiping her eyes. 'I didn't mean to go on so. It's just that – well, it must be telepathy, I suppose, because ever since you told me about your ambition, I've had the same kind of thought in my mind. Business partners, I mean. I know you never meant it that way at the time, but it seemed quite a sensible thing to do, with me investing, and you doing the work – well, I suppose that's what you mean, isn't it? I'm never been much good with figures and suchlike, so you'd have to explain everything to me, Bert, and I'd *want* to be a part of it all, not kept in the background . . .'

She stopped for breath because she was laughing now. Sensible, clever, gullible little Amy, he thought jubilantly, who hardly knew an Australian pound note from a kangaroo's backside, and was about to launch him into dreamland. He seized both her hands in his, smiling at her with what he knew always charmed the girls – his eager boyish look.

'You mean it, Amy? We've really been thinking the same way? Well, if that don't beat everything. And you'd really risk going into partnership with me, would you? I'd never do you out of your money, love, you know that.'

'Well, of course I do, otherwise I wouldn't agree to it, would I?' Amy said smartly. 'Naturally, we'd have it all on a proper business footing, though, with some sort of contract written up by a lawyer. It's protection for both of us, isn't it?'

'Oh, of course. We'll have to find somebody to get it all done legal-like,' Bert said, who had never intended any such thing. He was slightly surprised too. Little Amy Moore wasn't quite as naïve as he'd thought, and he certainly hadn't wanted any shark-nosed lawyers poking into his business . . .

'We could try Mr Charles Rugby of Welles Street,' Amy said suddenly.

Bert gave a short laugh. 'You do come up with some surprises, Amy gel. Have you been holding out on me all along, and moving in high places with lawyers and such?'

'No. I just heard his name somewhere, that's all.'

'Well, I don't know any, so he'll do.' Bert scribbled down the name and address. 'I'll go and ask his advice, and then I dare say he'll want to see us both.'

'Will he?'

'Well, unless you just want to hand over the money

without involving an outsider,' Bert said nonchalantly. 'We could easily sort it out by ourselves, Amy.'

'No. It wouldn't be right. If I have to see Mr Rugby as well, then I'll have to see him.'

She couldn't remember where she'd heard the name. She'd had no need for lawyers, but the information had just tripped off her tongue. It didn't matter anyway. The flush of excitement from parading in the new bronze frock had died down, and now that she and Bert had come out in the open and made a sort of commitment to each other, she began to feel a bit flat. There was no one to advise her on whether she was doing the right thing or not.

She forgot her doubts and made herself determinedly bright. After all, it was something of an occasion, the day she became a business partner, which made her highly respectable, and far removed from a humble skivvy. She refused absolutely to think about Daniel, or the fact that her new status might even make her acceptable in the odious Frank Easton's eyes now. It was a closed chapter in her life, and with more resolution than Amy knew she possessed, she simply erased Daniel from her mind. Because everyone knew that crying over what might have been was a waste of good energy . . .

'Shouldn't we celebrate our new partnership in style?' she asked.

'What kind of style?' Bert laughed back at her, catching her reckless mood and thinking what a stunner she could be, given the chance. 'You don't have a bottle of champagne hidden away with all your other treasures, do you, sweetheart?'

'Not champagne, just Mrs Coggins' bottle of brandy,' she said triumphantly. 'I'm not too keen on the taste, but we ought to seal our bargain properly, and I feel a bit like getting tipsy tonight.'

It wasn't really night-time yet, but darkness had fallen softly while they'd been talking, and a great yellow moon slid in and out of the fast-moving clouds. Amy got up quickly and drew the curtains across the window. Mrs Coggins had a habit of peering inside when she went to fetch her Len's tonic bottle from the public, and she didn't care to be seen drinking brandy with a handsome young chap in her own parlour.

Bert watched her through lazy eyes. A partnership with Amy Moore, with her putting up the money. It was an attractive proposition all right, and he wondered how soon he could put the next idea to her. A more permanent proposition . . .

Only to himself did Bert admit that he wasn't all that keen on the thought of marriage. The idea of making love made him somewhat queasy, for all his boasting and flirting, and the fact that he'd steered clear of it so far only enhanced his reputation as a bit of a ladies' man. But even though he'd got over the first hurdle and acquired the money – or nearly – he could see the advantages of marrying Amy. Once she became Mrs Figgins, all her assets would become his with no effort at all.

He knew it would have been hopeless asking her to marry him before the business deal went through. Amy wasn't that gullible and she'd have known very well it was the money that was the main attraction. Besides, he still suspected that she hadn't got the other chap out of her system yet, even though she never spoke of him now.

Amy fetched the brandy bottle and two glasses. This was the way posh people sealed contracts. Fill your head with alcohol and your boots with optimism.

'To us,' Amy said. 'May we be a rousing success.'

'To us, and especially to you, Amy,' Bert said earnestly. 'I won't let you down, I promise.'

At that moment he really meant it.

Mrs Coggins paused outside Amy's house on her way to the public. The curtains were drawn at the parlour window, but they were made of cheap thin stuff. Two silhouettes could clearly be seen against the gaslight above the mantelpiece and the glow of the fire. Two people, a tall man and a slender girl, held glasses and touched them together, the way people did when they toasted each other.

'Well, I'm buggered,' Mrs Coggins muttered to herself. 'It didn't take you long to find out what was what, and good luck to you, gel. We all need a good man to keep us, and any of 'em's better'n none.'

Expansive with her own thoughts, and disregarding her useless lump of a husband who hadn't worked more than spasmodically in years, Mrs Coggins went on to the public, commenting to anyone who would listen that it didn't look as if little Amy Moore would be mourning her gran for too long.

A week after he'd moved out, Daniel went home to see his mother, choosing his time carefully when he knew Frank would be occupied at the Roxy cinema.

'I know you did what you felt you had to do,' Helen said tearfully. 'But life's even more impossible now, with that girl acting as if she owns my home.'

'You mean she's still here?' Daniel said, outraged. 'I was sure she'd find some other fool to harass when she knew she couldn't win. Hasn't Father seen through her yet?'

'He thinks he's doing the right thing . . .'

'Mother, don't you believe me when I tell you Tess's child has nothing to do with me?' He felt even more betrayed by her unwilling acceptance of Tess Loveridge's accusation.

'If you say so, then I believe you, but Frank says where there's smoke there's fire, and a girl wouldn't make up such a wicked lie unless there had been some relationship between her and a man.' Her face coloured, totally unused to uttering such things, especially to her son.

'There's been nothing,' Daniel said savagely. 'Nor could there be, when it's Amy I love.'

'Well, that's a nice thing to hear and no mistake!' Tess's shrill voice said from the doorway.

Even now, she knew everything might go wrong, and she didn't know how long she could depend on Frank's support. She tried desperately to keep up the charade that she and Daniel had been lovers, but even Frank was starting to be sceptical.

'I've heard about men who deserted a woman in trouble,' she said, forcing ready tears to her eyes.

'When are you going to stop this wickedness?' he snapped. His eyes assessed her quickly. She looked no more pregnant now than when she'd first come to the house, and he felt a sudden suspicion. 'Have you seen a doctor yet? Are you sure of your facts?'

She gave a high-pitched laugh. 'Go on, try to get out of it another way! You ask your mother if she ain't heard me retching, morning, noon and night, and if that ain't a sure sign of a bun in the oven, I don't know what is.'

Her coarseness sickened him. He hardly noticed his mother disappear hastily from the room, and wouldn't have blamed her if he had.

'I'm taking you to see a doctor tomorrow,' he said coldly.

'And I'll see one when I'm good and ready,' she retorted. She hated doctors and all that probing around and the horrible clinical stink of their surgeries.

Daniel felt his temper snap. Without warning, he seized her by the shoulders and shook her cruelly.

'Listen, you bitch! We both know that if you're pregnant, it's nothing to do with me. We both know it was Giles Beaumont, and I'll not be blamed for it.'

Caught unawares by his physical assault, she blabbered wildly. 'Even if it was him, he'd never admit it – you know his sort. I'm sticking to what I told your father. You had your pleasure, and you don't want to pay for it.'

Daniel's hand was halfway to her face as she flinched back. He'd never struck a woman in his life, but he came nearer to it at that moment than ever before. God, how could he ever have thought her beautiful? She was nothing but a calculating bitch.

'Have you thought what you're doing to Amy?' He tried a new tactic. 'You were supposed to be her friend . . .'

Tess's eyes gleamed, her voice was full of spite now. 'Amy's doing all right, by all accounts! I saw Fanny from Aveley Square the other day, and she said Amy and Bert Figgins were getting very cosy now, and Bert was bragging about a partnership with Amy.'

'What kind of partnership?' he demanded. 'Is this more of your lies?'

'You didn't know she's come into money, then?' Tess taunted. 'Bert's getting his hands on some of it. Setting themselves up in business, Fanny said. Next thing they'll be getting wed, I dare say, so you may as well forget all about her, because it didn't take her long to forget you!'

He didn't believe any of it. Amy had said nothing about any money to him. Amy had shown him the door as soon as he'd told her the terrible thing Tess had done.

'You're a liar,' he said savagely.

'I'm not! Go and find out for yourself if you don't believe me. You never believe anything I say. You're hateful to me, and I wish I'd never set eyes on you.'

She spoke with the self-righteousness of knowing that at least there was some truth in this tale about Amy and Bert. Fanny had taken great delight in passing on the bit of kitchen gossip, highly elaborated by Bert himself.

'*You're* wishing it? Dear God, nobody could wish it more than I do,' Daniel said harshly.

At that, Tess resorted to noisy tears.

'You don't know what it's been like for me, with my

mother running out on me and leaving me with all her debts, and then having nowhere to turn when I found myself in trouble. Do you know what happens to girls like me with no man to protect them? They end up on the streets or in the workhouse. You were always kind to me, buying me afternoon tea that time, and giving me rides in your car. I didn't think it would be impossible for you to like me a bit . . .'

She overlooked the fact that each of those times she'd been with Daniel, it was because of Amy. She looked at him between half-closed lids, through which ready tears squeezed out. She ran to him, pushing against his chest and letting him feel as well as hear her ragged sobs. He stood rigidly, determined to stay unmoved by her histrionics.

'I'll get at the truth of this from Amy,' he snapped, pushing her away. 'I want to find out just what's been happening these last weeks. And who is this fellow?'

Tess's eyes glittered, suddenly triumphant that she could still turn things her way.

'Bert's the Beaumonts' chauffeur and he and Amy were quite a pair until you came along. *Everybody* knew they was soft about one another.'

Everybody except Daniel, the words implied. His eyes hardened. He thought himself pretty astute, but girls could twist a man around their little fingers these days, and despite his love for Amy, if this Bert Figgins had been as important in her life as Tess suggested, he began to wonder if he could trust anyone any more.

He was furious with himself for letting Dr O'Neil persuade him not to contact Amy these last weeks. It had been his first instinct to go back to her immediately and find out what was wrong. But he wasn't waiting any longer to try to put things right.

He drove his car to the end of Stratford Lane, cursing the slanting rain that glossed the cobbles with a slippery sheen and blew the smoke from the crowded chimneys into his face worse than a pea-souper. It reminded him far too much of the devastating day of Gran Moore's funeral.

It was the middle of the afternoon, but the day was dark with heavy rain-clouds. In the narrow lane, it might have been night-time, Daniel thought, remembering painfully how much he'd wanted to lift Amy out of these surroundings. Some of the houses were already gas-lit, but not Amy's.

He tried not to recall the sweet nostalgia of other Saturday afternoons that seemed like part of another life. The closeness of the darkened Roxy, where they had held hands, transported into a fantasy world of tinsel and romance no more wondrous than their own; Flannery's dancing-rooms, where they'd held each other as close as they dared in the waltz, or thrown themselves into each new dance craze, loving and laughing over their stumbling footwork . . .

'She ain't in, young sir,' a voice said as he knocked for the third time on Amy's door

Daniel turned to see the gossipy woman in the cotton overall, arms folded across her ample bosom, as she stood in the doorway of her own house and looked him over keenly.

'Do you know where she is?' he asked.

Mrs Coggins sniffed. 'Oh, fair popular is Amy Moore these days, wi' young men calling at all hours of the day and night. Shall I take a message?'

She gauged his reaction to this. He was haughtier than the sandy-haired gent, and it wouldn't hurt him to know he had a bit of competition where young Amy was concerned.

'Do you where Miss Moore is right now? I have to see her.' He spoke impatiently, disliking her immensely.

'Well, I might,' Mrs Coggins said cagily. This one hadn't been near Amy as far as she knew since the day of the funeral, and he'd been attentive enough until then. Leaving the poor dab to fend for herself all this time, while the other one had been fussing around like a mother hen.

'Well then?' Daniel said, tired of her hedging.

'She went off for the weekend to some place in the country with her young man,' Mrs Coggins said, as if it was an everyday occurrence for the inhabitants of Stratford Lane. 'It wouldn't surprise me if they didn't come back at all, the way they were carryin' on, and her buyin' all them flashy new frocks. Amy said summat about an engagement too – 'ere, don't you want to hear the rest of it?'

Whatever else she was going to say was lost on Daniel as he brushed past her and stormed back up the lane. It was true then. Amy and that chauffeur fellow. He felt as if the earth had suddenly cracked beneath his feet. He knew Amy had felt the same when he'd told her what Tess was trying to do to him, and he could hardly believe that Amy could have forgotten him so soon.

She must know that this business with Tess was all a terrible mistake, and that somehow he was going to put it right. However many lies Tess Loveridge told, it couldn't touch their love . . . and he'd have staked his life on Amy feeling the same way. He would never betray her with another woman. But Amy hadn't waited, and he hardly knew how to face the thought of her and this Bert Figgins spending a weekend together.

14

Bert collected Amy on Friday afternoon, and it was still daylight when they reached the Derbishams' estate. As soon as Amy caught sight of The Gables in the rolling Sussex countryside, she took fright. It wasn't just the house, though that itself was impressive enough to frighten the daylights out of her. It was more like a palace fit for kings and queens, she thought hysterically, with row upon row of mullioned windows that must dazzle the eyes in mid-summer, and which now looked down contemptuously on these two upstarts daring to drive towards them in the small borrowed car. The house was magnificently set off by its surroundings, being centrally situated in a huge sprawling country estate of parklands, woods and streams. And long after they had found the signpost pointing the way, they realized they had already been on Ronald Derbisham's land for a considerable time. Bert stopped the car briefly while they both looked at the house in some awe.

'Whew!' Bert said reverently. 'Looks like we're coming up in the world, gel.'

'Bert, let's go back,' Amy said at once. 'We'll say I was ill or something. There's plenty of flu about, and all this is far worse than I expected.'

'What do you mean, go back! And what's worse about all this?' He threw out an arm expansively, causing the car to wobble for a minute until he righted the wheel again.

'It's all wrong, that's what I mean. I don't mind seeing Ronald at Flannery's, where everybody with the price of a ticket is equal, but it'll be different here, you know it will. They'll guess in a minute we're who we are.'

'So we're *who we are*. We're the up-and-coming Fig-ginses, aren't we?' he said, daringly including her, as if they were already married. It didn't do any harm to dangle the idea in front of Amy, however obscurely. The more she heard it, the more likely she'd be to accept it as inevitable. 'We're business partners about to start our own car sales firm, remember? Respectable and solvent.'

Thanks to Amy's gran, he thought silently, blessing the old girl for leaving this unexpected windfall. He opened his mouth to continue the argument for definitely staying, when the sound of hoofbeats made him turn his head sharply.

A rider was reining in an enormous grey horse along-side them, a young man dressed in immaculate riding jodhpurs who sat astride the animal as if he was part of it. His fair hair was ruffled by the exertion of the ride, his cheeks glowing. He was a younger version of Ronald Derbisham, Amy thought at once, and guessed that this must be the brother Ronald had spoken of at Flannery's.

'I say, have you lost your way? This is private property, you know,' the young man said, leaning towards them. The tone was firm if not unfriendly, but all the same Amy felt embarrassed at once. She and Bert obviously didn't look like the kind of people who would be arriving at The Gables for a weekend house-party!

'We do know,' she heard Bert say cheerfully, immune to the implication in the other's voice. 'We're guests of Mr Ronald Derbisham.'

The young man looked slightly flustered.

'Oh Lord, what a gaffe. I'm Ronald's brother, Archie Derbisham. Please forgive me, but I didn't expect . . .'

His eyes flicked over the car, and mortified, Amy silently finished his sentence for him. He hadn't expected any guests at The Gables to turn up in a humble little motor like this! She could hardly blame him. Ronald and Jane,

173

and now this Archie, were obviously of a far grander station than themselves.

'Fun, isn't she?' Amy heard Bert say enthusiastically, patting the side of the car as if it was as prestigious as Lord Beaumont's Rolls-Royce. 'I'm giving her an airing for a friend this weekend, just to test her out. I'm quite handy with the mechanics if anything goes wrong, but I'm not expecting trouble. She's got a very efficient and useful little engine inside this small body.'

Archie Derbisham's eyes gleamed with interest, and immediately Amy remembered Ronald saying that Bert and his brother should get along famously since both were interested in engines and the like. There was no doubt in her mind that Bert remembered it too. He had an uncanny memory for things which could be of use to him. Especially anything to wheedle his way into the kind of life-style to which he'd like to be accustomed. She didn't know whether to be annoyed or amused, and decided it was easier on the nerves to let Bert have his moment of glory than to get in a state about it.

Archie was down off his horse now, and Bert was out of the car, flexing his fingers inside the gauntlet gloves he habitually wore for driving, and pointing out the intricacies of the workings beneath the bonnet of the car.

After about five minutes' conversation, the two of them remembered Amy and came back towards her, flush-faced from bending over the motor.

'Do please forgive my lack of manners, dear lady, but your friend's enthusiasm for the mechanics of motors clearly matches my own. Won't you please introduce yourselves, and then I shall be happy to escort you the rest of the way to the house.'

'I'm Amy Moore,' she murmured, extending her hand to his, thankful that since leaving service in Aveley Square the roughness of the skin had vanished and her finger-nails had grown longer and kept in better shape. 'And this is Bert Figgins.'

It sounded so plain and dull and ordinary. Why couldn't she have announced grandly that she was Lady Elizabeth Ponsonby-Smythe, and her companion was the Honourable Willoughby Huntley Winters the third . . . The wildly invented names drew a smile to her lips, and Archie Derbisham smiled back, thinking she made a very pretty picture framed by the backdrop of Derbisham trees, and wondering just where Ronald had met these two odd people.

Not that it mattered a damn. The Gables was often filled with bohemian characters, and if the Derbisham parents had been alive to see it, they'd probably have had a fit. But now that Ronald had inherited the family millions, he did as he pleased and allowed Archie to have his head.

'I say, you're not the chap who's interested in flying, are you?' Archie said, as he allowed the grey to trot alongside the car and conversation became awkwardly non-existent. 'Ronald was saying that he and Jane had met a chappie at the dancing-rooms in town who had a fondness for the machines.'

'That's me,' Bert enthused. 'Not that I've ever been up in one of them flying machines, mind you. I might have had the chance if I'd been old enough in the war, but it didn't last long enough for me.'

The two of them guffawed as if Bert had said something very funny. Amy thought they made a good pair. They were both stupidly insensitive if they could refer so glibly to the horrors of the war to end all wars, and aristocratic or not, Archie fitted that description as perfectly as Bert.

'You can have a try in my flyer sometime over the weekend if you like,' Archie said casually, at which Bert almost lost control of the steering again.

'Do you mean you have your own plane?'

Bert stared straight ahead, this time completely out of

his depth. Owning a car was one thing, but he'd never met anyone who actually owned their own plane. No more had Amy.

'I do,' Archie said quite comfortably as if it was of no great importance. 'Would you care to come up for a spin as well, Amy?'

'No, thank you,' she said quickly. 'I prefer to keep my feet firmly on the ground.'

Archie laughed. 'Well, I'm sure you won't mind if I steal this dear boy away from you for a couple of hours to show him the rudiments, will you? I can see he's just itching to have a go.'

'Of course I won't mind. Bert's free to do as he likes. He doesn't have to ask me,' she said, and her voice was a little sharp, because for some reason she decided she didn't altogether like Archie Derbisham.

She certainly wasn't jealous of Bert's obvious delight at the instant camaraderie the two of them seemed to have found, but there was something about Archie that vaguely repelled her. He wasn't dashing and open like his brother. There was a veiled secretiveness about him that made Amy shudder. When he'd shaken her hand, that slightly clammy palm had had the same effect on her, she remembered. It was as easy to dislike him at first sight as it had been easy to like Ronald.

At once, she wished she hadn't compared the two. It brought to mind the very first day she'd spoken to Ronald Derbisham. It had been at Flannery's, and she and Daniel had held hands across a table, and he'd been about to speak the words of love to her she had so ached to hear. Unwittingly, Ronald had broken into their closeness, and it had never come again, nor ever would . . .

'I'll leave you here for the moment and get the horse to the stables for a rub-down,' she heard Archie say as if from a long way off. 'You can leave the car wherever you like and it'll be put away for you, Bert. Just give the keys to Sampson and he'll see to it. He's the butler, but he'll pass the message on to the chauffeur. Sampson or Mrs Sampson will know which rooms you're to have, if Ronald's not around, and I'll see you later. Come down to the drawing-room for a snifter when you're both settled in.'

He rode off, and Bert and Amy looked at one another. He gave an ecstatic chortle.

'That's rich, ain't it, gel? A chauffeur putting Bert Figgins' car away for him. Now that's what I call poetic justice. I'm starting to feel like a reg'lar gent already. Come on, it's time we went inside to see what the accommodation's like.'

He hauled their suitcases out of the car, carried away by his own elation, and Amy knew it was too late to wish she had something smarter than the old brown cardboard suitcase that was battered and worn. She'd bought everything else for the weekend, but she'd never thought of a new suitcase . . .

Sampson was a butler well used to the Derbisham brothers' varied assortment of house-guests, and greeted the new arrivals with the same deference as anyone else. It wasn't for him to speculate on whether these two chugging up to the front of the house in their peculiar vehicle were eccentric millionaires or not. He and his wife were paid a fat salary to attend to whatever the house-guests required, and that was all that concerned them.

Ten minutes later, Amy sat on the largest bed she'd ever had all to herself and gazed around her bedroom dumbfounded. The carpet beneath her feet was soft and deep, and on the dressing-table were implements for her use, a silver-edged brush and comb set and matching trinket boxes, and even a perfume spray filled with essence of wild violets that she sniffed at delicately. The furnishings were richly plum-coloured, and the wallpaper followed the same theme, with great bunches of mauve grapes on lush green stems trailing down the walls.

After the briefest of knocks, Bert came into Amy's room, sprawled on her bed, hands locked behind his head, and beamed at her.

'I reckon we've struck lucky, Amy gel. If we keep our heads screwed on right and cultivate these new acquaintances, we can probably do ourselves a useful bit of business this weekend too.'

'Bert, we can't!' she said, appalled. 'We can't take advantage of Ronald Derbisham's invitation to try and drum up business. We don't even *have* a business yet.'

'That's just the point. If we can get some firm orders from these toffs while we're here, think what a godsend it will be to take to the bank for a loan.'

'What loan?' she said faintly.

Bert sat up, trying to be patient.

'Amy, I don't think you've thought everything through properly yet. How far do you think your money will go? It will buy us premises and a showroom and maybe one or two cheap cars to sell, but that's no good! We must have a good stock, and that means a loan, see? The bank will recognize that we mean business by the very fact of having premises, but with definite written orders for motors, we can get anything we want!'

'You mean we're going to be in debt?'

She, who like her gran had never been in debt in her life . . .

Bert sighed. 'It's business, Amy. 'It's the way all businesses are run, on credit. I'd have thought you knew that. Unless you're as well-heeled as the Derbishams, for instance, there's no other way to get started. Don't worry. It can't fail.'

He gave her a quick kiss on the cheek and wandered around her room, picking up bits and pieces, assessing everything, while her thoughts whirled. They were going to be in debt for a great deal of money if Bert's intentions were realized, and it terrified her. What if anything happened to him, and she was the partner left to pay the debts? How could she do that, knowing nothing about engines and motors? Unwillingly, she remembered Tess's distress at paying the debts her mother left when she ran off with her Italian. What Bert was contemplating was a far bigger gamble than the piddling little debts that a housemaid might struggle to pay . . .

'I'm in the room next door,' Bert went on, blissfully unaware of her boiling anxieties. 'Considerate, these nobs, aren't they? I suppose some of them do a little bit of canoodling at these places. Not that I've got anything like that in mind, Amy,' he said hastily, seeing her look. 'Have you looked at it all? There's a bathroom attached, same as mine. That's real swank, isn't it?'

His words lulled her fears for a while as she inspected every bit of the room and agreed that it was real swank. And then he held her shoulders and coaxed her into smiling and said they were here to have a good time, and he hoped she wasn't going to be miserable, and wasn't it time they went down to the drawing-room, or Archie would think they didn't know what was what.

'All right.' She gave a small sigh. 'But Bert – just don't be blatant about the business, will you?'

'As if I would!' He treated her to his wide-eyed boyish look, which made her laugh, because she knew very well he'd do anything if he could get away with it.

She held in her stomach as they walked down the elegant wrought-iron staircase tipped with gold inlay, to the drawing-room. She needn't have bothered holding herself in, because she'd lost so much weight in the last weeks that her shape was sleek and quite fashionable now, apart from a natural curve at the bustline.

For a second she thought how ironic it was. Here was she, without even trying, almost the epitome of the flapper look that was all the rage, when she'd always been so infuriatingly plump . . . and there was skinny Tess, forever dieting and tightening herself in, presumably getting rounder and heavier with every week that passed now, and undoubtedly hating it.

To their relief, the first people they picked out in the chattering crowd of people in the drawing-room were Ronald and Jane, though they were too busy talking to notice the newcomers. Drinks were thrust in their hands and they took them automatically. Amy saw uneasily that everyone looked terribly chic and well-groomed, except for one couple who were so unkempt that she was positive they could only be filthy rich.

She and Bert managed to make small talk for ten minutes without ever catching the eye of their hosts, and then Jane appeared from the midst of a small group and came to link her arm in Amy's, while Ronald lifted a finger to a manservant bearing a silver tray of yet more drinks, who brought them over at once.

'Amy darling, how lovely to see you, and Bert too,' Jane said gaily. 'Have a drink to loosen you up, and then I'll introduce you to some people. You won't remember any of their names, but that doesn't matter. By Sunday afternoon we'll all be old friends, and I gather you've already met Archie on the way. He was telling us he's taking Bert up for a spin in his flyer tomorrow morning.'

'Well, yes, if that's all right,' Amy put in when she drew breath, since Bert was already drinking so deeply from his second glass that Amy guessed he was as bemused as she was. 'I mean, I don't know what other plans you and Ronald might have for the weekend, Jane.'

Jane's indulgent laugh stopped her.

'Amy, you're so frightfully sweet. We don't have any *plans* at all. We just invite a crowd of people, throw them together like a stew, and see what happens!' She roared at her own joke, and those near enough to hear roared with her.

They were like a crowd of sheep, Amy thought at once, and hoped her incredulity didn't show on her face.

'Oh, I see.'

Ronald hovered near. 'Jane, stop being so naughty.'

He turned to Amy. 'She's teasing you, Amy, though actually, the dear girl's partly right. In the evenings we all get together and socialize, eating, drinking and merrymaking, but in the daytime we each do as we please. I mean, if Archie and Bert want to go up in the flyer, that's fine. If some of the chaps want to come shooting with me, then that's fine too. The ladies do what they want to do – play croquet, or wander around the grounds, or sit and take tea and gossip the way you young things do. We don't stand on ceremony here, Amy.'

It all sounded *frightfully* civilized and bohemian at the same time, Amy thought, unaccountably bristling. Ronald had obviously meant it in a spirit of geniality, but in Amy's opinion he had managed to denigrate the entire female sex by his discriminating remarks.

'And what if I wanted to go shooting with the men?' she enquired blandly. 'Would that be allowed?'

It was one of those moments when everyone seemed to have stopped talking at once, and several shrill laughs could be heard at this audacious suggestion. Progressive as Ronald Derbisham's bashes were, it simply wasn't done for the sexes to mix on what was essentially male territory.

'Oh Amy, you are funny.' Jane began to laugh, lightening the moment of tension, and as expected, everyone followed suit. The women glanced curiously at this new guest with such odd ideas, and the men's interest varied. Some turned their backs, while others smiled and moved nearer with deceptively casual steps, assessing this vibrant girl with eyes that suddenly flashed as golden as pulled toffee, whose soft blue woollen frock

181

couldn't disguise the alluring curves of the svelte figure beneath.

'What's so funny about it?' she demanded to know, and Ronald joined in the laughter.

Amy realized she was suddenly the centre of a small crowd that mostly consisted of young men in country tweeds, some sporting a monocle or twirling moustache.

Where was Bert? she thought frantically. She saw him over by the window, talking animatedly with Archie Derbisham, the wintry sun outside making a halo of each fair head. A fat lot of good Bert was going to be in helping her to keep her end up, Amy thought irreverently. He'd found a kindred spirit, and she wouldn't see much of him this weekend!

'Amy darling, ladies don't shoot,' Ronald explained patiently, his eyes twinkling with gentle humour at this delightful girl. There was nothing he liked more than a bit of controversy and some heated exchanges at one of his house-parties. 'The thrust of the gun would damage your delicate shoulders, don't y'see? You wouldn't want to go back to London all black and blue now, would you?'

'Well, not from the butt of a gun, anyway,' she heard a male voice mutter from somewhere behind her, and her cheeks suddenly burned.

'I was only joking, actually,' she said in a clear voice. 'I don't believe in blood sports, but it just seems to me unfair that there's one law for men and another for women. After all, we're all people, aren't we?'

'Good God, you're not one of those accursed suffragettes, are you?' a man's voice said indignantly.

'Don't be ridiculous, Percy,' another answered as if she wasn't there. 'She's not old enough to have got involved with those damned Pankhurst women. Besides, none of them can have a vote until they're thirty, and that's not a day too soon in my opinion for some addle-headed females.'

Amy couldn't believe what she was hearing. She'd never had an ounce of interest in politics, but there wasn't much that a man could do that a woman couldn't do better, including cutting these two down to size! She turned on the speakers, two young men that Bert would undoubtedly describe as well-heeled chinless wonders, and looked them straight in the eyes.

'You think women are incapable of dealing in business affairs too, I suppose?'

Their indignation vanished, and their wide superior grins made them look incredibly foolish, Amy thought seethingly.

'Show me a businesswoman and I'll show you a dried-up old biddy too strident to be called female!' the one called Percy drawled. Amy gave him her most seductive smile and heard him draw in his breath at the unexpectedness of it, and she made her voice a little huskier than usual when she challenged him.

'Is that how you see *me* then? A dried-up old biddy too strident to be called female?'

In the startled silence, Jane squealed with excitement.

'Amy, are you telling us you've gone into some kind of business? How frightfully exciting. Do tell!'

How the blue blazes had she got herself into this, Amy wondered. The last thing she'd intended was to advertise on Bert's behalf, and she'd sternly instructed him not to embarrass her this weekend by trying to drum up business. And here she was, trapped by her own arrogance into doing just that. But she could hardly back down now without looking a complete fool and making these county toffs think she was just playing out a line.

'It's only at the planning stage as yet,' she said coolly. 'It's a car sales business, and Bert and myself are going into partnership. It should be the most enormous fun,' she said recklessly, falling into the jargon of the group and rounding out her vowels in the process. 'As soon as we get premises and stock, we'll be getting cards printed, and we shall expect all our friends to come and patronize us for their new motors.'

Bugger me, Amy thought, reverting to Gran's patois when anything befuddled her thinking. *Did I really say all that! Next thing I know, Ronald Derbisham will be throwing me out on my ear, with Bert following . . .*

'Oh, of course we will, Amy!' Jane said, her face glowing with excitement. 'Oh, how exciting, isn't it, Ronald? And when we've bought our motors, we could get some of those little plaques put up at your premises. You know, "Suppliers to Ronald Derbisham Esq" – just like royalty! What d'you say to that, Percy?'

'Good-oh, of course, old girl!'

Suddenly they were all caught up in the novelty of this slender girl in their midst who was brightening up the day no end, daring to enter a man's world and not afraid to say so. The charm of it was that she looked so damned feminine too, and was proving that she was perfectly capable of holding her own with the best of them.

Amy gulped, hardly able to comprehend what was going on. Only that Bert and Archie were joining them, and Bert was looking as stunned as she felt at the little group surrounding her now.

'You must advertise, of course,' Ronald declared at once. 'One weekly advertisement in a newspaper will sell more motors than waiting for casual buyers to inspect the new premises. Leigh-Jones can help you there. His father owns a prominent country weekly. He'll tell you the form before you leave on Sunday.'

'It's – uh – frightfully good of you,' Amy heard herself murmuring, her poshed-up accent slipping slightly, and for some reason this set them all laughing again. But it was kindly laughter, and she and Bert found themselves joining in, if somewhat hysterically.

15

Late that night Amy lay in bed in the darkness with her eyes wide open, thinking back over this extraordinary day. To her amazement, she and Bert appeared to be quite a hit with Ronald Derbisham and his friends. It was *her* venture into business that tickled them all pink, Bert said jubilantly, and if it benefited them to play on that, then play on it they would.

Amy was surprised at his reaction, since it had been all his idea. She'd quite expected him to be jealous of the way the house-guests had crowded around her, wanting to know as many details as possible. She didn't tell them all of it, of course. She didn't tell them what she had been doing until very recently, or that Bert had still to give in his notice as a chauffeur to a titled family, or how she'd come into the money, or the fact that it had been disappointment in love that had allowed Bert into her life at all.

She moved restlessly beneath the soft sheets, turning her face towards the window. She'd left the curtains drawn back, so that she could see the stars in the blue-black of the sky and hear the whispering sigh of the breeze among the trees. How beautiful it was here. How wonderful to live one's whole life in such surroundings and never have to scratch for pennies the way less fortunate folk did. How Daniel would love to see it . . .

His name slid into her mind before she could stop it. She didn't want to think of him. It was no use. He was lost to her now, and she had to make the best of it. Her brain habitually formed the words, but her heart always refused to listen. And then she was unable to stop the silent tears flooding her cheeks, because none of this meant anything without Daniel to share it, not moving up in the world, or the excitement generated by the thought of going into business, or anything at all. Without him she was only half-alive . . .

'Amy, are you awake?'

She jerked round at the sound of the hoarse voice, remembering too late that she hadn't turned the key in her door. She dragged the sheet up to her neck as she saw Bert's shadowy outline swaying gently from the quantities of spirits he'd drunk. Dear God, this was all she needed!

'Go back to bed, Bert,' she said, hoping she didn't sound too wobbly. She didn't want him to know she was upset and start making useless platitudes. She certainly didn't want him getting all soppy and amorous over her. She had definitely made up her mind about that.

'Amy, we've landed ourselves a big fish.'

He took no notice and came and sat on the side of her bed. To her relief he hadn't undressed, and still wore the clothes he'd had on for the evening's dinner and dancing.

'What do you mean?' she said, irritated.

Her head ached with all the talk, and the cigarette smoke that had got into her eyes and made them smart, and with the sweet memories of Daniel. Part of her was enraged because Bert had interrupted them, even while the saner part knew she should be glad.

'Archie Derbisham, that's what I mean. He doesn't have the kind of money Ronald sports, but he's got his own generous allowance, and he's offered to stand the loan for Figgins' Car Sales to save us the trouble of going to the bank. What do you think of that!'

'*What!*' Amy sat up, not even noticing when the sheet fell away from her. The bedroom was lit by moonlight, but she was covered from head to toe in her cambric nightgown, so it hardly mattered. 'Bert, how could you . . . ?'

'Now don't go off half-cocked, Amy. It was all his idea,

not mine. We've been down in his den talking the night away about his flying machine and engines and the plans we've got for the business, and he suddenly offered the money, just like that. I'm telling 'em I'm leaving Aveley Square on Monday and starting to look round for premises straight away. Archie's putting up the money for stock, so there's no need to glare at me, gel. I thought you'd be glad.'

'Are you sure you need me at all now?' she asked, with more than a trace of sarcasm. 'You and Archie seem to have everything all sewn up between you.'

Her heart sank, knowing it had been the thought of doing something positive that had prevented her going completely to pieces after Gran died, then discovering Tess's treachery and losing Daniel. She'd at least felt able to hold her head up a little, being a business partner. If that too was taken from her now . . .

''Course I need you, gel.'

You and your five hundred quid, he thought swiftly. It had been his boast to Archie Derbisham that he had money of his own, and that Archie's involvement would merely help him out without troubling the old bank manager, don't y'know . . .

'Archie thinks it best to keep it a private arrangement between us, only I said you'd have to be involved too, since we'd already made an agreement. He'll be a "sleeping partner", see?'

'It sounds odd to me.'

'It's the best offer we'll get, and we'd be mad not to take it,' he said sharply, then added more softly as he leaned over and stroked Amy's cheek, 'Come on, gel, don't spoil things by getting all uppish. It's fallen into our laps, so let's make the most of it. It's still you and me, ain't it?'

'I suppose so,' she said slowly, and then he leaned over still farther and pulled her into his arms.

'Amy, I'd like to make it legal between us. You know

that, don't you?' Bert was reckless now. The drink was making him bold, pushing away the memory of the insidious suggestions from Archie Derbisham. He'd always wondered uneasily about his own inclinations, but he'd never put them to the test. And when they were as blatantly matched as they had been in the last hour or two, he took fright, needing to remind himself that he was still a man.

'Oh Bert, don't – please don't.'

'Why not, Amy gel? Don't you think there's plenty of it going on in bedrooms tonight? Take pity on me, Amy. You don't know how it hurts to be frustrated all the time.'

To Amy, the word sounded almost wicked. She didn't want to be silently wrestling with him here on her bed, and she didn't want to think of him as a sexual partner. He was just Bert, harmless and friendly and kind, and she was so in need of someone who cared for her and understood her . . .

Hardly realizing what she was doing she allowed herself to relax and kissed him without passion, the way a girl kissed an old and trusted friend. Bert was encouraged to experiment, forcing open her mouth and placing his tongue against hers. Women were supposed to like that, according to the manual he'd studied and the occasional girl he'd tried it on.

Amy didn't like it at all. She wriggled away from him at once, just when he was getting warmed up and feeling himself stir down below.

'Oh Amy,' he moaned. 'You won't push me off like that when we're married, will you?'

'Who said I was going to marry you?' She began to laugh a little, because he looked so comical sitting there all dejected, like Charlie Chaplin.

'Well, you are, aren't you?'

She didn't answer. She could hear the sound of her own breathing, and his, ragged above her. She supposed she'd known all along this was coming, and just hadn't wanted to face it. She wished he hadn't asked the question, because it could make things awkward between them if she refused, which naturally she would.

'Perhaps,' she capitulated, taking the easy way out. 'I'm not saying yes or no, Bert, and you shouldn't be asking me yet, with me still in mourning over me gran, as you very well know. I couldn't think of marrying anybody yet.'

He moved away at once. "Course you couldn't, gel, and I've been so busy trying to cheer up you these last weeks that I'd nearly forgotten the reason why. But at least you'll think about it, won't you? I mean, we could be sort of engaged. It'd make it all seem more proper-like, us working together and all?'

'I'll think about it,' she said, and thankfully he got up from the bed and went back to his own room, unsure if this was a triumph or not.

Still, an engagement could go on for ever, Bert thought in some relief. It wasn't the same as tying the knot and being intimate with a woman for the rest of your days. An engagement was a sign of respectability without all the rest. It would be without getting his hands on Amy's money completely too, but with Archie Derbisham behind him, that hardly seemed so important any more.

He would have been affronted to know that Amy's thoughts almost matched his own. An engagement needn't mean total commitment, unless one of them broke it off and sued the other for breach of promise, and she dismissed any such idea. She didn't want to marry Bert Figgins. She didn't want to marry anyone except Daniel, but an engagement would certainly make her feel that she was able to hold up her head again without feeling like a cast-off glove.

The weekend was a great success. On Saturday evening Jane and Ronald formally announced their engagement, and Bert made veiled hints that theirs might not be the only one in the offing. The others frankly found the idea charming, and Ronald insisted that when they decided on the formal date, it would give them another excuse for a party at The Gables to celebrate.

Bert was flushed with success. He hardly knew what Amy had been doing with herself all day, but he'd had a marvellous time with Archie. He'd found a pleasure he'd never known before, soaring into the sky in the little two-seater plane and cruising over the treetops of the Derbisham estate, catching sight of the shooting party in the woods and the ladies playing croquet on the lawn, wrapped up against the chill November air. He and Archie had a rapport that was both exhilarating and charged with double-entendres, and if Archie became a little too familiar too soon, Bert told himself it was time he became more broad-minded if he was to mix with these sophisticated folk, and took it all in his stride.

By Sunday afternoon when the house-guests began to depart, it was with several more gilt-edged cards in Bert's pocket and invitations to various other homes. And Archie was coming up to town during the week to introduce Bert at his club and discuss business matters.

'We made it, gel,' Bert almost sang as they drove back to London. 'No more bowing and scraping to the Beaumont pack. After I go to Aveley Square and tell 'em what to do with their job tomorrow morning, we'll go and see this lawyer chap you mentioned, right?'

'All right,' Amy said woodenly, remembering all in a rush why she knew the name. Charles Rugby was the Easton family lawyer, and it had been Daniel who'd mentioned him when she'd wanted to contact Tommy in Australia to tell him about Gran's death. It all seemed so long ago now, and everything had changed since then . . .

Bert glanced at her. 'You've gone quiet. Everything all

190

right? They loved you in that bronze frock, Amy. The chaps were calling you their little ray of sunshine. Did you know that?'

'No,' she said, uncaring if it was patronizing or not. She smiled slightly, because she'd realized she should have brought two evening frocks, since every other girl had worn a different one on the second evening. Apparently it hadn't mattered, and her bronze-coloured glittery frock had given her a certain image . . . though to Amy it seemed ironic to call her a little ray of sunshine.

She didn't feel very sunny right now, but she knew she must make an effort to climb out of the depression sweeping over her again. Bert was on top of the world, and he expected her to be there with him. It was partly the thought of going back to Stratford Lane that sent her spirits plummeting. Not from any sense of snobbery, but because it was too full of ghosts, of Gran, of Tommy . . . of Daniel.

'I suppose we'll be looking at premises with living accommodation?' Amy said suddenly.

'Well, I thought so. You're not wanting to leave Stratford Lane, are you?' Bert tried to keep up with her quicksilver mind. 'We could always move in together, of course,' he said cheekily, chancing a look at her face.

'*I* could move in,' she said calmly. 'You could get rooms nearby.'

'That's daft. Supposing the premises were broken into. What chance do you think you'd have to defend yourself, a woman living there alone?'

'It seems to me that having a bit of money and a business is more trouble than it's worth if you're scared to go to bed at night,' Amy retorted.

'But you wouldn't be scared if I was there as well, would you?' He hardly knew how he was talking himself into it, nor if it was what he really wanted.

Amy was silent for a minute. 'I'll think about it,' she said

191

at last. 'I'm not having my good name ruined, mind. It'll have to be two bedrooms and both our names above the business sign. Miss Amy Moore and Mr Bert Figgins.'

Bert wondered how the hell he had got into this situation. He'd intended keeping Amy well out of the way, using her money and doing things his way, not having her moving in and poking her nose into business affairs. It wasn't what women were meant to do . . . He caught her eye and sighed. He knew by now that where Amy Moore was concerned, Amy Moore did exactly what she wanted.

'Hadn't we better get engaged then, even if it's only for the look of things?' he said.

'I suppose so,' Amy said slowly. 'All right, then. We'll get engaged, but just for the look of things.'

Daniel made daily visits to his old home now, always avoiding his father, and finally Tess agreed to his insistence that she saw a doctor. In the Easton household, the atmosphere was brittle, and Tess never admitted her real anxieties to anyone. The truth was that she felt weaker and more ill with every day that passed. She was often so light-headed she thought she must be going mad, and she simply couldn't eat anything. If she tried, she was physically sick.

In an effort to make the best of things, Helen had assured her it was perfectly normal for a pregnant woman to be nauseous every morning, but Tess had nearly snapped her head off and said it wasn't bloody normal to throw up, morning, noon and night. After that, Helen gave up trying to be friends with this difficult girl, and merely took away the plates of untouched food. And since it was a waste of good food, Helen put less and less on her plate. She did her best to make it attractive and nourishing, but nothing tempted Tess's appetite.

Tess had always tried to keep her wafer-thin shape,

constantly crowing to Amy that she'd rather die and be fashionable than fat. While Amy had raided the larder in the kitchen at Aveley Square, Tess had starved herself, ignoring her stomach rumbles, and persuading herself that it was all worth it when she could span her waist with her hands. One of the most hated penalties for being pregnant was that her figure had begun to fill out, and she'd kept that at bay for as long as possible by her fanatical dieting.

But now she had stopped filling out. She should be glad, but instead she was becoming alarmed. She had all the other signs of pregnancy, the missing monthlies, the retching at the smell of food, the vomiting . . . but that was all. She didn't need to step on Helen's weighing machine to know she was losing weight alarmingly fast. Her face was so thin it had changed shape entirely, and without her clothes on she could count her ribs. There was no longer any visible bulge where the baby should be. It wasn't normal. It bloody well wasn't normal . . . and nobody in this house seemed to notice it. Nobody cared.

She felt ill with fear. Contrarily, she was almost desperate now to see a doctor and confirm her date. In reality she was frantic to know that there was nothing wrong with her other than pregnancy.

She had resigned herself to the knowledge that her story wouldn't wash with Daniel. He'd made his stand in moving out of the house and resisting his father's ultimatum, and she knew she was never going to get him to marry her.

She'd have to carry her shame with her to the grave, but she wasn't bloody well moving out of here now that she'd got her feet under the table. Frank still blustered that it was a damn scandal that a man couldn't stand by a girl in trouble, but he was more disturbed by his son's show of independence than he let on, and wasn't too sure which way to turn for the best.

He resorted to preaching about the wickedness of his

son, and that he'd get his just deserts in heaven. If Tess had known Frank better, she'd have known that his moods were as unpredictable as his temper, and the pseudo-godliness would wear off as quickly as it had appeared.

Daniel took her to see Dr Harding, their own family practitioner. Harding would see Tess sooner or later on one of his visits to his mother, so they might as well get it over with straight away.

He sat in the waiting-room impatiently while Tess was with the doctor, hating it. Hating the deceit to which Tess had made him a party, and most of all for putting Amy out of his life. He didn't want to know the date of the expected birth. He didn't want to see Tess growing bigger and insisting on bringing the child into his family, where it didn't belong. The nightmare soared ahead of him relentlessly . . .

The door of the consulting room opened and he stood up, retrieving Tess's coat from the chair where she had carelessly slung it. Harding appeared in the doorway, and Daniel tried to read his expression. There had to be censure and disappointment in a young man he'd known since childhood, but he saw at once that there was something more.

'Come in, please, Daniel,' the doctor said. 'I need to talk to you.'

He went without enthusiasm, not wanting to be involved in details. Whatever medical problem Tess Loveridge had with her pregnancy was no concern of his. Inside the consulting room he took one glance at her stricken face and felt a strange sense of alarm. The girl looked almost out of her mind, and he freely admitted he'd been nothing short of a bastard to her lately, but with just cause, he reminded himself grimly.

'Miss Loveridge is not expecting a child,' the doctor said, without wasting words.

Daniel's heart stopped for a minute and then raced on. He felt relief, elation, suspicion, and finally worry. She wasn't expecting a child, but there was obviously something else badly wrong. He could see it in their faces.

He found himself talking angrily to cover his feelings. 'But she swore it was true – and there's the sickness – my mother assured us the sickness came with pregnancy . . .' He stopped, seeing the doctor's grave face.

'Miss Loveridge has been a victim of two things. The first was a compulsion to keep herself as thin as possible in this ridiculous female fashion. She's been starving herself for a long time, and her body has finally revolted against the abuse, with the result that it can no longer tolerate food at all. And the pregnancy is one of sheer imagination, probably brought on by the dread of being in such a state after indulging in sexual intercourse.'

Daniel flinched at the accusation in the doctor's voice. *Not with me*, he raged, but one look at Tess's ashen face and he couldn't get the words out.

'It's not an unknown phenomenon. Even a woman's monthly occurrences can stop through a lack of bodily nourishment, which accentuates her conviction that she's pregnant.'

The doctor went on using pompous long words as if discussing an interesting case for a medical journal and not for the benefit of a living, breathing woman quaking with fear in the chair opposite him.

For the first time, Daniel felt real compassion at the sight of her now, so unlike the bright brash Tess of old. It was the same raw pity he'd feel for an animal hopelessly cornered by something bigger than itself.

'What complicates matters is the body's rejection of food,' the doctor went on clinically. 'The weight gain, due to the imagined pregnancy, is minimal and mostly fluid. It soon disappears, and then the true extent of the condition makes itself known. I fear that from what

Miss Loveridge tells me it has already progressed considerably.'

This was all getting beyond Daniel. If Tess was ill instead of pregnant, why couldn't the doctor give her some medication to make her well again? Even as he thought it, he realized that Tess wouldn't be able to keep up the pretence with his parents any longer. She had no more false claims on him, and he was free . . . For an ecstatic moment Daniel felt as if he had been unshackled.

'Daniel.'

He looked at Tess, trying to concentrate on her face through his wild thoughts.

'He means that I'm going to die.' Her voice, normally strong and raucous, shivered into the silence.

'Don't be stupid, of course you're not going to die,' he said roughly. He glanced at Dr Harding, hearing him clear his throat and shake his head. Daniel felt shock ripple through him.

'I'm afraid there's nothing I can do now that she's totally unable to keep food down. It's too late for treatment. She'll refuse whatever she's given unless she's force-fed. Even then, if she doesn't vomit naturally, she'll make herself vomit. I've seen it happen before with young women who starve themselves. It's the condition.'

If he says it's the condition once more I shall throttle him with his own words, Daniel thought savagely.

'So what's to be done?' he said, gritting his teeth at Tess's helpless sobbing.

'Just care and rest for as long as she needs it.'

And then? Daniel didn't need to ask the question. It was all there in the way the doctor closed a folder on his desk, as if closing the book that was Tess Loveridge.

'It would be best for her to be taken care of in hospital,' Dr Harding went on briskly. 'Your mother's not strong enough to look after her, and I presume there will be no problem about the hospital fees?'

He could hardly think straight. The callousness of the discussion in Tess's hearing washed over him. But it was clear that the doctor simply assumed what everyone else assumed – that Daniel Easton and Tess Loveridge had been lovers, and that therefore he must stand by her now until the end. And it was certainly not in Daniel's make-up to deny her the right to die with dignity. He'd done it for Gran Moore, and he must do it for Tess.

'Of course there will be no problem with fees,' he said firmly. 'She must have every care.'

She had done him the most terrible wrong, but after all her lies and bravado, Tess was going to die, and the inescapable knowledge was all there in her shrunken face. There was nothing anyone could do to stop it, and the words drummed around in his head, filling his brain until it felt as if it would burst.

16

Right after Christmas, Bert riffled through the newspaper until he found the page he wanted and handed it jubilantly to Amy.

'What do you think of that then? By tonight, everybody in London will know that Bert Figgins and Amy Moore are in business!'

'Everybody who bothers to read advertisements, you mean!' She grinned, but felt a surge of pride just the same.

She had never felt so important in her life, and Edward Leigh-Jones, the friend of the Derbisham brothers, had done them proud. There it was, in black and white, with a smart sketch of a Daimler motor-car at the foot of the square-edged advertisement. There was even a small paragraph about the two of them, with a photograph of herself and Bert standing outside the show-room. The photographer had suggested she link her arm through Bert's to show off the engagement ring, and bemused by the whole thing, she had complied without objection. Even ignoring the thought that Gran Moore would have snorted contemptuously, telling her she was making a poppy-show of herself . . .

'New car sales business, in elegant premises off Claymore Street, and run by mechanical expert Mr Bert Figgins and his charming partner and fiancée, Miss Amy Moore. For all the best in the latest motors, you won't do better than to patronize these premises, where it's whispered that nobility already shows a keen interest,' Amy read out, and then looked at Bert, clucking a little. 'It's bending the truth a bit, isn't it?'

'Not at all,' Bert said. 'Leigh-Jones had it on the best authority from his father's staff that the best way to couch an advertisement is to go for the jugular. And nobility *does* have an interest. Leigh-Jones's father is a lord, and he's taken the trouble to print this, so it's not exactly a lie, is it? And as long as it brings in customers, you shouldn't complain, Amy.'

He stuck a cigarette in the long tortoiseshell holder he'd taken to sporting lately, cursing when he couldn't quite get it to fit. Amy hid a grin, more used to seeing Bert nip out the end of his Woodbine, blow on his hand and tuck the half-smoked ciggy in his vest pocket for later. Oh yes, they had definitely come up in the world.

And it was true that they had to act the part. Things had moved apace since Archie Derbisham had sponsored them. Archie was used to snapping his fingers and getting things done, and before the turn of the year they had the grand show-room premises with six gleaming motors inside the glass frontage, and they had already sold two at a handsome profit. Nineteen twenty-six was going to be a bumper year, Bert said gleefully, practising his new falsely upper-class voice, which he often forgot, except when speaking with customers or staying at one of the country houses to which he and Amy were now frequent visitors.

'Amy, this is all so quaint!' Jane Broome squealed when she came to inspect the rooms above the premises. 'And how daring and progressive you are to share living quarters with Bert! I'm frankly amazed, and not a little envious.'

Her eyes had twinkled, and Amy had told her smartly that there would be no hanky-panky going on when they moved in at the end of the week, and that the bedrooms were at opposite ends of the long living accommodation.

'Well, it's no concern of mine.' Jane smiled. 'But you know how people talk, and it might put a few people off a teensy bit from buying their motors from you, darling.

Why don't you let me send you one of my little maids to offset the tongue-waggers? She could have the box-room, couldn't she? And you really should have someone here, Amy. You can't be doing housework yourself. It's so vulgar.'

Amy almost laughed out loud. Amy Moore, housemaid, solemnly discussing employing a young girl to do for her! But Jane wouldn't hear of anything else, and the cost would be almost nothing, she said airily. Just keep the girl fed and watered, and they would hardly notice she was about. And before she knew it, Amy had stifled her mirth and agreed, and Maisie Legge was installed in a room halfway between hers and Bert's, assured that when they went on weekend trips to the country, Maisie would go with them.

Leaving Stratford Lane had been something of a wrench for Amy after all. So much of her past was wrapped up in the small dark rooms and the centuries-old cobbled street. So many memories . . . She pushed them stalwartly out of her mind, instructed Mrs Coggins that if ever she should need to get in touch, she'd now be living up West in Claymore Street, and gave Dr and Mrs O'Neil the same information.

She now wore a modest little ring on her engagement finger, and they were all privately glad that Amy Moore seemed to have got herself settled nicely at last, unaware that inside, her heart still hadn't mended. That the shock of Gran's death and discovering the truth about her parents, followed by losing Daniel in that terrible way, had never really left her and was merely buried for the time being beneath the need to survive.

On the surface she was seen to be surviving very nicely. She wore smart clothes, because to keep up the image of successful business people, Bert had insisted that they look the part. And once the ackers started rolling in from the car sales, they'd be well and truly laughing.

If Amy was more or less content with the way her life was going, it was due to a great extent to a feeling of security and a need for self-preservation that had been with her since childhood. Once the dealings with Mr Charles Rugby had been completed, and the legal partnership between her and Bert made proper by a document with a red seal at the foot, she'd gone back to the lawyer in Welles Street on her own.

At one time she'd never have done such a thing, but there was a confidence about Amy now that was new and attractive. Amy the little mouse was far removed from Amy the business partner and friend of the wealthy. She asked Mr Rugby to arrange an annual insurance policy on account of the money she'd put into the business, and to cover the cost of the stock and premises, just in case . . . It took a good part of her remaining money, but she felt it had to be done. It was also nothing that need concern Bert, she told Charles Rugby, looking him straight in the eye.

Frank Easton was bored with visiting Tess in the hospital. Daniel went every evening, which was only right and proper, but there was really no need for Helen and him to be dragged along once a week on a duty visit. He'd lost all interest in the girl. He was sorry for her plight, and she certainly looked a sorry sight now, thin and wasted, and nothing like the vivacious miss who'd caught his eye and caused him to fancy his chances.

He no longer urged Daniel to marry her. There wasn't going to be any sprat, but it was obvious to him that the boy must have got his oar in there for her to accuse him so vehemently. The Bible called it fornication, whether there was anything to show for it or not, but vying with Frank's new-found piety was the reluctance to have Tess back in his house as part of his family. He had to admit that it was a calmer place without her.

Daniel hardly had time to eat his meals any more, always

dashing off somewhere, Frank thought irritably. If it wasn't to visit Tess and sit with her, with neither finding anything to say to one another, then it was putting in extra hours at the library. His boss had had a stroke, but was quite stable and passively content to let Daniel take over as chief librarian.

He was practically running the show, Frank scowled, and thought his son should push himself forward to buy the old man out. But Daniel no longer seemed to have any interest in advancing himself. Still missing the other one, Frank suspected. The girl with the fudge-coloured eyes and pert little nose, who'd dared to put Frank in his place in his own front parlour.

He was out in the hospital waiting-room now, taking a breather from the hospital smells that nauseated him, while Daniel and Helen sat beside the silent, staring Tess. Somebody had left a newspaper on a chair and Frank picked it up and glanced through it. It was all political stuff these days. All about the miners and the government and the threatened strike, which would probably never happen . . .

Of more interest to Frank were the tantalizing references to bringing sound to the motion pictures, instead of the idiotic mouthings and exaggerated facial expressions of some of the so-called stars. Frank eagerly awaited the age of the 'talkies', as some of the Americans already referred to them. Frank read the filmgoers' publications avidly, and although the breakthrough seemed as far away as ever, he intended to make the Roxy one of the first picture palaces in the area to show these new 'talkies'. He'd splash out on advertising, and he envisaged it as his own personal stepping-stone to fame and fortune.

'Good God!' Frank suddenly said out loud, staring at the newspaper as if he couldn't believe his eyes. He scanned the words in a fever of disbelief, studied the photo a moment longer and then rushed along to the private ward where he was paying out good money for his son's dalliance with the Loveridge girl. Since he felt he owned the ward, he rushed in without knocking and thrust the newspaper under Daniel's nose.

'What about that then? It didn't take your other piece long to find her feet, did it? Engaged to this Figgins chap and a partner in a new car show-room. Where'd she get the money, I'd like to know, unless he's putting up the lot and took her along as a bed partner, which is probably more like it,' he sniggered.

Daniel snatched the newspaper from his father, and his mother peered over his shoulder. Her heart ached at the stark misery on Daniel's face.

'Dear God, Amy, what have you done?' he said hoarsely.

Frank laughed triumphantly. 'I'll tell you what she's done, you dolt. She's got her feet under the table, same as this one tried to, only it seems as if Miss Amy Moore's struck gold.'

'Amy?'

Tess spoke so rarely now that it took them all by surprise to hear her quavering voice. Her cheeks, normally as white as the bed-sheets, showed two bright spots of colour as she stared at the newspaper, trying to comprehend what they were saying. She was so muddled that it was difficult to understand anything in these twilight days, and Frank Easton thrust the newspaper closer to her face.

'That's right, darling, little Amy, your friend, remember? The little housemaid who thought she was good enough for my son. Well, it seems she's done a bit better for herself now, what with nobility taking an interest in her and all.'

'Bert Figgins!' Tess said, feeling hysteria rising up in her and unable to stop it. One minute she was staring stupidly at the photo and the next she was screaming with wild, uncontrollable laughter. 'My God, if that ain't a turn-up.

That's Bert Figgins, Lord Beaumont's chauffeur! He never had two 'a'pennies to rub together, except what he filched from his lordship, so how did the cheating sod ever scrape together enough for all this, I'd like to know.'

'It says he and Amy are engaged!' Helen exclaimed, hardly daring to look at Daniel, while Tess screamed even louder with laughter.

'She always said he fancied her, the little frump, just because he wanted to take a look at her knickers and she was star-struck.'

'Shut up, Tess,' Daniel snapped furiously.

'Well, she ain't so bloody frumpish now,' Frank said suddenly, as if only just noting the change in Amy. 'She's quite a tasty dish, with that fur collar up around her neck, and looking a damn sight thinner than she used to. I'd say she's quite a beauty.'

'Don't be fooled. She always liked the winter so she could cover up the bulges,' Tess snapped. 'She was a real fattie underneath.'

'Well, it's obvious that she's not fat now, and for someone who used to be her friend, you're not being very kind, Tess,' Helen said reproachfully.

Tess's burst of energy was diminishing very quickly. The spots of colour had gone and the usual pallor took its place. Her eyes were huge in the wasted face, with great deep smudges beneath them. Without warning, her mood changed, and great tears slid down her cheeks and into her mouth.

'You're the one who's being unkind to me,' she mouthed at Helen. 'I'm helpless, and you all hate me.'

'We don't hate you, Tess, otherwise we wouldn't be here,' Daniel said curtly, his mind still warped by the newspaper item. Amy engaged to that smug-looking chauffeur. Amy, looking happy and affluent, and clearly not missing him at all. Amy, his beautiful Amy, his once-a-week love, his once-in-a-lifetime love, out of his life for ever . . .

204

'Christ, I can't stand any more of this.' Frank stood up as Tess's sobs became noisier. He folded the newspaper and stuck it inside his coat to take home. 'We'll wait for you outside, Daniel. Don't be all day.'

He went out without another word to Tess, and Helen said goodbye quietly, getting no reply. Once they'd gone, Tess looked desperately at Daniel, too self-pitying to see his despair.

'Daniel, I don't want to die all alone,' Tess sobbed.

'You're not alone. You have doctors and nurses to care for you.'

'Did you mean what you said, about not hating me?' She seized his hand in hers. Her grip was claw-like and, guiltily, he felt nauseated.

'Yes,' he said, for what was the point any more? His life and Amy's had grown too far apart to waste time on hating Tess. She was too pitiable a creature for that now.

'Then take me home, Daniel. Don't leave me here. Let me die in bed at home. It's not much to ask, is it? It won't be for very long.'

It was on the tip of his tongue to make some glib reply. But he looked into her eyes and saw death there, as plainly as if the word was printed across her face.

'I'll arrange it with the doctors,' he heard himself say. 'You won't have to die all alone.'

The words flooded out. 'I know I don't deserve it, Daniel. You don't owe me anything, but I've got nobody else, and I'm sorry for all I've done to you. There's no child, but being Mrs Daniel Easton would have saved my pride.'

Talk exhausted her and her breath was thready. He hadn't prepared for this, but he asked himself what he had to lose now that he'd already lost everything. It was little enough to do. After a long moment he spoke roughly.

'Do you want to get married, Tess?'

* * *

'You've done *what*?' Frank roared at him in the car.

'I've told her we'll be married as soon as I can arrange it, and she'll come back to the house until the end. Love doesn't come into it, and I shan't sleep in the same room as her, but at least she'll know that people are caring for her when the time comes. She needs to feel that she belongs to somebody, and she's got no one else, so it's the least we can do.'

'And your reward will be in heaven, Daniel,' his mother said quietly.

For a so-called religious man, Frank Easton had a colourful selection of phrases at his disposal when necessary.

'And you'd bring that fornicating trollop back to the house, knowing that she tricked you with her lies and tried to pass off her bastard as yours? Have you forgotten the way she fawned and ogled men at the Roxy? She even tried it on me, the dirty little slut.'

He saw the coldness in Daniel's eyes and knew that his son knew all about his little pastimes, and his voice dwindled away.

'I haven't forgotten the look of a frightened and pathetic girl who's going to die before she's twenty-two years old,' Daniel said. 'I'm going to marry Tess and bring her home to make her last days comfortable, and there's an end to it. God knows, you've been trying to blackmail me into it for long enough.'

Frank eyed him warily. Daniel had become harder since the Tess Loveridge episode, and when he'd made up his mind to do a thing, he did it.

And Daniel couldn't quite forget the ease with which he'd allowed Tess to go to hospital, as good as washing his hands of her. She wasn't his responsibility, but she had no one else, and if he didn't do what he could for her, she'd be on his conscience for the rest of his life. So three weeks later, Tess Loveridge became Mrs Daniel Easton, and was brought carefully back to the house where she'd caused such turmoil. All the people there knew there was only one way she would be leaving it.

There was no question of Daniel sharing Tess's bedroom. Her condition was serious by now, and knowing that it couldn't last much longer, he employed a nurse to be with her at all times. Helen couldn't possibly nurse a sick girl, and the men had their work to attend to. In the evenings, Daniel relieved the nurse to sit and read to Tess. She liked the melodious sound of his voice, even when she didn't always understand the words of the classics.

'Amy was always better at reading than me,' Tess said suddenly, in her wandering voice. 'Amy was a good girl. She deserved better than Bert Figgins, and if he's come into money it can't be honestly. She really loved you, Daniel, and I took you from her.'

She spoke as if only just discovering the fact. Daniel kept his eyes on the book he was reading.

'I don't want to talk about Amy. Do you want to know what happened in *The Arabian Nights* or not?' he said, gently bullying.

'No. I want to see Amy.' With sudden feverish passion, her voice rose. 'I want to make my peace with her. I want to know she forgives me.' ·

'I don't think it's a good idea –'

'Yes it is! Daniel, do this last thing for me. Bring Amy to see me. I miss her. Don't you remember the times we had? Every week at the Roxy, done up in our best frocks. Douglas Fairbanks was my favourite. He was so handsome. But I do miss Amy, Daniel. You'll let me see her, won't you?'

Her mind switched from one thing to another with lightning speed. He hoped she'd forget this new idea, but she didn't. On and on she persisted, until he knew it had become an obsession with her. Sometimes she awoke sobbing in the night, begging the nurse to send for Daniel, and always it was for the same reason. To bring Amy to see her so she could make her peace.

In the end he said he'd think about it. He doubted that Amy would want to see Tess. Though he knew that when he explained what had happened, her soft heart would relent. The real truth was that he didn't want to see her himself, knowing she belonged to someone else. Engaged to this Bert Figgins, who looked prosperous enough, whatever Tess had to say about him . . .

'I shan't die until I've seen Amy,' Tess screamed at him one night, her eyes burning. 'You won't be rid of me until you've brought her here. You owe me that, Daniel.'

He didn't think he owed her anything, but finally he gave in and told her he'd go to Claymore Street on Saturday afternoon and see if Amy would agree to come. He was a strong man, but he quaked in his shoes as he drove towards the new car show-rooms. He hadn't seen Amy in a long while now, and he had no idea how she would receive him.

The sandy-haired man with the boyish face came towards him, thinking he was a potential customer. Daniel heard the plummy accent, and knew it was as false as the man himself. He didn't like him on sight.

'I don't want to buy a car,' Daniel said briefly. 'I want to see Amy – Miss Moore.'

'Does she know you?' Bert said to give himself time, preparing to bar the way from this good-looking chap whose identity he half-guessed.

Daniel gave a tight smile. 'She knows me,' he said.

At that moment she came through a door, and Daniel caught his breath. He had never seen her look more beautiful, in a soft cream wool dress and glowing amber beads that almost matched her eyes. She was thinner than he remembered, her face finer-drawn, but she was still Amy. His Amy, whom he loved and longed for every minute of every day. If he had ever doubted it, he never

208

would again, when one glimpse of her could start his heart thudding like that of a schoolboy.

'Daniel.' She breathed his name, and he realized the colour had gone from her cheeks one minute, then flooded back the next. He was aware of Bert glaring, standing carefully between them, and he tried to speak sensibly.

'I need to see you, Amy. Can we talk – privately?'

'My fiancée has no secrets from me,' Bert began pompously.

'Shut up, Bert,' Amy said. She seemed unable to say anything else for a minute, as if she was deciding what to do, and then she nodded slowly. 'Come upstairs to the parlour, Daniel. We can talk there. Bert will be busy down here in case of customers.' She dismissed him as easily as swatting a fly.

Daniel followed her, thinking that this was a new and different Amy. She was more confident and self-composed. And despite all that had happened, he was still wildly in love with her . . .

He had always behaved like a gentleman towards her, but once they were inside the parlour it was more than he could do to stop himself taking her in his arms. In a moment he was holding her close and kissing her lips, feeling the blood run fast in his veins as she responded involuntarily. And then he heard her sob as she pushed against him.

'Don't – please,' she said hoarsely. 'This is all wrong. I know everything about you and Tess, remember. It's no good, Daniel. Did she get you to marry her?'

'Amy, it's not what you think. Nothing's as you think it is, my dearest girl.'

'You mustn't call me that,' she said with a touch of hysteria. He was stirring up all the emotions she had tried so desperately to hide, and after the first ecstatic moments of seeing him, she was bitterly resentful that he should come here.

'Amy. Tess and I were only married a week ago.'

He had to be brutal, sensing that she wouldn't listen if he didn't get the words out quickly.

'Then it was all true.'

'None of it was true. Tess and I were never lovers, and there was never any baby, despite what she thought. She persuaded my father to believe her cock-and-bull story and I moved out right away, although I've moved back there now.'

'I don't want to know the sordid details,' she said shrilly.

He seized her hands. 'But you must know, and they're not sordid, Amy, only pathetic. Tess needs you. She wants to see you.'

'To see *me*? What for? To crow over me because she's got you and I haven't? That's really rich, that is!' Her voice broke and her mouth trembled. She was unable to believe that Daniel had come here pleading for Tess's sake.

'She wants to make her peace with you before she dies, my love, and the doctor says it can only be days now.'

17

Bert heard Amy cry out and came rushing up the stairs from the show-room to find out what the devil was going on. He found her near to collapse, and the newcomer holding her in his arms as she wept uncontrollably.

'All right, that's enough,' Bert snarled. 'What d'you want to come here for, upsetting her like this? You're the *ex*-boyfriend, I presume, the one that did the dirty on her with Tess. How is she, by the way? Blooming, I dare say? In the pink and about to pop?'

He went on coarsely, completely nonplussed by the sight of Amy continuing to weep, and not knowing what was wrong or how to go about putting it right. These two seemed to be one unit at that moment, and it both infuriated and frustrated him. He was fly enough to know that Amy was turning to this well-dressed good-looker for some pretty important reason. He could see it in her face. He recognized the signs, and was going to stop it before it began. He hadn't worked and schemed to get this business and everything else underway, just to have it knocked from under his feet. However superficial his personal feelings towards Amy, they were intensified now, when he sensed a danger of losing her.

'Bert, you don't understand,' Amy gasped at last, when she could find enough breath to speak.

Bert strode across the room and physically pulled her out of Daniel's arms, where she seemed to lean as if her bones had melted and wouldn't hold her up without support. He kept one arm rigidly around her shoulders, the fingers pressing hard into her flesh, and tried to stay calm.

'No, I don't bloody well understand,' he said, giving up any pretence to plum up his vowels and reverting to the old Bert Figgins, would-be charmer and rogue. 'All I see is my girl – the one I'm supposed to be marrying – being cuddled by a man who walks in off the street. What's any decent bloke supposed to think?'

'Oh, don't be stupid, man.' Daniel was angry at the insensitivity of the other. 'Can't you see Amy's just had a terrible shock! Do you have any brandy?'

''Course I've got brandy. We ain't paupers,' Bert began grandly.

'Then get it, for God's sake, and let Amy sit down before she falls down.'

Bert looked down at her chalk-white face and frowned. But he still intended digging in his heels and proving to this Easton chap that he was the boss here.

'Not until somebody tells me what's happening. I've got a right to know.'

Amy suddenly shrieked out the words.

'Tess is dying, that's what's happening.'

'*What*!' Bert moved away from her so fast she almost stumbled and fell. 'Are you out of your mind, gel? You're not going to be taken in by a tale like that, are you? Tess ain't dying, no more'n you or me! It's all a trick to get back in your good books. I suppose one gel ain't enough for him, and he wants both of you. Or else he can't cope with our flashy Tess, and wants somebody less demanding in certain departments –'

Daniel hit him so fast he never saw the fist coming until it connected with his jaw. He went down like a ninepin and Amy began to think it must all be a nightmare. Daniel had come here to tell her the worst of news, and of *course* it was true. Daniel wasn't the kind of man to make up such a wicked story. He was honest and upright, and very dear to her, despite all . . .

And Bert was behaving at his very crudest, the way

he did when he felt that all the odds were against him. She knew him well enough by now to know it was all bravado, all self-defence, but he'd gone too far this time. She couldn't even feel pity for him as Daniel dragged him to his feet again, dazed and bleeding from a split mouth.

Daniel still had his hands round Bert's throat, forcing him to pay attention.

'Listen, you guttermouth, you can thank your stars I don't finish you off. If it wasn't for Amy, I'd probably do just that. I came here with one purpose today, much against my will, because Tess is so desperate to see Amy that I swallowed my pride. And Tess has very little time left in this world to see anyone.'

As Daniel let him go, Bert rubbed gingerly at his throat. There was no doubting now that at least the fellow believed what he was saying.

'We'd all better have some brandy. Then tell me exactly what you've told Amy, and just why I should allow her to enter your house after what you did to her.'

He side-stepped quickly as Daniel made a move towards him again, and went to the kitchen for the bottle of brandy.

'Don't waste your energy, Daniel,' Amy said wearily. 'It's not worth it, and he doesn't mean half of what he says. The words leave his mouth before they've had time to get sorted in his brain.'

She tried to make a small joke of it, but she grieved too deeply for what had become of Tess to make more than a poor show. She sat down heavily on the sofa, and Daniel wanted nothing more than to sit beside her and comfort her, but there was such a remoteness about her now, and the oafish Bert Figgins was coming back with the brandy bottle and three glasses, and the moment was lost.

Besides, how could he make vague promises about the future right now? How could he beg her forgiveness for all the unhappiness he had caused her, saying that they might

213

yet be together, if Amy wished it? He was saying in effect, that when Tess died, he and Amy . . . He didn't love Tess, but it was still ghoulish to have such thoughts, and besides, there was still Bert, and the ring on Amy's finger.

'Now then, why do you say Tess is dying?' Bert said briskly, when they all had a filled glass in their hands. 'She looked well enough last time I saw her, and as cocky as ever. Is it something to do with the child?'

'Bert, you're such a pig-ignorant man at times,' Amy spoke up more forcefully, taking him by surprise. 'Why won't you listen to what other people are saying, without putting your own interpretation on it?'

'Well, me lady, pardon me for breathing! Have you swallowed a dictionary or summat?'

God give me patience, Amy thought. She took a quick mouthful of brandy, hating the stuff that always reminded her of death. Which was quite appropriate in the circumstances, of course. The burst of censure vanished, and dully she repeated everything Daniel had told her, parrot-like.

'Tess was never expecting a child. It was all in her imagination. The doctor said that such a thing can happen. First she put on a little weight, and believed the worst, and even then she wouldn't eat properly. You know how thin she always was – I always told her she was daft about keeping herself thin.' She gulped back the tears. 'She ended up starving herself, and now she's got some condition where she can't eat at all. She can't keep any food down, and she's just wasting away. And she's going to die.'

She looked at Daniel, her eyes huge with tears. 'Is that just about right?'

'That's just about right, my love,' he said gently, hurting with her, wishing he could spare her this, wishing he could take her away right now for them to start a new life where pain and sadness didn't exist. And knowing he might as well ask for the moon as wish for such an impossibility.

'I never heard of such a thing,' Bert began to bluster, feeling uncomfortable at the raw pain on Amy's face, and not knowing how to cope with any of this. Her gran dying was one thing. She'd been old and it had been her time. Tess Loveridge was only a girl, and a beautiful one at that, or had been . . .

'Tess wants to see me, to make her peace, and nobody's going to stop me,' Amy said in a low voice.

'No. All right. Of course not. I'll take you sometime,' he went on vaguely.

'We can't wait for "sometime". Amy's coming with me now.' Daniel dared him to argue. 'You needn't worry. I'll bring her back safe and sound.'

They all heard the tinkle of the show-room door-bell, and knew that there were customers downstairs. Bert hovered, not wanting to leave these two alone any longer, but finally being overcome by his natural business instincts.

'Well, see that you do. And – er – give my best to Tess and say that I hope she'll get well soon.'

He completely failed to notice the misplaced irony in his words, banged his brandy glass down on a table and went down to resume his best sales manager-cum-owner's face and voice, and found it easy enough to forget Tess Loveridge for the time being.

'You know how very sorry I am to bring you such news, Amy,' Daniel said into the silence between them. He ached to hold her and transform the little marble statue she seemed to have become into the warm and vibrant girl that he loved. But she had the look about her that he knew of old. The look that said she was building an impenetrable barrier against all the hurts life threw her way, and, God knew, she was getting her share lately.

'Tell me how she is, so that it's not too great a shock. I

don't want her to see me back away.' She was practical, considerate, afraid, not looking at him . . . and by God she was strong, Daniel thought. She was stronger than she looked, dealing with this new situation. Looking at it, deciding it had to be faced, and facing it.

'I won't pretend she's a pretty sight. She's a bag of bones, Amy,' Daniel couldn't think how to put it any other way. 'She's like one of the starving millions in India we're always being told about.'

'Like the ones Gran always said would be glad of the scraps I left on my plate.' Amy gave a wan little smile.

'Just like them.' Daniel knew she didn't mean him to smile back. She was somewhere in the past with Tess now, remembering the good times. She looked up, her eyes focusing on him more clearly.

'I'll fetch my coat.'

As she went to pass him he caught at her hand.

'Amy, this is one hell of a mess. We should never be in this situation. You and me and Tess – and this Bert Figgins. How the devil did you come to be set up here with him like this?'

For the first time he looked about him, seeing the cosy little home Amy had made of the place. There were touches of Gran Moore's parlour in a couple of the pictures on the wall. On the mantelpiece there were two framed photographs he'd never seen before, a young woman looking remarkably like Amy, and a young man. She caught him looking at the room and at the photographs. Was he suspecting her of living over the brush with Bert already, she wondered with a burning shame.

And then there was that other shame – that of knowing the truth about the two people in the photographs.

She still wasn't sure just why she had framed them and kept them constantly on show. It was what everyone did. Family pictures gave her a past, a respectability, even if the reality was very different. Daniel's glance reminded her of it all too well.

'*Set up*, Daniel?' she said bitterly. 'I'm not sure just what you mean by that, but I had to do something after Gran died and you – and you went your own way. Bert offered me security and a fair living, and I saw no reason not to take it. I don't have to depend on any man's charity. I'm a partner in Figgins Car Sales, quite legitimately. When I went through Gran's things, I discovered that my – my father left me provided for.' She felt an extraordinary, unexpected burst of pride as she said the words. 'And that reminds me. I'll pay you back the money you loaned me for Gran's hospital expenses.'

'You damn well will not!' he said angrily, still reeling at all she was saying. He was quite sure now that this Bert Figgins had got wind of Amy's money, however much it was, and had cashed in on it. He knew his sort. Before he could say any more, he heard the change in her voice, shocked and upset.

'Oh Daniel, what are we doing, arguing like this when we should be on our way to Tess! Forget what I was saying, please, all of it. None of it matters any more. We've each made our bed, and we have to lie on it.'

And if that wasn't telling him plainly that she was sharing hers with this other chap, Daniel didn't know what was. It made no difference to his feelings. He still loved her, and he understood her need to be loved by someone at a traumatic time in her life. But if she was as attached to Bert Figgins as it now appeared, then he couldn't try to take her from him. He wouldn't break up any man's home, and it seemed to him now that he'd come back into Amy's life too late.

He told her his mother was out for the afternoon, for which she was very thankful. After that, there seemed nothing to say as they sat beside each other in his Austin motor-car. The only other sad time they had been together

217

like this was going to her Gran's funeral. Other times, there had been that glorious feeling of happiness, of loving and being loved, sitting beside the one man in the world who could lighten her day and make her feel the warmth of the sun in her heart when there were only dark clouds overhead.

She had never expected to be sitting in Daniel's car again, and she was beset by memories that wouldn't be denied, spiced with the sadness of knowing why they were making this journey.

She remembered the very first time he'd given her a lift to Aveley Square, when Amy had been genuinely amazed as Daniel ushered Tess into the back seat, smiling as she arranged her skirts so prettily. And then opened the front passenger door for Amy.

She remembered other times . . . but tried desperately to stop such thoughts. They did no good, and it wasn't seemly when Tess was so ill . . . but the recollections wouldn't be stopped.

They were passing the Roxy cinema now, its posters blaring out the news that as the start to the new year, and by popular demand, they were reshowing Mary Pickford in *Little Annie Rooney*, ringlets and all. Frank must be confident of good takings at the box-office, Amy thought cynically.

The lyrics of a certain song began to run through her head. She hadn't thought of them in a while, and she didn't want to think of them now.

'She's my once-a-week love, my once-in-a-dream-time love, all so del-i-cate and lovely . . .'

A noise that was suspiciously like a sob escaped from her throat, and angrily she pretended it hadn't happened.

'Life can be bloody at times, can't it, Amy?' Daniel said in such a low voice that she wasn't even sure she'd heard him speak at all. It was better not to answer. If she did, he'd know she was near to crying, and she purposely

218

looked the other way so that she didn't have to see the Roxy and remember another kind of life that had been so briefly wonderful.

Tess had hardly looked away from the bedroom door since Daniel left the house. It wasn't Sunday, as far as she knew, but somewhere outside the Sally Army was banging tambourines and singing its heart out. Unless the sounds were all in her head, as they often were nowadays, ranging from the buzzing of a thousand bees to the declarations of love from a dozen Douglas Fairbanks all talking at the same time, and sometimes even the rollicking music of the charleston, or the solemn beat-beat-beat of drums . . .

Sometimes she had weird hallucinations too, and the worst was that of an enormous, stern-faced cleric bearing down on her like a grotesque black crow about to blot out the sun. She hated that sensation more than the noises in her head. She'd never had time for religious rot, especially seeing how farcical it had been with Frank and his Bible-thumping. He'd lost interest in that now, and Daniel said he spent more time collecting and organizing his moving-picture magazines, like a great adolescent kid clinging to childhood.

More likely getting a thrill out of seeing pictures of half-dressed Hollywood tarts, Tess told him. She saw no reason to hide what she felt, if she ever had, because she wouldn't be around much longer, and when she was gone they could say what they liked about her. She'd never forgiven her mother for running out on her, and with the total selfishness of the invalid she had no feelings for anyone in this world, except Amy.

It was funny how the thought of Amy could still make her wince. They'd been bloody good mates for a long time, and she knew very well she'd treated her rotten. She was already tired of Daniel and his family. The father, who was the biggest bore in creation, and the mother, nice enough, but a real soft 'ap'orth. And Daniel, still in love with Amy and putting up with the lot of them because of devotion to his mother. Tess didn't know whether to admire him for it or despise him.

It had been the biggest shock in the world to find she wasn't pregnant after all, and that that bastard Giles Beaumont hadn't done for her. For one stupendous moment in the doctor's consulting-room, Tess had thought she could be rid of them all and start living properly again – and then had come the death sentence. She'd accepted it now, because she simply didn't have the strength to fight it, and all she wanted was to see Amy and ask her to forgive her.

When the door opened, she even managed a grin that wasn't half bad, though to Amy it was more like a grimace. Amy hid her shock, and also the revulsion at the smell pervading the room. She knew it at once. It was the death-smell, and Tess was enveloped in it.

'Hello, ducks,' Tess croaked. 'This is quite a turn-up, ain't it?'

Amy's throat tightened. One minute she was standing awkwardly by the door, and the next she was rushing across the room to take the wasted body of her friend in her arms.

For minutes they rocked together without speaking, the painfully gaunt girl with the frame of a child, and the smartly dressed young lady oozing style and affluence. The contrast couldn't have been more marked, and Daniel couldn't bear to watch the reunion. It should be private anyway, but although he stayed outside the room he could hear all that was said.

'Amy, I know I did you a terrible wrong, and there's no changing that, but I was scared out of me wits at the time, and I couldn't think of no other way.'

'Tess, I forgive you,' Amy said, unable to bear Tess's

revelations. 'You don't need to say anything. It's past. It's over.'

'Nearly over for me too, eh, gel? Oh, you don't need to be embarrassed. I know what's happening. Can't keep any food down, see. Funny, really, after all me dieting. Me figure ain't so special now, is it? Not much left of it now. You've improved though, gel. True love suiting you, is it?'

Amy blinked, hearing Tess's shrill laugh.

'We saw it in the newspaper. Quite the lady now, eh? And old Bert turned out to be the one for you. Maybe I did you a favour after all. You are happy, ain't you, Amy? It's all worked out all right in the end, ain't it?'

For a second Amy wanted to shriek at her that *no*, it hadn't worked out all right, that the engagement was all a sham, and that there was only man in the world for her, and always had been . . . But she looked at the mute appeal in Tess's eyes and said what the other girl wanted to hear, the only thing it was possible to say.

'Of course it has. Me and Bert have got a fine little business together, and we've got lots of influential friends too. We even go to weekend house-parties in the country, just like real toffs, Tess.'

'*Go on*! Blimey, gel, who'd ever have believed it of little Amy Moore. Tell me all about it.'

She looked so animated that Amy elaborated on the weekends at The Gables until it seemed as though her whole life was one gay round of parties. Tess loved it all. It almost made up for the fact that she'd never go to another party in her life . . .

'Sorry I shan't be around to be your bridesmaid, but when are you tying the knot?' Tess wanted to know next.

'Oh, we haven't decided. In the summer, perhaps. We're too busy with the business at the moment.' Amy said it brightly, not knowing how much longer she could sit here pretending this was an ordinary visit to a sick friend. It wasn't. It was the most awful ordeal she'd ever had to go through.

'Get off back to Bert now, gel. I'm tired of talking and too tired to listen any more.' Tess lost concentration quickly, and closed her eyes for a second. When she opened them again, she gave a brief smile. 'Don't come back, Amy. We've said all there is to say. Promise me now. And I don't want no crying over me grave neither. Save your crying for the pictures, and enjoy it!'

Amy bent and kissed her. There was no point in saying she never went to the pictures now. No point in anything, and she promised blindly.

Daniel drove her back to Figgins' Car Sales in Claymore Street without saying a word, and when she went to get out of the car, he thanked her for seeing Tess and shook her hand. He was so formal that no onlooker could have guessed they had once been on the brink of becoming lovers.

She asked him to let her know when the inevitable happened, and then she watched him drive out of her life without looking back – never knowing that her caring lies to Tess had given him totally the wrong idea about herself and Bert Figgins.

18

'Guess who was here while you were away!' Bert caught her in his arms and swung her around as soon as she went inside. Still immersed in the sad little scene at Daniel's house, Amy couldn't think sensibly, and pushed Bert away in disgust.

'Aren't you even going to ask about Tess? You know where I've been, Bert – and you seem to have recovered pretty quickly from your daft attack of jealousy!'

'Oh God, I forgot. You've been gone so long and people have been coming and going all afternoon. Well, how is she?'

He was obviously bursting to tell her his own news, and Amy sighed. He probably couldn't help being the most insensitive man she'd ever met. He could be charming or ingratiating or downright boorish, depending on the mood of the moment, and she'd learned to accept it by now. If she had once thought Daniel was her rock in any storm, then Bert was more like shifting sand, she decided. Yet in a strange way, each of them had become more than friends. She recognized the strong tie between all three of them. All four, counting Tess . . .

'She's exactly as Daniel said. She's dying. We made our peace and she doesn't want me to go there again.'

Amy swallowed quickly, because somehow that had been the saddest thing of all.

'It's probably all for the best,' Bert told her, undeniably glad to hear it. He hoped the episode with Daniel Easton was now well and truly over. It was a bloody shame to start upsetting Amy like that, just when they were beginning to enjoy life. 'Anyway, how do you fancy going down to The Gables next weekend, old girl?'

Couldn't he see that such a suggestion was just about the last thing on her mind right now! She grieved for Tess and for Daniel, who had seemed to shut her out of his life with that formal hand-shake, and it was all too much . . . and yet, and yet . . . without warning, Amy found herself laughing hysterically.

'Why not! It sounds wonderful! Let's have a weekend in the country and forget that my friend is dying. She may even be dead by then, so we needn't think about her at all while we're enjoying ourselves –'

'Here, steady on. People will think you've gone potty.' Bert said anxiously, as a motor slowed down outside and the occupants peered in through the windows. 'Let's go upstairs and I'll give you another drop of brandy.'

'I don't want brandy. I don't want anything,' Amy snapped. 'I just want to be left alone.'

'All right.' For once, Bert didn't probe. 'I'll ask Maisie to bring you a nice cup of tea and some of her ginger snaps. She asked if she can go and visit her mother while we're away, by the way, instead of coming with us. I didn't think you'd mind. Old Ron has plenty of maids to do the necessary.' He chuckled. 'You go and put your feet up, old girl, and I'll tell you what Archie had to say later.'

'What on earth are you talking about?' Amy said in exasperation as he rattled on.

'I told you. Archie called in this afternoon and said we're invited for next weekend. Oh well, you might as well know it all now. Ronald and Jane want to give us that engagement party they promised us ages ago. It's to be next weekend, to brighten up the winter, Archie said. And now that people know all about the business, who knows what useful contacts we might make? Good-oh, ain't it, gel?'

She laughed shrilly, exaggerating her accent.

'Oh yes! I should say so! It's bloody good-oh!'

And nearly an hour later, when he'd dealt with the interested couple in the show-room and got their assurance that they'd be back during the week to see the new model he was expecting in, he went upstairs to see how Amy was doing.

By then, she had faced the fact yet again that everything between her and Daniel was over. Guiltily, she had even hoped that someday . . . They had always been destined to be more than friends, always, *always*, she thought passionately, but from his manner when he left her, it had seemed obvious to Amy that all the softness in his eyes and his voice when he'd arrived was only on account of Tess and what was past. And now there was nothing left.

'Shall I buy a new frock for next weekend or take the bronze one again, do you think?' she asked Bert when he came cautiously into the parlour, never sure of her temper these days.

'Buy two new ones,' he said recklessly, relieved and delighted that the haunted look was leaving her and she looked more like his perky Amy again. 'Let's show 'em we're the up-and-coming Figginses, sweetheart. Perhaps we can sell a Roller on spec, and get some lordship or even a duke to pose with it outside the show-room for the paper. How about that for an idea?'

She couldn't stop her mouth twitching at his cheek, and then she was laughing out loud and telling him he was too outrageous to be true. And later, when she began to show an interest in who was invited to The Gables for the weekend as well, he really began to think she'd got that Easton chap out of her system for good.

The note was delivered by hand two days later. Tess had died peacefully the day after Amy had been to see her, and Daniel said he was sure she'd only been hanging on because of her need to see Amy. He thanked her sincerely for her generosity in making Tess's last hours easier. He didn't invite her to the funeral. And remembering how Tess had begged her not to cry over her grave, Amy merely sent him a short note of condolence by the same messenger, did her crying in private, and went up West to buy two new party frocks for the weekend. It hardly mattered. She already knew that mourning was more a matter for the heart than for outward show.

They had their own car now, a snappy little Ford that got them to The Gables in record time, considering the damp slippery roads and the threat of January pea-soupers in and around London. There would be no chance of taking the flying machine up for a spin this time, Bert said regretfully, eager to try it out again.

'I can't say I'm all that sorry. It seems a very dangerous sport to me,' Amy commented. 'And you and Archie don't strike me as the most careful drivers, either.'

Bert laughed. 'You don't have drivers in planes, old girl, you have pilots. I thought a clever one like you would have known that.'

'I did know it. I just forgot.'

He glanced at her and put his hand on her knee. Her skirt was several inches above it when she was sitting down, and he felt the warmth of her skin inside the beige silk stocking. She didn't bother pushing his hand away, knowing that if she didn't react, Bert soon got tired of the experiment and took it away.

'Amy, I know you thought I was an unfeeling swine over Tess, but the only thing to do now is look to the future. We can't undo what's past – and we are going to have a good time this weekend, aren't we?'

'Well, I hope so. Don't worry, I won't let Ronald and Jane down, if that's what you're thinking.'

'I wasn't, exactly.' Bert cleared his throat. 'I mean that

I want us to have a good time – the way some of the others do.'

With a little shock, Amy realized his hand hadn't left her knee, as it usually did. It was still there, caressing the soft silk, and it was only the appearance of another car coming the opposite way around a corner that made him put both hands on the wheel again. She turned her head slowly to look at him. He kept his eyes straight ahead, concentrating on steering the car, but she could see a nerve pulsing at the side of his neck.

He had a very elegant profile, especially when his mouth was held tightly together, as it was now, and the rather fleshy lips weren't so prominent. His nose was as straight as a Roman soldier's, and the lock of sandy hair that always flopped over his forehead accentuated the boyish and somewhat roguish look he cultivated. There were plenty of girls who'd be happy to marry Bert Figgins. Amy didn't happen to be one of them. She gently removed his hand from her knee.

'Don't be daft, Bert. You know we don't have that kind of relationship.'

She spoke in a no-nonsense voice. She didn't pretend to misunderstand what he meant. She'd heard the creeping footsteps along the landings at The Gables long after the lights had gone out, the suppressed giggles and deeper seductive murmurings. She knew that for some, it was an accepted part of these sophisticated country weekends, even if it was never ever mentioned.

'But why not?' Bert persisted, finding her resistance more alluring than the thought of actually *doing* anything, but determined to try.

'Because we're not properly engaged, are we? All this is just for show, isn't it?' When he didn't answer, she spoke more sharply. 'Bert, we did agree. You're not going to try and hold me to anything, are you?'

She saw his lower lip jut out. Sometimes he could be just

like a great sulky kid when he didn't get his own way, she thought.

'I don't see why we couldn't make a go of it. It would be more respectable, and think what a splash we could have in the papers. We could even hire a Roller to take us to church, through the business, of course.'

'Bert, for God's sake! I think the thought of the *business* has made you a bit loopy in the head. And I don't want my picture splashed across the papers all the time, thank you very much.'

The last time, it had provoked Daniel into coming to see her, because of Tess. She didn't want the next picture he saw to be of herself and Bert Figgins tying the marital knot, committed to spending a lifetime in each other's company, in each other's bed . . . She shivered, wishing she didn't always think in terms of how things would affect Daniel. She still couldn't stop it.

'Well, it doesn't change what I was thinking about this weekend, Amy. You like me a bit, don't you? Damn it, I thought we was good mates.'

'We are. And that's all I want us to be. Please don't try and change things, Bert.'

'I suppose you think that Easton chap will come sniffing around now that –'

'Don't you dare say it,' she whipped out. 'Don't you dare, Bert, or I shall get out of this car right now and go back to London – if I have to walk every step of the way!'

She would too. He saw that she meant it, and tried to bluster his way out of it.

'I didn't mean anything. I'm just jealous, like you said. I do love you, Amy. You know that, don't you?'

'I know.' She supposed she loved him too. As a friend or a brother, no more. And who in their right minds could contemplate making love with their brother? Even as she thought it, Amy felt the world slip sideways. She'd never told a living soul about her parents, who *had* been brother and sister.

She knew in her heart that if she'd had to, she could have confided in Daniel. He would have understood and not condemned. And she knew just as certainly that the last person in the world she would tell was Bert Figgins, who would undoubtedly find some way of cashing in on the situation. And that must surely mean something.

They arrived at The Gables late on Friday afternoon, and Ronald and Jane greeted them as old friends. They used the same rooms as previously, and were quickly included in the frivolous atmosphere of The Gables. Archie and Bert soon had their heads together, discussing topics that only they understood, the intricacies of aerodynamics and wind speeds and flying procedures, and the girls in the group admired Amy's engagement ring and tried to get her to name the date for the wedding.

'We really haven't decided, but it will almost certainly be a long engagement,' she said, fencing them off. 'We're just too busy with the business at present.'

God, now she was doing it too, bringing the business into every conversation. But if it stopped these bright, flirtatious young things making daft comments and twittering away like idiots, then she didn't care. They weren't dressed up in their evening glitter yet, but to Amy, they still resembled bright, vivacious butterflies, beautiful, decorative and empty-headed, flitting from party to party, with rarely a serious thought in their heads.

And how contemptuous she was being now, she thought guiltily, superior and sneering, an inverted snob with no right to criticize these generous people who had taken her under their wings, so to speak. The unintentional simile made her smile. Butterflies taking her under their wings . . .

'Hello, little Amy below-stairs with the smiling face. I see we've become quite the social climber these days.'

For a few seconds, her heart felt so tight in her chest she could hardly move. The soft voice that was posher than royalty was only too familiar. She had heard it many times. At the bottom of the servants' stairs at the house in Aveley Square . . . in the elegant dining-room when she'd served soup from the huge silver tureen with trembling fingers that felt like thumbs . . . at the front door of the house, where she'd swept out like a lady after telling Giles Beaumont just what she thought of him. She turned slowly, composing her face, but unable to hide the burning colour that swept up from her throat to her forehead.

Giles was standing with a glass in his hand, already slightly unsteady on his feet so early in the evening. He was the typical city gent dressed for the country, tweeds and brogues to the fore, and a speculative look in his eyes as he assessed this new and beautiful Amy Moore. He'd been staggered to see the business advertisement in the newspaper and the photograph of the two of them as bold as brass, and had toyed with the idea of confronting the jumped-up ex-chauffeur and the snotty little housemaid in their brand-new premises, and wiping the floor with them for causing his family no little inconvenience at the way they'd run out on them.

But he'd had second thoughts, because servants weren't really worth the bother, however much they fancied their chances among their betters, and he thought it hardly likely that he'd ever have to see the pair of them again.

And now here they were, larger than life, and playing the part of toffs not half badly, to his annoyance. And Ronald Derbisham, whom Giles hadn't seen since his days at Oxford until they happened to run into each other in the city, was actually entertaining that Figgins fellow in his home. *The Beaumont chauffeur, for Christ's sake!*

He glanced across to where his fiancée, the Honourable

Thelma Parkes-Leighton, was in semi-animated conversation with one of the horsey set. Giles regretted the day he'd ever set eyes on Thelma, who was as dull as pond water and twice as boring. The country didn't interest him. He was far more at home in the city, but he'd suffered many tedious weekends plodding through mud and worse with his family, and seemed destined to spend even more among Thelma's awful connections.

He was still deciding how to handle this new situation when he realized that Bert Figgins had caught sight of him. He saw the fellow's jaw drop slightly, before he moved out of sight in the company of that pansy brother of Ronald's. Hoping he hadn't been recognized, obviously, though he could hardly expect to remain undetected for the entire weekend. And at that moment Giles decided it would be more fun to play with these two than to expose them for what they were.

'So how are things with you, Amy?' he went on more sociably. 'You don't mind if I call you Amy, do you?' he added innocently, with a meaning only she understood.

'Of course not. It's my name.'

He smiled, enjoying her discomfiture, which was quite apparent to him despite her lifted chin and bright eyes. She was a beauty all right, he thought in some surprise, and only now did he see it. It was a pity he hadn't cottoned on to her before, instead of the other one – what was her name?

'Tess died, you know.' She said it suddenly, brutally, meaning to shock.

Giles cleared his throat, looking at her uneasily. How much did she know? There was a quality in her voice he didn't like – almost threatening. Which was ridiculous, because what could this chit do to threaten him? Except poison Thelma's mind against him by mentioning Tess – the thought came instantly. Thelma was already becoming suspicious of his dalliances, and he couldn't risk jeopardizing the marriage plans now. He needed Thelma's money to indulge his life-style . . .

'Good God. What a tragedy. She was such a pretty girl.' He pretended a concern he didn't feel. He hadn't even known her full name. What had Tess been to him but a quick hop between the sheets – until she told him she was pregnant.

'What about you and your – er – partner, isn't it? Are you selling plenty of motors?'

She knew at once what he thought about her relationship with Bert.

'We're doing very nicely, thank you. And yes, Bert is my partner – my *business* partner.'

Giles smiled, blowing smoke into the air from his expensive cigar. Not for him the common cigarettes that even the Derbishams and most of their friends flaunted, whether in holders or not. A true gentleman always smoked cigars.

'Good. Perhaps I'll come and see you there one of these days.'

He smiled boldly into her eyes, and Amy could hardly believe what she saw there. He couldn't have made it plainer if he'd shouted it aloud. *You be nice to me, darling, and I'll keep quiet about what I know.* Well, she knew one or two things, too, that the Honourable Thelma double-barrel might care to know . . . She was cold with anger.

'Oh, I don't think we have anything in your class,' she said icily. 'Unless your fiancée would be interested, of course?'

His face darkened, and the moment was very sweet. They understood one another perfectly, and Giles turned abruptly as Thelma led him away from the attractive young woman who seemed to be claiming all his attention. She looked vaguely familiar, but Thelma freely admitted that she had a rotten memory for faces, unless they sat above the neck and shoulders of a horse.

Bert made his way across the crowded room to Amy as soon as he could.

'*Christ*, did you see who that was?' he hissed. 'Everything will be up if he starts spouting –'

'He won't. I've seen to it,' Amy said calmly.

Inside, she was wilting, but she would never let anybody know it. Bert had no idea that Giles had caused such disruption in Amy's life, and was only worried about his own skin and the business he'd schemed so hard for. She couldn't blame him for that. It was the most important thing in his life, and it didn't matter to her that she knew she came a poor second.

'What do you mean, you've seen to it? He knew us, I tell you.'

'Of course he did, but you know as well as I do about his little games with the servants.' She went as far as she dared. 'I hinted that Thelma might be interested as well, and that was enough to scare him off. Thelma's daddy has pots of money, you see.'

'Does he now?' Bert's thoughts were diverted at once, his eyes narrowing. 'I wonder –'

'*No*. You try anything, Bert, and I'll walk out on you, and that's a promise. *And* I'll tell the papers what a swine you can be for tricking your way into people's good books,' she said recklessly.

'All right, gel. It was only a joke. We'll just enjoy the weekend, right?'

'And don't try anything with me, either,' she muttered. She was quite sure that neither he nor anybody else would bother her, because she intended locking her door very securely each night.

Giles Beaumont's presence was disturbing, but Amy was convinced she'd got the measure of him now. And she sensed that Jane Broome didn't care for him too much, so it was safe to assume he wouldn't be included in the regular Derbisham set at The Gables. In fact, as the weekend went on, it became fairly obvious that most of the guests disliked him, and merely tolerated him because of Thelma.

Amy refused to think of him as a threat to her well-being any longer. Instead, she marvelled at how much she had changed. Perhaps until meeting Giles Beaumont on a social level, it had never really come home to her how easily she had slid into the skin of a lady. She fitted in, and these people liked her company. The occasional arguments she put forward, giving as good as the men on social issues, stamped her as a woman with a brain in her head as well as a delicious sight to see.

On the Saturday night at dinner, when they toasted her and Bert with genuine affection, she laughed at the teasing references that they'd better hurry up and tie the knot and start producing junior motors to go with the big ones in the show-rooms.

It was all the usual screamingly hilarious fun, and Amy stared Giles Beaumont straight in the eye and silently dared him to add anything to the daft jokes about babies. He didn't even know the truth about Tess, and she wasn't going to tell him. He didn't know Daniel had married her to give her a saving grace before she went to meet her Maker. He didn't know he had ruined Amy's life.

And nobody knew that on the night of her official engagement, Amy wept into her pillow, because if only things were different, there was one man in all the world she wouldn't refuse entry into her room that night. The one man to whom she had given her heart, and that, to Amy, meant being faithful unto death. And if she was destined to be like those poor unfortunate women left alone after the war to end all wars, then so be it. Better no life partner at all than living intimately with one she didn't love.

Bert was echoing something of the same sentiments when he finally found his true role in life. Long after the house had quietened down for the night, he heard his door-handle being opened. For a moment he thought it might be Amy. His heart fluttered erratically, wondering if he could do as he'd rashly boasted so many times. And then the bed dipped and he recognized Archie's scented aura, and gave himself up to the inevitable.

19

By the middle of a wild and stormy February, when most people shivered indoors over oil heaters and spitting coal fires as gusts of wind blew the sparks back down the chimneys, Helen Easton couldn't stand the misery on her son's face any longer. He'd done his duty – more than his duty – by the Loveridge girl, and it was time he started thinking about himself.

'Daniel, love,' she said gently, when he'd stood at the window watching the rain slide down the pane for a solid fifteen minutes without moving a muscle. 'When are you going to put things right between you and Amy?'

He made a shrugging movement with his shoulders. Her tall strong son, who'd made such a sacrifice for her. It wasn't fair. She ached to take him in her arms and tell him so, but he was no longer her small boy, running to her with grazed knees. He was a man, with a man's deep feelings, and so far he had kept them private. But if he kept his hurt to himself, Helen didn't need telling that it went very deep.

'Amy has her own life now.'

'With this chauffeur fellow? I'm convinced it's only a business arrangement, Daniel. I can't really believe she prefers him to you. Anyway, you'll have to see her sometime. There's Tess's things . . .'

He ignored her last remark. 'Your loyalty touches my heart, Mother, but Amy's made up her own mind about her future, and there's an end to it. You weren't here the day she came to see Tess, but if you'd heard what I did, you'd know she's perfectly content with things the way they are. How can I break up another man's life? God knows, my own has been broken, and I wouldn't wish that on anyone.'

It was the nearest he had come to revealing his feelings, even to her.

'Daniel, it's wrong. I know Amy loves you, and if you let her marry this Figgins –'

'If I *let* her? Listen to what I'm saying, Mother. I won't interfere in her life. I've got no right to, after what's happened.'

'If you let her marry this Figgins,' Helen went on doggedly, 'you'll be condemning her to the kind of life I've had with your father. Would you wish that on *her*?'

She had his attention now.

'Daniel, when I married your father I was the happiest woman alive. I loved him so much, I thought the sun shone out of his eyes. I wasn't sickly and nervy then. I was as bright and alive as Amy. I loved him so much I was even prepared to overlook his little – lapses, shall we say? Oh yes, my dear, I'm not blind! But that very devotion, that very *love*, made your father despise me. Because I let him have his little flings, he turned on me. He *wanted* me to object, you see, to scream and shout and make scenes, but it was never my way. I know now that it might have fed his ego sufficiently so that he didn't need his little extras any longer. But I didn't see that then. I thought that by playing the martyr, waiting until he came back to me – which he always did – that I was being the clever one. Instead of which, he merely carried on humiliating me, mentally and verbally, and physically too, losing all respect for me, and never seeing that it was because I loved him. Because I still love him –'

'Mother, don't,' Daniel said. He'd never seen her as emotional as this before. 'You're torturing yourself needlessly. And nothing you're saying has any relevance to Amy and Bert Figgins.'

'I think it does. I loved Frank, but Amy's caught in a

237

different situation. From what you say, this Figgins man is also something of a womanizer. Don't you see what's going to happen? If Amy marries him when she doesn't love him, he'll know it, because you can't hide it. He'll turn to others to prove himself, and she'll know that too. He'll flaunt his affairs, just to show her that other women find him attractive. That's where the two of us will end up the same, but Amy's made of stronger stuff than me. She won't whine and give in to bouts of mysterious illness that are none the less real at the time. She'll grow hard and embittered, and know that she's wasted her life, and it will be on your conscience, Daniel. You must go to her.'

'I think you're being ridiculous.' He was rarely angry with her, but he was angry now as her impassioned words ended. 'What Amy does with her life now is no concern of mine. She didn't have to get engaged to Bert Figgins, did she? And she did it before she knew anything about Tess, remember. Don't talk about her being on *my* conscience. As far as I'm concerned, it's over, and I want to forget her.'

He strode out of the room, pushing his arms into his overcoat and banging out of the house. He walked blindly through the streets, uncaring of the rain that was fast turning to sleet, and the chill winds whipped around his legs. He didn't care about anything, except the cruel blows fate had dealt him.

Go to Amy? How could he go to her and say everything that was in his heart? How could he implore her not to marry Bert Figgins, not to do this to him, to them, to the bright, feverish love that still burned so fiercely in him?

Daniel suddenly felt sick of the whole rotten mess. He had never thought himself violent, but he'd already struck two men in the name of love. One was his father, when he'd accused him of fornicating with Tess Loveridge. The other was Bert Figgins, who'd taunted him for wanting Amy . . .

Daniel stopped walking, leaned on a parapet and closed his eyes as his thoughts washed over him. He felt a surge of wanting so strong that it almost bowled him over. Of course he wanted her. Wanted and needed and loved her, with an ache in his soul that was physically painful. He wanted her sweetness and innocence. He wanted to lie with her in his arms and possess her as he'd never possessed any woman. He wanted to make her part of him. He wanted the mystical union that was heaven-blessed by the sanctity of marriage. He wanted children with Amy, and to grow old with Amy, because to live without her was to wither and die.

"Ere, are you all right, mate? You look a bit queer-like. And it ain't going to solve anything, you know. It'd be mighty cold in there on a day like this. Best go home now and sit by a warm fire.'

Daniel started at the sound of the rough voice. A man in workman's clothes was looking at him in alarm, and he followed the man's glance. He must have walked farther than he realized. How he came to be standing on this bridge overlooking the river, he couldn't even remember. Below him the water swirled, black and turbulent with the wind and sleet, and he supposed he must have looked suspiciously like a man contemplating suicide, staring unseeingly into its depths.

'Thanks, yes, I'm all right,' he said heavily. 'Just felt a bit groggy, that's all. Don't worry. I wasn't going to throw myself in the Thames.'

'You don't look too good to me,' the man said, peering into his face. 'Had a drop too much, have you?'

'I reckon I have,' Daniel agreed.

'Best get a tram and get orf 'ome, then,' the man advised. 'Or a cab,' he added, seeing Daniel's good overcoat and deciding he was swank enough to pay for such things.

'You're right. Thanks.'

The man was evidently going to stand firm until Daniel moved on, and when he saw a taxi-cab trundling over the bridge, Daniel waved it down and got inside thankfully, not realizing before how exhausting the wind could be.

'Where to, guv?' the cabbie asked. 'Cold enough to freeze a brass monkey, ain't it?'

'Over the bridge, then I'll decide,' Daniel said. He didn't want to go home yet. He still felt too churned up.

'It's your money,' the cabbie said cheerfully.

'Take me to Claymore Street. Figgins' Car Sales,' he said suddenly.

'Righto. Thinking of buying a new motor, are you? Seen a nice little Morris Cowley in there meself that I wouldn't mind getting when me ship comes in.'

Daniel listened half-heartedly. He could still change his mind. He could ask the cabbie to turn right round and take him home. But his mother was right. He had to see Amy again. Tess had wanted her to have a few trinkets, and he owed it to them both to see that her last wishes were carried out.

Archie and Bert seemed to be enjoying themselves enormously, Amy thought that afternoon. They were in the parlour, tinkering with the brand-new wireless set Bert had bought. It stood in pride of place on the sideboard, huge and cumbersome, emitting the most horrendous noises as they tried to make it work satisfactorily. It wouldn't really matter if it never did, Amy suspected, as long as those two could twiddle with knobs and take things apart and put them back together again. They were two of a kind, grown-up boys playing with mechanical toys . . .

They hardly noticed her at all. She might as well have been part of the furniture when Archie came calling, as he did quite regularly now. Bert seemed to come to life whenever Archie was around. It surprised and pleased her, because he'd stopped the nonsense about making their engagement a real one. She didn't know if he'd told Archie or not, but if so, he was keeping it to himself. Archie knew how to keep a secret, she remembered Bert telling her smugly over their financial arrangement. So as long as he kept this one as well, it was all right.

She heard the show-room door-bell while they still had their heads together over the innards of the wireless set.

'It's all right, I'll go,' she said to thin air. 'If anybody wants that new Austin I'll let it go for fifty quid, shall I?'

'Mm?' Bert said vaguely. 'Whatever you like, Amy.'

She heaved a sigh and ran down the stairs. It would serve him right if she did just as she'd said and sold the car at a huge loss – only she wouldn't, of course. It would be her loss as well as Bert's . . .

'Daniel!'

Involuntarily, her hand went to her throat as she felt her heart race. Why must the sight of him always knock the stuffing out of her! Why must he turn up without warning like this, tying her stomach in knots, just when she was beginning to reorganize her life without him? Before he spoke, she took a good look at him.

'You look terrible. What's happened to you? Have you been out walking in this weather?'

'I'm all right,' he said abruptly.

'No, you're not. Come into the little office. It's not very big, but there's an oil stove there and it's warm and cosy.'

She spoke severely, shocked at the way he was beginning to shiver. There was plenty of flu about, and it could kill if people didn't take care of themselves. From Daniel's wild eyes, she doubted that he'd been doing much of that lately.

'I have to talk to you, Amy.'

'In a minute. First you're going to sit there, and I'm going to fetch you some of that brandy. Don't argue, Daniel,' she said.

241

'You've become very bossy,' he murmured, with the ghost of a smile.

'So do as you're told,' she said briskly, and ran upstairs to fetch the drink and call out to Maisie to make some strong tea.

'Are you giving drinks to customers now?' Bert asked, hearing her.

'It's not a customer, it's Daniel. And I'd be glad if you'll keep out of the way while I'm talking to him.'

He remembered the last time his jaw had come in contact with Daniel Easton, and didn't argue. Besides, he no longer cared whether Amy was having a bit of a fling with the fellow or not. Bert Figgins was in love, and it wasn't with anyone in skirts.

'Drink this, Daniel,' Amy ordered, handing him the brandy. Their fingers touched, and she snatched her hand away as if he was red hot. As indeed he was, she realized swiftly. 'Whatever it is you wanted to say to me, it had better wait. You should get home and go to bed. It looks to me as if you're in for the flu.'

'You're probably right,' he said, feeling his limbs ache and a shivering inside him that wasn't entirely due to being in such close proximity to Amy.

All the passionate feelings he'd had earlier were dwindling, merely because he'd begun to feel so ill. He didn't love her any less, but it was hard to feel anything when his head was throbbing and his legs seemed as if they were turning to jelly.

'What did you want to see me about?'

What indeed. They were sitting here, making the most inane conversation, in what was potentially an intimate little room, as warm and cosy as Amy had said, and he couldn't gather two sensible thoughts together.

'Oh yes,' he said, making a supreme effort. 'Tess's things. She wanted you to have your pick, Amy. She made me promise to let you go through them all before I – well, before I disposed of them to the charity.'

He wished he hadn't said all that. It would remind her of Gran, and Mrs Coggins' pickings . . . He wished he could read her mind, but her eyes were shadowed, and suddenly she wouldn't look at him.

'I see.' If she had hoped that, in some glorious way, Daniel had come to sweep her off her feet, the hope was dying a quick death. Not that he was in any fit state to do any sweeping, but she certainly hadn't expected this.

'Look, I'd better go. Would it bother you to come to the house when it's convenient, Amy? It would obviously be better when I'm there myself. Perhaps on a Saturday afternoon?'

'When your father's out of the way at the Roxy, you mean,' she said, the words twisting her gut.

He caught at her hand for a second.

'They were good times, weren't they, Amy?'

'Yes. Good times,' she said thickly, and then she heard Bert and Archie clattering down the stairs. Bert poked his head into the office, nodding briefly at Daniel.

'I'm going into town with Archie to see about getting some new valves for the wireless. You know what to do if any customers turn up, though I doubt if many will in this weather. We'll call in at his club for a while and eat there, so don't bother about dinner for me. See you when I see you.'

'Yes. Fine. Goodbye.' As Amy spoke, the door closed. He'd gone back through it like a dose of salts.

'Amy,' Daniel croaked, sensing that something wasn't quite right, but unable to work anything out now with the buzzing in his head. 'You do know that if anything ever worries you, that you – well, you know you can always count on me, don't you? I'll always be your friend. If ever you need a shoulder to cry on, and all that.'

'Why should I? Don't you think I've got everything a girl could want?'

She was instantly defensive, needing to prove to him that she was happy and successful, because she too had an uncomfortable feeling that something wasn't quite right. And however sophisticated she pretended to be among her new friends, she wasn't worldly-wise enough to recognize a bit of buggery when she saw it.

'Do you want this tea in here, miss?' Maisie hovered at the door with a tray, privately thinking this gent was a bit of all right. and she knew which one she'd choose if it was up to her.

'Yes please.' Amy made a decision. 'Then I'm going out for a while. I'll close up the show-room when I do, Maisie, and any customers will have to come back on Monday.'

She encouraged Daniel to drink the hot sweet tea. *Good for shocks and good for knocks*, Gran used to say. And probably good for influenza too. When he'd finished, Amy stood up.

'Come on. I'm taking you home.'

He looked at her dazedly. There seemed to be two of her . . . or four, depending on how far he opened his eyes. She caught his arm and dragged him to his feet. He leaned heavily on her, knowing that by rights Amy should be dependent, one of the weaker sex, not this capable woman ushering him to the back of the building where a neat little Ford car stood at the kerbside.

'Get in,' Amy said, opening the passenger door.

'You're not driving!' he said, aghast.

'Yes I am. Bert's been giving me lessons.'

It had only been a few so far, but if she took it slowly and carefully, she was sure she could manage. And Daniel needed to be home and in bed as quickly as possible. She concentrated on that and not on her nerves, and managed reasonably well, stopping the car outside the Eastons' house with a wrench on the brake.

'That was the most hair-raising ride I've ever had,' Daniel mumbled with an attempt at humour, feeling more than choked at this brave, wonderful girl who still had to take the car back to Claymore Street through the heavy sleet.

'Never mind – it got you here. Come on. I'll get you inside, and then I'll be off before this weather sets in for the night. I haven't done any night driving yet.' She grinned for the first time.

Helen opened the door to the astonishing sight of a more self-assured Amy than she remembered, helping Daniel inside and saying she'd call round the next Saturday afternoon to see if he was better, and to look at Tess's things then, if that was convenient. And advising Helen to get the doctor to Daniel right away.

And as Frank battled his way along the street on his way home from the Roxy for his tea, deciding it was wiser not to take his car home on the greasy roads, he thought he must be seeing things. It couldn't have been Amy Moore slipping gracefully into the driving seat of not a bad little motor, and driving the thing off at a break-neck speed, just like one of them flash Hollywood tarts in the pictures.

Amy hardly knew how she drove the motor back to Claymore Street. She'd taken it out because it had been necessary to get Daniel home as fast as possible. His need had been of prime importance. Now that she was on her own, she felt the power of the engine beneath the bonnet. She felt the wheels skid, and the snatch of the steering-wheel in her hands. She felt the dampness of her palms, and the thudding of her heart. She was simply terrified, because she had never driven without Bert beside her, ready to grab the wheel and help her to steer it safely. By now the sleet was blinding her vision, and she was sure she was never going to get the car back in one piece, and then Bert would be furious and she'd be in for a slice of tongue pie all right, if she banged up his precious machine.

At last the welcome sight of the show-room came into sight, and she'd got there without mishap. She put the car back exactly where she'd found it and hurried indoors with trembling hands, shivering from nerves and cold. Thankful Bert wouldn't be back for hours yet, she hollered out to Maisie to make some more tea and stoke up the fire, and then come and talk to her.

Ten minutes later, both of them were toasting their feet in front of the fire, and Maisie suspected, as she often did, that Miss Moore probably hadn't always been the lady she was now. It didn't matter a toss to her. She liked her new position more than the old, and even if Miss Moore hadn't been *born* a lady, she was a lady in spirit all the same. And she never minded inviting Maisie into the parlour for a sit-down and a chin-wag, which was nice and friendly, especially when Bouncy Bert was out.

In private, Maisie always thought of him that way. Bouncy Bert was a bit of a ladies' man, she'd reported to her old mum in Hackney. Bouncy Bert had chucked her under the chin once or twice, but never tried to do more, and she'd decided he was harmless. Bouncy Bert had a nice gentleman friend with a smooth face and oodles of money, and a way of looking at Bert as if they shared lots of secrets. And her old mum had told her the gentleman friend was probably a nancy boy, which probably meant that Bouncy Bert was too, and proceeded to spice up a wet Sunday afternoon by finishing Maisie's education.

'That was a bit of turn-up today, weren't it?' Maisie asked comfortably now, wiggling her feet in front of the coal fire and hoping they didn't smell. Miss Moore was a stickler for cleanliness, always washing and powdering herself, and splashing on that lovely ashes-of-roses scent that Maisie borrowed now and then.

'What was?' Amy said, leaning back in her chair,

exhausted with the strain of driving, and more so with the strain of seeing Daniel again and trying to behave normally.

''*im* turning up again. The other one, I mean. The one that punched Bou – Mr Figgins.'

'You don't miss much, do you, Maisie?' Amy grinned.

'Nah. Like a fly on the wall, me old mum says I am. So which one d'you reckon then, miss?' she asked daringly, seeing that Amy was in a mellow mood now she'd got some good hot tea down her, and the tempting smell of simmering stew was wafting in from the kitchen.

'Which one do you think? I'm engaged to Mr Figgins, Maisie. You know that.'

'I know which one I'd pick! And I know I'm 'ere as a kind of chaperon, only 'tain't really necessary, is it? I mean – well, I mean –'

'What do you mean?' Amy said lazily as she floundered.

The girl didn't answer, and Amy opened her eyes. Maisie's face was all flushed, and not only from the heat of the fire.

'Maisie, you're beginning to annoy me. If you've got something to say, then say it.' She was still too wrapped up in the way Daniel had looked this afternoon to deal with riddles. He had looked just terrible, so ill and weak, and if she hadn't kept her wits about her, she'd have smothered him with love and kisses, and probably ended up getting the flu herself . . .

'It's what me old mum said, really.' Maisie took refuge in somebody Amy was never likely to meet. 'About Mr Figgins's gentleman friend. Mr Derbisham, I mean. The one he calls Archie.'

'What about him?'

'Me old mum reckons he's probably a nancy boy, and there, I've said it, and I'm ever so sorry if it offends you, miss, and I think I'd best see to that stew now before it burns to a crisp.'

247

She dashed out of the room while Amy was still staring after her. She wasn't entirely sure what Maisie's old mum meant, though she was intelligent enough to guess. And why should it offend her? Such things had been going on way back into history. It certainly wasn't a very nice thought, but you had to live and let live, and as long as it didn't affect her, Archie could do as he jolly well pleased . . . and then her heart jolted. Unless Maisie was insinuating that Bert too . . .

20

A few days later, Amy silently handed Bert the letter that had come through the post that morning.

If she had been unusually quiet since Maisie's insinuations, Bert hadn't noticed it. Business was slack, and he constantly fretted over it, as if the loss of a few customers because of the bad weather would make or break them. Amy had thought hard about the suspicions Maisie had put in her mind, forcing herself to decide if it made any difference or not to her own life.

She finally decided that as long as Bert kept his part of the bargain and didn't try anything on with her, it did not. But naturally, there was no way Amy could question him about his relationship with Archie Derbisham, and she was no longer sure that she'd choose to. It was Bert's life.

Amy was seeing so many things clearly now, though, that she hadn't seen before. Things about Bert and Archie, the little laughing glances they shared, the touching hands, the arms around shoulders, holding glances across a room and then looking quickly away, the way lovers did . . .

The realization had given her several sleepless nights while she grappled with the new idea that Bert too was obviously what Maisie's old mum described as a nancy boy. Amy wondered why she hadn't suspected it before. But she had been totally naïve in those matters, and now that she did, her feelings were a mixture of repugnance and a sneaking kind of relief, because she was quite sure now that Bert would leave her alone as long as they were outwardly seen to be respectable partners. And the so-called engagement could continue indefinitely, as far as Amy was concerned.

But now there was this new little problem . . .

Bert drew the folded letter out of the envelope and stared at the printed words, his face going a sickly colour as he took them in. Amy studied him in those few moments. Charming, bland, a little fleshy now with the good life, and never in a million years the man for her . . . and clearly outraged by the words dancing in front of his eyes, words which, unknown to the sender, were an ironic lie.

'Christ, it's an anonymous letter!' he spluttered unnecessarily.

'I know that.'

'But the bugger who wrote it accuses us of living in sin and asks how we think business would be affected if it was splashed all over the newspapers!'

'Yes. Funny, isn't it?' Amy said sarcastically. She didn't know why she was suddenly so coldly angry, or why she was so certain she knew who had done this. Giles Beaumont, of course. Nor did she know why she felt so inclined to take it all out on Bert at that moment.

'What's that supposed to mean? Not that it matters. I can't be bothered with your clever tongue right now. We've got to think, Amy.'

'What's there to think about? Throw it on the fire where it belongs. That's the only thing to do with rubbish.'

Bert stared at her. The letter hung limply in his fingers. Amy could almost see Giles Beaumont's gloating face as he penned the words and pushed the letter into the posting-box.

'Ignore it, do you mean?'

'Well, what else? Unless you want to go to the police with it.' But she knew how he would react to that.

As she expected, Bert flinched at the thought, with his inborn mistrust of anything to do with the law. After a few seconds, his sallow face took on a tinge of colour.

'All the same, I think we should take the implications seriously, and act on it.'

'Oh, Bert, don't be ridiculous. It's some crank.'

He spoke all in a rush. 'We've got the business to consider, Amy. I'm not throwing it all away for the sake of some crank, if that's what you call the swine who did this. We'd better get married. Make our situation open and above board. Then we'll be seen as perfectly respectable. Even if it's – well, not a proper marriage, because I know that's what you'd prefer.'

He stopped, flushed and breathing quickly, avoiding her eyes, as if he knew that she knew all about him and his paramour, and was taking the easy way out. A respectable marriage would solve all his problems . . . Amy took a deep breath at the damn gall of him and swallowed quickly. The last thing in the world she wanted was to marry Bert Figgins, but before she could say a word, he'd dropped the offending letter and grasped her hands.

'I know you don't love me, Amy, and I accept that. But I'm talking about a marriage in name only, for the sake of what we've built up. Isn't that worth something? You could still be as free as you like, and it would stop any wagging tongues.'

'And you could still be as free as you liked too, of course,' she stated, poker-faced.

'We'd have the best of both worlds.'

'I'm not deciding anything until I've had time to think this out,' she said, refusing to let herself be pushed into it.

'Don't take too long then,' Bert said sulkily, thankful enough that at least she was thinking about it, after all. He wasn't losing his good name now, not after all he'd been through to acquire it. He knew he'd better be patient . . .

And Amy wouldn't decide anything until she'd seen Daniel again. Until she'd been to the Eastons' house and chosen something of Tess's, just as Daniel had asked. Then, she might just be able to gauge if there was any future for them both or if she was still chasing rainbows . . .

The following Saturday afternoon, she sat stiffly opposite Daniel's mother, while he went upstairs to fetch Tess's box of trinkets. Fleetingly, Amy could almost imagine it was like that other time when she'd come here to tea, and she and Daniel were on the brink of love . . . until she heard Helen Easton ask awkwardly if she was all right, as she looked so pale . . .

Helen spoke in some distress, seeing the shadows under this lovely girl's eyes, and the fined-down cheek-bones that were so attractive. This was a different Amy from the girl she had first met in this room, slender and confident and sophisticated now, but Helen could see that she wasn't happy. She wasn't a girl bubbling with joy because she was engaged to be married. To Helen it was obvious that she wouldn't be marrying for love.

'I'm fine, thank you,' Amy said quietly, and turned to Daniel as he came back into the room.

'There's not a great deal here,' he said, handing her the cardboard box. 'Tess didn't have much, except for some bright glittery stuff that you may not like.'

Amy opened the box, and a wave of nostalgia swept over her. Daniel wouldn't consider – no man would – how well she knew all these baubles. The long strings of beads, the hair combs, the beaded headbands, the cheap fake pearls from a market stall, the gold-coloured bangles that had left green rings around Tess's arms. Amy had seen Tess wear them all a hundred times. She'd been with her when she bought most of them. And in the end she couldn't bear to take any of them, except for a small cameo brooch with a butterfly imprisoned inside it.

'I'll just take this. It's all I need to remind me of Tess.'

It seemed to epitomize them both, Amy thought in a flash. They had both been trapped, as the butterfly was trapped, unable to spread their wings and fly . . . That glorious freedom of choice had been denied to her and Tess.

'You're sure that's all you want?'

'Yes, thank you.'

In the awkward little silence, when Tess's ghost seemed to hover between them, Helen went out to the kitchen to make some tea.

'Your mother looks well,' Amy said.

'It's more than I can say for you.'

'I'm fine. You're the one who had the flu. Has it gone now?' she asked, making small talk and unable to think of anything more scintillating to say.

'I'll survive,' he said roughly. 'I've packed in my job. Did I tell you?'

'No, you didn't. What are you going to do now?' At least this was on safer ground. She could show polite interest in his future, even if it wasn't a future that included her.

'I've already done it. My father's slowing up, and he's retired from the Roxy and handed it over to me.'

'But you always said it wasn't what you wanted.'

'Well, we don't always get what we want. If we did, I'd probably get out of London and take Mother to live in the country,' he said. 'Anyway, Father's nagged me into not letting the Roxy go to the highest bidder. It was my first reaction, of course. You of all people must understand that. Still, there's plenty of life in the old Roxy yet for pretty young girls who want their heads turned at the pictures and dream of being film stars.'

She heard the bitterness in his voice and wondered how much he regretted ever setting eyes on two particular young girls who'd been picture-mad every Saturday afternoon. She was stunned by his words, and the small hope she'd cherished of their getting together again slowly flickered and died. He was as good as telling her he didn't want her any more.

She tried to think instead that it would be good for the Roxy to continue under the same management. The memory of the old days could still enchant her when she let it, and so could the way two particular young girls had been so swept away by the magic of the movies . . .

'Do you remember that Douglas Fairbanks picture that Tess was so mad on?' Before she had time to think, the words rushed out. 'We must have known every word by heart.'

A swift image of her and Tess, wide-eyed and carefree, munching their boiled delights every Saturday afternoon as each dreamed secretly of Douglas Fairbanks belonging exclusively to her, soared in front of her eyes as if she was watching it on a cinema screen. Unreal, fleeting, ephemeral, immortal . . .

'I don't want to remember. I'm taking on the Roxy as a business proposition, and nothing more,' Daniel said harshly, and she saw how changed he was too.

She'd never thought him less of a man for working at the penny lending-library, even though it had surprised her at the time. She'd always known there was a great deal of the intellectual in him, undoubtedly from his mother's side of the family.

But if he'd chosen now to step into his father's footsteps, it was probably the right thing for him, after all. There was a piquancy and pride in following family tradition. All the best families did it, from the nobility down to rag-and-bone men. It was something Amy herself had never had the chance to do.

Helen brought the tea-tray into the room, and glanced at the sky outside the window. Only three o'clock in the afternoon and it was quite dark, with heavy clouds overhead. The lamplighters were already at work, and the small pools of light were stringing the streets like amber necklaces.

'You'd better not stay too long,' Daniel said abruptly,

as if he couldn't bear her presence here much longer. 'I'll drive you home.'

'Don't trouble yourself. I came by tram and I can go home by tram.' For some reason she felt defiant. He didn't need to patronize her like this. 'Besides, you don't want a recurrence of the flu.'

'I've said I'll drive you, and so I will.'

Helen looked at them both in exasperation. They were so obviously meant for each other, and so obviously refusing to see it. Half an hour later she showed them both out of the door, and sat down, wilting.

She had been feeling much stronger lately. It was a strange phenomenon, but now that Frank was slowing down, Helen's own health seemed to be improving. He was becoming more dependent on her, and subtly but surely it was restoring her strength in a way she had never expected.

Perhaps someday they could even follow her own dream and retire to the country, whether or not Daniel stayed in sole charge of the Roxy, Helen thought wistfully. Perhaps someday Frank might even revert to being like the loving young man he had been when she first knew him. Dreams weren't only for the young, though she knew it would take a miracle to shift Frank out of London . . .

Amy sat beside Daniel in the car in which he'd first taken her and Tess back to Aveley Square. The time that Tess had sat so indignantly, relegated to the back seat, while Amy had sat beside him in damp-palmed excitement, and known for the first time that a young man was interested in her.

She sat stiffly now, wanting the ghosts to go and leave her in peace. Wanting this journey to last for ever, yet wishing desperately that it would end. When it did, Daniel kept the engine running as he reached across her to open the passenger door for her.

255

She could feel the warmth of his breath. She could smell the special, personal scent of him. She could touch him if she wanted to. She only had to put out her hand. If she dared, she could even throw herself into his arms and beg him to take her back, away from this waste of a life she had chosen . . .

Both of them saw Bert hovering behind the glass window of the show-room at the same time. He had a client with him, and he was almost bursting with pride as he showed off the latest Austin car. Just like a bantam cock on a dung-heap, Amy thought irreverently, knowing it was how her old gran would have described him at that moment.

'Goodbye, Amy,' Daniel said.

'Goodbye,' she said in a muffled voice, and scrambled out of the car, hearing it roar away as she went indoors and rushed up the stairs before anybody could see the stinging tears in her eyes. And even before she'd climbed the stairs, she'd come to a decision.

'If you want us to be married, Bert, then I accept,' she said without expression.

She had nothing to lose by it. And the alternative was to brazen it out if Giles carried out his threat, and hope to survive the scandal of a newspaper story. But why bother, when this was simple and effective and would put a stop to his little game? She'd already lost Daniel, so what did anything else matter?

'You mean it?' he said, startled at her forthright manner, after he'd fretted over the time it was taking her to say anything more on the subject.

'When did I ever say anything I didn't mean? But we'll have it in writing that it's to be a marriage of convenience, and nothing will ever change that. Separate rooms, just like it is now. And I want it all done legal-like, witnessed properly and all.'

'You and your legal-like,' he said, smiling and uncaring

and indulging her with a nod, because a bit of paper wasn't going to change anything. He didn't want her as a bed-partner anyway. He just wanted to keep his pride intact and his business flourishing. There was more of the ambitious entrepreneur in him than he'd realized until recently, and he wasn't throwing all that away for some cowardly sod who was trying it on with him through an anonymous letter.

He felt a flutter of relief. At least the bastard hadn't discovered his real secret, the one that would throw a cat among the aristocratic pigeons.

And Amy steadfastly refused to dwell on the fact that what she was about to do would push real happiness even further out of her reach. Happiness was a state of mind that seemed destined to elude her for ever, she decided stoically. She just had to make the best of it. It was exactly what Gran Moore would have said. Though if there was any blame attached to anyone for forcing her into this sham of a marriage with Bert Figgins, it lay squarely on Giles Beaumont's shoulders.

Hatred for him was the uppermost emotion in her mind as Bert set about making immediate plans for the wedding, which was to be small and private and quick. Hatred was a safer emotion than any other, Amy discovered. You had nothing to spare for weeping when you hated.

At the end of February Amy became Mrs Bert Figgins at the register office – by special licence, which Gran Moore would have called a shameful hole-and-corner affair, and one that was only resorted to by folk who had something to hide.

They had told no one of their plans but the two witnesses, but of course Bert had insisted on putting a notice in the column of every London newspaper, so that any interested parties would be sure to see it. Including the anonymous letter-writer, he told Amy jubilantly. The witnesses were Maisie and Archie, which Amy considered an indignity, but by now she was too uncaring to argue.

They treated the pair of them to lunch in the dining-room of a nearby hotel, seated among the potted palms and with a ladies' three-piece orchestra playing discreet music. Bert and Archie sniggered together and behaved like overgrown school chums, while Maisie sat in silent, miserable embarrassment, too overcome in their company to say a word.

'We must see about getting the sign above the show-room changed as soon as possible,' Bert announced when the meal was over. He and Archie were awash with brandy while Amy and Maisie merely sipped cold water.

'In what way?'

'Oh, come on, Amy gel,' he said impatiently. 'It'll have to be "Figgins' Car Sales – Props. Bert and Amy Figgins" now, won't it? Have to let the public know of our new status, don't we? Though I don't suppose it's likely to be "Figgins and Son" in the foreseeable future, is it?'

Amy heard Archie giggle, and knew that Bert must have told him everything about the anonymous letter that had produced today's farce of a wedding. She was filled with a sudden acute shame. A marriage should be sanctified by God, not arranged at speed because of one man's vindictiveness and the lecherous needs of two others. She suddenly saw that this was a marriage of convenience for Bert and Archie more than herself. Bert could play the charade of the respectable married man, while continuing his disgusting double life . . .

'Are you all right, miss – madam?' she heard Maisie whisper. 'You've gawn fearful white.'

'I feel a bit faint. I'll be all right in a minute, but I think I'll just go to the ladies' cloakroom.'

'I'll come wiv yer,' Maisie said, glad to get away from these two men who spoke in riddles half the time and didn't seem to notice anything but themselves.

And on the wedding day too, the girl thought indignantly. Not that she was under any illusions about that! Miss Amy was still keeping to her separate room, to Maisie's certain knowledge, and a bloody good thing too. Maisie for one wouldn't want a chap who mucked about with other chaps making up to *her* after lights-out. The thought of it made her shudder.

'I'm all right now, Maisie,' Amy said with a little smile. 'It was so hot in there, that's all. We'll be going soon, anyway. My – husband will want to open up the show-room this afternoon.'

If she said it enough times she might be able to believe it. Bert Figgins' wife. Mrs Bert Figgins. Bert Figgins was her husband, for better for worse, until death did them part, to love and honour and obey. She smothered a sob in her throat and lifted her chin. She'd made her bed and she had to lie on it, and just as long as it wasn't Bert's bed, she'd cope. She'd bloody well have to.

That evening, Frank Easton bought a newspaper on his way home through the freezing yellow fog, and it was Frank who saw the notice in the hatches, matches and despatches column of the newspaper.

'Well, I'm buggered! So your little lady-love has got herself hitched. Seems like you'll have to be looking around for a new bit of skirt, Daniel, unless you intend to stay a mother's boy all your life.'

Daniel ignored the sarcastic words, said with less gusto than of old, and snatched the newspaper out of his father's hands. The words wavered in front of him, and all that registered was that Amy had got married to Bert Figgins. There was no going back on that. His senses reeling, he decided she must have felt something for the fellow, after all.

'She could have told me,' he said savagely. 'She must

have known what she was planning when she was here to look at Tess's things.'

Frank guffawed. 'Why should she? You're nothing to her now, boy, and the sooner you realize that the better. You're wasting your time thinking of her. One bit o' skirt's the same as the next, and you'll soon find another if you put your mind to it.'

Daniel caught his mother's glance and pitied her for putting up with this oaf all her married life. But apart from the sympathetic look she gave him, he was surprised to see her go to Frank and put her arm round his shoulders as he began a bout of harsh dry coughing.

'Will you take a glass of brandy, Frank? These pea-soupers do your chest no good at all, and the doctor's cough medicine doesn't seem to help much at the moment.'

For a few seconds he clung to her as the bout of coughing racked him. It was incongruous, Daniel thought, to see his mother supporting a man who had briefly changed from an ogre to a child.

'Brandy then,' he wheezed, as soon as he could speak, his eyes streaming. 'You're a good woman, Helen. You know what a man needs better than any damn fool of a quack.'

'I always did,' Daniel thought he heard her say pithily as she went to the kitchen to fetch the spirit.

But all his thinking for the rest of the evening and far into the night was concentrated on Amy. This was Amy's wedding night, and long before now she would be wrapped in Bert Figgins' arms and he would be having his fill of her.

The thought of them together tormented him. She belonged to Bert now, and Daniel wondered if he should have been more aggressive and taken her away from him when he had the chance.

There was no need for them ever to meet again now. As

his father had said, he should look for someone else to share his life. But far from giving him comfort, the thought of it merely turned his stomach.

After their wedding lunch, Amy discovered that Bert had no intention of working that afternoon. He and Archie had other plans. When they arrived back at the show-room, she gaped with surprise.

'It was all done for you, gel, while we was getting spliced. What do you think?' he asked, as she saw the bunting draped across the large picture windows – and the hand-painted notice placed inside, where no one could fail to see it:

> Due to the marriage of Mr Bert Figgins and Miss Amy Moore, this establishment will be closed for one week while the happy couple have a well-earned honeymoon. We look forward to seeing all our clients on our return.

She read it out loud, her cheeks burning now at the implications of the words. They were completely untrue, but they offended her all the same. And it was more for Bert's face-saving than for her, she thought in a fury. She whirled round on the pavement after they had all alighted from Archie's motor.

'I'm not going anywhere with you,' she raged, and Bert caught her arm and hurried her inside, followed by the others.

'Oh yes you are,' he hissed in her ear. 'It will underline our new status. When Archie told his brother about our marriage, he insisted on laying on a spread for us tonight. We're invited down to The Gables for the week, and Ronald will be asking a few chums for the weekend to liven things up and give us a bit of a celebration. We don't want Ronald to suspect things ain't as they should be. You're my wife now, so just you behave like it, at least in public.'

His fingers gripped her arm cruelly as he pushed her ahead of him up the stairs, and she felt a moment's panic. In other words, she was bought and paid for, and the lawyer's bit of paper stating that this marriage was in name only counted for nothing if Bert decided to change things. Not that she believed he ever would, especially while he was enmeshed with Archie Derbisham. It would have happened before now if it was ever going to, but still . . .

'Naturally I'll put on a show in public,' she whipped back at him. 'Just behave yourself in private, and I'm changing the lock on my door just to make sure!'

His easy laugh and change of mood told her she didn't have anything to fear on that score. And it wasn't such a bad idea to get away for a week. A honeymoon would be expected from all the friends who clearly assumed this was a love match. It was dear and kind of Ronald Derbisham to do this for them, just as he'd done for their engagement, and she could hardly throw his generosity back in his face.

And it would be best if she wasn't here, just in case Daniel Easton came storming round to Figgins' Car Sales, demanding to know just what she thought she was playing at to tie herself to a man she didn't love.

Not that he would, of course. But if he ever did, she knew she wouldn't be able to face him without breaking down, and The Gables suddenly became a sanctuary she could run to. It was the only place left to her.

21

As the days following the wedding became weeks and
then months, Amy made herself believe that Daniel
hadn't cared, after all. There was no word from him,
not even a note. It was no more than she had any right
to expect, but she felt bereft now, knowing she had made
her choice and there was no going back on it. Everything
had changed . . . so many changes since she and Tess were
carefree together.

She no longer hated Tess. She missed her more than
ever. Tess had been her one real friend, and she had no
one now to whom she could talk really freely. Maisie had
her place in the world, and since she wasn't aware that
her mistress had been a maid herself such a short time
ago, it simply wasn't done for Amy to confide in the
girl whole-heartedly. Amy knew well enough that Maisie
would recoil from too much familiarity. There were limits
between mistresses and servants, and it was an unspoken
pattern that Amy remembered well.

Jane Broome called her on the telephone in the middle
of April.

'Amy darling, I wondered if you'd care to come trousseau shopping with me in town on Friday. Ronald and I
have finally set the date, and the wedding's to be in early
July, which is quite ridiculous of course, since there's such
masses of things to do and I can't *possibly* be ready in
time . . .'

Jane's musical voice trilled on and on, implying total
panic but with the underlying assurance that of course she
would be ready on the due date, since there would always
be a little man or a little seamstress to pick up any pieces

that still needed to be done. And naturally the sun would shine and the day would be perfect for this couple who were so much in love and were to be married in church with pomp and ceremony, so different from the wedding that had been shunted in between several other shot-gun affairs at a register office . . .

'I'd love to come trousseau shopping with you, Jane,' Amy said brightly.

'Good. It will be tremendous fun. I'll pick you up in my motor about ten-thirty, darling. We'll have lunch somewhere in town, and when we've finished we can take tea at the Ritz. See you then.'

The phone went dead and Amy replaced the instrument slowly. Tea at the Ritz. Trousseau shopping, at the best and most expensive places, naturally. Jane's world.

For a moment, she felt like crying. It was a fine and wonderful thing to have fitted in so smoothly and to be invited to share a day with this nice girl who had simply assumed that Amy was one of her set, despite Bert's obvious working-class manners and speech. Jane had first seen Amy at Flannery's dancing rooms, in the company of Daniel Easton, who could pass for a toff any day of the week . . .

Without warning, Amy gave up the struggle to keep her chin up and not let the buggers get her down, as Gran used to say, but the tears flowed unchecked as she stood in the cramped little office of Figgins' Car Sales.

Bert found her there.

'Good God, what's wrong, gel? I thought it was a cat wailing. We've got customers in the show-room. Don't wanter frighten 'em off, do yer? There's a new spring coat in it for yer if we sell this model.'

For a minute Amy couldn't speak, and then the tears changed unexpectedly to laughter. Shrill, high laughter, because it was all so daft.

What a bloody, mixed-up world she lived in, where she

was married to one man and loved another; where her husband had a fancy-man, and the two of them pretended to be something they were not; where they spent their nights in separate rooms and half the time neither knew what the other was doing. It was all a mockery, and there were times when she thought she should go down on her hands and knees and say sorry to God, or whoever was looking down on them, for mucking up His whole bloody scheme of things . . .

'Christ, now what's up?' Bert said irritably, which sent her off into more peals of laughter.

He banged the door of the office shut and went back to what he understood best: his beloved motors and his grovelling to the customers, which none the less produced excellent results. Amy would get her bloody new spring coat, he thought grimly, if he had to drag her around the shops himself to buy it. They had to be seen to be prosperous and happy. It was good business.

Once he'd made the expected sale, he went upstairs exuberantly to tell Amy the good news. He waved a cheque in front of her nose. By then she had recovered herself, and was bent over a cushion case she was embroidering. He ignored her red-rimmed eyes and pinched face and sat beside her smilingly.

'What did I tell you? Shall we go up West on Monday morning sometime and see about that new coat for you then?' They closed on Monday mornings. It was the worst day of the week for car sales.

'If you like. I'm spending the day in town with Jane on Friday, buying her wedding trousseau. She and Ronald are getting married in July.'

'Are they?' Bert said carelessly. He looked at her sharply. Christ, but she wasn't having second thoughts about their arrangement, was she? She didn't want him to start getting amorous or anything, did she? The thought made him go cold inside. He was already wondering how he could get around to telling her that he and Archie wanted to go to Switzerland together for a week next winter, but he'd cross that bridge when he came to it.

'Amy, are you all right? You do look a bit off-colour, gel. In any other circumstances I'd ask if there was going to be the patter of tiny feet.'

'Don't be stupid, Bert. I'm fine. Women have certain times when they feel a bit weepy, that's all.'

She'd never resorted to such feeble tactics before, but she knew it suited the moment as he sprang away from her in a kind of horror. Clearly, Bert had no wish to know anything about a woman's physiology.

He changed the subject quickly. 'By the way, I'm going for a spin in Archie's flyer on Sunday, did I tell you? I'll be gone all day. You'll be all right, won't you?'

'Of course I will. I don't need wet-nursing,' she said, resenting the fact that he thought she did. And knowing very well, as he did, that he'd never mentioned going flying with Archie until that moment. She hardly cared what he did, anyway. If he wanted to risk breaking his neck, it was up to him. All the same . . .

'You will be careful, won't you, Bert?'

He gave her a beatific smile. 'Don't you worry about me, old girl. I've got a charmed life, or so they tell me.'

Amy didn't bother asking who had ever told him that. But she supposed it was true. Bert Figgins had come up smelling of violets all right. What with meeting the Derbishams and getting his share of her money to start up this place, and then becoming 'respectable' by marrying her, Bert Figgins wasn't doing so badly. She paused in her sewing, realizing how much she had done to help him on his way, and her mouth twisted.

Anyway, she wasn't going to worry about any of them any more. Not Bert or Archie or Daniel. On Friday she was going to spend a day with Jane and pretend to be posh.

What she hadn't reckoned on was that Jane was genuinely concerned at her peakiness when they'd done a morning's shopping and were seated in a little restaurant, tucked away in an alcove for a quick lunch.

'Amy, tell me if I've got it wrong, but are you and Bert already – you know?'

Amy looked at her blankly.

'Oh, you know what I mean, darling! Are you knitting little bootees?'

Amy's face filled with colour. 'Good Lord, no!' she said, and laughed.

'Well, all right, but I don't see why it's so funny, darling. I mean, it's hardly impossible, is it, now you're a married lady, even if it is a bit soon.'

'It is for me. For us.'

Jane stared at her, but Amy knew she'd already said too much to retract. She gave a small sigh.

'Jane, I'm sorry, but I'm afraid we've deceived everyone a little. Our marriage isn't a proper one, you see. There won't be any babies, not ever.'

Jane went pink now. Her voice was hushed. 'Oh dear, I'm so sorry. You mean there's some problem? I've heard of such things, Amy. And if it's any help, I know of a marvellous man in Harley Street who can –'

'No, it's not that kind of problem.' Amy bit her lip. 'It's not a problem at all, really. Bert and I are friends, Jane, and nothing more. Business partners and platonic friends. It just seemed a good idea to be married, partly to save any unnecessary gossip.'

'Good heavens. Then you aren't – you don't –'

'No, we don't.'

Jane was shrewder than Amy gave her credit for. Her voice softened after a moment, and she put her hand over Amy's as it lay tensely on the table-top.

'Tell me to mind my own business if you like, Amy, but I think you should have married the other one. The one

267

who was so mad about you the first time we met you at Flannery's. What was his name?'

'Daniel.' Amy almost choked on it, and there was hardly any need to say more. She took a deep breath and looked Jane straight in the eye.

'Will you promise to say nothing about this to anyone, Jane? It would be humiliating if people knew the truth – about Bert and me.'

'Of course I won't say anything. You didn't need to ask,' Jane said at once, and they both knew it wasn't only Bert they were talking about.

Jane changed the conversation quickly. This day might have been a bit of an ordeal for Amy, she saw now, buying satin underwear and nightgowns, and the elegant evening wear for Jane's honeymoon with Ronald, which they would be spending in Italy.

'What do you think will happen about the political situation and the miners?' she asked casually.

Amy blinked. She knew little about what was going on, except that the words general strike were being bandied about everywhere.

'I'm an ignoramus about it, I'm afraid,' she said, feeling guilty not to be following the fortunes of the brave miners who wanted a proper wage for a horrible job.

'Ronald is very politically minded,' Jane said. 'It wouldn't surprise me if he decided to stand for Parliament one of these days. He says the coal-owners are getting fat while their workers are forced to take lower wages and work longer hours. The government subsidy for the coal industry is only temporary, and it expires on April the thirtieth. What happens then is anybody's guess.'

What was happening, Bert told Amy later with relish, was that from midnight on 3 May, the workers in iron and coal, transport, printing, metal and building industries, electricity and gas supplies were to come out on strike in support of the miners.

'Me and Archie were at a big rally in Hyde Park yesterday,' he said excitedly. 'The TUC's behind it all, and so is the rest of the country. We plan to go up in the flyer on the day to see what's happening. Think of it, Amy. No trams, no lorries, no trains or newspapers, no anything.'

'No food?' she said sarcastically, thinking he was more animated over this than almost anything.

'Oh, the government's seen to that. There are plenty of volunteers ready to distribute food. Nobody's going to starve.'

'Only the miners.'

'Well, that needn't worry you. We've got plenty of coal and, anyway, the winter's over. They picked the wrong time to do it, if you ask me.'

He was so complacent these days. So bloody complacent, Amy thought. He had never felt so good about life . . . he and Archie. While she limped along, knowing what a mess it all was. And this strike probably wouldn't solve anything. In the end, strikes rarely did. Daniel had always said that, from his book-learning.

'Why are you so damn pleased about it, anyway?' she asked, over their evening meal.

'Because if it goes on for any length of time, people will get fed up with trams and trains that never arrive, and think about buying their own motors. Why do you think I put an extra-large advertisement in the newspaper, gel?'

Amy looked at it in disbelief as he thrust the paper at her. In large letters in the middle pages, it announced that Figgins' Car Sales would be open through strike or blizzard, and that wherever you wanted to go, a private motor got you there quicker. It was crude and obvious, and reeked of Bert's clumsiness. She felt ashamed at his cashing in on the strike before it had even begun.

'I'm putting another poster in the show-room window, advising strikers that if it ain't no fun relying on shanks's pony to get about, they can always rely on Figgins' motors. Quick thinking, eh gel?' he said in delight at his own cleverness.

'Quick as a rat,' she agreed dryly.

When the strike began, it was as if some areas of the city had become frozen in time. Around Claymore Street nothing moved, not even the occasional private motor, or street urchin whizzing past on a bicycle or pushing a barrow, or horse-drawn cab. It was eerie. Even pedestrians seemed more inclined to stay indoors at first, for fear of legions of pickets at tram depots and factory gates suddenly pouncing on them and accusing them of being blacklegs.

'It's so quiet,' Amy said. 'It's like a ghost town.'

'Not for long,' Bert assured her. 'You give it a coupla days, and see if business don't pick up. There won't be any more papers to advertise us, but folk will remember the last one they saw, you see, and plenty have taken note of our poster in the window.'

He disgusted Amy. He saw no further than what was in it for him. The wireless bulletins assured people to stay calm and that everything was under control. Food was plentiful and would be distributed by troops, volunteers would keep the essential services going, and special constables would ensure that no unnecessary hazard affected life or property.

'Special constables!' snorted Frank Easton when the strike was six days old and already folk were getting restless and uneasy. He eyed his son up and down as he got ready to go out on his late afternoon and early evening shift. 'I hope you ain't planning to take this job on permanently, boy!'

Daniel ignored him, shrugging into his thick overcoat. It

would be late when he returned, and the nights could still be raw, even at this time of year. His father needn't have any fears, he thought. This was a temporary measure, but something he was keen to undertake, since the Roxy was now closed for the duration.

It sounded a bit like a war, he realized, and hoped that wasn't prophetic.

'You'll be careful, won't you, Daniel?' his mother said as he made to leave the house.

'I'll be all right. Don't worry. I'll see you later.'

He wasn't taking his car. There was no point in risking it. He'd seen roughnecks rocking private motors violently, shaking the guts out of the machines and injuring the occupants who were suspected of being scabs on their way to work. He hadn't told his mother about that. He reported to his makeshift unit at the local police station, where the specials were just about tolerated by the regulars.

'Nothing much doing around here at the moment, though there's reports of plenty of open-air meetings and banner-waving in the parks, and one lot marching through the streets over Bermondsey way looking a bit ugly,' his sergeant said laconically. 'Nothing that need concern us, though.'

'What's your opinion of all this, Sarge?' Daniel asked him. 'They can't win, can they? The government's too well prepared. They've covered everything, and they'll win in the end. Even the wireless only gives out the news the government wants people to hear, so why do the strikers prolong the misery for their families?'

The thick-set sergeant looked at him sourly. He'd come up in the police force the hard way, and didn't want any snot-nosed young feller who looked as if he'd be more at home acting in one of them Hollywood pictures telling him about the rights and wrongs of society.

'Don't waste my time with questions, boy,' he growled.

'Just follow orders, and you'll do well enough. Opinions are best left to those who understand politics.'

In other words, Daniel decided, he was one of those bull-in-a-china-shop policemen who was probably one hundred per cent good at his job as long as it didn't involve thinking too much. He was a follower, not a leader, except when it came to doing something physical.

There wasn't time to think about anything from then on. Instructions for the new shift were being allocated before the old one had been dismissed, and almost simultaneously a runner came in with news of an outbreak of violence nearby.

'Right, men,' roared the sergeant. 'Forget all last orders. Everybody get round to Claymore Street, and don't spare the bastards. You'll get reinforcements from other units, so lay into 'em and disperse 'em as fast as you can.'

'Did he say Claymore Street, Harry?' Daniel said sharply to the man beside him.

'Yeah. Some car show-room or somefin'. Weren't you listening? The windows have been smashed and the motors wrecked. Silly buggers should have pinched one of them fine machines if they'd had any sense. I don't fancy getting tied up wiv 'em. Can we get out of going?'

He was talking to the air and being pushed along with the rest, as Daniel ran blindly out of the building and into the direction of Claymore Street. Dear God, it was Figgins' Car Sales the bastards were wrecking. It was Amy's life that was in danger.

''Ere, where do you think you're off to?' one of the regulars yelled at him. 'Stay with the others, Easton. There's safety in numbers.'

He didn't care about that. What was his safety compared with Amy's? The thought of her being terrified by thugs vandalizing her premises was enough to put wings on his feet, and as if pushed into action by the sight of him, the rest of his unit thundered after him.

As they turned into Claymore Street, it was to see a uniformed group from another unit approaching from one of the side streets, whistles screeching in warning of their arrival. There was a large mob at the car show-room, and the road was littered with broken glass that crunched under the feet when the constables moved in, wielding their truncheons. In the crush of people, there was no telling whether Amy or Bert was among the crazed mob.

The vandals turned on the police. Their leader had a gravelly voice that reverberated above the din.

'Get the rozzers, boys. Kill the buggers!'

Daniel felt a frisson of fear, and heard Harry Bacon begin to sob beside him. He glanced towards him.

'Don't let them see you're scared,' he hissed. 'Stick close to me and behave like a man.'

It was an ironic word to use, when these bastards were behaving like animals. They used fists and sticks and knives, and as one of them closed in on him Daniel felt a keen piercing pain on his cheek and then the trail of hot blood trickling down his face. But there was hardly time to register it.

'Daniel!' Suddenly he heard Amy's voice screaming his name and jerked up his head to see her leaning from an upstairs window. At the same moment he saw Bert Figgins try to haul her back inside. A stone went hurtling upwards and narrowly missed her, sending a shower of glass inside the room where she stood. Daniel roared at her to get back.

'Do you know these people, Easton?' his sergeant shouted at him as he dodged the flailing fists of a smaller man than himself and twisted him easily and cruelly into submission in his great hands.

'Yes,' he shouted back.

'Then you and the blubbermouth will stay behind and get all the particulars when this is over, seeing as you're such a book-learner.'

He could hardly refuse, and at least he could see for himself that Amy was all right, Daniel thought grimly.

Gradually, as more police reinforcements appeared, they outnumbered and overcame the mob. A police vehicle was on hand to bundle those who weren't knocked senseless off to the lock-up. Casualties were put into an ambulance manned by volunteers and taken to the nearest hospital.

When everything was quiet again and a soft dusk hid the brutality of what had taken less than an hour to control, the shattered glass in the street shimmered like diamonds in the yellow gas-light. How long before there was no street lighting at all, Daniel wondered briefly, as he and Harry Bacon climbed the stairs to the living quarters above the show-room. How long before everything of value in the country dwindled and died -- or would his father be proved right, and the government's strength and foresight make a mockery of this whole futile strike?

Bert Figgins met him at the top of the stairs, bristling with anger more than nerves.

'Christ, what are they recruiting for the police these days?' he whipped out, seeing Harry's pale thin face, and needing to hit out at somebody verbally since he hadn't had the guts to face the mob physically. He rounded on Daniel. 'Have you seen what they've done to my motors? Christ knows how I'm going to get compensation. I just hope the bloody insurance will cough up, that's all.'

'Is Amy all right?' Daniel said shortly, since it was obvious that all this oaf was interested in was his precious business.

Bert scowled. 'The silly bitch might not have been if I hadn't dragged her away from the window.'

Daniel pushed past him as Amy came rushing towards him, ashen-faced, her eyes wide and dark with fear.

'Oh – *Daniel*, thank God you're safe!' she choked. 'I was so frightened. I kept losing sight of you, and I thought they were going to kill you. Your poor face is bleeding.'

It dawned on him that she was voicing fears for him, not for herself. For a second they stood apart, separated by a yard of space, by all that had gone before, by Tess's treachery, by her forced marriage to Bert Figgins. And then they were in each other's arms, and later when Harry Bacon was boasting to his girlfriend about his part in the day, he was able to report the extraordinary sight of seeing his fellow constable clasping the lady in his arms, while the husband stood scowling by and never said a word.

But Amy and Daniel each acknowledged secretly and separately that one thing had never changed, and that was the love each had for the other.

'The insurance will pay for this,' Archie said expansively. Bert seemed to be little more than a shivering jelly in the clear light of morning when he saw exactly what had happened to his beloved motors. 'You're making mountains out of molehills, Bert.'

'Molehills! Thousands of quids' worth of damage!'

'Don't exaggerate. There's only one motor really dented and another scratched. It's nothing that a good repair man can't put right. As for the show-room window, I've always thought that we should have tougher glass in it with more divisions between the panes. It was asking for trouble to have those great sheets of glass.'

'You're taking all this mighty calmly.' Bert scowled, more than miffed that Archie hadn't come rushing up to town last night when he telephoned, and didn't seem too upset now. After he'd spent a couple of hours boarding up the damaged windows too, so that no more vandals could get at his expensive motors.

He was just as miffed because Amy had shut herself away in her room and refused to come out until Bert had got control of himself. The fact that she'd accused him of acting like a hysterical prima donna did nothing for his ego at all.

'There's no point in doing anything else,' Archie said. 'Buildings and machines can be repaired. As long as you're not hurt, then the rest can be taken care of. People are more precious than possessions, my dear.'

Bert looked at him blindly. How wise and clever he was, this almost aristocrat who was the most important person in his life now. And how ironic that sharp-tongued Amy should have said the same thing. He let out his breath in a long sigh.

'I know. I just panicked when that terrible crowd started throwing stones. You'd think they'd be pleased they could buy their own motors and beat the striking trams and trains.'

'Not if they couldn't afford them,' Archie said dryly. 'And you made a mistake in advertising so blatantly. Still, there's no real harm done, and I suggest you come down to the country for a while and let somebody else get on with putting it all to rights.'

'Amy probably won't go,' Bert said disagreeably. 'She's giving me the great silent treatment, as if all this was my fault.'

'I wasn't asking Amy. If she wants to stay here and supervise things, it's up to her, isn't it?'

Bert cheered up at once. He could get away. He could abandon the strikers and the moaners to their own devices, and be in the peace and tranquillity of the country. He soon rid himself of the stab of guilt at leaving Amy behind, but she knew the way things were when they were married. She was the one who insisted they should still lead separate lives, so she could hardly complain when Bert did just that. He had no doubt that if she pressed it, Archie would say that of course she could come too. The Gables was so large that they didn't ever need to come into contact except for meals. But Amy didn't press it.

'My goodness, you mean you're trusting me with Figgins' Car Sales?' She didn't try to hide her sarcasm. 'You don't really intend leaving the place in the care of two women day and night, do you?'

'Two women? Oh, you're including the maid,' Archie said, in the manner of one to whom servants were invisible. 'If it makes you feel easier I'll install a caretaker from dusk until daylight, and the workmen will be here today, of course.'

'Of course. They'll break the strike to do your bidding, will they?'

Archie looked at her coldly. She was too outspoken by half, this pretty wife of Bert's, and too damned canny as well . . . If she'd been born ten years earlier, he had no doubt she'd have been campaigning with those irritating Pankhurst women . . .

'They'll be estate workers. We employ our own builders and repair people on the Derbisham estate. They don't belong to any union.'

'How nice. I hope any passing picketer realizes that. Do they wear special labels or something?' Amy asked innocently, at which Archie simply turned his back on her.

'It's time we were leaving, Bert. We'll take the flyer up for a spin this afternoon. You need something to take your mind off last night, you poor old thing.'

And *she* didn't, Amy thought furiously, still seething that afternoon at the way the Archie Derbishams of the world could pull whatever strings they chose. Already the broken glass in the street had been swept away, the small broken window upstairs replaced, and two men were busy at work on the show-room alterations. The damaged motors had been removed from public gaze and would be taken away later for repair when the insurance assessors had inspected them.

A *Business As Usual* sticker was placed across the remaining show-room window, but so far there had been no customers to brighten up this dreary day. She didn't know when Bert would be back, and she had told Maisie to get off home and see her old mum, knowing it would take her hours to get across London on foot, unless she could thumb a lift with one of the few vehicles still on the road. If she couldn't get back that night, Amy told her, it didn't matter.

By late afternoon the workmen had finished for the day. Part of the outside of the show-room was still boarded up,

278

and the men promised to be back early in the morning. By the time they left, the caretaker was at his post in the office with last week's newspaper and a deck of cards, some bread and cheese and a bottle of ale for company.

The long night stretched ahead of Amy. Before eight o'clock she had a bath and got into her nightdress and dressing gown, intending to have an early supper and then go to bed. When she heard a footstep on the passage outside her door she assumed it was either Bert or Maisie coming back, and then she heard someone knock. Cautiously, she opened the door a few inches.

And then her heart leapt, because Daniel was standing there.

'I told the caretaker I was a relative,' he said. 'I had to be sure you were all right, Amy. I – oh God, I just couldn't keep away any longer. I've thought about you all night long, wanting you and cursing everything that's come between us. I still love you, Amy, you know that, don't you? You knew it last night.'

She felt the dryness of a little sob in her throat, and she was hardly conscious of either of them moving. She merely seemed to sway towards him, and the next moment she was in his arms and he had kicked the door behind him, shutting out the rest of the world.

'We shouldn't be here like this,' she sobbed against his chest, when she was dazed with his kisses and the passion that seemed to have burst like a flame between them after months of repression.

'Where else should we be?' he demanded, the masculine aggressor now that her responses had told him everything he needed to know. Whatever she felt for Bert Figgins, it was nothing compared to this. Never had been, nor ever could be.

She didn't try to deny the unspoken truth of it. She

spoke in a brittle, high voice, as if she had to try and put everything right at once.

'Daniel, I'm so sorry – for everything. For making such a mess of things.'

'Hush, sweetheart. You didn't make a mess of things. It was – well, it was fate playing with us.'

He couldn't bring Tess's name between them, or blame her for what she had done. Poor, foolish Tess, who had let her life slip away in her craving to be fashionable. He couldn't condemn her now. But Amy could.

'Tess began it all, and we can't hide away from the truth of that.' She raised a tear-blotched face to his, and he saw how pain darkened her lovely eyes to a deep honey colour. 'I suppose she couldn't help herself. She'd never had much love in her life, and it was all she wanted, really. Just to be loved.'

'Isn't that what we all want? I love you, Amy, and if you knew how tortured I've been since you married that Figgins chap. Why did you do it? Why didn't you wait?' he asked in a deep voice that smouldered with sudden anger.

'As you waited?' She sprang away from him, her face flushed. 'You rushed into marriage with Tess, didn't you? You couldn't have been all that repelled by the idea!'

They stared at one another, the distance between them widening again, until Daniel seized her hands in his and held them so tight that she couldn't move away from him.

'You rushed into it with Bert Figgins, didn't you?' he said. 'Do you know why I married Tess? Just because she wanted to die respectable. Unbelievable, isn't it?'

He heard her gasp, and went on ruthlessly. 'My mother was suffering because I'd left home, but even that wouldn't have forced me into marrying Tess when I knew I had nothing to blame myself for. I never loved Tess – but you wouldn't listen to anything I said. Anyway, what does any of it matter now? She went to pieces when she heard that she was going to die, and it seemed little enough to do to give her my name. We both knew it wouldn't be for long, and all she wanted was the status of a married woman.'

Amy felt choked now. 'I thought I knew her, but I'd never have guessed that. But we never really know people, do we? We only let them see what we want them to see. Perhaps we can never really trust anybody but ourselves.'

She shivered. She had her own family secret, and it could still awaken her in the night in a burning sweat, the shame of it overwhelming her. She'd never trusted anyone else with that knowledge. Daniel's arms folded around her, and without realizing it, she melted against him.

'You can trust me, Amy darling. I'd never hurt you.'

In her thin cotton nightdress and dressing-gown, she became aware of the erratic beating of his heart against her own, and realized how little there was between them. So little keeping them apart . . . Her head lifted slowly to look into his eyes, and her breath caught.

'Oh, my Amy, I want you so much.' The words seemed to be dragged out of him.

'And I want you,' she whispered, knowing exactly what he meant, her need soaring to match his own.

'Is he here?' He couldn't speak Bert's name now.

'No one's here except the caretaker, and he won't disturb us.'

She was giving her consent and they both knew it. She wanted to feel his body become part of hers, to be whole and alive at last.

She was drowsy with the aftermath of love. She had never known it could be like this – the fusing of body and mind, the completeness with a man. Even the first sweet pain when he entered her body was her own special offering to love. At that moment Daniel had looked into her eyes with some dismay at her smothered cry, and she had admitted in a mumbling voice that he was the first . . .

Even while he felt a great tenderness in the knowledge, it was a shock to him. He'd truly believed that her marriage was a proper one. It was only later, arms wrapped around each other in the soft darkness of the night, that Amy told him the marriage was no more than a legality, a sham.

'You're not to stay with him,' Daniel said doggedly. 'You're to come away with me, and we'll start a new life together. We belong together, Amy.'

She moved restlessly in the bed. It sounded so perfect, so idyliic, and so impossible . . . She took a deep breath.

'I can't do that, my love,' she said, her voice low. 'I made a promise to stay with Bert as his wife, for better for worse . . . till death us do part. Whether it was said before a preacher or a registrar, it was still said before God.'

'What are you saying? You know we should be together. I won't let you go on living this lie, Amy.'

'I'm married to Bert, and nothing can change that. Would you want me to throw away my good name to live in sin? You know what they call women who live with a man without being married to him.'

What was wrong with her? She asked herself the question a dozen times, and couldn't answer it. She was still blessed – or cursed – with the poor-but-honest mentality of the little maid wanting to make good, she thought bitterly. Despite the trappings of middle class she had assumed so easily, deep down she was still little Amy Moore, whose gran would be scandalized to know what Daniel Easton was asking of her.

Perhaps that was it, she thought with misery. Her own parents had let Gran down so badly, Amy knew it was up to her to stay on the straight and narrow, come what may. Even if she suspected that her own husband was a nancy boy with a life of his own . . .

'You could get the marriage annulled,' Daniel said

savagely. 'A doctor could prove that you've never been with a man.'

'But I have, my dearest,' she answered him huskily. 'I've been with you.'

Daniel leaned on one elbow in the bed, looking down at her. In the dim light from the window, she could see the outline of his body, the clean-cut muscular chest and arms faintly glistening with the exertions of passion, the strong shape of his head. She couldn't see his face, but she didn't need to to know that her pain was his too.

'Are you telling me you're prepared to throw all this away for the sake of Bert Figgins and his business?' he said deliberately, and she realized he was angry.

'It's my business too. It's something we've built up together. I've put money into it.' Defensively, her pride came to the fore.

'And that's important to you, is it? I never realized how commercially minded you were, Amy.'

'I'm not – at least, not in the way you mean. I'm just trying to be sensible. If I did as you said – moved out of here and in with you – what would your parents think? We'd never hear the end of it from your father, and what respect would your mother have for me? You haven't thought further than the moment, my love.'

'Do you think I give a damn about what people think?' He was still angry, and she put a hand on his arm, feeling how taut it was.

'But you must, darling. It was because of the damage other people could do that I agreed to marry Bert. I never told you about the blackmail letter, did I?'

It was clearly time to tell him now, so that he'd understand why she too had been pushed into marriage. He listened intently, and then pulled her back into his arms.

'I'd like to kill the bastard who did this to you,' he said, and Amy silently agreed with him, knowing in her heart that it was the same man who was responsible for all their

283

troubles. He rocked her close to him for long minutes, and then murmured against her hair.

'Then if you won't come and live with me, at least I must see you often. I'll come to you.'

'No. I don't think I could bear that,' she said softly. Once, she had thought it romantic and wonderful and sophisticated to have a secret lover, the way those heroines of the silver screen did. Now, she could only see the shame of it, and the constant anxiety that went with it.

'Are you pushing me out of your life, Amy?'

She shifted gently out of his arms. They still shared the same bed, and felt the warmth of each other's body, yet already Amy knew how far apart they were, and how far apart they had to be.

'I believe I am. I can't risk seeing you and knowing you're only a part of my life, you see. If I can't have all of you, it has to be nothing at all, Daniel. I can't bear the thought of secret meetings, or the risk of being seen or caught, or the risk of having a baby.'

'I would see that nothing like that happened,' he said at once.

'Did you see to it tonight? Did you plan any of this?'

'No, of course not.' He looked away from her. God, it could happen, and that would be disaster for Amy, because Bert would know she had been unfaithful to him. Unfaithful, in a marriage like this! It was so ludicrous it was almost laughable, except that Daniel had never felt less like laughing.

'But I'm offering you all of me,' he said urgently. 'In everything but name, we'd be married, my darling. In our hearts, we'd be married.'

She shook her head slowly. 'I can't. I've already made my vows, Daniel, and I can't cheat on them. Don't ask it of me, please – and we must both forget that tonight ever happened.'

He knew that she would never change her mind. She

was too strong-willed for that. If it meant cutting him out of her life for ever, she'd do it.

'Don't ask me to forget about tonight,' he said bitterly, throwing aside the bedcovers and reaching for his clothes. 'And don't tell me you'll ever forget it either. But don't worry. You won't see me again, if that's what you want. I'll go out of your life for good.'

'It's not what I want,' she said through dry lips. 'It's what has to be. What will you do?'

'God knows, but I'll probably get out of London,' he said grimly. 'Perhaps I'll sell the Roxy while it's still a going concern. I doubt that I'll have the stomach to bother with fairy-tales from now on. Perhaps I'll take my mother to live in the country, and my father can do as he damn well pleases. Don't worry, Amy, we'll all survive.'

She bit her lips hard. Didn't he know he was hurting her with these accusing words? As if she wanted to throw away every chance of happiness. Didn't he know she'd give her soul to be going with him, to some faraway place to share his life? And, oh God, she was so tempted, knowing that this could be the answer.

Who would know the truth, except for themselves and his parents? But she was too afraid. Fate seemed to have a habit of catching up with her. Daniel thought her strong, but she wasn't strong enough to take the chance.

She slipped out of bed and tied her dressing-gown tightly around her waist as Daniel thrust his arms into his overcoat.

'Will I ever see you again?'

He pulled her roughly to him. The scent of outdoors was on his clothes, and she closed her eyes as he kissed her almost brutally.

'I told you once that if you ever needed me, you only have to ask. You don't need me now, Amy.'

*　　*　　*

She didn't move for a long while after he had gone. She seemed to be transfixed, hardly able to believe that Daniel had been her lover for such a brief while, that they had been as close to heaven as two people could be, and now he was gone. If ever she needed him, she only had to call . . . but if he meant what he said and left London, she would have no idea how to find him.

She made no attempt to stifle the sobs welling up inside as she stumbled back to bed. She threw her arms across the pillow where his head had lain. but already the warmth of his body had gone.

Bert came back to town four days later. By then the general strike was over. Despite all the fuss and the banner-waving marches and protest meetings, one by one the striking organizations had gone back to work, knowing that the government had been better prepared than the unions, and that they couldn't win. Only the miners vowed to hold out, however long it took to get their demands met, and feeling betrayed by the unions.

'It gives the newspapers something to talk about, anyway,' Bert said. His main pleasure was that the printworkers were back in production and running his usual business advertisement again. He was more than pleased at seeing that the work on his premises had been done satisfactorily, with Archie footing the bill, and that Amy looked none the worse for staying in town alone.

Although she did look a bit pale, he observed, as if she'd been having too many late nights. Feeling expansive after his spell away, he tried to jolly her up.

'And what have you been doing with yourself, old girl? Have you and Maisie been burning the midnight oil?'

'No. Maisie stayed away for two nights, because her mother wasn't well,' Amy snapped.

'All right, don't bite my head off for that. Well then, did you see anybody or go anywhere?'

'Who should I see and where would I go!'

'Bloody hell, I think I'll go out and come in again. I was only trying to be friendly. What's got into you today?' he asked in genuine amazement.

Amy bit her lip. 'I've got a rotten headache, if you must know.'

She'd had it ever since Daniel left her. Tension and unhappiness and the arrival of the curse had ensured a miserable few days. She should be glad of the appearance of her monthly, but cussedly she knew she wasn't.

Terrible though it might have been explaining it all to Bert, at least a child would have been something of Daniel's . . . In those moments of despair, she had a sudden affinity with her mother's feelings when Tommy went away, leaving her with Amy. Leaving her with something of himself.

'I'm sorry, old thing. Can I get you anything for it?' Bert said, in quick sympathy.

She looked at him, her eyes blurred. He wasn't all bad. He cared for her in his own way, and she had gone into this marriage with her eyes wide open. They had to make the best of each other. And if he'd been a man with carnal desires, it might have been much worse.

'A hot cup of tea and a lie-down for a while should do the trick,' she said huskily.

'Coming up right away,' he said cheerfully. 'And I'll get you a hot-water bottle as well. A bit of comfort won't come amiss, eh?'

'Thank you, Bert,' she murmured. She really did feel unwell, and a sleep in the afternoon still felt like something of a luxury. Gran used to say that only actresses and tarts slept in the afternoons. Some might say ungenerously that Amy was a bit of both. She dismissed the thought and snuggled down beneath the bedcovers.

It seemed a long while before Bert brought her the tea and hot-water bottle. She was in that dazed half-state between waking and sleeping, the headache already partly dulled, and she groaned at the sound of his excited voice.

'Listen to this, Amy. I just popped out to buy an evening paper, and it's on the front page.'

'What is? Can't it wait?' she muttered.

He ignored her and read out the large black headline and the meaty bit of reporting beneath. 'Scandal of lord's son. The Honourable Giles Beaumont has been apprehended for embezzlement. Lord Beaumont's son has been forging cheques amounting to considerable sums of money to pay his gambling debts. The disgrace has put an immediate end to the engagement between Beaumont and the Honourable Thelma Parkes-Leighton, whose family have stated publicly that they no longer wish to be associated with the rogue.'

Bert couldn't get over it. 'What a turn-up, eh? Old Giles has been doing a bit of embezzling. So much for his airs and graces. I wonder what he'll get? Years, I shouldn't wonder, and good riddance. He'd once have been transported to Australia for far less of a crime – it's a pity they can't send him there now.'

He stopped in astonishment as Amy's startled exclamation changed to hysterical laughter. He'd never understand women if he lived to be a hundred, Bert thought, and thanked God fervently that he didn't really have to try.

23

Exactly six weeks after Amy had made her decision clear, Daniel signed over the ownership of the Roxy cinema to new people who were quick to sense a bargain when they saw it. The estate agent had known some likely buyers as soon as Daniel approached him. They were two middle-aged brothers keen on the prospect of talking pictures coming in very soon and making them a fortune. They were prepared to pay handsomely for the picture palace in a prime position in town, and their eagerness suited Daniel perfectly.

All his interest in the cinema had vanished, and the further away from the celluloid images he could get, the better. Since the cinema was now solely his, he had said nothing of his plans to his parents until the thing was done. And now he was on his way back from the solicitors' with the deed of sale in his pocket and a large cheque to wave under his father's nose. All the same, he didn't expect the next half-hour to be easy.

'You've done *what*?' Frank bellowed as soon as Daniel had said his piece. He began coughing and spluttering at once, and Helen moved anxiously behind his chair.

'I've sold the Roxy, and before you go off half-cocked, my next suggestion is that we sell this house. It's far too big for Mother to manage, for one thing – and for another, the London smogs get worse every year and do your chest no good at all. I suggest that we buy a place in the country, well away from town, where we can all put some clean fresh air in our lungs.'

Helen caught her breath. Daniel had become sharper and more aggressive of late, though not in a bad way, she thought approvingly. He had seemed to be in the wilderness for a long time, ever since the unfortunate affair with Tess Loveridge had damned any chance that he and Amy would get together.

But in these last few weeks he had seemed more positive in his thinking, and it was obvious to her now that he had been planning this move for some time. It was a good plan, because Amy was out of his reach, and he had to build his life without her. To Helen's relief, he seemed to be doing just that. All the same, his announcement about the Roxy had taken her by surprise.

'You young devil!' Frank spluttered. 'Doing this without so much as a kiss-my-arse or by-your-leave.'

'You handed over the Roxy to me,' Daniel said calmly. 'I decided I didn't want it and that the money from its sale could be put to good use.'

'And what's that, may I ask?'

'We could buy a small-holding. We'd get a couple of men in to teach me the rudiments of farming. We could go in for dairy-farming, or chickens.'

'God give me patience!' Frank snapped. 'Do you think you can learn to be a farmer in a few weeks? It takes years, boy.'

'I've got years. And you might have a few more if you agree to this.'

Helen put her hands on her husband's shoulders, breathing quickly.

'We'd both have more time to relax in the country, Frank. You know it's what I've always wanted.'

He turned to look up at her, seeing the faded prettiness that still shone through when her eyes became animated the way they were now.

'You think you'll have time to relax when this young fool has you running around feeding chickens?'

'And we'd be able to go for long walks across the fields,' she said blissfully, as if he hadn't spoken. 'In the spring we could pick the first catkins, and in the autumn there'd be blackberries in the hedgerows and I'd make my own preserves. You could make your own wine, Frank. Remember that bottle of home-made elderflower champagne we sampled once? You said at the time it must be grand to make wine yourself from the trees growing round about.'

'Good God, woman, you're as besotted as the boy with all this country talk. What of the winters when you're snowed in? Chickens still have to be fed and cows have to be milked. Farming doesn't stop because of a bit of bad weather.'

Daniel sat back in his chair, arms behind his head, letting the two of them talk themselves into it. Truth to tell, he was still a bit staggered at the way he'd thrown everything to the wind, made his decision and acted on it.

His very authority had seemed to affect everyone he approached, from the solicitors to the cinema buyers, and it had all gone through with amazing ease. Even now, in the midst of his father's wrath and predictable objections, he knew he was going to win.

'You can see it's what Mother wants.' He stood up, deciding that Helen was going to be badgered no more. 'How much longer are you going to make her put up with your bullying? It's time she had a say in how she wants to live her life.'

Frank glowered at him. 'You take a lot on yourself, boy. Selling my picture palace –'

'*Mine*,' Daniel reminded him. 'The minute you signed it over to me, it was mine to do as I liked with. I put money into it and spruced it up, and gave it a fair chance. Then I decided to sell, and I made a good profit. I'd have thought your calculating little brain would have appreciated that, Father.'

In the old days, such a challenge would have had Daniel dodging to avoid the crack on his head from his father's fist. Now he stood his ground, staring Frank out, as each recognized that the son was now the stronger, and finally Frank gave a crooked smile.

'You've a lot of me in you, boy, and don't ever forget it,' he conceded.

'So what of Daniel's idea?' Helen came round to sit beside him on the sofa, holding his hands in hers. 'Shall we sell up, Frank, and become farmers?'

'More likely we'll become bankrupt,' he muttered.

'No we won't. I've told you, we'll get reliable men in to advise us. A farm manager for a start, and somebody to teach me the ropes. We can easily afford it,' Daniel said relentlessly, giving him no loop-holes.

'I suppose you've already got somewhere in mind?' Frank said sarcastically.

Daniel moved over to the sideboard and produced several folios from a large envelope.

'We can go and look at any of these properties at the weekend. Any one of them will be suitable for what we want. They're all in Somerset, and none of them is far from the seaside, so that will be a bonus. We'll be able to motor to the seaside in the summer and Mother can paddle her toes.'

'You haven't been dragging yours, have you?' Frank said, as Helen began leafing through the information leaflets and exclaiming rapturously over the sight of the white-washed farmhouses in idyllic green fields.

Eventually he was persuaded to study them too, and Helen willed him to agree at least to take a look at the properties. In the end he nodded, and she looked at Daniel in delight. It wouldn't take a miracle to shift Frank out of London, after all; just the foresight of her son, and she loved him all the more for it.

And only Daniel knew that it had really been Amy Moore's rejection that had set him on this course of action. He had to get right away, to put as much distance between them as possible. It wouldn't make him forget her, but it was better than staying here and knowing that he might turn a corner one day and walk right into her. Ironically, it was Amy whom Helen really had to thank for making her dream come true.

'Well, that's one person we can cross off our invitation list,' Jane Broome said feelingly, when news of Giles Beaumont's five-year prison sentence was finally made public about a month before her wedding to Ronald Derbisham. 'I never did like him, and I always felt there was something untrustworthy about him, but it's Thelma I feel so sorry for. She must have been fond of him, despite the off-hand way he treated her.'

She and Amy had been to the dressmaker's for their final fittings, and were having afternoon tea at Brown's when a newsboy went by outside, gleefully shouting the news of Giles's sentence.

'It must be awful for his family too,' Amy murmured, remembering that Lady Beaumont had always been kind to her from the usual distance shown to servants.

'Did you know them, Amy?' Jane asked, her eyes showing sudden interest at the note in Amy's voice.

'Oh no. I think I did speak to them on the odd occasion, but I didn't really know them.' She said quickly, praying that the heat in her cheeks wouldn't give her away. The only times the Beaumonts had spoken to her was when she had served them tea, or asked for her release from their employ!

'Well, we won't think about any of them any more. Ronald says we must still invite Thelma to the wedding, of course, but I rather doubt that she'll come. It will be too embarrassing for the poor dear. Did I ever tell you that she and Archie were once rather attached to one another? Perhaps there'll be a chance for them now that horrid Giles is out of the way.'

Amy hoped her face didn't alter its expression as she agreed politely. Thelma and Archie indeed. That would put the cat among Bert's pigeons all right.

'We haven't had much of a chance to talk lately, Amy, and I didn't think you looked too well when I collected you today. Are you sleeping properly?'

'I'm fine, really,' she said brightly. As fine as anybody could be when their heart was broken, she thought.

She had wished a hundred times that Daniel had never come to her that night. She wished she had never known the ecstasy of loving him, because then her dreams wouldn't have such substance, knowing how it felt to have his arms holding her in such intimacy and to be a part of him. She wouldn't have to feel this sense of guilt every time she longed for him, knowing that it was wrong, that whatever arrangements she and Bert had made, in the eyes of God she was a married woman, and as such she had sinned.

'You don't look fine to me,' Jane went on. 'When Ronald and I go on our honeymoon, I'd like you to stay at The Gables for a while, darling. You look as if you need a break away from town. Even if Bert doesn't want to come, you're to go there and relax. Promise me, Amy.'

'Of course I promise! It's lovely of you to suggest it, Jane. I'm sure Bert will want to come too, though.'

'Well, he and Archie can go off on their little shooting jaunts or up in that wretched flying machine, and you can just enjoy yourself quietly. If it would interest you, I might even ask Thelma if she'd care to spend the odd day with you. What do you think?'

'Oh. I don't think so. I don't know her at all well, and it might be terribly embarrassing, Jane,' she said quickly.

'You're probably right. I won't mention it then. If she and Archie want to resume anything, it's up to them, isn't it?'

Amy gave an audible sigh of relief. God only knew what she'd have done if Thelma double-barrel had been invited to The Gables while Amy was there alone, and the two of them had been expected to make polite conversation together. She could just imagine the wheels of memory slowly turning in the other girl's head, and the sudden awful realization of just where she had seen Amy before.

She began to feel the throb of a headache begin. She'd been getting so many of them lately, she had begun to wonder fearfully if there was anything wrong with her. A growth in her brain or something. *Good God, gel*, Gran Moore's voice seemed to censure her, *what's that imagination o' yours putting you through now?*

'Amy darling, I'm taking you home,' she heard Jane's voice say as if from a great distance. 'Sit right where you are and I'll send someone for a cab.'

'Jane, there's something I've got to tell you.' She said it all in a rush, before the other girl could move. She couldn't bear any more lies. There were some that she couldn't do anything about, that were no fault of hers. But there were others that were a constant nightmare, and she could no longer live with them.

'What is it, darling?' Jane said gently, thinking that she looked as pale and fragile as she had ever seen her. It didn't detract from her loveliness, but it gave her an ethereal quality that didn't seem quite healthy.

'You may not want me to be your bridal attendant when I tell you.'

'What nonsense. Why on earth should I not?'

'Because I'm not what I seem, that's why. I said I knew the Beaumonts slightly, and so I did. But not as equals, Jane. I – I worked for them. I was their housemaid, and I know it will shock you and you'll hate me for deceiving you.'

Unbelievably she heard a sympathetic laugh.

'Is that all? I think I half-suspected something of the sort when we first met, but it makes no difference to me. I love you for yourself, Amy, and there's no need to mention it again. Goodness me, it's not a crime to have done honest work in the past. It's not as if you've murdered anyone, is it? Now sit there while I call that cab.'

Amy sat numbly. She had confessed, quite needlessly, she supposed, and it all seemed a bit of an anti-climax now. The headache still throbbed and her limbs felt as heavy as lead. She ached all over and she longed to be home and in her own bed. The dining-room seemed to move and sway like the waves of the ocean, and as she saw Jane coming back towards her she stood up too quickly, and the next second she folded up and slid to the floor.

She awoke in bed. Someone was holding her wrist, and when she focused her eyes properly she saw a man she presumed was a doctor taking her pulse. Jane and Bert were at the far end of the room. Was it a wake? Was she already dead, or near to death?

'You've got a severe chill, young lady,' the doctor said cheerfully. 'A week in bed with the medicine I'll prescribe for you and you'll be as right as rain. I understand you're to be matron of honour at a wedding in a month's time, so we've got to get you fit and well for that, haven't we?'

He spoke to her as if she was a child, and it was exactly how she felt. She didn't have a brain tumour and she wasn't about to die, and the weak tears gathered in her eyes and ran down her cheeks and into her mouth. However bad life was, she wasn't ready to die, she thought fiercely.

Jane leaned over her while the doctor went to instruct Bert about the medicine.

'Don't worry about a thing, Amy. I'm sending one of my maids to help Maisie while you're in bed, and to make sure that you stay there and get properly well. I'll come and see you in a couple of days.'

When she and the doctor had gone, Bert stood looking down at her awkwardly. Illness made him uncomfortable, and Amy never normally got ill.

'Don't worry, I'll live,' she mumbled at him. 'You could

ask Maisie to bring me some cocoa though, Bert, and one of her coconut buns, and then you'd better get back to the show-room, hadn't you?'

'If you're sure you'll be all right?' He tried not to show his relief at being able to escape.

'I'm sure,' she said. She lay back and closed her eyes when he'd gone, glad that she hadn't betrayed his little secret to Jane – not that she thought Jane or Ronald would be in any doubt about Bert's background.

She was a good mimic, and it hadn't been difficult for her to talk nicely without poshing up her accent too ridiculously, but it was something Bert could never do. And even if he managed that, he'd simply always be common. She wasn't being snobbish; it was just a fact of life, and even though she'd never bothered to think much about it before, she was quite sure Jane and Ronald would have seen through him long ago.

She wondered if Archie had too. Didn't people say darkly that some of these toffs liked a bit of rough? She'd always assumed it meant they took a fancy to the street-girls, but now she supposed that it applied to the nancy boys as well as anybody else.

Figgins' Car Sales was doing very nicely, Bert told Archie with satisfaction. They were showing good profits, and there was plenty of custom. In fact, the trouble during that miserable general strike had stood them in good stead, because some weeks later Bert had arranged to be interviewed by the newspapers, commenting bravely that business had continued as usual and he hoped that justice would be lenient to those who had been driven to vandalism out of desperation.

Somehow Bert managed to come out of it as the knight in shining armour, and in the weeks following the strike there had been no shortage of customers in the show-rooms, or people calling to congratulate him on his good fortune in suffering no real damage.

'Marvellous, ain't it, madam?' Maisie said to Amy, looking over her shoulder at the newspaper report. 'He's a clever one, Mr Figgins.'

Amy wasn't sure whether she was being sarcastic or not, but in any case it wasn't Maisie's place to read over her mistress's shoulder, and Amy snapped the paper shut.

'I'm getting up today, Maisie. Miss Broome's maid is going back to The Gables this afternoon, and I want to be back on my feet again. I shall be getting foot-rot if I don't use my legs soon.'

Maisie grinned, pleased that the other snooty maid was leaving and her domain would be all hers once more. It would be good to have Madam moving around again too. It had been like a morgue without seeing her cheery face.

'Is it still all right for me to have Saturday afternoon off, madam?' Maisie said hopefully. 'Me and my young man are going to the pictures.'

'Of course it is,' Amy said evenly. 'You go and enjoy yourself.' *And don't remind me of Saturday afternoons in those lovely days of long ago . . .*

'Did you know the old Roxy's changed hands?' Maisie said suddenly. 'They had workmen in and out all one Monday, and ever so different it is now, with white and gold paint on the doors, and the name changed to the Globe. Daft name for a picture palace, if you ask me.'

Amy's heart leapt with shock. Surely Daniel hadn't done as he'd said so soon! She hadn't thought it was so definite, and to do it without telling her . . . The thoughts hammered around in her head as she tried to sound no more than casually interested. 'No, I didn't know. What's happened to the people who used to own it, then?'

'Dunno.' Maisie shrugged, uncaring. 'Sold up and moved away, so somebody said.'

*   *   *

She knew it was extremely foolish, but she had to see for herself. It was like the murderer's compulsion to revisit the scene of the crime. She told Bert she needed a change from seeing the four walls of her bedroom, and that because she had been in bed for a week, she would go for a drive in the motor to avoid a further chill. In reality it was because the Roxy cinema, and Daniel's house, were more than a walk away from Claymore Street.

The exterior of the Roxy cinema, now grandly renamed the Globe, was exactly as Maisie had described it. All white and gilded and a world away from the familiar picture palace Amy and Tess had visited every Saturday afternoon.

She pushed down the pang of nostalgia, determinedly feeling glad that it was different. It meant she no longer had to imagine herself and Daniel in the intimate flickering confines of the cinema . . . She didn't have to remember that first magic moment when she had slowly turned her head to find Daniel looking at her, speaking to her . . . while the strains of a contemporary tune ran in and out of her head . . .

'She's my once-a-week-love, my once-in-a-life-time love; all so del-i-cate and love-ly . . .'

Amy switched off the memory with alacrity and put her foot down on the accelerator of the car. A few streets away was the house where the Eastons lived. If what Maisie said was true, another family would be living there now. She was filled with indecision. She could hardly walk boldly up to the front door and enquire, just in case Maisie had made a mistake. If Helen or Frank Easton answered – or Daniel himself – Amy would be too embarrassed to speak.

She sat in her car in the road outside the house for more than an hour. There was no *For Sale* signpost in the garden and, as far as Amy could remember, the curtains looked exactly the same. And then at last, when she had almost given up hope of knowing the truth, and passers-by had begun to look at her strangely, a young woman opened the front door, pulling a perambulator behind her. An older child danced around her, and Amy heard the woman tell the girl to be patient and they would go to the park and Victoria could push baby Sarah if she was very careful.

It was true then. This little family was living in Daniel's house, and new people had taken over Daniel's picture palace, and Amy didn't have the faintest idea where Daniel and his family had gone. She might be able to find out by asking the young woman, and she was almost tempted to get out of the car and run after her. But what was the point?

If Daniel had wanted her to know of his movements, he would have told her. Sickened, Amy accepted that. She had told him to go, and he had done just that, but in a far more final way than she had imagined. He had simply vanished from her life.

The daylight seemed to spin in front of her eyes for a minute, and she realized how tightly her hands were gripping the steering-wheel. A constable patrolling the streets peered in at her, touching his fingers to his helmet as she gave him a half-nod and started up the car engine again.

She tried to get her thoughts in order. All right, she had asked for this, and she had got it. There was nothing left for her now but to go under or go up. And she knew what Gran Moore would have told her to do.

By the time she got back to Figgins' Car Sales, her chin was higher, and no one would have detected what an effort it was to keep it there. She'd been doing some hard thinking on the way back to Claymore Street.

She didn't want to be a drone, doing nothing and raking in the profits on her investment, which was more or less all that Figgins' Car Sales was to her. She needed to be useful. Even as a housemaid she'd been useful, and the glimmerings of an idea had begun to take shape in her mind. She marched into the little office, where Bert was drinking a cup of tea. He clattered the cup into the saucer.

'Blimey, gel, I thought you'd gone for good. I was getting worried about the motor.'

'Thanks, Bert.'

As usual, he didn't notice the sarcasm in her voice. 'Where've you been, for Gawd's sake?'

'Shut up and listen, will you? What do you say to expanding a bit? I don't mean buying more cars, but you've often heard people say they've come here from quite a distance, and they ask about a tea-room in the area to revive themselves.'

'Go on,' he said, his eyes narrowing.

'There's nothing of that kind around here, but we could open a tea-garden on that bit of grass at the back, and have a sort of canopy thing over the top in case the weather's bad. We could have a few tables and chairs and sun umbrellas, and Maisie and me could run it with a bit of help. I wouldn't wait on tables, being one of the owners, but I'd be in charge and make the cakes and fancies, and we could advertise in the papers and over the show-room window. *Figgins' Car Sales and Tea-Garden*. Folk who were only out for a drive might call in for refreshments, and browse in the show-room at the same time. What do you think, Bert?'

For a second he just stared, then he put his arms round her waist and planted a jubilant kiss on her cheek.

'I think you're bloody brilliant, Mrs Figgins, that's what I think! We'll start planning it straight away!'

24

'This is my department, don't forget, Bert,' Amy insisted, when they had gone into the small matter of fitting out the patch of grass at the back with wicker tables and chairs, and enquired about sets of matching crockery. 'You can see to the cars, but the tea-garden is my responsibility.'

'Weli, of course it is.' He was only too willing to agree. 'It's women's work, and you're a clever old duck for thinking of it, Amy.'

'Not so much of the "old",' she said pertly. Truth was, it had been a bit of an inspiration, but it had given her no end of a perk. It was something interesting to do. She liked baking, and even if it was only making fancies and fruit scones, it would be an interest of her own.

Maisie was filled with enthusiasm. 'You're a blooming wonder, madam,' she declared. 'It's just what's needed around here, and we'll soon have Tildy shaping up.'

Tildy was the young girl coming in to help Maisie wait on tables. Maisie was in charge of her, and Amy was in charge of the whole thing. Everyone had their place and everyone knew exactly what was expected of them, Amy thought with a stab of humour.

Summer was just round the corner, and she hoped to be so busy there'd be no time to wonder what Daniel Easton was doing now, or where he was, or if he ever thought of her . . .

Jane thought it was a perfectly charming idea. They were having tea at the Ritz again.

'I don't know why men never expect women to have brains,' she commented. 'You've got plenty, Amy, but more important than that, you're not afraid to put your ideas into action. I do admire you for it, darling.'

Particularly as Jane knew very well that if Amy's personal life was not exactly the way she would have chosen it to be, at least she had risen from being a housemaid. She was a survivor.

'It's a very modest venture,' Amy protested laughingly at all the praise being heaped on her. 'My little afternoon teas will hardly compare with this, Jane – or with the wonderful wedding-breakfast in the marquee they're putting up at The Gables!'

Jane laughed, setting the bone-china cup down in its saucer for a moment and delicately touching her lips with a table napkin. 'Do you know, I do believe I'm starting to get nervous. Only a week to go, and I'll be Ronald's wife.'

Amy saw her give a small shiver of excitement, and impulsively put out her hand to give Jane's a squeeze. Despite their vastly different backgrounds, they were genuinely fond of one another.

'I only wish you and Bert could be as happy as I know Ronald and I are going to be,' Jane said softly.

Amy gave a short laugh. 'What's happiness? We're content enough, and plenty of folk have far less than that. We suit each other very well, as a matter of fact.'

With no demands on either side . . .

'Where are you and Ronald going for your honeymoon? I know it's supposed to be a secret from everyone, but I'm just dying to know.'

Jane laughed, eyes sparkling like the brilliant jewel she wore on her third finger.

'I wouldn't tell anybody else, but because you're so special, Amy darling, I'll tell you. I'm bursting to let someone know, anyway!'

Amy felt her throat thicken as the other girl leaned forward to give it away. How kind Jane was, how unsnobbish and unpretentious . . .

'Well, well, well, what's all this? A cosy little tête-à-tête if ever I saw it. I didn't know you were in the habit of consorting so closely with housemaids, Jane dear.'

They both jerked up their heads at the sound of the brittle, caustic voice. Neither had seen the woman approach, and Amy felt her face flood with colour in a mixture of shock and embarrassment and finally shame as she looked into the accusing, hurt eyes of Thelma Parkes-Leighton.

The current gossip being bandied about town in the smart upper-set slang was that the girl had become a wasp since the unfortunate ending of her engagement to Giles Beaumont, and it was advisable not to be at the receiving end of her sting.

And it was obvious now that she had finally remembered exactly where she had seen little Amy Moore before, and intended making the most of the knowledge.

'Thelma, how lovely to see you. Do come and join us. It's been far too long.'

In an instant, Jane was mistress of the situation. As Amy mentally floundered, gauche as a child, hands as clammy as if they'd just wrung out a house-cloth at the Beaumonts', Jane took command, raising an elegant finger towards a waiter, who rushed to attend her.

'A chair for the lady, and another cup and saucer and serving of pastries, please.'

'Certainly, Miss Broome.' The young man snapped his fingers at another, who glided away to do Jane's bidding, and a chair was placed behind Thelma before she could utter a word. In seconds another cup and saucer, plate and pastry knife were set in front of her, and a further cake-stand of pastries appeared on the table.

Jane went on talking brightly, giving Amy a chance to catch her breath and recover her composure a little, and giving Thelma no chance to blunder on for the benefit of anyone nearby. Fortunately the area was fairly empty that afternoon, so Thelma's poison was unlikely to be the prime subject at any dinner tables that evening.

'Thelma, I do so wish you'd change your mind about coming to the wedding. There are so many interesting young men Ronald would like you to meet. Do tell me you've decided to accept our invitation, after all.'

Thelma sat down abruptly on the elegant pink velvet chair, her eyes narrowing at having the wind taken out of her sails so adroitly.

'Didn't you hear what I said?' she asked sharply. 'Your – *friend* – is an imposter.'

There was a small silence, and then Jane spoke very softly so that only the three of them could hear.

'Oh, I think not. If you mean did I know that Amy once did an honest job for the Beaumonts, then yes I did. I value my friends for their sensitivities and loyalty more than their social background. And I'd have thought the less you made any reference to *that* name, the better. A certain member of that family was less than honourable, and one will always be associated with him unless one chooses to drop all mention of him.

'It's such a pity to ostracize oneself from one's friends and acquaintances because of an unfortunate incident, and to drag up the past unnecessarily is also the mark of someone less than honourable. I think it unworthy of you, Thelma dear, and will hardly encourage sympathy towards you if you attempt to blacken the name of one of my dearest friends.'

Thelma stared in silence, taking in the words and knowing the significance of them as well as Amy.

Jane was on her best aristocratic platform, Amy thought, and Thelma had better not forget that Jane was about to marry a man whose aspirations to become a Member of Parliament would undoubtedly meet with success. The friendship of the Derbishams was to be coveted, not tossed away, and if Thelma wanted to remain a friend, she had best curb her tongue regarding Amy Figgins *née* Moore.

Amy could see Thelma wrestling with her own feelings, and because she herself knew so well how it felt to suffer what the popular papers called 'unrequited love', she felt an unexpected sympathy towards her. And because she could no longer sit still and do nothing, while Jane battled in her defence, she took the initiative.

'Won't you have a pastry?' She offered the cake-stand, willing her trembling hands to be still and controlling her wavering voice with a huge effort. 'They're truly delicious, and if you're ever in the vicinity of Claymore Street, perhaps you'd care to take tea at my own new tea-garden at the back of the car show-rooms.'

'Oh, *do*, Thelma. Amy's fancies are to be thoroughly recommended. When Ronald gets his seat, I'm going to try and persuade her to supply the House with afternoon teas. What a lark that would be!'

Thelma Parkes-Leighton's angry face crumpled suddenly, and she looked down at her hands in their white kid gloves, taut on her lap.

'I'm sorry,' she said in a muffled voice. 'This has been such a terrible time for me. I don't know what I'm saying half the time. You don't know how it feels to be so rejected, and to feel yourself a laughing-stock.'

'I do,' Amy said simply. 'And every woman with any gumption will understand how a man can turn your mind as well as your head. It'll pass, believe me.'

Thelma looked up, curiosity mixed with a flash of resentment. This little chit was daring to offer *her* comfort. It was an impulse, no more, that had sent her storming across the elegant carpet of the Ritz Hotel, to confront Amy and dear Jane, to put an end to this unlikely friendship.

And she had failed. She had failed miserably and utterly, and now she felt completely wretched. Jane was right. It was unworthy of her. A most unseemly and un-*honourable* thing to do. To her horror she felt a huge tear threaten to fall from her eyes, and blinked it back. It was so infra dig to be seen crying in public.

'Look, do you want a pastry or not, because me bleeding arms are going to fall off before long if I have to hold out this cake-stand much longer.'

Amy heard herself say the words with something like horror. It was the way Tess might have spoken irritably to her in a cheap tea-room long ago. It was how Maisie had been instructed *not* to address the elegant customers at Figgins' Tea-Garden. It was exactly the right way to force a smile to the corners of the Honourable Thelma Parkes-Leighton's mouth and to have Jane laughing out loud.

'Oh Amy, I love you!' Jane said. 'And for heaven's sake, Thelma, take off your gloves and do as Amy says, before her bleeding arms fall off.'

And Thelma capitulated, knowing when she was beaten.

'Guess who's coming to the wedding, after all?' Amy said to Bert that evening, when they were having a dress rehearsal of their new finery in her bedroom, and admiring one another in front of the long mirror in the door of her wardrobe.

Pale grey morning coat and tails with pin-striped trousers for Bert, together with a shiny grey topper and patent leather shoes; the most elegant cream silk jacquard suit for Amy, the jacket worn over a plain silk chemise, the skirt tied low at the waist with a gleaming satin sash. There were cream stockings and palest cream shoes to match, and for her head, the most chic little Parisian hat, tiny and head-hugging, with the gleam of a jewelled brooch at one side, from which curled a beautiful bleached peacock's feather to match the overall cream effect of the outfit. Only the eye of the feather was the original kingfisher blue and matched the jewelled brooch exactly.

She looked a real toff, Amy thought, admiring herself in the bedroom mirror, and so did Bert. She had to give him that. They looked the most successful, elegant couple who ever lived . . .

'Who?' Bert asked.

'The Honourable Thelma whatsit.'

He looked blank for a minute. He was still too caught up with his own splendid appearance, and gauging with satisfaction the effect it would have on Archie, so Amy explained in more detail.

'You know, the one Giles Beaumont was engaged to before he fell from grace.'

Even saying his name made her shudder, but she made herself do it to prove to herself that he meant nothing in her life any more.

'I'd have thought she'd want to keep out of sight for a bit,' Bert said carelessly.

'Why should she?' Amy sprang to her defence. 'It wasn't her fault Giles was such a fool. Why should she hide away because of his disgrace?'

'Well, you've changed your tune, haven't you?' Bert was still fiddling with his necktie and wishing he had the knack of getting it beautifully straight the way Archie did. 'I thought you never had much time for her. Isn't she the one you always thought might recognize you?'

'She did.' Amy said abruptly.

Bert stopped fiddling, staring at Amy in the mirror and finally noticing how fast she was breathing. A pulse was beating crazily in her throat and, beneath the soft silk jacquard of the smooth-fitting suit, her breasts were peaked with tension as the memory of those awful moments at the Ritz swept over her. She had intended telling him casually, but it wasn't proving easy, after all.

God, but she was a bloody cracker, Bert thought, surprised by the small surge of arousal the thought evoked inside the pin-striped trousers. And she was his wife. He'd never yet sampled a woman's charms fully, but any time he wanted to, he could sample this one, and she couldn't deny him. She'd promised to love, honour and obey, and there hadn't been much obeying yet from this wilful woman.

He ignored the thought for the moment.

'What do you mean – she *did*?' he demanded.

'Just what I say. Jane and I saw her at the Ritz today and she came and accused me of being an imposter.'

'*Jesus Christ!*'

Amy could read so well all the flickering emotions chasing across Bert's face. If this woman denounced Amy and him to the newspapers, or even just let her little drops of poison filter through the ranks of society in which they'd tried so hard to be accepted, they'd lose everything: custom, good will, the patronage of people like the Derbishams and all their connections . . . In an instant, Bert could see everything he'd fought so hard for dwindling faster than his momentary lust.

'Don't worry, she's not going to give the game away,' Amy said witheringly, turning from the mirror before she could see the obvious relief in Bert's eyes. 'It seems Thelma's as much of a social climber in her own way as some others I could mention, and she decided that Jane's friendship was worth more to her than showing us up. She might even come round to the tea-garden one afternoon with some of her chums.'

She wasn't prepared for Bert's sudden anger. She had removed the jacket of the jacquard suit and was laying it reverently across her sofa. She felt Bert's hands on her bare shoulders, cruel and insistent, and then they slid over the silk chemise, pressing against the hardening nipples. She tried to pull away from him, but he was gripping her breasts as if they were lifelines, fondling and squeezing until she felt physically sick at his touch.

'What the blazes do you think you're doing?' she gasped. 'Let go of me, Bert. You're hurting me.'

'Not as much as I'd like to! Leading me on like that and letting me think the tart was about to expose us,' he snarled.

'I never did. I was about to tell you the rest of it if you'd given me the chance.'

She realized suddenly that he smelled of drink. He'd been drinking steadily all evening, and since it wasn't unusual she hadn't thought anything about it. Now she saw that because her sudden fear of him must be showing in her eyes, he had become extra-aggressive. He saw himself as a real man, imposing his power over her, and she knew how easily that power could become sexual.

'Bert, don't be ridiculous.' She tried to be calm as his fingers brushed against her nipples, and realized how the mere chemical reaction of her body to a man's touch excited him. 'Don't do this. It's not what we both want.'

'How do you know what I want, sweetheart? You invited me into your bedroom, after all.'

His voice had become guttural, as a new and unexpected passion was surging through him. He was a man, after all, and if he wanted his wife panting beneath him, then, by God, he would have her. There was no law that said he had to be faithful to his lover, and there was no need for Archie ever to know . . .

As if she could read his mind, Amy knew exactly the right words to say. She spoke slowly and deliberately.

'The only way you'll get me to submit to you is by raping me. If you force me into it, I shall tell everyone I'm pregnant. How do you think your *friend* will like that? And if you think I'll stop at that, I may even hint at how unexpected it all was, since you're hardly the most normal of husbands, are you, Bert?'

His fingers stopped moving over her breasts, and his handsome face was pale. His mind glossed over the fury Archie would feel if he thought Bert had got Amy pregnant. The rest was more important. So far Amy had never said she guessed at his preferences, and he had never wanted her to know. Perhaps she still didn't, he comforted himself. He had always bragged about his prowess with the ladies, and she had seemed to believe him.

And while it was fine and dandy for him and Archie to cavort in private, it was the last thing either of them would want for it to be made public knowledge. He'd be hounded out of town, and his business would be in ruins. He didn't need telling that it wouldn't be Archie's name that would be disgraced. These people had a way of covering things up and putting the entire blame on somebody else. In this case, it would be Bert who went to jail for buggery.

He let go of her so fast she staggered and banged her hip against the dressing table. She didn't care. It was worth it to see the lustful look leave Bert's eyes. For a second, she'd been terrified. She snatched up her dressing-gown with shaking fingers and wrapped it around her body tightly, over the smoothly-fitting jacquard skirt.

'Why don't we just forget any of this ever happened, Bert?' she said, far more calmly than she felt. 'It's late and we're both tired. We've tried on our wedding outfits, and we both look the part. We'll hold our own with all the honourables and lords on Saturday, and we can both be proud of each other.'

He didn't speak for a long moment, and then his voice was thin, like that of a petulant child, grudgingly wanting approval and not expecting to get it.

'Will you be proud of me, Amy?'

Tentatively, not wanting to touch him any more than she had to, she leaned forward and shook his arm gently.

'I always have been. We're the successful Figginses, aren't we? We'll show them, Bert.'

She spoke with a kind of desperate bravado, wanting, needing to be alone so badly, before she broke down and wept. She didn't want to have to console this child-man who had been so aggressive minutes ago, and looked so pathetic and unsure of himself now. He had to sort out his own problems.

Bert cleared his throat and moved towards the door.

'All right. We will too. And Amy – I am fond of you, you know.'

'I know. Good-night, Bert,' she said evenly. She tossed his topper towards him, and he caught it involuntarily, sticking it on his head at a jaunty angle before he went out of the room and along the passage. Quickly, Amy went to the door and locked it. Not that she thought he'd come back; she just felt safer that way.

She leaned against the door for a moment, as tense as a spring, and then she wilted, sliding down the door to the floor in a slither of silk as if she was suddenly boneless. Weak tears filled her eyes and ran, salty, into her mouth, and she barely noticed. Nor did it matter that the wedding outfit that was in danger of getting soiled and creased had cost more than she had ever spent on clothes in her life before.

Nothing mattered but the feeling of being bereft, and acutely aware of everything she had lost. Bert's clumsy overtures seemed to make her even more aware of it than usual. And if he had carried out his unmistakable threat and forced her into submission, she knew she would have felt that she betrayed Daniel.

She realized it was ludicrous. It was wrong. It was against all that marriage stood for . . . But if her husband, whom she had promised before God to love, honour and obey, had made love to her, she would have felt shame at betraying her lover.

Amy got undressed and hung the clothes carefully in the wardrobe, putting the little hat back in its own box.

She wouldn't let herself think too deeply about Daniel, or imagine how she was going to feel on Saturday, attending a real wedding, where two good friends who loved each other dearly were going to repeat the words of the marriage service in the spirit in which they were meant. She was Jane's attendant and would receive the bouquet of pink roses, which were the real flowers of true love, and all the time she would be aching for Daniel, and God would know it.

In His eyes, she had sinned in marrying Bert and never intending to carry out the words that bound them together. She didn't love him. She could never truly honour him because of the things he stood for. And never, never would she obey him, especially if he was going to start getting crazy notions that their marriage should be consummated, after all.

But after her ultimatum, she knew he wouldn't press the idea any further, and as she curled up like a foetus in her lonely bed, she began to breathe more easily. When all was said and done, her will was stronger than Bert's, and if it meant being celibate for the rest of her life, that was infinitely preferable to betraying the love she felt for Daniel.

25

Daniel Easton began to discover a surprising affinity with his new surroundings whenever he was striding across the farm in his stout country gum-boots. It tickled him pink to think he was now a landowner in this picturesque part of Somerset. All around him the scents and sounds of the country invaded his senses, permeating his lungs and nostrils and filling him with an unexpected kind of peace.

It was albeit a temporary peace, because whenever he allowed his mind to roam further than the immediate here and now, his thoughts flew at once to Amy, seeing everything through her eyes.

Amy would love all this. Amy would adore the way the wild flowers and grasses grew in such profusion in the scented meadows. In his mind's eye he could imagine Amy running through the sweet green fields, gathering armfuls of daisies and cuckoo flowers as she went, and filling the farmhouse with their simple beauty.

Amy would love the pearly pink and golden sunrises that were more awesome and mysterious than those barely to be glimpsed by early risers among the crowded buildings of London. Here there was space to see and breathe and be, and here was nature at its most spectacular, with the hazy spread of the blue Mendip Hills not a spit and a throw away, according to the country vernacular he was learning. And the sand and sea within easy driving distance for a day's outing at the fashionable watering-hole of Weston-super-Mare.

Amy would love the early evenings, when the muted lowings and bleatings of animals safely bedded down for the night spoke of ancient rituals and traditions that existed through and beyond time. When owls in the dark silhouetted trees hooted into the twilight and turned their huge eyes unblinkingly towards you, soft eyes like those of the patient cud-chewing cows, reminiscent of Amy's own . . .

But then, everything reminded him of her . . . a look, a sound, a gesture. And if he wasn't reminded of her, then everything he did or saw was something he wanted to share with Amy.

Days and nights . . . when the glowing gold of the sun turned to vibrant red and sank below the horizon, and the soft evening shadows turned everything to a scene from an ancient painting, and that magical mist rose from the fields to transform it all into a wonderland . . .

'Be 'ee day-dreaming again, Squire? 'Tis twice I've asked 'ee how youm liking it down here among us.'

Daniel started, finding his way squarely blocked by one of the locals he'd hired to run the farm. He'd realized very quickly that it took a countryman to deal with milking the cows and understanding the seasons for harvesting and ploughing, and he was very glad to let his hired men get on with it and be merely the overseer.

It was the way they wanted it, and they respected him more for not interfering with their ways. He knew, because both he and his father had overheard one and another say so approvingly in the village pub.

'I was miles away then, Mick, and that's probably because I like it here very much. There's time to stand and stare.' He smiled at the burly cowman. Mick Hillson was a plain-speaking man, like most of his farm labourers. They had all surprised Daniel at first by the way they called him Squire so naturally, when his father was still Mr-Easton-sir, and his mother referred to as the missis.

Except for Ed Rowlands, Daniel's efficient farm manager, who lived in one of the cottages nearby and knew the land as well as the size of his boots and called him Mr Easton – until he'd told the older man gruffly for pity's sake to call him Daniel.

Mick spat noisily now. 'You know your trouble, don't 'ee? A good-looking man like yourself needs a wife to take care of 'ee. Mothers be fine and necessary, but they don't keep 'ee warm at nights, if you'll pardon the familiarity. I'll say good-day to 'ee then, Squire, and get along.'

Grinning to himself, Daniel watched him go, plodding squarely towards the cow-sheds for the afternoon milking session, legs bowed so wide you could nearly drive a herd through them. At first Daniel had tried his luck at the milking, but he was all fingers and thumbs, and the cows protested at his alien, awkward hands, and finally he'd left it to the experts who could squirt the pure pale liquid rhythmically and unerringly into the bucket and carry on a ribald conversation at the same time.

All the same, he needed to be useful. He had Ed Rowlands to deal with the men, but he'd decided to work closely with Ed himself. Daniel needed to be involved in the accounts of the farm, which required minute attention, since the last owner had been abysmally lax. There was feed to be ordered and marketing to be organized, and besides the secretarial work, Daniel made a point of walking over his property every single day, with or without Ed's company, since his own father seemed disinclined to do too much mucking about in farmyard filth, as he called it. Daniel checked on fences and stock, and simply enjoyed the fresh clean air. How long he would be content to live the simple life he wouldn't let himself think.

But there was a nagging truth in what Mick Hillson had just said. A farmer needed a wife . . . and children to inherit the land. It was the way of things. He accepted that much. His mother had hinted enough times that she'd like to see grandchildren before she died, and to see Daniel settled and happy. Once, that had been his goal too, until Amy, his beautiful, adored Amy, was out of his reach . . .

Well, he might be settled now, but happy wasn't a word that came into his vocabulary too much these days. He accepted that he was content, more content here than in London, where he might get some news of Amy from some source or other. Where he might run into her unexpectedly, or be tempted to go and see her, despite their decision. And it was far better not to be tempted, not to see or hear of her. If each of them had to get on with their lives independently of the other, then a clean break was the only way.

But content wasn't much of a word to describe a healthy virile young man of twenty-three years. As his father and Mick Hillson might say, it wasn't a word to go to bed with . . . So far, since arriving here, he hadn't come into contact with any young women, or sought them out. But without even trying, he knew that was about to change.

They were to visit a nearby farm for Sunday tea. Helen had got talking to a farmer's wife at a local fête, and as the Eastons were new in the area, the other woman had invited them all to tea. Daniel hadn't been concerned about going, and Frank had flatly refused, grumbling that the new people would all have hayseeds in their hair, and he'd rather sit in the sun in the back yard and listen to his wireless.

'*We're* the new people, Frank.' Helen reminded him. 'The Stevenses have been living at the same farm for generations. Still, if you don't want to go, I can always say you've got a touch of the rheumatics.'

She sneaked a small smile at Daniel. To her delight, Frank had become amazingly adaptable to the lazy life, and enjoyed nothing more than his own sunny back yard and the beloved wireless that was his current craze. She waited for him to say he supposed he'd better go with them, but all she got was a grunt, and she knew when to desist.

'Oh well, if you want to be unsociable, Daniel and I will go, won't we?' Helen asked.

'If I must,' he said half-heartedly.

'Of course you must. Mrs Stevens is a very nice woman, and she has two daughters, Sophie and Philippa. I'm sure you'll like talking to people your own age, Daniel.'

At the time, his look had dared her to start matchmaking. But he remembered the conversation now, as he strode back towards the white-washed farmhouse in the lee of the Mendip Hills, master of all he surveyed, watching the herd of black-and-white cows being shepherded in a crocodile towards the milking sheds, and the swaying, foot-high grasses in his own fields waiting to be harvested and glinting with health in the summer sunlight.

It was good to own all this, to be part of the land and heritage that was England. It would be the right and sensible thing to do to find himself a wife and family to continue that sense of husbandry which went with it. To forget the past and concentrate on the future . . .

He allowed himself a moment of honesty. It would be the perfect answer if he really was as steeped in the country life as he pretended, even to himself. But his roots were still in London, his roots and his heart . . .

Helen had certainly blossomed here, and for that he was thankful. She belonged here more than he or his father, and it was as much for her sake as his that he'd abandoned the bright lights. She wanted to see him married, to find someone who would make him forget all about Amy Moore . . . but she should have known that Daniel was not the kind of man who could ever settle for second best.

Bert drove Amy down to The Gables on the night before Ronald and Jane's wedding. Jane and her family were staying there too, and to avoid Ronald catching sight of his bride the next morning, which was considered very bad luck, Ronald and Archie, who would be his best man, were to leave the house and spend the night at their club. Bert was to escort Amy and Jane's mother to the church, while the bride arrived last with her father. All the Rolls-Royces had been hired, and the weather promised to be beautiful for the huge marquee reception on the lawn of The Gables when the wedding party and guests returned.

The ceremony was to be conducted in London, but there would be plenty of time for Jane to get ready before the cars arrived to take them to the church for the wedding at noon. Her personal maid helped her to dress after her bath, and when she was finally ready she turned round slowly for Amy's reaction.

'You look as lovely as Gloria Swanson,' Amy said simply. 'You'll take Ronald's breath away, and if he wasn't so mad about you already, he'd fall head over heels in love with you all over again.'

They gave each other a quick hug, careful not to disturb their finery, then each looked at the other and gave a small laugh.

'How absurd it all is,' Jane said softly.

'What is?'

'All this.' Jane spread her hands. 'The ridiculously expensive dress, the ritual, the bean-feast afterwards – all to tell the world what Ronald and I have known for months.'

'But this makes it right and proper, doesn't it? It makes it all – oh, you know I don't have the words to say it! It's – beautiful and ordered, fitting into the pattern of things,' Amy said, wishing she were clever with words to express properly what she felt.

Jane's eyes were tender for a moment. 'Poor Amy. How I wish it could all be beautiful for you too.'

'Never mind. As long as one of us is blissful, that's fifty per cent of us, isn't it?'

'Do you know, I suddenly feel nervous,' Jane said, changing the subject quickly at the shadow on Amy's face, despite the determinedly perky voice. 'I do wish the car would hurry up. Daddy's probably prowling about like a tiger downstairs, helping Bert to calm Mummy down. I suppose we should go down, but I want to stay here a minute longer.'

'You're bound to be a bit nervous, Jane. You've never been married before!'

A flush of colour crept over Jane's cheeks. 'I've never – well, you *know* – before, either. If yours had been a proper marriage, I might have asked you if it's going to be too awful – the first time. Forgive me for saying such things, Amy, I know I shouldn't.'

She bit her lip slightly. Normally so confident, Jane looked like an angel in her cream silk gown, with Ronald's flawless wedding-gift diamond collar around her neck; the heirloom Brussels lace veil that had been in her family for generations floating away from her shoulders, and held fast on her head by a tiara of pearls and diamonds. But Amy saw only the scared young girl that she now was. She put her arms around Jane's shoulders, feeling the slight tremor in them, and made up her mind.

'It will be all right, darling, I promise you,' she said softly. 'My marriage is not as it should be, but there was one night, one glorious night, when Daniel came to me, and showed me what heaven was meant to be. And if I never have another night like that in my life, I'll never regret it. As long as you love one another, there's no need to be afraid, and no two people in the world ever loved more than you and Ronald.'

'Except you and Daniel.'

'Yes,' said Amy. 'Except me and Daniel.'

*   *   *

The church where the wedding of Mr Ronald Derbisham to Miss Jane Broome was to take place was filled to capacity. The ushers stood opposite one another at the door and handed everyone a hymn book and a printed order of service as they entered. Bert left Amy in the porch while he importantly escorted Jane's mother to the front pew of the church. As Amy waited with the verger until the bride and her father arrived, she realized Jane wasn't the only one who was nervous.

The sight of that sea of colourful chic hats and gowns – and the sheen of the grey morning suits – stretching away into the body of the church, suddenly terrified Amy. Far away, beyond what seemed like miles of dark blue carpet, the minister stood awaiting the bridal party, while the organ music played softly, and right at the front, she could just glimpse the two dark heads of the Derbisham men.

This was a society wedding, and as such was to be reported in all the best newspapers. Reporters jostled for position outside the church, taking down names for their lists of those attending, and the photographers were already clicking away like mad, regardless of who the guests were.

Anybody who looked like anybody had their photograph taken, and when Amy had stepped out of the car with the bride's mother and their handsome escort, it was assumed by one eager novice that she was the bride.

And then Jane was stepping out of the silver Rolls-Royce, ethereal and lovely in her bridal gown, and no one could doubt that she was the star of the day. Proudly, her father offered her his arm, and Amy felt a lump come to her throat. How different from her own hasty marriage to Bert. She ached for Daniel in that moment with a pain that went far deeper than the mere physical.

She mustn't think of him, today of all days. And then, as Jane's father leaned over to whisper a few encouraging words to his daughter, Amy's thoughts went beyond

Daniel . . . How poignant and how dear it would have been for Tommy to give her away to a loving bridegroom – Tommy, her boisterous, dearest uncle, her father . . .

A discreet signal was given to the organist and the appropriate music swelled out and alerted the several hundred guests to rise as one person, as Jane began the long slow walk towards her bridegroom.

And Amy walked behind, demure, perfectly attired, acting the part of bridal attendant superbly, and no one would ever have guessed that throughout the service when Ronald and Jane plighted their troth, each to the other, her heart was breaking.

To love, honour and obey – how easy it was to say those words to someone who gazed down into a woman's face as Ronald Derbisham gazed down into Jane Broome's. How wonderful to know the meaning of being cherished and to be so certain that the man who entrusted you with all his worldly goods was the one man in all the world with whom you wanted to spend the rest of your life . . .

She caught herself before the thoughts of her own sham of a marriage made her totally maudlin. This was a day for sharing in the happiness that flowed like wine from these two dear people who had given her their love and support so generously.

And afterwards, when the official wedding photographs were taken for the family albums and the newspapers and society magazines, Amy smiled and held her head high, and Bert stood proudly behind her. They were as handsome a pair as the main attractions themselves, their girl Maisie, watching from the back of the pavement crowd, loyally told her old mum afterwards.

Once the serious part of the day was over, the bridal party was only just allowed to get away in their Rolls-Royces before the entire two hundred guests tore off at high speed in their cars for The Gables, intent on having their bean-feast. It might be a different sort of knees-up from anything Stratford Lane would put on, Amy thought, but the guests still went mad with excitement, and it would be champagne being drunk by the bucketful instead of beer from the barrel . . .

'This is the quiet before the storm, so make the most of it.' Ronald grinned as the bridal party took a quick breather before the line of cars began appearing. 'And I wanted a moment to say a special thank-you, Amy, and to give you this little gift from Jane and myself.'

He drew out a long narrow case from his inside pocket, and Amy gasped as she opened it. Inside was a long rope of perfect pearls that were undoubtedly real, and the costliest thing Amy had ever owned. She gaped at them and she simply couldn't speak.

'Don't say anything, Amy darling,' she heard Jane tell her. 'We both wanted you to have something special. Call it an heirloom, if you like.'

'One to pass down to your children, eh?' Ronald teased, and Jane quickly covered the moment as Ronald turned away to shake Bert's hand.

'Or to sell if you ever need the money,' she said quietly to Amy. 'You never know.'

'I'd never sell it. It's too precious and wonderful of you both,' she said, choked.

Jane hugged her and whispered so that no one else could hear.

'Possessions aren't as precious as people, darling. If their sale meant a new life for you, don't think twice, and do it with our blessing. That's my first bit of advice as an old married lady. Think about it.'

Amy couldn't think at all. It was such an odd thing to say. Was Jane telling her to sell out to Bert and use the pearls as collateral to start a new life without him? The car-sales business was doing so well now, it was worth far more than the original money Amy had put into it.

Did she want to leave him? They jogged along very well most of the time – and the other business with Archie needn't concern her. Besides, where would she go? She wouldn't even think of Daniel. He'd gone from her life, and she had no idea where he was. She certainly wouldn't humiliate herself by chasing after him and asking him to take her in. She had more pride than that, and she wasn't prepared to live the rest of her life on the wrong side of the blanket either, thank you very much.

She wished Jane hadn't put the idea into her head, though when Ronald suggested gently that it might be wise to place the pearls in the Derbisham safe until she was ready to leave, she couldn't underestimate their value.

A trusted servant took the slim case from her hands and spirited it away, and she concentrated very hard on forgetting all about it and standing in line beside Ronald and Jane for the ordeal of receiving these posh guests who reduced her to being little Amy Moore again, despite the elegant trappings . . .

Her heart jolted as Thelma Parkes-Leighton's lace-clad finger-tips reached out and touched hers. Thelma looked quite stunning in a powder-blue suit, in long silk lapels edged with lace to match her gloves.

'You looked lovely, Amy,' she said coolly. 'Well done. I intend coming to see your establishment very soon. Is it open yet?'

Amy felt as if she was smiling properly for the first time since taking part in the long receiving line. She knew it was quite daft and illogical, but this one girl's approval made her feel accepted, a part of the proceedings. She was no longer the little renegade housemaid, in terror of being exposed.

'We're opening at the end of the month. I'll look forward to seeing you – Thelma.'

'I may be bringing someone with me to sample your wares,' she said somewhat coyly, and Amy looked beyond her to where a young officer was busily congratulating Ronald on his charming bride. Amy breathed a sigh of relief. The best thing to cure Thelma Parkes-Leighton of her waspish ways after the shock of Giles Beaumont's imprisonment was to find a new escort, and this one apparently fitted the bill very nicely indeed.

Jane heard Thelma's remark, and added her piece.

'Yes, do patronize the tea-garden, Thelma, and tell all your friends. It will give Amy such a boost if we all show how much we think of her enterprise. Ronald and I will go there as soon as we return from our honeymoon.'

They were so kind, and once one fashionable personality was seen to patronize an establishment the rest would follow, and Amy's tea-garden would be all the rage with the smart set. They were like sheep, Amy thought, but the very nicest kind of sheep, she added hastily.

The rest of the day passed in a haze of champagne, with caviar on little round water biscuits, smoked salmon and pâté de foie gras, little things on toast Amy had never heard of, every kind of meat and fish and salad imaginable and tiny boiled and glazed potatoes, followed by delicious frothy concoctions of fresh strawberries and meringues and cream, and an enormous table of fresh fruit and cheeses from every part of the world. If the king and queen themselves had turned up, they wouldn't have looked down their noses at such a feast, Amy thought irreverently.

And then it was time for the newly weds to leave. Jane asked Amy to help her change into her going-away outfit, and once they were alone in the bedroom, Jane flopped down on the bed, radiating happiness, and looking for the moment less like the coolly detached and beautiful bride than the exuberant Jane Amy knew so well.

'Well, that was quite a day, wasn't it? I wish I could put it all in a bottle and keep it for ever and ever!'

Amy laughed. 'That sounds more like something I'd say than you!'

'Daft, you mean?' Jane grinned, using one of Amy's favourite down-to-earth words. She stretched out a hand, and Amy caught hold of it.

'Oh Amy, how I wish the whole world could be as happy as I am right now. And especially you, my dear friend.'

'I am happy,' Amy said. 'It makes me happy just to be around you.'

'But that's not what I mean.' She sat up. 'And Amy, remember what I said earlier, because Ronald and I have discussed it thoroughly. If ever you need to sell the pearls, *do* it – but let someone who knows their value handle the sale for you. I'd hate you to be robbed.'

'I know what you're saying, but I'm sure I'll never sell them. Anyway, don't let's be serious. This is your day, and hadn't you better start getting ready to go off into the sunset with Ronald?' Amy said, before she started dreaming impossible dreams.

'All right. Help me off with my veil then, and be careful – Mummy will have a fit if it tears. It's terribly old.'

'I'll be careful,' Amy said.

Something old, something new, something borrowed, something blue. Jane had done all the right things, ensuring a bright tomorrow and happy-ever-after. Not that she needed all those old superstitions for that. Some girls had all the luck. Others ended up with none.

'You never did let on where you're going on your honeymoon, did you? Are you still insisting on keeping it a secret?' she asked quickly.

'I'll tell you, but you're not to say anything until after we've gone. Ronald wanted to keep everyone guessing. We'll be away for a whole month and we're going to

Switzerland to stay in one of those dear little hotels in the mountains.'

'Oh.' Amy felt mildly disappointed, having expected something far more spectacular with all the cloak-and-dagger secrecy regarding their destination. 'But I thought people only went there in the winter.'

'Summer in Switzerland is wonderful, Amy. The pale-coloured cows with their huge soft eyes are brought down from the mountains to graze in the meadows and they have tinkling bells around their necks which echo around the hills as they move. The streams are so clear you can see your face in them, and the air is so fresh it invigorates you with every breath. Ronald and I are going to hire some horses and go riding and walking and fishing. We don't intend to do what's expected of us at all. We're going to live the simple life, which is why we haven't told anyone. They call the water that comes down from the mountains "snow water". It's a translucent green, and so pure and tingling, and it's reputed to have special qualities for lovers.'

She gave a soft laugh, and Amy knew at once why this would be such an enchanted place for two people so much in love. They already had the world at their feet here at The Gables, and needed nothing else but each other. If she had ever envied Jane at all, she could envy her now a hundred times over.

26

'Not a bad old shindig, was it?' Bert slurred as he finally stumbled behind the wheel of the car in the early hours of the morning when the reception finally broke up.

They were the last to leave, waved off by a more than distracted-looking Archie as the car lurched drunkenly off into the darkness. They were both wound up by the day and the occasion, and neither was willing to admit to exhaustion.

Amy looked at Bert's clammy, tremulous hands and was thankful that there would be little traffic about in London at this hour of a Sunday morning.

'Don't you think you'd better let me drive back?' she asked. 'First thing we know, you'll be wrapping the car round a tree.'

His mood changed abruptly. 'Are you trying to tell me I'm drunk?' he said belligerently. 'I know when I've had enough, and I ain't that way yet, not by a long way, gel.'

Bert turned to scowl at her, and the car slewed alarmingly over the grass verge at the side of the road before he straightened it again.

'I think you've had more than enough! Be sensible, Bert, and let me take over!' Amy gave a little scream as Bert pushed his foot on to the brake and jerked it to a halt, nearly throwing her through the windscreen.

'So as well as calling me a drunk, you think I'm incap – incap – able of driving my own car, do you? P'raps you think I should be needing my own chauffeur, like the Derbishams! You know your trouble, don't you, Amy? You've gone all toffee-nosed since you got so friendly with them. I bet Tess would never have put on so many airs and graces. Still, you never did think I was capable of *anything*.'

The mention of Tess took Amy by surprise, and she had to swallow the sudden lump in her throat. And then, as he stopped babbling, she realized to her horror that he was putting his hand on her silk-clad knee. Dear God, he wasn't going to start getting amorous at this late stage of their arrangement, was he? She couldn't stand that.

'You're a bloody attractive woman, Amy,' he went on, the words thickening and tripping over each other. 'I reckon it's about time you showed a bit of grat – grat – were a bit grateful to me. I've built up Figgins' Car Sales, and made a good life for us, and let you get started with your little tea-garden hobby. There's not many men would indulge their wives the way I indulge you.'

She clamped her hand over his so hard she bruised her own leg. In a blinding rage, she brought her other hand round with such force it was still stinging minutes after she struck Bert's face with the flat of it.

'Christ, what was that for?' Bert howled.

'That was for insulting me by saying *you're* indulging *me*, you bastard,' Amy screamed. 'Whose money was it that got Figgins' Car Sales started in the first place? Who sold herself to the most useless lump of buggery merchant that ever lived –'

'*What* did you say?' Bert hissed the words at her, his face very close to hers, his breath foul and stinking. His hands were on her shoulders, shaking her so furiously she could feel her teeth rattling in her head. If he went on much longer her brains would be like scrambled eggs, she thought wildly . . .

'Did you really think I didn't *know*?' she screamed contemptuously at him, uncaring now. There was nobody around to hear. The road was deserted, and they were isolated in this mechanical box that was Bert's pride and joy. 'If anybody's indulging anybody, it's *me* indulging *you* with your nasty little secrets. What kind of a blind fool do you take me for?'

He let her go so fast she fell back against the side of the car. Now that she had got used to the dim light inside the car, she could see that his face looked murderous, the chiselled good looks seemingly carved from stone. His breath was coming very fast, and she could see the wild glitter in his eyes. She had never feared Bert Figgins before, but she feared him now.

Sobs gathering in her throat, Amy cowered against the leather upholstery of the car as one hand still gripped her shoulder cruelly and she saw the other one whip backwards. She wasn't sure if he intended to strike her, or to rip the beautiful cream suit from her body and rape her. But it wouldn't be classed as rape, would it? Not when a husband lusted after his wife, that was considered right and natural – as if there was anything natural about Bert Figgins . . .

The dull yellow lights of another motor approaching from behind them lit up the road, and Amy heard the welcome chugging of another engine. To her intense relief, the engine note slowed down, and the car stopped right beside them. Bert let go of her again and turned on the charm as the driver leaned out of his window and spoke in some concern. Amy could see the shadowy figure of a lady passenger beside him.

'I say, old chap, is everything all right? Have you had an accident? Is there anything we can do to help?'

'Thanks, but we're perfectly all right,' Bert began, but before he could say anything more, Amy had grabbed her handbag, leapt out of the car, slammed the door and walked quickly round to the other driver.

Rightly or wrongly, she intended throwing herself on the mercy of these people. They looked respectable enough, which was more than could be said for the man she'd sworn to love, honour and obey. He'd forfeited that right for good and all now, if he ever had it.

'Oh, please, are you going to London?'

'Well – yes, we are,' the gentleman began, glancing at the lady beside him. She spoke up in a cultured voice.

'What's wrong, my dear? Do you need assistance?'

Amy was thankful that the early hours of the morning hadn't yet given way to the dawn light. She would be doubly humiliated for these fine people to see the state she was in, her reddened, distressed eyes and dishevelled clothes. But she sensed that the lady saw all that there was to see anyway, and felt an unspoken sympathy in her voice.

'Yes, I do. My – a relative of mine has been taken ill, and I need to get to London in a hurry. My – my friend doesn't have enough petrol to get me there, and has to return home for more,' she invented wildly. 'Could you possibly help me?'

'Of course.' The driver got out of the car at once and opened the door for Amy to climb in the back.

She was shaking all over. Bert hadn't said a word, but she didn't give a cuss about that. He'd probably go back to Archie for the night, and good riddance. She didn't even look at him as she heard the gentleman tell him he would see the young lady reached her destination safely.

The next minute she was speeding along the road towards London, and as she glanced out of the back window, she could see the lights of Bert's car receding into the distance. She was so upset she couldn't speak for a moment, and then she realized the lady in the front seat was holding out a handkerchief to her.

'Is your relative very ill?' she said sympathetically. Amy looked blank for a moment, until she remembered her garbled story.

'I'm not sure yet. I – I think so. My friend didn't really understand, you see.'

Why was she making excuses for him? she raged. He wasn't worth it, but the Bert Figginses of this world

331

always seemed to escape blame. It was part of their make-up.

'Men often don't see things as we women do,' the lady said, as if to reassure her. 'Now, whereabouts does your relative live?'

Amy went dumb. How *stupid* she had been to invent such a story. Now she had to invent relatives too . . .

'Stratford Lane. In the East End.'

The minute the words left her lips she knew she had made a mistake. Here she was – dressed to kill in her extravagant outfit, although it was less than pristine now, her chic little hat at a crazy angle and the peacock feather bent. Her voice had been slightly tarted up for the occasion, and Bert was undoubtedly looking a million pounds in his posh motor car – and she'd just given an address in a narrow side street in a miserable part of London.

The couple glanced at each other, and Amy could almost read their thoughts. They were probably wondering now if she was some kind of villain, and if Bert's car might come screeching up behind them very soon, accompanied by a constable and accuse them of kidnapping . . .

'I'm sorry to be such a nuisance,' Amy said, aware that her best accent was slipping and she couldn't control it any longer. 'But that man was being horrid and I had to get away from him. He got the wrong idea, see –'

'You don't have to explain any more, young woman,' the gentleman said, but to Amy, his voice had gone several degrees colder. 'We'll find the place you want as quickly as possible, and I'd advise you to be more careful about your gentlemen friends in future.'

She was too mortified to reply. She sat huddled up in the corner of the motor car, with the whiff of soft expensive leather strong in her nostrils, imagining Bert running his hands over it and whistling admiringly. After asking her for general directions to Stratford Lane, the couple in front sat stiffly, totally ignoring her.

Why hadn't she given Dr O'Neil's respectable address? she thought wildly. Why not ask to be taken to Charles Rugby of Welles Street, the lawyer Daniel used, and who had advised her what to do with Tommy's legacy? Why had she been so bloody reckless as to ask these posh people to take her to Stratford Lane and throw herself right back where she came from?

She was immediately ashamed, remembering Gran Moore. Gran would be ashamed of her too, asking in that caustic voice of hers if she thought she was too good for the likes of her own kind now. Her own kind. Servants and washerwomen and housemaids. That was what she was at heart, and would always be. She stifled a sob in her throat before she let herself down any more.

'Is this the place?'

By the time the driver began slowing down the car, Amy hadn't even noticed how far they had travelled. Already the sky was a mite lighter, and remnants of moonlight cast a pale glow over the cobbles of Stratford Lane. It had been raining slightly, and Amy recognized in the cobblestones the pewter sheen that had fascinated her as a child. It was a long while now since she had been here, and she hardly knew why she still regarded it as a haven to run to.

'Thank you,' Amy said, with as much dignity as she could, considering that her legs felt like jelly and knowing that she too had drunk too much champagne that day. 'You've both been very kind.'

Amy felt the lady soften towards her slightly, seeing the dark lane that was little more than an alleyway between the tall crowded buildings. There was not one light to guide the way, and the eerie morning mist was spectral as it curled around the foundations of the houses.

'Will you be all right? Would you like us to wait until you find the house?'

'No, thank you. I know my way blindfold.'

Perversely, she wanted no more help from folk who

obviously thought her no better than she should be and had their own opinions about a young woman seen clambering out of a gentleman's car at such an ungodly hour.

That was a laugh too, when it was Bert Figgins who was the nancy boy and the drunk, who had schemed after her money and married her to ensure that he'd look respectable.

Amy smarted with rage at the thought, and at the fact that it should be obvious to anyone that the clothes she was wearing cost a pretty penny, yet that didn't mean a thing once she mentioned this address. Stratford Lane was where she was born, and she felt unaccountably affronted that these people considered that Stratford Lane was where she belonged.

'Good-night to you then,' the gentleman was saying severely, 'and I'd advise you to be more careful in future, young woman.'

He drove off at speed, leaving her with the wisps of mist fondling her skirts, the wheels spraying dirty rain from the street on to the lovely silk stockings.

A sudden screeching of tom-cats among the rubbish made her scuttle quickly down Stratford Lane with her heart palpitating. She had to get to Gran's house, where she'd be safe, as fast as she could . . . She ran, head down, until she reached it. And she only stopped when she realized she had her hand raised to bang on the door.

Gran was dead. Amy gulped. What a *fool* she had been, asking those people to bring her here. She turned quickly, eyes blinded by tears, and almost fell over one of the prowling cats. It yelped as she trod on its tail, and disappeared in the darkness. Somewhere in the distance she could hear the sounds of drunks singing and bellowing at the tops of their voices. She didn't need to know she'd be fair game if they caught sight of her standing there so aimlessly. And no taxi-cabs would be cruising around Stratford Lane, either . . .

Before she knew what she was doing, she was banging on Mrs Coggins' door and calling out her name. The door wouldn't be locked, and in the old days Amy could have rushed in and nobody would have shown any surprise. But these weren't the old days, and Amy wasn't the old Amy any longer . . .

It seemed an eternity before she saw a light in the upstairs window. Next minute she heard the rasp of a window-pane being lifted, and Mrs Coggins' familiar head was poked out, a hedgehog of rag curlers.

''Ere, who's there? Do you know what time it is, fer Gawd's sake? What do you want?'

For a second Amy couldn't speak, and then she gasped out the words.

'Mrs Coggins, it's me. It's Amy – Amy Moore. Can I come in, please?'

'Oh, my good Gawd! What the blue blazes are you doing round here at this time of night?'

With that, the woman sounded so much like Gran that Amy felt the tears flow even faster.

'You stay right where you are, gel, and I'll come down. Fair scared the daylights out of me, you did.'

It was unnecessary to tell Amy not to move. Her legs threatened to fold up beneath her. This lovely, lovely day had turned into a nightmare, and already the hazy perfection of Ronald and Jane's wedding seemed somewhere in the distant past, part of a dream that had seemed so beautiful.

She hated Bert Figgins all the more for being the cause of it all.

The door of the house opened, and Mrs Coggins stood there in a voluminous flannel nightgown, a candle in her hand, gaping at the sight of Amy Moore done up so posh and looking as if all the demons in hell were after her. She felt a mild resentment that her old man wasn't here to take in the sight. Len was upstairs sleeping the sleep of the dead. as usual, and snoring fit to bust a gusset.

''Ere, what you done?' she said in sudden suspicion. 'You ain't got the law after yer, 'ave yer, gel?'

'No, nothing like that,' Amy said wearily. 'I've just had a – a kind of accident, that's all.'

The woman opened the door wider and pulled Amy inside. She lit the popping gas mantle and blew out the candle before she turned to take a proper look at the girl.

'Blimey, you look a proper mess, and no mistake. Your old man slung yer out, 'as he? I never did trust that one. Too slick by 'alf, I always said, wiv 'is long gloves and that fancy cap on 'is head.'

Amy felt a wild urge to laugh.

'It was nothing like that, Mrs Coggins.'

'Well, you sit down and I'll make yer a nice cup of cocoa – and how about a drop of summat in it for luck, eh?'

'No thanks. I've had enough for one day.'

The woman looked surprised. 'Bin drinking, 'ave yer? I'm not sure yer old gran would have approved of that.'

Not even the best champagne that money could buy?

Amy sat down quickly on the old sofa with the springs threatening to poke through everywhere, and closed her eyes. It was so cold in here. She remembered that nobody in Stratford Lane kept a fire going all night unless they were dying.

While Mrs Coggins put the kettle on the stove in the kitchen, Amy opened her eyes again and looked slowly around her. She saw Gran's picture of wild geese, now in pride of place above the Coggins mantelpiece, and its presence made her eyes sting.

Everything here was so familiar, so like Gran's house. Was that too so small and crowded, as if the old furniture itself was bursting to get through the walls and find enough space to breathe?

'Not what you're used to now, I dare say, gel,' Mrs Coggins said, bringing in two cups of thick dark cocoa and a plate of shortbread. Amy felt her face colour, and knew that her expression must have betrayed her.

'It's where I always come back to,' she mumbled, sipping the bitter liquid.

The older woman had slipped her arms into a threadbare coat now. She prodded the embers of last night's fire into a semblance of life, scattering enough ashes into the room to make Amy cough and feel starved of air.

'You going to tell me why? I don't suppose this is a social call at this time of a night.'

Amy felt all the hurt washing over her.

'I've left him,' she said baldly. 'He's a pig and a drunkard.'

Ma Coggins snorted. 'You ain't done too bad fer yourself, by the looks of yer. That ain't no cheap stuff yer wearin'.'

When she didn't answer, Mrs Coggins dunked her piece of shortbread in her cocoa and sucked it through the gaps in her teeth. Amy tried not to be disgusted, remembering how fascinated she'd been by this feat when she was a child.

'Anyway, you can't leave 'im, whatever 'e's done. 'Tain't right and proper for a wife to leave 'er 'ubby, and if yer gran was 'ere now, she'd tell yer to turn right round and go 'ome where yer belong.'

'I thought I belonged here!'

'So yer did once, ducks, but not any more. One look at yer fancy clobber, and yer posh hair and yer feathers, and folks around 'ere won't know 'ow to talk to yer. They'll think yer a duchess or summat.'

Amy knew she was right, but it was all so daft. The people who'd given her a lift thought her a tart, and the people in Stratford Lane would think her a duchess . . .

'Can I sleep here tonight, Mrs Coggins?' she said in a small voice. 'I'll decide what to do in the morning.'

Her spinning thoughts wouldn't let her think what her decision would be. Go back to Claymore Street? Right now that was impossible! Throw herself on the doctor and his wife, perhaps. But for how long? She had to live somewhere, be *some*body . . .

If only Jane and Ronald were in residence, it would be so easy. She knew there would always be a welcome for her at The Gables, but since Archie was now in sole charge of the estate while the newly weds were on their honeymoon, that was the last place she could go.

"Course you can stay, ducks. You can curl up on my sofa and I'll fetch yer a blanket. Will that do yer?'

'It will be wonderful, Mrs Coggins. And – I'm sorry I woke you up the way I did.'

It all seemed so foolish now. The old woman patted her shoulder awkwardly, hardly knowing how to deal with this different Amy Moore with the same wide eyes and gentle voice she'd always had, but with the new posh manner and clothes the like of which old Ma Coggins had never seen before.

The new shape too . . . Amy was far too thin and reedy to Ma Coggins' mind. She'd always had a lot of flesh on her in the old days, the kind of flesh a man liked to get his arms round. Still, perhaps her handsome chauffeur chap liked her that way. As for what brought her here tonight, it was none of her business what married folk got up to, and no doubt the girl would have come to her senses by morning.

Amy spent the most restless night of her life on the lumpy sofa. From upstairs she could hear Len Coggins' snoring, like the hooting sound from one of those ocean liners that she'd seen on the silver screen.

She wished she hadn't compared it to that. Thoughts of the moving pictures always brought Daniel to her mind, and she was trying so hard to shut him out. It was no use thinking of him any more. He was gone from her life.

A clean break, gel. That's the only way to deal with things you can't change . . .

That's what Gran would have said, despite Ma Coggins telling her she should stick by Bert. She'd made the clean break from Daniel, and now everything told her she should do the same with Bert. Start afresh. Go to Australia, perhaps, as Tommy had done. But that was daft talk for a woman on her own, and she'd no doubt fall by the wayside the minute she stepped off the boat. The very thought of it frightened her to death.

Anyway, she'd already begun her independence with the tea-garden that was due to open at the end of next week. Everything was ready, tables and chairs and umbrellas bought, and Maisie and Tildy all primed to do their bit while Amy swanned around as the manageress. Was she going to forget all that because of Bert Figgins' moment of madness?

She still hadn't slept when Stratford Lane began to wake up. She heard the bed upstairs start to creak protestingly, and Len Coggins began his early cough and spit that used to be heard right through the wall in Gran's rooms. He came downstairs, dressed in his vest and trousers and tugging his braces into a more comfortable position. And even when Ma Coggins bustled about, trying to make them all seem like one happy family over the porridge and tea, he was clearly embarrassed at having to make breakfast talk with this different Amy Moore.

By then Amy's head was throbbing and her eyes sore and aching, and she could only play around with the food. But one thing was clear. She didn't belong here. You couldn't ever go back. And she'd be damned if she was letting Bert Figgins take everything she had.

27

'So you've decided to come back, have you?'

Bert blustered as best he could through his hammering headache, arms folded tightly across his chest, wishing he could still the unsteadiness in his pins. His heart pounded unpleasantly and his palms were damp. Every now and then he felt the most violent urge to spew up his guts, all of which did nothing to further the wronged-husband image he was trying to convey.

He looked at Amy narrowly, not wanting her to guess that he'd been watching for her for hours – once he awoke – and was more than thankful when the taxi-cab turned up outside the showroom late on Sunday morning.

The scandal of a missing wife was the last thing he could afford, especially since he wasn't at all clear just what had happened between them last night.

'I won't ask where you've been, but you look terrible, as if you slept on a bench in the park.'

She was as cold as ice, noting that he was still in the striped morning trousers he'd worn to the wedding, with his shirt and tie all askew and everything looking very creased and slept-in.

'Well, I didn't, and if you'll get out of my way, I'm spending the rest of the day in bed. We'll talk later.'

Bert was indignant. ''Ere, just a minute, my gel. You can't come barging in here like nothing's happened and then go off to bed.'

'I can, and that's exactly what I'm going to do.'

She brushed past him and up the stairs. Nobody spent days in bed unless they were ill, but although she wasn't physically ill, she was sorely wounded in spirit. She was so tired she was nearly dropping with sleep. It had taken a long time for Len Coggins to find a taxi-cab and persuade the sceptical cabbie that there really was a client in Stratford Lane in need of his services, which had left her humiliated and numb as well as tired.

Thank God she didn't have to see Maisie's round saucer eyes. They had given Maisie the whole weekend off to watch the wedding guests outside the church and then visit her old mum. Amy usually did the cooking herself on Sundays, but food was the last thing that interested her today, and for all she cared, Bert could starve.

In her bedroom, she undressed with shaking hands, not bothering to lock the door. If he dared to come storming in here now, she'd kill him, and he knew it. What a mess. What a bloody unholy mess.

For some incongruous reason the last thing on her mind as she crawled blissfully between the sheets of her own bed was the recollection of calling Bert a bastard. That was a real laugh, that was. Going back to Stratford Lane had reminded her that that was exactly the name polite society would use for her.

Even if nobody knew the truth, *she* was the bastard, the unwanted child of incest between a brother and sister. Searing tears blinded her eyes, and then sleep drugged her mind.

She awoke unwillingly, aware of an enticing smell in her nostrils. She wanted to stay in her twilight world, where she would never have to face up to reality again. But the smell wouldn't go away.

Good Gawd Almighty, she thought, opening her eyes wide without moving her head from the pillow, it was Bert coming into the room with a trayful of food. Amy couldn't have been more startled if the king of England had walked into the room.

'Sunday dinner,' he announced, as if nothing had ever

been amiss between them. 'Roast beef and gravy, with spuds mashed the way you like 'em, and boiled cabbage. I couldn't manage a Yorkshire pudding, so I didn't try. How does this suit your ladyship?'

She sat up slowly and looked at him speechlessly. Since she came home – however many hours ago she couldn't imagine – he'd washed and shaved and changed his clothes. He looked presentable and moderately cheerful, though he still gauged her reaction warily.

'What time is it?' she finally managed.

'Nearly five o'clock.'

Amy gasped. 'In the afternoon?'

Bert grinned. 'In the afternoon, my lady. Now then, do you want this tray on the bed or are you going to sit out to eat it?'

She looked at the tray. It looked mouth-wateringly good, and Amy realized she was starving.

'Where's yours?'

'Downstairs.'

She was almost tempted to say he could bring it up and have it with her at her little table, but she changed her mind. She hadn't forgiven him yet, and it wouldn't do for him to think she had. She pulled the bedcovers up to her neck and flattened a space on her lap.

'I'll have it in bed then, like a proper lady. And afterwards, I'll come down and we'll talk.'

'Yes, ma'am,' Bert said humbly, but his heart was singing because he knew he'd done the right thing in offering her a cooked meal. The old saying that a way to a man's heart was through his stomach didn't only apply to a man – not that he wanted her heart, just her continuing companionship.

He'd discovered this through the muddle of his thinking this morning when he'd finally realized she hadn't come home. Damn it, he was fond of her, so why couldn't that be enough? They'd struck a bargain, and he hadn't welshed on it – at least, he didn't think he had.

The memory of his hand on Amy's knee in the car and a stinging blow across his cheek seemed to hover at the back of his mind. He *couldn't* have been unfaithful to Archie, could he . . . ? The thought of that really made him sick.

Half an hour later, Amy put him right. She had dressed primly in a beige linen house-frock that was buttoned right up to the neck and fitted snugly around her spare figure. Her soft brown hair waved gently into her neck with no glitter pins to enhance it. Without a bit of rouge and a dab of lipstick, and no jewellery to brighten it up, the frock did absolutely nothing for her, and that was just the effect she wanted. Bert knew, without the telling, that he was about to get an earful.

'Now then, Bert. First of all, thank you for cooking the dinner. It was very nice.'

He muttered something, and waited. Amy got up and walked about the sitting-room as if unable to keep still, picking up this ornament and that, and glancing from time to time at the two photographs she kept on the mantelpiece. Finally, she put down the china dog she was holding, and Bert, fearful that she'd fully intended throwing it at him, breathed a small sigh.

'Last night I had every intention of leaving you for good,' she said severely. 'But today I've changed my mind. I don't see that it would serve any useful purpose. We both need a home, and the arrangement we have here suits us admirably. You're doing well with the car sales, and I intend to do well with my tea-garden.'

'Thank Gawd for that. You always were a sensible woman, Amy,' Bert murmured, unable to stop the tide of relief he felt now, and letting it show in his eyes. He saw her mouth twist into a strange smile.

'I am, aren't I? Sensible Amy – unlike beautiful Tess,

and darling Jane, and aristocratic Thelma and all the rest. Sensible Amy, that's me.'

He knew he'd said the wrong thing.

'None of them hold a candle to you, Amy,' he said indignantly. 'They might all have their charms, but you've got the lot – beauty and brains as well.'

'So did Tess, didn't she? She had everything.'

Bert shook his head, not understanding.

'Hold up, gel, Tess is *dead*.'

But before she died, she'd worn Daniel's wedding ring on her finger. The euphoria of that one night with Daniel had faded, and Amy couldn't rid herself of the suspicion that during his brief marriage to Tess, they would have made love together. Could any red-blooded man have resisted, however much he was coerced into marrying through pity? Without him near, all the doubts were back.

'Sit down, for Gawd's sake, Amy. You're as white as a sheet around the gills.'

She managed a crooked smile as she sat down on an armchair. 'You make me sound as desirable as a piece of cod,' she muttered, knowing it didn't matter.

Unless she was desirable to Daniel Easton, nothing mattered. And he'd gone from her life, leaving no forwarding address, and it was all her own fault. She could have kept him near, if she'd only said the word, but she was too proud, too intent on keeping up a front, to accept that real love was worth any sacrifice, even her good name. She'd give it all now, just to have him back.

'Why don't we leave any more discussion until tomorrow, Amy?' Bert was saying now.

'There's not much more to say. We go on as we are, but with one difference. You never take strong drink in my presence again, do you hear me?'

'That's easy enough. You know I don't drink much,'

he lied easily, 'unless I stay the night at Archie's club, of course, or it's a special occasion like a wedding . . .'

He was blustering again, and then stopped as last night became clearer in his mind, and everything she had no intention of saying was mirrored in her eyes.

'Christ, Amy – I didn't, did I – *we* didn't . . . ?'

She let him wait a full minute before she answered him with heavy sarcasm. 'Don't worry, I didn't besmirch your slender body, but if you *ever* try to touch me again, I shall go for good.'

She turned away, because it was suddenly sad and terrible, and so against nature, to see the relief in a man's eyes at knowing he hadn't made love to his wife.

'I think I'll go out for some air,' she said. 'It may help to clear my head a little.'

'Do you want me to come with you?'

'No. Even if you were with me, you wouldn't really be there, would you, Bert? Do as you like. I'm surprised Archie hasn't come calling as usual.'

She wished she hadn't made it sound as if Archie was a regular beau, and evidently Bert thought the same, as a blush went up into the roots of his sandy hair. It made him look silly and simpering, despite the pale good looks.

Amy put on a light jacket over the dull frock and set out, with no real idea of where she was going. She walked for a long while until she realized she had come to the old Roxy cinema, all white and gold frontage now, its posters blazoning the name of the latest moving picture to come from Hollywood's glamour factory.

She didn't want to look at it and feel the excitement that would have come in other days. The ambience of the place was too wrapped up with Daniel and dreams that could never come true. She hadn't really wanted much anyway. Not artificial stardom and her name in lights. All she had wanted was the love of a good man who had touched her hand in the darkness of a cinema seat and stolen her heart . . .

There was one other thing she'd decided on about her relationship with Bert. He wasn't going to know anything about the pearls Ronald and Jane had given her. He'd only start calculating their worth and wonder what he could raise on them. She was going to keep them in Ronald's safe as a little nest-egg, if ever she should need one. It was a bit like the way Gran had kept Tommy's letters with the money – except that Gran hadn't even known what they contained. It would have eased her old life considerably if she had, Amy thought sadly.

As the daylight shadows lengthened, she turned back the way she'd come, towards Claymore Street. Instead of Daniel and what-might-have-beens, she concentrated on her new resolution. Superficially, she and Bert were back where they started, and they had to make the best of it. The future might not be perfect, but at least they had a future.

Amy told herself so over and over as she neared the windows of the show-room, with its selection of glossy, lovingly polished motors inside. They were the status symbol of the successful Figginses, friends of the aristocracy, photographed at society weddings for all the big national newspapers. Who could doubt that they were a well-matched and normal loving couple?

Frank Easton gave a weak chuckle that was a vestige of his former belly-laugh, cursing the red-streaked phlegm that threatened to choke him before he spat it into the receptacle the doctor had left him. He banged the floor with the walking-stick he'd been provided with, bringing his wife hurrying upstairs to the bedroom.

'There's summat here you'll be interested to see,' he wheezed painfully. 'And summat for young Daniel to think about and all. He's well out of that trap.'

Helen walked quickly across the low-ceilinged farmhouse bedroom, and surreptitiously covered the disgusting spittoon for the doctor's nightly inspection, while she tucked the bedclothes firmly around her husband. Ever since he'd fallen heavily in the farmyard mud a week ago, he'd complained of pains in his chest; and now the doctor had ordered him to bed, saying he had a touch of pneumonia.

'What is it?' Helen asked.

Frank was surrounded by the pile of newspapers he had sent down from London every month – so he could keep up with what was going on up the road, as he called it.

The newspapers reached him long after they were out of date, but Frank went through them assiduously, reading out bits of information that were of no interest, just to impress on the others that his heart was still in the smoke and they'd better not forget it. By now, he was heartily bored with country life, and he suspected that Daniel was too, despite spending a bit of time over at the Stevens' farm now, courting that young Sophie of theirs.

'There – look. That young madam that was once a housemaid like the other one!' He never mentioned Tess's name now. 'Look at it, all done up like a dog's dinner at some toff's wedding, with a chap standing behind her and holding on to her like he owned her. Probably does, too. Didn't I tell you she knew what she was after?'

He stopped talking, needing time to regain his breath, while Helen read the piece beneath the wedding photo silently. It was Amy all right, huge-eyed and smiling, and looking as lovely as the bride, and the chap with her must be the man she'd married. Helen saw far more than her husband did, and noticed how reed-thin Amy had become now, so changed from the blossoming girl Daniel had first brought home. For all her superficial aplomb in the photo, this girl wasn't happy, she decided. Any more than Daniel was, even though he and Sophie Stevens had started walking out together. She wasn't the girl for Daniel, while this one smiling out of a London newspaper, in Helen's opinion, most definitely was.

The society wedding had been six weeks ago, Helen read. She realized how quickly the days here went, now that she was settled and happy, and becoming involved in country life, its closeness and small day-to-day dramas.

She often wondered how much of Frank's grumpiness was genuine boredom with their new life, or merely a token protest to remind her and Daniel that none of this had been his idea. She resolved that when he was better she'd suggest going for an outing to the sea. They hadn't done that yet. It would be fun to walk along the promenade at Weston-super-Mare, and Ed Rowlands had told her that very often the early September weather was balmy and mild in this part of the world.

It was the best time of the year, Ed had said, in his lovely rich country voice that Helen found quite fascinating, when all the leaves turned to gold and russet and there was that hint of frost in the air that set your blood to tingling.

Helen had another guilty thought. It wasn't only the hint of frost that set her tingling when Mr Ed Rowlands was around. It was absurd at her age, and somewhat wicked when Frank was her lawful husband, but Ed Rowlands could put the sparkle back into her eyes faster than blinking these days.

'*Well*, woman?' Frank said irritably. 'What do you think of your plain little Amy now?'

Helen started, lost in her own day-dream. She studied the faces in the newspaper photo again, conscious of the colour staining her face at the thought of how Ed Rowlands had swung her around in a square dance at the recent harvest supper at the nearby village hall.

'I think Amy looks lovely,' she said. 'Perhaps it's best not to let Daniel see this.'

'Why ever not?' Frank said as belligerently as he could, while desperately trying to stifle another bout of coughing. 'Let the boy see how the tart's turned out with her fancy friends. She'd think herself a mite too good for him now, I reckon.'

He gave up the fight and grabbed for the spittoon, and Helen rushed from the room, unable to bear the sight and sound of him a minute longer. She knew she shouldn't leave him like this. She should stay and hold his head and comfort him . . . but apart from the fact that he didn't want her witnessing his revolting exhibition, she was in danger of disgracing herself by retching, and that would do neither of them any good.

Early September in London was fresh and keen, but Amy's tea-garden was having a fine flush of success after the initial opening. The season for outdoor snacks would be a short one, and she had no plans for expanding any further. There was no room, and although they had the light canopy on a frame ready to roll down over the tables and chairs in damp weather, Amy didn't really like it, thinking it took away the whole effect of the garden idea.

As it was, Jane Derbisham declared that the whole thing had a delightfully continental look, with its gay yellow umbrellas and white wicker tables and chairs, and the yellow checked tablecloths Amy had found on a market stall.

'You're a genius for colours, Amy,' Jane had enthused when she saw the finished area. 'It looks marvellously fresh and clean, and makes one think it's always summer.'

Amy revelled in her praise, and that of the other ladies and gentlemen who decided to patronize these quaint friends of the Derbishams, who were none the less attractive and vivacious in their own way. Bert preened himself on the coat-tails of Amy's success, and since the way in and out of the tea-garden was th.ough the car show-rooms, more than one extra bit of business was conducted on either side.

'It's a pity you have to close it down for the winter, Amy,' Jane said at the end of the month, on her umpteenth visit since coming home from her honeymoon. The afternoon clients had all gone, and she and Amy were enjoying the last of the lingering sunshine together.

'Oh, I don't know. Folk don't want to turn out from their own firesides so much in the cold and damp, do they? Not even to buy new cars. Business is never very good in the winter months.'

'You and Bert should think about closing up after Christmas and going abroad to get some winter sun. Why don't you, Amy? Nobody stays in London once the New Year celebrations are over.'

Amy laughed at her enthusiasm.

'Nobody? You mean the city just empties of people and becomes a ghost town?' she teased.

'Well, you know what I mean. Those who have to work at menial occupations stay here, of course, but not people like us.'

She caught Amy's look and stopped short.

'Dear Lord, I should get a medal for putting my foot in it, shouldn't I? What must you think of me?'

Amy kissed her lightly on the cheek.

'I think you're a dear sweet friend for accepting me and Bert into your social circle, and it's still wonderful to me that you're ever able to forget what we were,' she said huskily.

'Don't be a goose. I only think of you as my friend, Amy. Nothing else matters to me. And as my friend, I'm going to let you in on a little secret.'

But she hardly had to say the words. Her glowing colour and shining eyes said it all for her, as did the protective way she put her hand over her abdomen. Once she had blurted out the words and she and Amy had got over the initial excitement of sharing the secret, Jane went on rapidly.

'Of course, I haven't seen the doctor yet, but I know I'm right, and Ronald's beside himself with joy. He's even given up the idea of trying for Parliament for the present, until after I produce our son and heir, since he wants to be around every minute of the time. I'm not sure what my mother's going to say yet. Not that we ever discussed such things, of course, but I know she'll think it an indecently quick time to become *enceinte*.'

'What the blue blazes is that?' Amy exclaimed. 'It sounds like some horrible disease.'

Jane laughed and hugged her quickly.

'Sorry, old thing. It's my mother's way of describing a lady's "delicate condition". The word simply means pregnant! I'm *pregnant*, Amy, and if it wasn't socially frowned on, I'd go around shouting it from the roof-tops!'

There'd be nothing socially frowned on about being in the pudding club down Stratford Lane way, Amy thought. Either you'd been caught before you were properly wed, in which case you hid the bump as long as you could, or you were proud of it and joined in all the ribald jokes the neighbours put about at your expense.

For one sharp, crazy, nostalgic second, she missed all that camaraderie. And then she remembered Tommy, and knew how very different it would have been for her own mother in these circumstances. It wouldn't have been dressed up with some fancy French name that nobody around Stratford Lane had the remotest idea how to pronounce.

'So next May there will be a new member of the Derbisham family,' Jane concluded, and there was such a light in her eyes now that Amy had to look away, feeling she was intruding on a very private moment.

'You won't be going abroad this winter then?' Amy

pointed out, needing to bring the conversation down to a normal level again.

'Oh, I'm sure we will. January and February are traditional months for us to get away. Do think about joining us, darling.'

But Amy shook her head, smiling.

'I don't think so, but thank you for asking, all the same. But you take care, won't you? No skiing down the mountains or wild tobogganing, or whatever else you do. You've got to think of the baby now.'

'Yes, ma'am,' Jane said solemnly, and then they were both convulsed again.

Bert was furious with her when she told him she'd declined Jane's suggestion of joining them on a winter holiday.

'Are you mad? Think of the opportunities we'd have. Meeting more people and spreading the word about Figgins' Car Sales . . .'

'That's exactly why I said no,' Amy said coldly. 'I won't let the Derbishams be shamed by your blatant attempts at salesmanship. We don't go, and that's final.'

He scowled, thinking her a short-sighted grouch. He had to admit her little venture with her teas and cakes was a howling success, and she was damn good at balancing the books too. She knew where every penny went – at least, she thought she did.

There was no chance of hiding much from Amy, except for the money he consistently filched from the business and ploughed into his visits to the bookmakers, running up huge gambling debts that would turn the air blue if she got to know about them.

And once he'd established that in any case Archie didn't intend going abroad with the others for the winter months, Bert lost all interest in the trip.

28

There had once been a time when Amy thought summer was the worst of times, when her unfashionably plump shape was tugged protestingly into the slender, figure-revealing summer frocks that exposed her shameful excesses to the world.

Now she knew that Christmas and New Year were the worst times, when all the memories of other days crowded in, and no matter how many jollifications you were involved in, if the one you wanted most of all wasn't there, it was all shallow and meaningless.

The Figginses were invited to The Gables for the Christmas and New Year celebrations. It stretched into an entire week of mad parties, drinking champagne, dressing up, playing charades and hunt-the-thimble, and singing songs around the pianoforte that brought tears or smiles, and generally having a wonderful, wonderful time . . .

'I don't know how much longer I can go on enjoying myself like this,' Amy said weakly, kicking off one buttoned shoe after the other and sprawling down on the enormous bed in the guest bedroom she was obliged to share with Bert for propriety's sake.

On the other side of the adjoining bathroom, there was a small dressing-room with a small single bed in it, and if the Derbisham maids sometimes wondered why both beds looked so obviously slept in, they were discreet enough never to discuss guests' habits.

Bert was untying the laces of his new shoes and busily admiring their glossy patent leather in the new Hollywood style, still wondering if it would be considered terribly bad form, don't y'know, to sport some of the two-tone ones the gangsters wore in the motion pictures.

He spoke idly, only half listening to Amy. 'How about our Jane then? Bit of a bombshell, wasn't it, announcing to everybody at dinner that they were producing a sprig so soon? Old Ronnie must have been quick off the mark.'

Amy looked at him with cold dislike.

'Why must you reduce everything to farmyard level?'

Bert laughed. 'And what's wrong with that? Hens do it, cows do it, birds and bees and fishes do it. Everybody does it but us, my dear sweet Amy,' he finished mockingly.

She no longer feared his innuendoes. After the fright she'd given him last July, he had taken her ultimatum to heart. He would lose more than just Amy if she walked out on him. He'd lose his good name, half his business, certainly Amy's business acumen, as well as the friendship of upper-crust people like the Derbishams who were so useful as contacts.

He'd heeded what she said about his heavy drinking, and although he was rarely seen without a glass in his hand at any of the parties they attended, few realized how seldom it was refilled when Amy was around.

Only when he and Archie stayed at Archie's club and went on one of their wild bingeing nights did the champagne flow like water, with both of them ending up completely legless, and invariably put to bed by an understanding and well-paid steward who knew just which bed to put them in.

So he was moderately sober when he made the mocking remark to his wife. She usually ignored such taunts but, for once, he saw the flash of anger in her eyes. For Amy, tonight had been a night for unbidden retrospection, and everything about 'Auld Land Syne', the meaningless kisses and embraces, the noisy, excited welcome to the brave new year of 1927, had seemed to touch a nerve deep inside her.

'Do you ever think what a sterile life we lead, Bert?' She hugged her knees, the silvery blue strands of the beautiful new shorter-length flapper dress falling away from her elegant limbs. She didn't even care about Bert seeing her like this. In their own way, they were as intimate as any two family members, with none of the blood-ties of affection that went with it.

And Bert might be going steady on the drink, but Amy had had more than her fill this evening, partly to drown the memories, and partly because people kept offering yet another toast to Jane and Ronald and the coming baby, or toasting out the old year and welcoming in the new . . . She wasn't exactly tipsy, but she felt more expansive than usual, needing to talk.

'Sterile? That's a bleedin' odd word to use, ain't it? I'd say we live a very full life, old girl. Better than some, I reckon. We can hold our heads up high these days. Would you rather be scrubbing pots and pans in Lady Beaumont's kitchen, or washing out dear Giles's bleedin' Sunday shirts?'

'I wasn't thinking of that.'

She didn't want to think of it now, but she'd asked to be reminded of it, and so she was.

'I was thinking about you, Bert. I always thought you were a bit of a lady-killer in the old days. Cut quite a dash in Aveley Square, you did, whether you were pedalling about on your old bicycle, or turning up in your uniform in Lord Beaumont's Roller. Ever so swanky, you looked then. Didn't you ever want a proper marriage, with children? And don't go getting any daft ideas, because we both know where we stand on that score! I'm just curious, that's all.'

That was the truth of it, wondering if he'd been what they called a pansy, even then, and his lady-killing ways had all been a front. She was curious, no more. Yes, she knew he was Archie's lover, whether he was aware that she

355

was certain of it or only suspected. But even so, he was a man, and surely every man must have certain natural urges and desires?

Bert laughed at the pertness in her last words.

'We're all what we are, gel, and I can't somehow see half a dozen snotty-nosed little Berts running around the place, can you? Half a dozen little Amys would be far prettier, but since neither of us intends any of it, I vote that we stop twittering and get to bed. We're out shooting early tomorrow morning. It's traditional.'

He dropped a platonic kiss on her forehead before closing the door of the dressing-room firmly behind him, and she groaned at his mention of the shooting.

New Year's Day was always the same among the gentry. The shooting parties, the men striding off through the Derbisham estate in their plus fours and long waders, rifles cocked beneath their arms, dogs yelping excitedly around their feet. And later on, the distant sounds of gunshots and triumphant shouting heralding the news that some poor bird or animal had had its life cut short, to be bagged and counted and drooled over, and finally brought to the Derbisham table, unless too many shots had blown it to bits.

To Amy, it was barbaric, almost cannibalistic, but it was the way these people lived, and nothing was going to change that.

Nor did it change the leisurely way the ladies spent their day while the men were shooting. It was too cold for tennis or croquet or picnics on the lawn, but there were always card games in the library, or chess, or jigsaw puzzles to finish, or books to read, or tapestry to work, or listening to gramophone records, or simply sitting about and gossiping, whiling away the hours with friends and acquaintances and people you hardly knew. And for Amy, being utterly bored . . .

This year, of course, there was the added domestic

excitement of Jane's coming confinement. There were names to discuss and mull over, even though nothing definite would be given away until after the baby was born. That was the Derbisham way. There was the choice of colours for the nursery to speculate upon, the élite shops to be patronized for the baby linen, the perambulator, the discussion about a suitable nanny and the jotting-down of recommended names, the description of the Broome family's heirloom christening robe to be oohed and aahed over . . .

The talk might be no more than delightful trivia among these eager ladies, ways of passing the day until the gentlemen returned and the usual evening festivities began on this last night of the Derbishams' hospitality, but it filled Amy with a pang of envy she hadn't expected.

Through it all, Amy began to realize just what she was missing. Perhaps it was what she had been fumbling to say to Bert last night, only the thoughts had never been properly formulated. It wasn't for him that she had been sad, but herself.

Because of her farce of a marriage, a real family life was always going to be denied her, and she would never know the most fundamental fulfilment of being a woman. There would be no babies to hold in her arms and cuddle to her breast. There wasn't a single thing she could do about it, because she would never, *never* try to persuade Bert to perform the sexual act with her to give her a child.

Her imagination soared alarmingly, the very thought of it repulsing her. Besides, once might not be enough. There might need to be many performances, and Bert might even discover that he liked it . . .

'Are you all right, Amy? You've gone quite pale,' one of the other guests said, leaning towards her with some concern. Amy started, as everyone in the room turned to look at her, stopping the conversation in full flood.

'I do feel a little warm. Would you mind if I went out for a breath of air?' she said, forcing a smile.

'Would you like someone to accompany you, darling?' Jane said at once.

But just as before, when Bert had wanted to walk with her on the day she gave him her ultimatum, she needed to be alone with her thoughts, and she shook her head quickly. Someone else murmured that she shouldn't go out by herself if she felt faint, but as if Jane sensed all that was going on in Amy's head, she spoke brightly.

'I'm sure Amy will be all right. Go along then, darling, but don't go too far from the house, will you? The ground is quite slippery and we don't want any accidents – and wrap up warmly.'

Amy escaped quickly. She fetched her long fur coat from her room and snuggled into it, ramming a cloche hat on top of her hair. Beneath it, she saw by her reflection in the dressing-table mirror that her eyes looked even larger than usual, and darker too, because she had been moved by a pain that hadn't occurred to her before.

She turned away from the tell-tale reflection and got outside the house as quickly as she could. The air was definitely on the chilly side and made her shiver, but it was brisk and bracing, and she needed its sting to make her face up to things. She'd never been one for refusing to do that. Gran Moore had seen to it.

And what she faced up to was the stark fact that she was tied for life to the wrong man and she was never going to have children.

She tried not to be self-pitying, but without much success. She tried being angry at herself. Until Jane was pregnant she'd never really thought about children anyway, so what was the difference now? The difference was, she answered herself miserably, that in a few months' time she'd be able to hold Jane's baby in her arms and smell the sweet baby smell of him – and she knew that the moment she did so she would be lost in longing.

And that was the price she had to pay, so there wasn't much point in fretting over what couldn't be changed. At least she could have a minor share in Jane and Ronald's child, see it and hold it and applaud its first stumbling steps and baby words . . .

She had everything else, didn't she? A good living, a nice home, money to buy lovely clothes, loyal friends. What else could she possibly need?

Daniel had known from the beginning that there was never going to be any romantic spark between himself and Sophie Stevens. He suspected very strongly that she wasn't particularly attracted to him either.

Sophie and her young sister Philippa found him a novelty, with his quick, rounded speech and the tall, dashing figure he cut in his country clothes – which sat on him very well, Sophie conceded. But that didn't mean she was ready to fall headlong in love with him, nor he with her.

To their mutual relief, they discovered the truth about each other's feelings one Sunday afternoon when they were out walking in her father's fields. They sat down for a breather beneath the shade of a large oak tree. A sluggish stream ran nearby, in one of those mysterious murky ditches that seemed fathomless but was probably no more than a few feet deep, its surface humming with dragonflies and butterflies and overhung with withies – the country name for the willows that grew so profusely in this area.

Sophie was what Daniel thought of as a typical country girl who would make a typical farmer's wife. He had always despised putting people into categories, and preferred to leave that to the fictional characters of writers like Dickens or Hardy, and he didn't like himself for doing it now.

359

But from the moment he'd seen Sophie, with her flying dark hair caught up in a ribbon, her cheeks as ripe as a rosy apple, and the sprigged cotton frocks she always wore that stated louder than words that she neither knew nor cared a fig for London fashion crazes, he had put her into a certain mould in his mind. Sophie would made the ideal farmer's wife – as long as he wasn't the farmer concerned.

'A penny for them, Daniel,' she said now, lying flat on the soft summer grass, her beribboned straw hat beside her, and she smiled at him without an ounce of coquetry.

'You wouldn't want to know them,' he prevaricated. 'Anyway, thoughts are private. Did you ever stop to think that they're the only things in this world that we can keep totally to ourselves? So why would I want to share them with anyone – even a pretty girl like you?'

He teased her then, because he'd suddenly become more serious than he intended. The words sounded pompous, even to himself, and the last thing he intended was to sound like a slick city type whose head was full of book-learning with which to dazzle a simple farm girl.

He picked a long-stemmed buttercup from the grass and tickled her beneath the chin with it. She sat up quickly, grabbed the stem and took it from his fingers, holding the sunshine bloom beneath his chin.

'You're to tell the truth now. It's an old country custom, Daniel. You hold a buttercup beneath someone's chin, and if they don't answer truthfully, it turns the skin yellow.'

'I don't particularly want my skin to turn yellow,' he began, laughing. 'And anyway, it'll only be the reflection of the sun, you ninny.'

'I don't think you feel enough about me to want to marry me,' Sophie said calmly, persisting with the buttercup beneath his chin. 'Do you?'

Daniel hesitated. In some ways this girl was as direct as Amy. She didn't fuss and flirt, and she'd make some man a good and faithful wife and give him lots of children. She

360

looked into his eyes clearly and directly, and he liked her too much to lie to her.

'No,' he said.

Sophie removed the flower and inspected the firm flesh beneath his chin carefully. 'No sign of yellow,' she said cheerfully. 'Now you can try the same on me.'

Playing her game, Daniel did as he was instructed. He held the buttercup close to the pink and white skin that was already showing little folds of an attractive plumpness.

'Do you want to marry me?' he asked.

He saw the sudden mischievousness in her brown eyes.

'Is this a proposal, as they say?'

Daniel felt a flicker of alarm until he saw that she was laughing at him.

'Oh, my lamb, your fright is showing in your eyes! Don't worry, I'm not trying to force you! The answer's no, and if you see any yellow beneath my chin, 'tis merely a trick of the light, as you say, and not of my doing.'

He dropped the flower, giving her a little shake. To any onlookers, they would seem to be very cosy indeed. To themselves, they knew they had crossed the barrier of pretence, and could slip into a more easy friendship.

'You're a witch, do you know that?'

'And I think you're already in love with somebody else,' Sophie said, with a woman's intuition.

Before Daniel could feel embarrassed, she went on airily, 'After all, what other reason could there be for you to resist my charms?'

She leapt up, calling to him that there were strawberries and cream for tea if he wanted to come back to their farm, and that if he didn't, it would be his loss and the more for her and Philippa.

Daniel snatched up her hat, forgotten in the gaiety of the moment, and tore after her, his long legs covering the ground far quicker, until he caught her and swung her round in his arms, planting a kiss on her cheek and the straw hat on the middle of her head like a cow-pat.

'Perhaps we'd better walk back more sedately,' she said, her eyes dancing with laughter. 'It is Sunday, after all. Friends?'

'Friends,' Daniel said.

As the year had gone on, the two families became quite sociable, especially after Frank Easton's unexpected demise at the end of September. His pneumonia had worsened, and Helen had woken one night from her vigil on the sofa in the bedroom, aware that something was different. For a few seconds she hadn't been able to think what it was, and then she knew. The harsh, rasping breathing had stopped.

She'd tip-toed across to the bed, and in the glow from the night-light she kept burning all night, she gazed down on the face of the man who had so often been cruel to her in the past. The man she'd once loved with all the passion of a young and eager bride, before that love turned sour because of Frank's dalliances.

There was none of the lecher in him now. There was none of the old man he had become, who could turn her stomach with his roarings and retchings. Death had taken away all of that, smoothing out the lines on his face and closing his eyes in a half-smile of serenity.

Helen looked down at him and saw only the young man he'd once been, her fiery young lover who'd promised her the earth if only she would marry him. She took his cold hands in hers and wept over him, kissing the mouth that had so often tormented her and would never speak to her again.

'Good-night, my love,' she finally said softly. 'Sleep well.'

She swallowed back the tears, straightened her shoulders and went out of the room to fetch his son.

It had been a shock to everyone, even though the labourers began to jaw privately among themselves that life at the Easton farm was a mite easier for all concerned now that the old man had gone.

The sadness of Frank's death had faded somewhat by the end of the year, but although Helen still had hopes for Daniel and the Stevens girl, he told her firmly that there wouldn't be any nuptials between himself and Sophie.

The two of them were spending a quiet Christmas Eve together and both rather dreading the next day. Frank had always made such a theatrical production out of carving the Christmas bird, and they'd always had such a laugh about the way he mishandled it . . .

Festivities always brought back memories, and even though they'd attempted to be cheerful and killed a goose for Christmas dinner, neither of them felt much like it. They were too close, too united in the past. They'd politely refused the offer to go to the Stevenses' farm, insisting that Christmas was a family time, and now that Daniel had told her the truth, she could see why.

'You're wrong, Mother,' he said, smiling slightly. 'Sophie and I have a perfect understanding. We just don't want to be married, that's all.'

'That sounds as if you've already asked her!'

'We discussed it a long while ago.'

'You *discussed* it?' Helen shook her head slightly. 'You young people these days! Even buried down here in the country, young people's ways are faster than they used to be. Everyone seems to have lost the art of romance. Are you telling me that marriage between you and Sophie Stevens is quite out of the question?'

Daniel's immediate reaction was to answer vigorously that it certainly was, and then he saw his mother's sad little face, and couldn't do it. She needed so desperately to have something to hold on to in her life, and her dearest wish now was to see her son happily settled. It was her recurring theme.

'Let's just say there's no wild passion between us, but we're fond enough of one another. Will that do for now?'

'So it's not impossible then?' she said hopefully, thinking in her innocence that marriage to a good country girl might put the ghost of Amy Moore out of Daniel's mind at last. She heard him give a short laugh.

'Nothing's impossible, Mother. We'd never be living here if it was!'

She had to be satisfied with that, as the sound of a traditional Christmas carol suddenly burst forth outside their farmhouse door. When Daniel opened it he found a great crowd of children and adults gathered there, led by his farm manager, Ed Rowlands.

The group were dressed up in Victorian costumes and carried lanterns, and in the still of the Somerset night, with the moon and stars forming a perfect backcloth, it was quite magical. Long after Helen had given them each a mince pie and Daniel had put some money in their collection boxes and sent them gratefully on their way, Ed Rowlands came back and apologized. Broad and handsome in his caped jacket and checked trousers, he looked far more the country squire than Daniel at that moment.

'I realize this is still a house of mourning, but the children kept saying it was so sad that Mr-Easton-Sir had died, and that they should come and cheer you both up. I hope it didn't upset you.'

'Of course it didn't, man,' Daniel said. 'It was good to have something happy to listen to. It's three months since my father died, and life has to go on.'

'And it's so good of you to come back, Mr Rowlands,' Helen added, her face brightened by the carol singers' appearance. And perhaps not only that. 'Won't you stay and warm yourself by the fire, and take a drink of port and another mince pie? There's plenty here.'

The man's eyes beamed at her. Their glances held for an instant and Daniel could have sworn that his mother's expression was almost girlish.

'I won't say no to that, missus. I've nothing to hurry back to my cottage for.'

'Of course, you've no wife waiting, have you?'

'Sadly, no.'

Helen made up her mind, disregarding the sudden quizzical look that Daniel shot at her. She'd never made any secret of the fact that she liked this rugged-looking farm manager with the iron grey hair, and she knew very well that there was no wife waiting at home. As Daniel poured out three glasses of port and she put another plate of her fresh-baked mince pies into the oven to warm, she spoke quickly.

'But you mustn't be all alone at home for Christmas dinner tomorrow!'

Ed laughed. 'A man on his own don't take too much notice of such occasions,' he said easily.

'Then you're not to be on your own,' Helen said firmly, just as Daniel knew she would. 'We've a goose that's far too big for the two of us, and I insist that you come and share it. Come to the farm about noon and we'll spend the day in each other's company. You'll be doing us a favour, Mr Rowlands, and save us from being gloomy.'

'Well, if you put it like that, missus . . .' The smile was getting broader every minute.

'I do. And it's time we stopped being so formal with one another, Mr Rowlands. You're to call me Helen from now on, and I shall call you Ed, unless you prefer Edward?'

'Ed will do fine.'

This time she definitely avoided Daniel's eyes. She knew he'd be amused at her sudden purposeful manner after the dark days following Frank's death. But she also avoided her son's eyes for a different reason. She was afraid he might have read the thought that was flitting through her mind.

She hadn't expected the words to be in her head, but if fate had put them there, then she wasn't going to argue with them. Fate had sent her here, hadn't it? Her thought echoed the man's own words. Ed would do fine for her too.

29

Amy welcomed the end of February when Jane and Ronald came back from the Continent. The winter had dragged. Bert and Archie had spent a lot of the time in each other's company, and although the tea-garden was closed for the winter, the car show-room still had no lack of customers, thanks to Bert's astute advertising. The moment business seemed to be slack, a picture of a brand-new motor, seen from a different angle from the last time and demonstrating a different feature to entice the enthusiast, would appear in one or other of the London newspapers, and down would come the clients to view.

'Like lambs to the slaughter,' Bert would say gleefully.

Amy had missed Jane's company, even though the exuberant letters about the splendid times they were having brought Jane instantly to her side. But as soon as the Derbishams had returned and sorted themselves out, the Figginses were invited down to The Gables for what Jane called one of their intimate little weekends. It was the middle of March by then, and the weather was looking up.

'Darling, you look so pale,' Jane exclaimed, smiling out of a face still glowing with health and continental sunshine. 'Let's hope the English spring is halfway decent this year. We're planning a welcome-home party for ourselves around Easter, before I get too jolly fat to enjoy myself. What do you think of the little chap's progress? He's growing by the hour, according to Ronald!'

She patted her swollen stomach and laughed delightedly. Pregnancy suited her very well indeed, and there was clearly to be no false modesty between friends about her condition. The fact that Bert was deep in hearty conversation with Archie and Ronald at the other side of the room didn't matter a jot.

'He looks marvellous,' Amy grinned, feeling slightly foolish to be talking about an unborn child that way. 'I hardly need to ask you how you feel – you look so well!'

'I feel absolutely spiffing. I went to see the doctor as soon as I came home. Ronald said I should, just to be on the safe side, so we shot off to Harley Street, and apparently I'm a wonderful specimen of womanhood.'

She imitated the ponderous tones of the eminent doctor who went by the title of Mr, which, as Amy discovered, was more important.

'And you'll both come down in April, won't you, darling? It'll be a quieter affair than usual – but only as far as I'm concerned, of course. The rest of you can dance until dawn if you wish, but my infant and I will be retiring slightly earlier.'

She gave a special smile that totally excluded Amy. With a shock, Amy realized that if marriage to Ronald had inevitably changed Jane's relationship with her a little, the presence of the new baby was going to do so even more.

Already Jane and the unborn baby shared a secret world of their own that no one else could touch. It was stronger than the bonds the child would have with its father, and would be undiminished by the child growing up and taking a wife. The bonds that existed between a mother and child were too deep to be severed by the mere cutting of the umbilical cord, and Amy had never been more aware of it.

She realized Bert was talking to her excitedly.

'Archie and I are going to take up his flyer as soon as the weather's more stable. It's been grounded all winter, but we mean to make the most of it this summer.'

'Just don't break your necks,' she said.

And if you do, hip-hip-hooray. The unworthy thought was in and out of her head even before she could be disgusted with herself for thinking it.

'Archie will see it never comes to that,' Bert said proudly. 'He's taught me a lot, and he's going to let me take the controls next time we go up.'

'I don't know about next time, old boy,' Archie said, with the kind of indulgent smile usually kept for babies or pet dogs that was totally lost on Bert. 'I said I might, if you're a good boy and behave yourself.'

God, can't any of them *see* it? Amy thought. There were the two of them, simpering and ogling each other like two vamps of the silent pictures, and nobody seemed to be aware of it except herself! *Thank God*, she added fervently. With his fleshy mouth and the coy sideways glances at Bert, alternating with the occasional quick embraces that were supposed to be manly and matey, Archie simply made Amy's flesh creep.

But she didn't have to spend her time thinking about Archie Derbisham with his fair hair and film-star good looks that obviously sent Bert into raptures the way Douglas Fairbanks had sent her and Tess . . .

Her nerves jumped at the unexpected memory, and the cup in her hand jerked, spilling a few drops of tea on the Derbishams' beautiful Axminster carpet. Nobody seemed to notice, and she surreptitiously rubbed it in with the toe of her shoe. She could just imagine Lady Beaumont's expression if she'd been caught doing such a thing . . .

She was doing it again – dredging up past memories without meaning to! It was starting to happen often lately, and she began to wonder if she was going mad. These last few winter months with Jane away and nothing to do, the tea-garden all closed up and the tables and chairs and umbrellas stacked away until the short summer season, had all combined to make her restless, longing for the unattainable again . . . and Jane's evident delight in her pregnancy was only accentuating that restlessness.

* * *

'Let's go dancing,' she said to Bert on the way back to town, when both of them sat in the car, together and apart, each silent with their own thoughts.

'What – now?' He started to laugh. 'You do come out with some daft suggestions, gel. For a start, it's Sunday, and there ain't no dance halls open.'

'No. Tomorrow afternoon. There's always a tea-dance at Flannery's on a Monday afternoon, for beginners, mostly.'

'We're better than beginners,' Bert began.

'Oh Bert, let's *do it*.' She said it with such urgency that he looked at her in surprise.

She was all flushed in the face, eyes as brilliant as if she'd been crying – or was about to. Bert, who knew nothing about the intricacies of the female sex and didn't want to, shrugged his shoulders. Better a quiet life than a scratchy one.

'All right, if you want to. But if you lose me a big sale, I'll demand compensation, mind.'

He was grinning, hoping to tease her out of the strange mood he was slowly beginning to sense.

'You'll never know, will you? Not if we shut up shop for the day.' Or for ever, as far as she was concerned.

The thought filled her head like a thunderbolt, and yet it was somehow inevitable, as if she had always been waiting for this to happen. Without warning, without reason, she lost all interest in Figgins' Car Sales and Tea Garden, in everything. Life was suddenly meaningless and grey, all the colours dimmed.

She felt the small sob in her throat. She'd wasted everything good that had been offered to her, and she had no one to turn to to spill out all her hurts. Jane – dearest Jane – had everything. Not just money and position, for Amy too had those things in a lesser way. What Jane had was beyond price. She had a husband she loved and who adored her; beneath her heart she had a

370

baby growing out of that love; she had a father who had so proudly given her into Ronald Derbisham's charge less than a year ago.

Amy gave a dragging breath. *Oh, Tommy, Tommy, why did you leave me? Even if I was never meant to know the truth, I loved you desperately as an uncle. Why couldn't we have gone on the way we were so that I had somebody to lean on . . . ?*

'You all right, gel?' Bert sounded uneasy. 'Look, if it means so much to you, I've said we'll put on our glad rags and go dancing tomorrow. How's that? Never let it be said that Bert Figgins didn't try to please his little wifey, and there's always another day for selling cars.'

She didn't dare say that perversely she'd already changed her mind, that dancing wasn't the answer. Because perhaps it was. Perhaps they should tog themselves up and go into town and pretend to be the bright young things they'd been such a short while ago. Well, Bert still was, of course. He still had his secret. Just as Amy had hers.

'Thanks, Bert. You're a pal,' she forced herself to say with a brittle smile.

And tomorrow she'd put on a pretty silky-thin frock and dancing slippers, and wear the most glittery, extravagant beads acceptable for an afternoon affair, and she'd be bright and frothy and gay and forget all her troubles. After all, she didn't really have any, did she? Not on the surface, anyway.

The weekend of the Derbishams' April party turned out to be two of those unexpectedly glorious days that delude people into thinking summer has come early. The guests flocked down to the estate, revelling in the sunshine and casting off layers of heavier clothes with complete disregard for the old saying that it was wiser never to cast a clout until May was out. Jane was hugely pregnant by now, the last few weeks having expanded her waistline almost beyond repair, as she moaned ecstatically to the ladies. Even that couldn't dim her radiance.

For the Saturday afternoon, when the last of the guests would have arrived, it was decided to have an enormous picnic lunch on one of the back lawns. The servants were instructed, and with all the smooth efficiency of an army manoeuvre, long trestle tables covered with white damask cloths appeared, and tartan rugs were spread over the velvet lawn for the guests to sit on while enjoying the feast being brought out by a regiment of maids.

Nothing the Derbishams wanted was ever out of reach. A garden chair was provided for Jane, who would be too uncomfortable on the ground. For the rest, it all had the beginnings of an enchanted afternoon, and when all the food had been eaten and the champagne had made them deliciously dizzy, Ronald ordered a gramophone and records to be brought outside, and there would be dancing in the open air.

'I say, what a brilliant idea of Ronald's. This will set a new fashion for summer weekends,' one and another exclaimed, and Amy looked around eagerly for Bert.

They had mastered the steps of the tango very well, and she had no objection to showing off her skills with Bert, who was a very good partner. She tried to find him among the kaleidoscope of ladies in their bright afternoon frocks and the men minus their jackets and looking casual and at home.

'Have you seen Bert?' she asked Jane.

'I think he and Archie have gone off to take a spin in the flyer, darling,' Jane said. 'I heard Archie say they were going to give us some entertainment.'

Amy fumed. He could have waited. He didn't know there was going to be dancing in the open air, but he still could have waited. He could have told her where he was going, not sneaked off with Archie like two errant schoolboys.

Anyway, once the gramophone was wound up and the metallic sounds of the music blared out, Amy didn't lack for partners. There were several unaccompanied men, and a few married ones too, who were only too glad to whisk the adorable Amy Figgins around in their arms with the excuse of the exotic tango. She felt the flat of her latest partner's hand on the small of her back as he bent her backwards, and she laughed at the earnest expression on his red face as he tried to keep his balance, so different from his everyday banker's face . . .

'Careful, Cedric, we don't want to end up in a dreadful heap on the grass,' she giggled, intoxicated by the sun and the music and the champagne.

The man righted her, thrusting her arm forward with his in the dramatic walk-step, his cheek pressed tight to her own.

'Why don't we?' Drunk on champagne, he flirted outrageously with her. 'I'd love to end up in a heap on the grass with you, beautiful Amy, and I promise you it wouldn't be dreadful at all!'

She giggled again as they twisted round the other way, their cheeks so clammy with exertion and the heat of the day they were almost fastened together like glue. And then they heard a great cheer go up from the rest of the company, and a whining noise began to come nearer and nearer. Everyone stopped dancing, but no one let go of their partners.

The flimsily built flying machine seemed to come right out of the sun, its waving occupants as daringly glamorous as those flamboyantly heroic aces of the vaguely remembered war. Amy held her breath as the aeroplane swooped right down towards them, and she could clearly see Bert's excited face as he held the controls. He waved madly as Archie leaned his fair head forward to shout instructions.

Amy felt her heart pound. Dear God, this was crazy.

The two of them had been drinking far too much – for once Bert had forgotten his good intentions when Amy was around.

Bert had also forgotten that Amy existed. It was too blisteringly hot to limit his intake of champagne during the picnic and, anyway, he needed it to give him extra courage, because every time he remembered Archie had finally promised to let him take up the flyer himself, his mouth went completely dry. Now, nothing existed for him any more but this marvellous, exhilarating feeling of power. He was God, he was almighty, all-powerful . . .

Up here in the blue, blue sky, without a cloud on the horizon, and with Archie's comforting presence to guide him, he felt himself capable of anything. He was part of the universe, he could conquer mountains . . . He swooped and dived, and skimmed the trees on the edge of the estate, before turning the plane around, curving the wings so that the earth swayed deliciously, and then righting them again to go straight for the crowd of butterfly people on the ground. He was laughing and thinking himself no end of a swell as they ducked their heads and cheered him. He saw the sunlit shadow of his own plane beneath him, and for a moment he stared, fascinated . . .

'Keep her level, Bert,' he heard Archie suddenly screech. 'Get her nose up! Don't let her drop, for Christ's sake! You'll never recover her lift –'

The watchers thought it was all part of the entertainment. One minute the plane was swooping and doing all kinds of fancy tricks. The next, it was hovering, as if it was waiting for something. And then it plunged to the ground, spiralling in a ball of flame.

For Amy, for one horrific instant, time seemed to be suspended. Her eyes refused to take in what she had just seen. Her ears refused to accept that all around her people were screaming, and in the background the tinny sounds of a tango tune blared on. And then someone was shaking her, and she realized she was screaming too, because the only way any of them could express their agony at what they'd just witnessed was to scream, scream, scream . . .

'Don't look, Amy love,' the banker was saying hoarsely.

'We've got to get them out!' She was still screaming, beating her hands against his chest. 'We've got to save them!'

'Amy, it's no use.'

Some of the men were beginning to run towards the inferno of the aeroplane – Ronald and his guests, and the impeccable butler, who was crying without knowing it. Jane was weeping uncontrollably, the ladies crowding around her protectively so that Amy couldn't see her properly, the queen bee whose well-being must be assured. But *she* was the bereaved wife, not *Jane* . . .

Amy registered everything minutely, as if she had to store it away in her memory to bring out later and relive the horror all over again. It was her penance. She'd been so wicked, half-hoping Bert would break his neck – it was a wicked and terrible thing to do, to wish somebody dead. And now it had happened. The reality of it washed over her anew, and she pressed herself into the banker's helpless arms while great gusting sobs were wrenched out of her.

It was all my fault. I wanted this to happen and now Bert's dead. The words shrieked through her head for the first time. *Bert's dead.*

'Give her some brandy and get her inside.'

'I think you'll have to carry her. She's nearly fainting.'

'See to Jane. I'll bring Amy.'

She heard the words as if through a great fog. She felt as if she was floating through space, and vaguely realized she was being carried into the house and laid on a sofa. Then someone pushed the stinging liquid she hated into her mouth, and it merely dribbled down her chin because she was simply incapable of swallowing it.

'I'm so sorry. So sorry,' she mumbled to no one in particular.

The arm around her tightened. 'It doesn't matter, darling. The frock can easily be cleaned.'

She looked up vacantly at the nice woman who had spoken, a friend of Jane's she hardly knew, calling her darling as if she was precious and important. And getting completely the wrong idea. Amy wasn't sorry because of a few drops of spilt brandy on her frock. She was sorry because it was her fault the plane had crashed. Her fault that Bert and Archie were dead . . .

She gave a sudden gasp as her head cleared slightly. Archie was dead too. The Gables was going to be a house of mourning, because Ronald Derbisham's brother was dead. She hadn't even registered that. She was shamed into quiet sobbing again, struggling to sit up and looking around her frantically.

'Where's Jane? I must speak to Jane – and Ronald . . .'

'Later.' Still holding on to her, the woman prayed that the girl wasn't going to be completely deranged over the terrible accident. She had such a wild, intense light in her eyes. 'Jane's gone up to her room to rest quietly. The baby, you know.'

'Oh God, nothing's happened, has it?'

'No, no, but she needs to stay calm, and her parents have been sent for. I'm sure they'll stay here tonight if they think it's necessary. You must stay too, Amy, although the rest of us will naturally be going home. But you shouldn't be alone, and I'm sure Ronald will insist on it.'

Amy didn't care what happened to her, as long as she didn't have to think for herself. She had known grief before, all kinds of grief. When Tommy went to Australia, when Gran Moore died, when Daniel married Tess, and then when Tess . . . But none of that grief had been mixed with guilt the way this was. She hadn't loved Bert, except as a sister would love a brother.

She turned her face into the soft plush of the Derbisham sofa. Even the innocence of that thought turned to shame, remembering the incestuous way her parents had loved one another. At that moment she couldn't think of any sort of love with anything but revulsion. The whole world was ugly and obscene, and she was part of it. Oh yes, she was part of it for wishing her husband dead.

The Derbishams' Harley Street doctor was spending an unusually quiet Saturday afternoon tending his roses. On such a splendid day as this, Sheldon Kemp was always thankful he didn't normally make house-calls unless summoned by his most important patients. The sound of the telephone ringing caused him to sigh a little, and he left his housekeeper to answer it, hoping it was one of those wretched wrong numbers.

He arrived at The Gables to find that most of the weekend house-guests had slipped quietly away to tell their own tale to friends and relatives. Already the press had got wind of it and was hounding anyone who was there for news, but mercifully his principal charges were well out of sight from prying eyes.

He switched off the engine of his Daimler-Benz motor and paused for a moment, admiring as ever the way this graceful old house lazed in the April sunshine, deceptively quiet and serene. But once he stepped outside his car, he breathed in air that was still rancid with engine oil and smoke and burning wood, and the stench of something only those who had smelled it before would recognize. Once smelled, never forgotten, he thought grimly, the stench of burnt flesh . . .

The debris was all cleared away by now, leaving only a wide patch of scorched earth, but the scars on the human mind would remain far longer than it took for the sweet young grass to grow again. Kemp sighed, wishing it was as easy to cure such ailments as to mend a broken limb.

The butler, eyes red-rimmed from weeping, opened the door at once. Kemp patted the old man on the shoulder. These old retainers took any disaster to their families very much to heart, and this was a disaster of some magnitude.

'Mr Derbisham is in the drawing-room, sir,' the butler said. 'Follow me, please.'

Kemp did so, wishing himself anywhere but here. Away with his roses or pondering over his stamp collection. This was a part of his career that he particularly hated, when he tried to comfort a bereaved person in shock, knowing that neither the most junior nor the best-trained physician in the world could ever be adequate for the task.

And knowing the truth of that old adage, time heals – but try to mention that to those in most pain, and they'd rage at you for daring to suggest that this would ever end. People needed the pain of grief. They needed the time it took to adjust to a world without their loved ones, and there was no hurrying it, nor any yardstick to measure one person's acceptance time against another's.

'My dear sir,' he said to Ronald now. In lieu of verbal sympathy, he clasped him by the elbow, and was somewhat relieved to see that the man was well in control of himself. It was the breeding, Kemp thought. It always showed. 'How is Mrs Derbisham?'

'As one would expect,' Ronald said abruptly. 'She's resting, and of course I'd be glad if you would take a look at her. But it's not Jane whose condition disturbs me most. It's the wife of Archie's friend who died in the crash with him. She will be staying here for a while . . . Mrs Figgins.'

Kemp tried not to raise his eyebrows too obviously. Figgins. It hardly sounded like a well-connected name. But if Derbisham was willing to pay his not insubstantial bill for attending to the lady, then so be it.

After attending to Mrs Derbisham and adminstering a

mild sedative, he was shown into another room, where a young woman lay prostrate on the bed, gazing empty-eyed at the ceiling. The maid seated near the window stepped forward and whispered to the newcomer.

'She's not said a word since being brought in here, sir, not a blessed word. No crying nor nothing –'

'Thank you.' Kemp cut her short, and moved across to the bedside. 'Will you please wait by the door while I examine my patient?'

The girl was obviously in deep shock. He shone a light into her eyes and felt her pulse and tested her reflexes, to reassure himself that there was nothing physically wrong. He studied her thoughtfully. Some of his methods were known to be unorthodox, but unless there was obvious physical disability, he believed in treating shock with shock, and making patients face up to reality as quickly as possible before any mental instability set in. He spoke deliberately, close to her face.

'Mrs Figgins, your husband couldn't have suffered for very long, if at all. It's quite probable that the two men were already dead when the aeroplane burst into flames. They undoubtedly broke their necks.'

There was no response, and Kemp repeated the same words over and over, five times, then ten, then twenty, and began to think that this time he'd failed. If patients didn't react almost immediately to his tactics, it was often a long haul to get them back to sanity again. And in these lovely eyes there was still the dull, still, vacant look of the manic-depressive . . . Then at last the eyes flickered and looked directly at him. They were blazingly alive again, angry and accusing.

'Don't tell me daft things I already know! Of course Bert's dead, and of course he broke his bleedin' neck, you gormless 'ap'orth of tripe!'

She curled up in a ball and began crying quietly into the pillow, while the maid gaped at this lapse into gutter-talk from the classy Mrs Figgins. But Kemp patted the young lady's back and told her more gently that he'd be leaving some pills for her to take, and he'd call again in a few days' time. Few things shocked Sheldon Kemp. He'd seen and heard it all before, and all that mattered to him was that his patients got well.

30

The London newspapers might have given it greater headlines, had the weekend not coincided with a bank robbery in which two policemen and a night-watchman had been killed. The matter of a small private plane crash had to be relegated to halfway down the front page, but was still given due coverage because of Archie being the brother of Ronald Derbisham of The Gables. Bert's credentials were given slightly lesser space, but a photo of them both, taken at Ronald's wedding, was featured prominently.

Amy forced herself out of her initial shock by remembering how bad Jane and Ronald must be feeling, though they were undoubtedly more stoical than she was. They were all thankful when the ordeal of the funerals was over. Amy remained at The Gables, wondering guiltily if they really wanted her there, since Bert had virtually killed Ronald's brother. She wouldn't blame them if they couldn't stand to look at her any more.

'Don't be ridiculous, darling,' Jane said, when Amy hesitantly said as much to them. 'We both love you, and you're to stay as long as you like.'

'I can't stay for ever,' she said with a wan smile.

Jane and Ronald exchanged glances.

'Why not?' Ronald said gruffly. 'God knows, there's enough room in this barn of a place, and you won't want to go back to Claymore Street . . .'

She looked at him as if such a thing had never occurred to her before. 'Of course I will. It's my home.'

'Amy darling, you can't run a car show-room by yourself,' Jane said gently. 'And the tea-garden wouldn't attract

381

any customers by being at the back of an empty window display.'

'It needn't be empty. I could get in a manager – somebody who knew something about cars. I – I can't just abandon it after all Bert's efforts.' She spoke with a kind of desperation in her voice.

Ronald cleared his throat.

'You do know that Archie was a sleeping partner in the enterprise, don't you, Amy?'

'Yes,' she murmured, not looking at him.

'You probably haven't considered the implications, but since I'm Archie's next of kin, then half of the partnership now belongs to me. You and I are partners in Figgins' Car Sales, Amy.'

No, she hadn't thought of it. She didn't want to think of it. She didn't want to think.

'And I'm suggesting that we sell the place outright to the highest bidder. There's a lot of valuable stock standing there, for which the suppliers will be wanting their money, and neither you nor I have the same interest in motors and engines that Bert had. You know now of the gambling debts to be paid out of the estate. I'm afraid that when everything's sorted out you won't be worth a fortune, Amy, but you'll be reasonably comfortable. And both Jane and I honestly believe it would be best to clear out the past, my dear, and make a fresh start.'

She stared at him dully. Yes, there had been the shock of Bert's gambling debts that she hadn't known about. There were bookmakers with outrageous bills to be paid, and outfitters calling in their money from the long-standing accounts Bert had run up. And none of the expensive shiny cars in the show-room was actually paid for yet.

Common sense told her to do as Ronald urged, to sell the business and the goodwill. Clear out the past. She seemed to be constantly doing that and getting nowhere. One part of her wanted to rebel, to get in a manager for

Bert's car sales and continue with her tea-garden, and prove something to the world. Or get rid of the motors and use the show-room as a frontage for an entirely new venture. *Amy's Tea Rooms, teas available outside or in, in hot or cold weather*, with a different kind of splashy advertisement in every newspaper . . .

Even as she thought it, she knew it wasn't what she wanted. That was Bert's style, not hers. She felt Jane's hands grip her cold ones.

'Please consider it, Amy. I can't bear the thought of you going back to that place on your own. Ronald will see to everything if you'll agree to sell up. Stay here with us and help me with the baby – please?'

At last she nodded slowly, unable to argue any more. What did it matter anyway? These good friends wanted her, and nobody else did.

She went back to Claymore Street once after that. Ronald and Jane went with her, and she directed everything as dispassionately as she could, donating Bert's clothes to a worthy charity and taking only what was her personal property. The rest was to be sold, the profits shared between herself and Ronald. And then their brief partnership would be at an end.

Helen Easton had never cancelled the bundle of newspapers that arrived from London once a month addressed to Frank. It was something she forgot to do, but life was so full and happy now, and, anyway, she enjoyed browsing through the pages, finding it a source of amazement that news which was of such importance to city folk seemed like something from another planet to her. She unfolded one that was dated early in April, and sat up with a jolt.

It was the middle of July by the time the letter reached Amy at The Gables, having been redirected several times. From the scribblings on the envelope, it seemed to have been sent all over London before finally reaching Sussex. There was something vaguely familiar about the hand-writing, but she had no idea who could be writing to her. The original postmark was completely obliterated by all the rest. She stopped rocking the perambulator in which the cherubic Derbisham son and heir now slept peacefully, and opened the envelope curiously.

'*My dear Amy*,' she read, and glanced quickly at the signature. She drew in her breath, her heart lurching at seeing the name of Helen Rowlands, lately Easton.

I've only just learned of your great tragedy, and had to write and offer you my sympathy. My dear, I do understand what you'll be suffering now, since I lost Frank in September of last year. As you'll see by my signature, I am recently married to a very dear man who is our farm manager, and although I would not want to be insensitive by saying that in time I hope you too will find happiness again, I assure you that it can happen, quite unexpectedly.

If you ever feel in need of a change of scene, do please come and stay with us. The country has a very beneficial and soothing effect on the nerves. If you feel disinclined to stay with those you once knew, then I can recommend Weston-super-Mare as a resort of great charm and bracing sea air. The Grand Atlantic Hotel is right opposite the promenade and you would be extremely comfortable there.

I do urge you to get away from your present surround-ings, Amy, as you will see things in a better perspective. If you do, please contact me by letter or telephone. If nothing else, I could join you at your hotel for tea. I would so like to see you again. Meanwhile, my sincere condolences,

Helen Rowlands (lately Easton)

Amy was taken completely off balance by the letter. Frank was dead, and Helen had married again . . . *and there had been no mention of Daniel*. That was the most startling thing of all. She scoured the letter, trying to read between the lines for any hidden message.

If you feel disinclined to stay with those you once knew . . . What inference could she take from that? Had Daniel instructed his mother to say he didn't want to see Amy and this was her way of softening it? Had time changed everything, after all?

The baby began snuffling, and Amy rocked the perambulator absent-mindedly. It was a lovely mid-summer afternoon and Jane had gone for a drive with Ronald to view some property he wanted to acquire. Here in the quiet grounds and affluent haven of The Gables, where she was slowly coming to terms with being alone, she could pretend that all this was hers. She was a movie queen with the world at her feet, and this was her adored child . . .

As he started crying in earnest, she plucked him out of his perambulator, keeping him well wrapped in his shawl, and began rocking him against her shoulder, crooning softly to him. He smelled of sleep, warm and fragrant, his soft mouth against her thin frock, and she knew she was in danger of becoming far too fond of him. He wasn't her child, but too often this pretence overtook her reasoning, and she understood just how nannies and governesses became attached to their charges to the point of obsession. She didn't want that to happen to her. She laid him back quickly, seeing his blue eyes blinking up at her.

'You just go to sleep, young Master Derbisham,' she said severely, 'while I think about all this.'

She smiled crookedly, knowing the decision had already been made. The moment she realized that Helen had never mentioned Daniel at all, she was burning with curiosity to know why. She suddenly went rigid. It could be because he was already married to somebody else. But she still had to know. She had to find out for herself, and by the time Jane and Ronald came home to take charge of their ewe-lamb, Amy had made two important telephone calls.

'Will you take me to the station tomorrow morning, Ronald?'

He looked at her in surprise. 'Of course I will, but whatever for?'

'I've decided to get right away for a little while. I think the change will do me good, and someone once mentioned Weston-super-Mare to me, so I thought I'd go there to get some sea air. You don't mind, do you?'

'Good lord, no. Jolly good idea,' he said, trying to hide his amazement at the new authority in Amy's manner. 'We could all go.'

Jane put her hand on his arm. 'No, we couldn't. This is something Amy needs to do by herself. Have you any idea how long you'll be away, darling?'

Amy shook her head, suddenly a little choked. Somehow Jane had known instinctively of her need, whether she guessed about the rest or not. Jane knew that the Easton family had packed up and gone to live in the country, and that was all.

'I thought I'd have a lazy time and come back when I felt like it. I'll let you know when I'm about to descend on you again, of course. Does that sound too inconvenient of me?'

Jane put her arms around her and kissed her. 'Of course it doesn't. This is your home for as long as you want it to be, Amy. You know that.'

Amy knew something else. These two were coping with the tragedy better than Amy herself. They had each other and their child. They were a complete unit. She still had to find something of her own to cling to.

Amy spent a solitary evening packing her clothes into a borrowed suitcase. She had no idea if this would be a short stay or a long one. She only knew she had to see for herself whether Daniel Easton still loved her.

'You did *what*?' Daniel asked his mother angrily.

She had moved into Ed Rowlands' cottage after their

quiet wedding, despite his efforts to get them to move in here. But they were at the farm most days, and always on Sundays, when his mother took over from Daniel's buxom housekeeper and did the cooking and baking herself.

'Mother, I can't believe you wrote to Amy and invited her to stay. And what about Bert Figgins? What do you think he's going to say about that? Or is he coming too? Because if that's the case, I can assure you I shan't be here to see him.'

'Will you stop shouting at me? You sound just like your father,' Helen said calmly. 'And before you say anything else, you'd better read this.'

She handed him the old newspaper she'd kept at the cottage all this time. Both she and Ed had decided there was no point in showing it to Daniel until they knew for sure whether Amy would even come, and until Helen was sure in her own mind that he didn't have fond feelings for Sophie Stevens. Then Sophie had announced her engagement to someone else, and Helen had almost decided that Daniel was destined to be alone for ever, since it was so long since she'd written to Amy and got no reply.

Then out of the blue, there had been a telephone call at the cottage, and Amy's voice saying she was at the Grand Atlantic Hotel in Weston-super-Mare. She'd been there a week already, and if Helen still wanted to see her, could she come to tea one afternoon?

'How long have you known about all this?' Daniel said at last.

'A while. I didn't see the point in telling you until I'd written to Amy. I didn't hear from her for a long time, and she's been staying with friends ever since her husband was killed. Now she's in Weston-super-Mare on a visit, and she's expecting me to turn up at the Grand Atlantic Hotel for tea this afternoon at four o'clock.'

They looked at each other.

'I'll be there,' Daniel said abruptly, as they had both known he would.

Amy sat on the warm sand, watching it trickle through her fingers like spun gold and feeling it slide deliciously through her toes. She had never been to the seaside in her life before, and it was an experience that enchanted her. The train-ride had been terrifying at first, noisy and rattling, then finally marvellous. She watched the countryside go past the window as if it were on a moving picture screen.

She loved everything about her new surroundings, though she'd been dumbstruck when she'd first seen the huge hotel with its elegant filigree wrought-iron balconies and its pointed turrets like the French châteaux Daniel had once told her about. But when she realized she was being treated deferentially as a lady of some importance, she relaxed and enjoyed the experience of being waited on.

She had decided she could afford one of the best rooms overlooking the wide crescent of the bay, where the sand stretched for miles and the sea came in twice a day and seemed to go away for ever before it miraculously returned.

She loved to hear the plaintive sounds of seagulls wheeling and dipping and screaming into the wind; she loved the tug of the salt breeze in her hair, the spray tingling against her face when the tide was in and the waves were rough; watching those who dared the quick dash into the waves and hearing the screams of mingled pleasure and horror as they dashed back again with the shock of the cold water thrashing against their legs; the bright little yachts that bobbed along the horizon in the afternoons, and the children who kicked up the sand and built sandcastles and roared and laughed with so much excitement.

And she loved her own early morning walk along the soft damp sand at the sparkling water's edge, leaving footprints behind her, and feeling like Robinson Crusoe; the sharp pang in her heart when she glanced back at them and saw how lonely one set of footprints looked; and, above all, the gradual realization that the tonic was beginning to work, and she was finding peace with herself at last.

She had been there a week before she found the courage to ask the hotel people to get her the telephone number Helen had given her. She clasped her hands around her knees now, gazing across the expanse of grey-blue water that was the Bristol Channel, to the distant hazy outline of Wales. The locals said that if you could see Wales clearly, it meant it was going to rain; if you couldn't see it at all, it was probably already raining.

It wasn't raining today. It was a beautiful day, with the breeze fresh off the sea, and an old friend was coming to the hotel for afternoon tea. She'd left a message, in case Helen got there early, that she was walking on the beach and would be back sharp at four.

Amy felt horribly nervous about seeing Helen again after all this time. The hour was almost here, but the hotel was just across the promenade. It would only take her a few minutes to go inside and brush her hair and wash her face and make herself look presentable . . .

She got to her feet and shook the sand from her frock, slipping her feet back into her sandals. She glanced at her watch. Just five more minutes . . . She walked slowly along the firm sand, breathing in the ozone that was supposed to have such marvellously restorative properties, if you believed everything you were told.

Her eyes squinted. The sun was dazzling against the blue of the sky, and sent spots before her eyes when she looked away from it again. She was half blinded for a minute, and side-stepped as she realized someone was walking purposefully towards her. He wasn't dressed for the beach, and nor was she. His shoes were Sunday shoes, as if he was here to meet someone. His clothes were country casual, but still too smart for the seaside. His walk was suddenly familiar, the cut of him acutely remembered . . .

Amy's heart was already thudding in her chest. Not six feet away from her and coming ever nearer was Daniel.

For one crazy moment she felt as though she was experiencing a sequence from every motion picture she had ever seen in her life.

The hero and heroine were running towards each other along a sunlit shore, straight into each other's arms, and seconds later the cinema pianist played them out with crashing chords meant to depict passion and fulfilment, and then the picture faded while the lovers drifted off into the sunset, happy ever after . . .

Daniel stopped a foot away from her. His face was unsmiling, awkward, seeing this lovely slender new Amy with the gossamer frock of muted blues and yellows, and the long elegant scarf wound about her head and trailing over her shoulders. He felt stunned by her, and for the life of him he couldn't rush this moment.

Amy saw only his indecision, and the crying started somewhere deep inside her. There were no lover's arms reaching out for her. There was no music, no thundering waves, only the cry of a gull soaring skywards, and the sad sound of a lisping sea.

'I – I didn't expect to see you,' Amy stammered.

'My mother thought it would be a good idea,' he said shortly. 'And we both wanted to say how sorry we were to hear about your husband's accident.'

'Thank you,' she murmured, shocked beyond belief that they could be standing here like this, two strangers who were once as close as each other's heartbeats. It was more than a year since they'd met and loved and been so intimately a part of each other, and that year suddenly seemed like an eternity.

'Amy.' He put his hands on her shoulders, and pulled her to him.

They embraced briefly, since they were in public, and she felt his mouth touch hers in a kiss that told her nothing. Her eyes burned with sudden suspicion. Did he think she'd come chasing after him, and felt obliged to come to tell her he no longer loved her? She was bewildered, numbed, unable to read anything in his expression.

'Did your mother come with you?' she asked, for want of something to say.

'No.'

She made an enormous effort to act normally, as any other lady would when a gentleman came to see her.

'Then perhaps we'd better go and have some tea at the hotel. I suppose a farmer can't stay away from his farm too long. Do you enjoy it?' She heard herself half-heartedly organizing him the way she used to organize Bert.

Daniel shrugged his shoulders as they went slipping and sliding over the yielding sand.

'It's not really my vocation. My heart's still in the city.'

And not with me?

'I was sorry to hear about your father.'

'Thank you. It was quite a shock.'

It was terrible. They were making the most inane small talk that was getting them nowhere. She hadn't thought beyond seeing his mother and finding out about Daniel through her. She hadn't expected this stranger who was holding her hand to help her across the expanse of shifting sand towards the promenade, then stamping his feet to rid himself of it before they went into the hotel.

Once inside, Amy showed him the way into the afternoon lounge.

'Will you order the tea and cakes, and I'll join you in a minute?' she said, and quickly escaped upstairs to her room. Inside, she leaned against her door, her heart pounding. She loved him so much . . . so much. But the barriers were still there. Tess, and Bert, and everything that had gone between . . . It was too soon, and yet, heartbreakingly, she knew it was too late. They were no longer the same two people.

She washed her face, conscious that she'd been in the sun too long, and that it was as red as if she was feverish. Her eyes were stormy, and she was angry at life, at fate, at everything that had made her and Daniel into what they were now, instead of the fresh young lovers they should be. She was still too wrapped up in grief, in guilt, and he . . . She went down to the lounge again, almost afraid he'd be gone.

'Have you met any nice people here?' she forced herself to ask when they had been served with tea and scones and iced cakes.

'They're all nice people. The type they call the salt of the earth.' He tried not to sound condescending, and cursed himself for coming at all. He'd imagined himself gathering her up in his arms and saying that everything was going to be all right for them from now on. But her bewildered, angry face had stopped him. And now that he was here, he didn't know what to say to her, because the ghost of Bert Figgins was still there between them. And so was the ghost of Tess.

'There's Mother's new husband, of course, who's a good bloke. And we're quite friendly with the people at a neighbouring farm. The two daughters come over quite often.'

'Oh?'

He didn't know why he'd said it, but if he'd hoped to see a flash of jealousy in her eyes, he was disappointed. She looked at him steadily, without flinching.

'Are you happy, Daniel?'

'Are you?'

She looked away. 'I'm not supposed to be happy. My husband just died, remember?'

It was months ago now, and yet it was yesterday. The horror, the pain, the guilt.

'Look, Amy, I can't stay too long, but Mother wants you to come out to tea on Sunday. Say that you will, or I'll never hear the end of it. I'll come and fetch you, of course.'

'Do you want me to come?'

He looked angry now. 'Don't be bloody stupid. I've never stopped wanting you.'

In the small silence, Amy saw several people glance their way, and hoped that he hadn't been overheard. Her heart was doing its jungle dance again, but his eyes were guarded and unsmiling, and she wondered if she'd imagined the words, because she wanted to hear them so much.

'Shall I call for you about two o'clock, then? I'll show you around the farm first.'

'All right. I'll be waiting outside.'

He leaned forward and kissed her cheek. For a moment she caught the tang of him, the outdoors freshness, the sharp clean scent of shaving soap, the newness of a freshly laundered shirt. And she wanted him. God, how she *wanted* him.

The next minute he was gone, and she was as empty as before. Had he really said those words? That he'd never stopped wanting her? She had to suppress the urge to run after him and beg him not to go. To stay with her, all day and all night, to spend every moment making love with the wild sound of the sea in their ears, imagining themselves to be those glamorous lovers on the silver screen for whom love never ended but went on into the sunset . . .

Sunday seemed an eternity away. Each day Amy walked the beach endlessly until she began to think her footsteps must have worn a groove in the sand. Except that twice a day they were all washed away . . . like feelings, like love . . . She asked herself again and again if she had been mistaken in thinking Daniel had said he'd never stopped wanting her.

She cherished the phrase in her mind like a sweet refrain, recurring over and over, warming her nights, tormenting her days. His expression had denied it, yet her heart told her differently. But then, you couldn't always trust what your heart said.

She was outside the hotel long before two o'clock on Sunday afternoon, but he was already there. He opened the car door for her and she slid in beside him. The sense of déjà vu was overwhelming.

It was a different car, a different place, and their lives had moved on. But a part of her was still the naïve little housemaid who had been so enchanted that this young man, this wonderful, intelligent, gloriously handsome young man, wanted *her*, Amy Moore, and not her friend Tess, who sat fuming in the back seat. She almost had to glance round to check that Tess wasn't there.

They spoke of ordinary things on the way to the farm. He told her about the vagaries of the weather, about dairy farming and harvesting and how pleased he had been that his mother had found contentment at last. She told him about Ronald and Jane's new baby, and Ronald's renewed ideas for going into politics, and how she'd started up her own little tea-garden, but decided not to go on with it. They talked of anything and everything but themselves.

He drove past the farmhouse, pointing it out in the distance and seeming so proud of it that Amy began to feel very depressed.

He finally stopped the car and they stepped out. They had come to the top of a ridge, where they could look down on the whole farm. Behind it was the shadowy blue-green range of hills that framed the white-washed buildings as if it was the focal point of an oil painting.

They sat down on the grass, surveying it all, and Amy hardly knew what to say. It was lovely, part of another world, but it wasn't her world. She knew that once and for all. And she had to say it, to let him know she wasn't expecting anything.

'It's beautiful, if you can stand all the silence.'

'Are you so desperate to get back to London already?' he asked.

'I'm sorry. I suppose that sounded rude.'

He leaned across her and she didn't know what he intended to do. To her surprise she saw that he held a golden flower on a long slender green stem in his hand.

'This is what we country folk call the truth game,' he said with a half-smile. 'You have to tell the truth when I hold the buttercup under your chin, or your skin will turn yellow.'

'That's daft,' she began, and then stopped, her heart beginning to beat very fast.

'Would you hate living here, Amy?'

'That depends –'

'You're turning yellow.'

'All right. Yes, I'd hate it,' she said angrily. 'I don't belong here. I belong in London.'

She didn't bother to take the flower. She didn't know how to play this kind of game. 'And where do you belong, Daniel?'

'Anywhere, as long as it's with you. I've tried hard to be a farmer and to forget you, but it doesn't work.'

She didn't hear the rest, only the beginning. And even though it was everything she longed for, she knew that for her, truth didn't end with such simple words.

'You might think differently if you knew the whole truth about me,' she said, very slowly. She didn't notice when his arms went around her, only that she felt warmed and loved by them. She only had to lift her mouth to his, and words would no longer be needed . . .

'What whole truth? That you loved Bert, after all? That we shouldn't think of loving one another so soon? Dear

God, Amy, how much longer do we have to wait for one another?'

She swallowed painfully. 'I didn't mean any of that. I mean the truth about me. Who I am.'

If she saw contempt in his eyes at the telling, she wasn't sure she could live with that, even now. Daniel's sixth sense told him to wait and not to make any protest as she slowly drew out two battered photographs from her bag. He'd seen them before. Her pretty mother, and that famous Uncle Tommy she'd adored so much.

And then she told him everything, the words hesitant at first, and finally pouring out of her, all the hurt and the love that was so mixed up inside her. And there was no hint of condemnation in his eyes as he held her close to his heart and spoke in a husky voice.

'Did you really think any of this would make any difference to my feelings, my darling girl? Who you are is *Amy*, my Amy, the only girl I've ever loved, the one I want to spend the rest of my life with. We've both done our duty to those who needed us, so don't you think it's time for us now, Amy?'

A long while later, when they had still not really come down to earth, they tried to talk sensibly about less heady things. They were going to be together for the rest of their lives, and they would start anew. Daniel had already decided on selling the farm, knowing there would be no problem in handing over to Ed Rowlands – and the bonus would be that he and Amy would always have somewhere to come for their summer holidays.

'And what will we do with our lives?' Amy wondered, in a blissful, rose-coloured haze because everything in her world was unbelievably the right way up again, and she was going to marry her own true love, in the tradition of all the best heroines.

He didn't say anything for a few minutes, and when he spoke, his voice was filled with amazement.

'A dozen ideas have been going through my head, and you know where they all end up? You'll think I'm crazy . . .'

'No, I won't,' she said softly. 'Tell me, Daniel.'

'I was remembering the way we met, and thinking that a new picture palace, one that belonged to the two of us, would be the perfect thing to buy, as a kind of thank-you, I suppose.' He gave an embarrassed laugh. 'Oh, don't listen to me, Amy – I told you I was crazy, living in a dream-world!'

'I don't think you're crazy!' Amy said, hardly knowing whether to laugh or cry, because it was such a spectacular idea.

'You don't?'

'No – I think it's a wonderful idea. And when the new talking pictures take over from the silents –'

'Exactly. Pretty soon people will be flocking to see these new talkies, as they call them, make no mistake about that. There's going to be a whole new era of pictures, and we could be in at the start of it! Just imagine it, Amy. You and me, back where we started, in a way, going to the pictures every day of our lives. What a thought – if only it could happen.'

'Why shouldn't it happen?' She was already caught up in the dream, and dazzled by it, the most exciting future she could ever have imagined.

'Because, my darling, there wouldn't be enough money from the sale of the farm. Unless I came into a fortune, I'm afraid we'll have to settle for something far less ambitious.'

She didn't say anything for a minute, and then she gave him the most brilliant smile, her eyes glowing and alive. He couldn't read her thoughts, but he could tell that his beautiful Amy had something stupendous in mind.

So she did. And he had to agree to it. She had been a businesswoman for quite a while now, and there mustn't be any silly nonsense about not wanting to take her money. It wouldn't demean him in her eyes in any way. It would make them partners in every sense of the word.

Of course, Daniel wasn't aware that she had any money to speak of. She had almost forgotten it herself until these last moments when the answer became gloriously clear in her mind. She could almost discount the fact that there was still some of Tommy's legacy left, and a fair bit of money from the sale of the Claymore Street business. Because none of it could remotely compare with something of immense value locked away in the Derbisham family safe for a rainy day.

And there could be no richer dowry for Amy Moore to bring to this perfect rainy day in which the sun shone so wonderfully than a fabulous rope of pearls that was going to turn all their dreams into reality.